Luke Pittaway

I0601926

Jenkins' Ear

Culicidae Press®
PO Box 5069
Madison, WI 53705-5069
culicidaepress.com
editor@culicidaepress.com

ISBN: 978-1-68315-180-7

Library of Congress Control Number: 2026933401

Our books may be purchased in bulk for promotional, educational or business use. Please contact your local bookseller or the Culicidae Press Sales Department at +1-352-215-7558 or by email at sales@culicidaepress.com

culicidaepress.bsky.social – facebook.com/culicidaepress
threads.net/@culicidaepress – instagram.com/culicidaepress
x.com/culicidaepress

Designed by polytekton ©2026
Edited by Sami Strait and Mikesch Muecke

For Isabella, Mia, and Zara
Never forget you're my favorites

*Alice: "Sometimes I've believed as many as six
impossible things before breakfast."
Imagine impossible things and
aim to make the impossible possible.*

Also written by the author:
Yamacraw Bluff, the prequel to *Jenkins' Ear*

Table of Contents

Part One: The Stono Rebellion

Chapter 1: Castillo de Santa Catalina

Achingly long, drawn out, and compressed, a muted belly-like squawk emanating from deep within the soul. It wasn't a scream he'd heard before. Hernando Perez had stood guard outside the inquisitor's iron door for longer than he cared to remember. He thought he'd listened to every scream possible, but no, this one was new.

Unable to draw blood, the inquisitors had dreamed up all manner of tortures, which created all manner of screams. There was the arrogant, tough man grunt, which usually accompanied the beginning. A man trying hard to show he wouldn't confess. Then, there was the high-pitched squeal that resembled a pig as it was taken to slaughter. That one always made him sweat profusely under his tunic and iron breastplate. In the hierarchy of screams, the squeal was a mere damp squib.

It couldn't compare to the blustering, contorted bellows of pain caused by the garrucha. Hernando had seen it once. The victim was hanging from the ceiling attached by his wrists, weights tied to his ankles, which were dropped violently, dislocating his arms and legs. Now, Hernando did more than sweat when he heard that one; a chill shot down his back as if his spine anticipated the inquisitor's touch.

There were other screams, though, even higher in his makeshift hierarchy. Next up was the gagging, spluttering, coughing, and muted sob brought on by the toca. He strained to hear it but often sensed it in the atmosphere. It was the silence beforehand that warned him. He hadn't seen the torture itself, but he'd been told. A wet cloth pushed into the mouth and slowly forced water down the throat, giving a feeling of drowning. Hernando couldn't swim, so whenever he heard it, his chest tightened, and his breathing became shallow. Twice, he nearly collapsed while standing on guard.

The apex of his hierarchy was the constant comatose groan that accompanied the potro. The torture involved a rack that slowly stretched the body, pulling the limbs apart. There were no longer any arrogant, controlled grunts. The man was always broken, barely alive, but making incoherent sounds nonetheless. The terror Hernando felt at this point was almost unbearable. It didn't matter how long he served as the inquisitor's guard; the screams always brought the same symptoms.

He often thought about it. After so many years and tortures, why hadn't he become immune to the noises, like his colleagues had? He considered that he might be a soft man at heart and had no business being a professional soldier. Like so many others, he'd been tricked into it, and he didn't know how he'd react if he got into a real battle. He hoped he would be brave and not a coward. He might find out soon now that war with the British approached and his regiment was to set sail for Florida.

This was his last day. Six long years, he'd stood to attention outside the inquisitor's rooms in the Castillo de Santa Catalina, listening to screams and trying to ignore the horrors from within. On occasion, he walked along the thick stone corridors of the Castillo for his lunch break or for the change of the guard. These moments of escape from the sounds that haunted him were always welcome. He often dawdled along the beach paths to its fortified ramparts from his Cádiz home, not wanting to hear more screams. It had been a tedious assignment, but he was relieved it was over. He would miss his wife Juana and his kids, Isbel and María when they sailed on the San Luis next week.

General Manuel de Montiano had promised the soldiers that their families could follow and settle in St. Augustine once his governorship of Florida was established. Hernando Perez was eager to start this new phase of his life. Though short, he was stout, strong, resilient, and resourceful. He felt he could build a good home for his family in St. Augustine while he served in the Castillo de San Marcos garrison. It seemed unlikely that such a far-flung outpost would become caught up in the coming war. He and his family would be safe there.

At last, it was over. Hernando took a long look at the oak and iron door, which had been his constant companion for the previous six years. He knew every inch of it. During those boring hours of his watch, it was all Hernando had to look at, along with the stone wall across from it. He collected all of his belongings from the guardhouse. Hernando stomped through the stone corridors of the Castillo de Santa Catalina one last time. Down the outer steps of the Castillo, he took one last look back at the castle. It sat imposing at the end of the beach with its bastions and irregular design, defending the city's northern flank. A fitting home for the local inquisitor. He turned away, never to cast a glance at the castle again.

Hernando swiftly left; he almost raced down the outer steps of the fortification, down the tracks that led from the Castillo to his house in Cádiz. He'd always loved the city and would miss its ancient history, beautiful buildings, and long beachfront. Hernando knew St. Augustine would be newer and less developed, and so he would take fond memories of Cádiz with him. Its meandering streets and horseshoe bay were dotted with rivers and inlets. It had been a stunningly beautiful place to live. As elsewhere in Spain, it was hot, particularly in the summer. The breezes off the Atlantic had made it bearable, even during the middle of the siesta.

As he arrived at his quaint Andalucian home along C. José Cubiles, Juana was waiting for him on the doorstep, and knowing how important today was, she embraced him. Hernando gazed into her dark, enigmatic eyes. Small tears were noticeable, tears of joy and sorrow—joy that their lives could move on from him being the inquisitor's guard and sorrow that they would soon be apart while Hernando built their new home in St. Augustine.

She was always beautiful in his eyes. Petite with a slim, curvy figure, dark brown, almost black hair that cascaded down her back in waves, and untouched olive skin. Her smile was perfection, while her face had the compelling dimensions of a proud Andalucian woman. He never knew what she saw in him, in his drab blue soldier's tunic, cross belt, breastplate, long black boots, and white pantaloons. His dark eyes mirrored hers in many ways while she made fun of his dark handlebar mustache that was flecked with grey. He held her tightly, appreciating their moment of intimacy.

They were soon disturbed as Isbel tugged at his left leg and María tugged at his right. Isbel was four and growing, the picture of her mother, with her almost black hair and dark eyes.

María was two but no less beautiful than her sister. She had lighter brown hair that was straighter and hazel eyes, quite a bit different from an Andalucian girl. He stooped down and picked them up. They giggled and squirmed as he hugged them and carried them into the house for their evening supper.

⧖ ⧖ ⧖

The following day, the preparations for his departure began. He packed the few possessions he was allowed into their oak family chest with its rivets and leather cross straps. His spare uniforms, work clothes, haversack, escopeta, and cockade were carefully packed. His escopeta, the long musket, would be necessary should there be war, so he cleaned it and carefully placed it into the gun case he had just acquired for his travel. It was handmade from deer hide imported from the colonies; the stitching was exquisite.

His daughters were constantly chitter-chattering around him as he packed, sensing some significant change in their lives. They wouldn't leave his side.

His last days with the family disappeared faster than he would have liked. His last night with Juana was quiet and cozy at first, but burst out into frenzied lovemaking late into the night, for they both knew tomorrow he would leave. Hernando's family bliss came abruptly to an end the following morning. His sergeant, Diego Moreno-Rodriguez, wrapped on their door, waiting outside with two soldiers; they were here to assist Hernando with his possessions, which were to be taken to the ship.

It was a challenging moment for everybody. The girls cried and clung to him, and despite her fortitude, Juana could not hold back her tears. They embraced as a family. He held both girls in his arms, and they all hugged Juana and wept together.

He tried hard not to show his weakness to Moreno-Rodriguez, but the sergeant just slapped him on the back. He'd already seen the same thing six times today as his men said goodbye to their families; each had experienced the exact moment. Diego himself bid farewell to his wife yesterday, but it was difficult.

Their journey would be long and dangerous, with British pirates waiting for them and an uncertain future in an unknown land. There was no guarantee that the families would be able to follow. If they did, they faced similar uncertainties getting across the Atlantic. Tears and hugs seemed entirely appropriate even to a battle-hardened veteran like Moreno-Rodriguez.

As they rowed the skiff out into the Bay of Cádiz' harbor, the shoreline receded, and the city's splendor only increased. Hernando Perez was sad to think that this might be his last time in Cádiz. He turned to take in their destination.

The San Luis sat in the harbor alongside several other Spanish ships of the line. Seagulls swarmed around the vessels as if the sailors had recently offloaded food waste. The San Luis was imposing; even when sat alongside its counterparts, it had sixty-two guns and three decks. Guns were being cleaned and ready for departure, and they poked out of the gun deck through the gunports. The forecastle strutted between the foremast and the ship's stem while the gallery rose out of the stern.

Hernando had seen the ships from a distance, but this was the first time they were up close. They looked even more prominent and loomed ever present as his small boat sculled towards them. The San Luis's three masts seemed to rise forever into the sky, and the rigging looked like a complex web of ropes and pulleys. He had no idea how the sailors understood the intricacy of masts, booms, ropes, pulleys, and sails. He was happy to be a soldier and not a sailor.

Many sailors were up in the rigging, checking and fixing, ensuring the ship was ready to sail. He didn't fancy that at all. Climbing and jumping in the rigging was a quick way to break a leg or two. Three other ships in the squadron would take the new governor's regiment across the Atlantic, and he was convinced there was enough firepower to ward off any British pirates. They'd only be at risk if the squadron was somehow split.

The skiff pulled alongside the San Luis's starboard, ropes were thrown down, and the soldier's luggage was hoisted aboard. Ten soldiers were in his party, ready to join their regiment alongside Sergeant Moreno-Rodriguez. They were hauled to the ship's side and disembarked onto the upper deck.

His squad was a good group of men. Juan the Joker could always be trusted to be the center of the conversation. Then there was Antonio the butcher, at least six foot three, a beast of a man rumored to have killed many men. Miguel and Rodrigo were inseparable, brothers in the squad, the incessant gamblers who fought when they lost. Gonzalo, Francisco, and Hernán were the stalkers, quiet men who could be sent out into the night to kill without a word and trusted as the best sentries and scouts. Then there were the new men, Alvaro and Benito; they were very young, barely sixteen, and Hernando didn't know them yet.

Their squad was one of many in a large regiment of men set to sail with the new governor and General de Montiano. Should war materialize, they were to strengthen the Castillo de San Marcos in St. Augustine against a suspected attack by the British. The British had already begun to settle the disputed lands that Moreno-Rodriguez called Guale. It seemed only a matter of time before they turned their attention to Spain's colony in Florida.

This wasn't their only worry. Hernando Perez didn't know what to expect, but he'd heard stories, just as all the soldiers had, and the tales seemed far-fetched. They were of strange dragon-like creatures that lured victims into the swamps, never to return, and of outlandish natives who flayed their victims and burned them alive. He didn't think the stories were credible. At least, he hoped not. The night before he left, he prayed to Mary, Mother of God, in case there was truth in the stories and lit a candle in the Cathedral de Cádiz to safeguard him on his journey.

The squad was taken to their quarters, a cramped space stuffed with bunk beds and a single latrine. There was no air. It seemed to Hernando that they were as likely to die from suffocation or disease as they were from dragons or natives. Despite himself, thoughts of the toca's drowning sobs imposed themselves on his mind and overflowed him with anxiety. Months in this space didn't seem like a great alternative to his guard duty, despite its horrifying noises. The risk of drowning didn't seem too attractive either.

⏳ ⏳ ⏳

The following day, the San Luis and its squadron set sail. He hadn't expected it to happen so soon. The soldiers crowded the ships' upper decks, hoping to glimpse a loved one before they left, perhaps never to return.

The riverside was a swarming mass of families waving, shouting, and crying. They hoped to catch sight of a husband, a father, a brother, or a son as they set off on their expedition on behalf of the Spanish crown. The crowd jostled and moved along the riverside as the ships pulled anchor and slipped their moorings.

Despite himself, Hernando looked for Juana. He knew she wasn't there; he'd told her not to come. It wasn't unheard of for the little ones to get crushed in the stampede of distraught families trying to get one last glimpse of their loved ones before they left. Hernando couldn't bear that risk for his little beauties Isbel and María. He didn't see her, and his heart sank just a little. This was it; they were on their way to strengthen St. Augustine's garrison of Castillo de San Marcos and fight the British if they had to.

Chapter 2: Uga

Tom Ellis sat on the riverside wharf, drinking a pint of Georgia's finest ale. It was a good beer with a light, elegant taste that reminded him of a beer he once had at a Gravesend pub called the Old Amsterdam. There were other similarities. The Old Amsterdam sat alongside the Thames River. Tom recalled a beautiful sunset with his feet up on a causeway overlooking the Thames.

He often had fleeting memories of England, but as time passed, they became rarer. Today, he was sitting in a new pub on the riverside in Savannah, a new colonial city he'd helped start. He gazed out across the river towards Trustees' Island. Some had begun to call it Hutchinson's Island after Oglethorpe's friend. It was not a name he cared for; for him, it would always be the Trustees' Island, where the colony kept its cattle.

Tom enjoyed this spot; it was his favorite location in the colony. The island had once been almost completely covered in pine forest, but the trees had been cleared to make way for the cattle's pasture. It was still a stunning view across the Savannah River. The undulating fields that crisscrossed Hutchinson's Island were dotted with cows. The river flowed through the channel, glistening as it sped on its path to Cockspur Island at the mouth of the Savannah, taking its fertile sediment load to the Atlantic Ocean.

He sipped his beer; it had a hint of zesty lemon to it. Of course, his memory of the island was tinged with sadness. The murder of little Clemy in Savannah, who had been killed by a stray bullet meant for him, and his vicious retribution of her killers Cameron and Horn on that island.

Occasionally, his dreams re-lived the moment. His tomahawk split Horn's skull, followed by his rifle marksmanship, pitching Cameron into the river. He never felt any guilt; they deserved it. Clemy's murder at such a young age would live with him for the rest of his life, and sometimes, he wished the bullet had hit him instead.

Sitting enjoying his beer, Tom looked away from Hutchinson's Island along Savannah's riverfront. What he saw continued to amaze him. When he arrived a little over five years ago, the riverside constituted a mile-long shingle beach below the great bluff on which Savannah was now situated. There were signs of small boats etched in the shingle, mainly traders' skiffs coming and going to the Musgrove's trading post to pick up furs, but there was little else. A small trail weaved its way up the side of the bluff to the top, which had been wooded in parts.

Now, the riverside was the hub of activity. Tom could count at least twenty small vessels moored along the quayside and behind them two British frigates, their hulls bristling with guns and their masts rising like great pine trees almost to the height of the bluff itself. The shingle beach had been turned into a permanent street.

Like he'd seen in Port Royal, ballast from the ships had been dumped onto the riverside and reused to lay a cobblestone streetscape. The small trail and its scrub-like wood had been obliterated in favor of a stone stairway constructed from the same ballast.

What astonished him the most was the sheer volume of people, traders, stalls, and even warehouses that now lined the mile-long wharf. This had become the primary trading spot for the city and where the sailors spent much of their time. He never realized that so many people could fit into such a small space. Now that Oglethorpe had passed his ordinance controlling trade with Georgia's native Indians, the Creeks, Choctaws, and Chickasaws, Savannah had become a trading center. It had proven to be an inspired decision but was still disputed and disliked by the South Carolinians.

The last six years had disappeared in no time, yet so much had happened. Tom was still a young man at twenty-three. Life had accelerated, and change was ever present around him as Georgia continued to develop at a breakneck pace. He reflected on how lucky he had been. At sixteen and destined for debtors' prison, life had taken an unexpected change. Spending his last shilling in a pub in Fleet Street, soon to be arrested, he had intervened in a fight. Not that he knew it at the time, but he had unexpectedly saved Oglethorpe from certain death and possibly changed the course of history itself in the process.

He smiled inwardly as he thought about Oglethorpe's machinations during their murder trial and his successful attempt to get Tom out of debtors' prison, committing him to a contract of indenture to serve Noble Jones and the colony of Georgia. It had been quite a whirlwind since then. He'd become the first Georgia ranger, a source of pride, especially now that the rangers were a proper colonial regiment with several hundred men and officers. He'd been involved in his first battle at Fort Argyle, broken up a smugglers' ring, and even found the love of his life, the beautiful shrew Mary Hicks.

Yes, indeed, quite a journey, and now he and Mary were to be married. It had taken some time. They wanted to do it much sooner, but both had to finish their indenture as servants first.

Due to his work with the rangers, he had accumulated enough funds to buy himself out, and Mary Hicks' family, the Cannon's, had been decimated. The baby James had died crossing the Atlantic on the Anne. Mary Cannon died of pox during the first year of settling in Savannah. The same disease and grief had pushed her husband, Richard, into an incapacitated state. Then Clemy's death, after a prolonged bout of illness, had eventually tipped him into his grave. Only Duke remained from the Cannon family; he was now fourteen and growing into a strong young man. Tom could see a future ranger in the making, and he had already begun to train him with the rifle and singlestick.

Tom smiled again; life had unexpected turns. They'd agreed to adopt Duke on their marriage since he had no family left. At twenty-three, Tom hadn't expected to have a fourteen-year-old son. Tom didn't begrudge Duke, and Mary was clear about where their responsibilities lay.

His quiet thoughts and slow drinking were interrupted. An old, white-haired, unkempt, and disheveled man ambled toward his table. The barman went to wave him off, thinking him a beggar, but Tom stopped him. The man had a deep, wrinkled face and a white beard and wore nondescript, drab, fawn-colored clothing. He tugged on two leads. Connected to those leads were two of the strangest, stoutest-looking dogs Tom had ever seen. Clearly, he was no beggar, just a tradesman, but maybe a poor one. As Tom scrutinized the man, he, in return, inspected Tom.

The trader saw a tall man, well over six feet tall, with dark, long, wavy hair. He was a tough-looking man who had gained muscle from carpentry work, his solid, calloused hands visible as he placed them on the table or when he lifted his beer. He was a good-looking man with piercing brown eyes and a naturally stern look that only lightened when he smiled. There was a clear-cut aura of confidence about him and body language that betrayed the professional competence of a trained soldier. The old man yanked his two dogs closer to the table to talk. Perhaps he could make a sale.

"Good day to you, sir. Be interested in a pup, would ya?" said the old man.

As the man spoke, Tom picked up an East London accent that was not unlike that of the hackney coachmen who used to hang out around the Fleet. Tom wondered if his Yorkshire accent was still noticeable while he took a close look at the dogs. They were small white dogs, not quite fully grown, with short chubby legs. Their tails had been docked, but their faces were most remarkable. They were all wrinkled like the old man's; the noses were squashed in, the teeth poked out, and the eyes and ears looked tiny compared to other dogs. When they panted, their big tongues lolloped around, firing saliva everywhere. Despite himself, Tom smiled. The man and the dogs looked awfully alike. "What are these dogs? I've never seen this breed before", he asked.

"These are bulldogs, good for fighting and baiting, but also good companions. I reckon this be the first two of this breed in Georgia." Pointing to the dogs, he continued. "Here, this one is Ug A, and this one is Ug B."

Tom looked at the old man quizzically, "Those are some strange names for your dogs. Why not more common names like Merryboy, Drunkard, or Younker?" He liked the idea of owning the first of a breed. The first Georgia ranger should own the first bulldog in the colony. Also, they looked symbolic of strength, determination, and courage. He had a premonition that they would be a meaningful symbol of something.

The man responded, "Simple governor, this be Ugly A, and this be Ugly B. They not be so good looking, see!"

Tom laughed despite himself; this man was a rare salesman. He was interested but didn't want to pay too much, "Which one stepped onto Georgia's soil first?" Though an odd question, it mattered to Tom; he wanted the one that arrived first.

"That's easy, Ug A. That's why he's A and not B!"

Again, Tom couldn't help but chortle. The man had a real knack for selling, but Tom hadn't negotiated well. "Well, I will have to have Uga A. Tell me how much you want for him." They haggled over the terms and eventually agreed on a price. The man handed over the lead, and Tom was delighted with his purchase. He needed a wedding present for Mary and Uga would be a great gift.

As the old man left, Uga took one glance at him and then curled up next to Tom's feet. As Tom finished his beer, Uga seemed happy with his new master even as he accidentally salivated all over Tom's boot. Tom wondered what Mary would say. Hopefully, she would welcome this latest addition to their growing family, just as she had welcomed Duke. He wondered if the beer had led him into a mistake he might regret. After all, a dog was for life, and he was about to get married.

Chapter 3: Chioke the Yamasee

The Yamasee village in Pensacola was a makeshift affair. Dotted over the open landscape amongst the oak trees were tent-like structures of a temporary nature. The area had once been a permanent settlement for the tribe, but a combination of pox and constant raids by the South Carolinians after the Yamasee War had destroyed it. Occasionally, they would find a burned-out cabin or an old firepit that spoke to this legacy of former occupation. Now, the Seminoles tolerated their occasional presence, as the roving band of Yamasee to which Chioke was attached moved around Northern Florida.

Pensacola had seen its fair share of destruction over the years and was now sparsely populated. The French and Spanish had fought over it, and the Creeks and South Carolinians had raided it. So now, only a few French and Spanish settlers, along with a small population of Seminoles, lived there. Chioke liked the place. It was hot, like his former home in Africa, and beautiful, with its untouched white sandy beaches and translucent cobalt blue water. He even appreciated its foul-smelling swamps and strange pointy-nosed crocodiles.

The plants appeared odd to him, though. Old laurel oaks with their thick trunks and broad leaves, Titi trees that occupied the swamps with white flowers and spiky seeds, and tall pines that dominated further inland—all alien to Chioke. He was used to African mahoganies, irokos, palms, and walnut trees, and he had rarely seen the sea or beaches before his enslavement.

He missed his home in Igboland, West Africa, but he knew he could never return there. This wasn't a terrible place to live and much better than South Carolina, where he'd been enslaved before his escape.

Chioke looked across the village. Yamasee warriors sat at several bivouacs, eating, drinking, and talking. He liked these men. They adored their wild hairstyles, many of which were very different, but a common theme was to have it short cropped on top and long down the back. They wore kiltlike cloaks over their deerskin leggings and sported comfortable moccasin boots. Chioke could never quite understand the goose-feather headdressings, but he knew they symbolized something important amongst the men. Beside them sat their guns and bows while their axes and knives hung from their belts.

These warriors had a fearsome reputation, which Chioke appreciated; the Igbo also cultivated such a status among its enemies. He knew many of the stories he had heard of flaying and burning before his acceptance were exaggerated. These were reserved for their worst enemies or for heinous crimes. He had never seen any such torture, and the Igbo tribe hadn't been known for its generosity to its enemies, either. The captured might be tortured or sold into slavery, so the stories didn't bother him, even if they were true. He'd been adopted by the Yamasee, and this was his tribe now.

When they found him escaping Georgia, they hadn't killed him or given him to the Spanish as he'd expected. They'd allowed him to join them and become one of them. It was an honor that he'd accepted. Better a freeman in a new tribe than a chattel, owned by a European.

Chioke didn't care for the whites, and he hated the British most of all, but he didn't like the French or Spanish much either. It was this hatred that had endeared him to the Yamasee. They had their own reasons for hating the British, especially the South Carolinians, who had warred against them and removed them from their ancestral lands. The Yamasee were more careful with the Spanish, and the French. They often allied themselves with these Europeans when needed. So, Chioke had learned to be more cautious with his hatred. He had learned to direct it at his new tribe's historic foe, the British.

Chioke was Igbo, a black man. He was very proud of his deep ebony blackness, much darker than his brethren from other tribes. They seemed half-white to him in contrast to his deep black hues. Take Lamine, his friend and escapee. He was Fulani with his strange briar-like tattoos, but he wasn't black; he was more brown than black. Chioke knew that he stood out. It had done him no harm amongst the Yamasee. The women were also free; they could choose amongst the warriors as they saw fit and change when they wanted to. Their freedom didn't bother the men, who accepted it without jealousy or fights.

Chioke was tall, somewhat skinny, with a bulbous stomach. Across the left side of his face was a series of parallel facial scratches from his forehead to his left eye. His eyes were dark and luminous, and his smile was wide and inviting. The Yamasee women seemed to like his look, as they often crept into his bed at night.

The tribe had learned to respect Chioke's fighting and hunting skills, and he suspected this might have helped with his allure amongst the tribe's women. He bought something new for them that they hadn't seen before. He was skilled with a spear or wooden staff. He could whirl it like a hummingbird's wings so that it disappeared before his opponent's eyes until it materialized again for the killing stroke. The speed with which he wielded it had shocked the other warriors, and he was known to demobilize three Yamasee men in a practice bout.

His speed with the spear transferred to his knife-fighting skills. He preferred a much smaller knife than was usual amongst the Yamasee; they preferred tomahawks or long knives. Chioke's knife was just under six inches. What he lost in reach he recovered in swiftness. In one fight, he had disarmed his assailant instantly. The tomahawk had flown out of the man's hand as his severed finger dropped to the ground, blood dripping everywhere.

It was his final skill that brought something new and significant, though. The Igbo fought with poisoned tipped arrows; this was particularly important when hunting large game. It took a lot of testing and experimenting, but Chioke had found an alternate poison in Florida. Now, the Yamasee took this new weapon into battle. The poison wasn't as strong as the Igbo's, but it could fester and kill and would be lethal in a fight, killing a man a day after a hit. Many of the Yamasee chose to fight with muskets now, though, so its value had limits. Chioke had tried the gun, but it wasn't for him. Too noisy and cumbersome.

Watching the villagers go about their day, he thought about his journey from Igboland. He didn't often make mistakes when hunting, but that day would live in his memory for a long time. He'd been so focused on his game, a small adolescent buffalo, that he didn't notice the trackers. It was a small group of Mandingo searching for people to capture and sell. He walked straight into their trap. In no time, he was trussed up like the game he had hunted and carried off to the coast for sale.

The slavers were efficient. It took no time for Chioke to end up on a ship to the Bahamas. He didn't like to think about that ship; it was a visit to Esu himself. Disease-ridden and pitiful, with the living piled up on the dead until the dead were thrown overboard to feed the sharks. He survived the ship only to be sold and shipped to South Carolina. After working for years on a plantation, his life took an unexpected turn. He was sold again to an owner in the new colony of Georgia. This was when he first met Lamine the Fulani.

Only a few days into their new duties in Savannah, a white man was thrown into their chamber and locked up with them. Chioke still struggled with English and was tongue-twisted trying to pronounce the man's name, Tom Ellis it was. He knew he didn't get it right; he was better at the Yamasee language. This white man had somehow managed to escape from their confinement. He took Chioke and Lamine with him, escaping the clutches of their owner and getting them out of Savannah. He'd never liked a white man before, but if he was going to, it might be this Tom Ellis. He seemed likable enough for one of them.

Ellis took them to a trading lodge, where they met two Creek Indians, Hillispilli and Sinlouchi. The Creeks smuggled Chioke and Lamine past Fort Argyle and out of Georgia. That was when Lamine and Chioke split up. Lamine headed for St. Augustine and the Spanish. At the same time, Chioke set out into the wilderness to find the dreaded Yamasee and take what he found.

Now, he was among them and an essential member of their tribe. They knew the value of people and had adopted many escaped slaves. If a man was strong and valuable, he would become a warrior. If he had nothing to offer, he became a thrall or was killed. It was a simple policy. Women and children were always welcomed and adopted into clans, replacing loved ones who had been lost to disease, famine, or war.

Chioke reflected on yesterday's clan meeting. The chiefs had talked for many hours in the council of warriors. He understood most of it but not everything. The Yamasee believed a great war was coming - between the British and the Spanish. It was rumored that a new governor and great warrior from Spain had set sail for St. Augustine, bringing with him an armada and a vast legion of warriors. They'd heard that the British, too, were mustering troops and sending them to Georgia. They'd argued for hours; they had suffered much, and some felt they couldn't afford to engage in another war with the British. Others were angry with the appeasers and the peace seekers and daubed themselves in paint to express their desire for blood, battle, and to call for war.

The debates seemed endless to Chioke. The freedom to speak, argue, and do so for so long was a unique feature of his new tribal life. It was a true gift to speak elegantly in these councils, and Chioke's language skills didn't stretch that far, so he listened. The Igbo hadn't been so vociferous. If the chiefs decided, then the warriors followed. After a long deliberation, it was agreed that if a war came, their traditional enemies, the Creeks, would join the British. So, the Yamasee must seek out an alliance with the Spanish. Several emissaries were chosen amongst the chiefs, and it was settled that they would leave in the morning for St. Augustine to meet this new governor and his army and to be ready to approve an alliance as soon as possible. The chiefs decided the tribe would break camp in the morning and head north towards the old Apalachee town, Tallahassee.

Chapter 4: Defender of the Frontier

Private Williams and Lieutenant Evans were playing dice. It could have been better for Evans; he'd wagered too much already and lost more than he'd won. Williams couldn't contain his smile; taking some winnings off Evans was a rare treat. Neither of them used their South Carolinian ranger's titles now. They were simply Williams and Evans, just two Welshmen who liked to play dice. Surrounded by the opulence of Colonel William Bull's house in Charles Town, they might not have titles, but they sure had influence. At least that's what they told each other.

It was a beautiful house with a three-story Georgian design, tall chimneys, and servants' quarters downstairs in the basement. The fixtures and fittings were the best in the colonies, shipped from the leading merchants in England. No expense had been spared; the colonel had just redecorated with gaudy wallpaper, new drapes, and the most expensive rugs the Welshmen had ever seen. They were downstairs, avoiding the colonel's wrath, for he wasn't keen on them playing dice in his house. Evans lost again. He decided to distract Williams, hoping he might end his winning streak, "Who would have guessed we'd end up here?"

Williams was perplexed. He seemed to sense what Evans was up to, but his curiosity got the better of him. "What, staying in Colonel Bull's house?"

"No, I mean clerks to the Governor of South Carolina," replied Evans. It sure had been a wild ride for both of them. They punted up the Savannah River only a few years ago, with Colonel Bull and Oglethorpe looking for the perfect site to start a new colony. They'd been young rangers serving their grisly old veteran commander. The colonel had helped pick a site for the new colony's first city on Yamacraw Bluff. Now, they were sitting in the seat of power for South Carolina, a prosperous colony with rich pickings when you knew where to look.

"Yeah, who would have guessed at this one. Just sitting down in Port Royal fiddling my thumbs and sitting on my arse, I was, when I got the note. Didn't think we'd impressed him that much," Williams had taken the bait that Evans had laid for him.

"Mind you, Evans, you can't go around calling him Governor; you'll get us all in trouble. Stick to Acting Governor; that's the correct term, I heard. What a farce it's all been."

Evans knew what he was talking about; the governorship of South Carolina had been in limbo for years. A political mess, if ever there was one. First, Johnson died, and then Broughton died. Then the Carolina Lord's Proprietors proposed Horsey to be Governor, which was overruled by the King, who suggested Glen. Now Glen was stuck in England fighting for his salary as Defender of the Southern Frontier. The title and funds had just been passed to Georgia from South Carolina, and Oglethorpe had gained them as the new Governor of Georgia. Just to rub salt into the wounds, Oglethorpe was made a general.

The mess led to the old stalwart Colonel Bull becoming Lieutenant Governor and then Acting Governor. Never a man to miss a slight, William Bull was apoplectic with anger. Consequently, Evans and Williams played dice in the cellar, as far away from the old man as possible. He was also fuming at the loss of income for the colony. Still, Evans suspected that Bull was angrier about Oglethorpe receiving a generalship ahead of him. After all, he was a veteran commander who had led a large body of rangers during two colonial wars. In Bull's opinion, Oglethorpe was a well-connected upstart with little to no experience; worse, he was a showman.

Evans had successfully distracted Williams from the dice and carried on. "I heard it was Viscount Perceval, Earl of Egmont. He's been Georgia's Lord Protector in Parliament and pulled this stunt off. That's what Bull was raving about last time I dared to go into his office!" They both laughed. Bull's temper was legendary at the best of times. This certainly wasn't welcome news in South Carolina and not for the new Acting Governor. They had been on good terms once, but Oglethorpe's and Bull's relationship had deteriorated, and the relationship between South Carolina and Georgia was undeniably on the rocks.

The Georgia proclamations started it. Banning rum and slavery were dumb ideas, but Evans and Williams didn't care much about those laws. They didn't really affect South Carolina. Monopolizing the Indian trade, though, and redirecting it to Savannah was a direct hit on South Carolina's economy. Now, they'd taken away the Parliamentary grant and generalship of the colony's defense and given it to Georgia. It was an outrageous affront to South Carolina's colonial sovereignty.

He'd be surprised if Bull didn't call out the militia and march on Savannah, with the South Carolina rangers as his vanguard, before Oglethorpe returned from London.

Williams saw it differently. He reckoned they'd all be fighting the Spanish soon, giving Bull a different target for his fury. A fighting man at heart, he just needed a battle or two to get over it. Their ruminations were interrupted. The bellboy, bouncing down two steps at a time to the basement, had a summons for Evans to attend Bull. "Well, here goes, I hope he doesn't throw anything at me!" Evans declared as he disappeared up the basement stairs.

As he opened the door Evans instinctively ducked; it was becoming a habit of his. It was good that he did, as one of Bull's leather shoes came flying at him out of nowhere and smashed into the door frame next to his head. "Where in damnation have you been, young man! Playing dice with that reprobate Williams again, no doubt!"

Evans picked up the shoe and carried it back to Acting Governor Bull, who took it from him. Bull's office was a mess; manuscripts and letters lay all over the place. His oak-paneled desk was piled high with them, and large leather-bound books lay on the floor. As he was accustomed to doing in the evening, he'd been smoking his clay pipe and enjoying a glass of port. The air in the office was stagnant. Fumes from his pipe circulated like ghostly apparitions dancing to the ceiling. Bull was in his mid-fifties, a tall, athletic-looking man growing a little portly of late. His years as a military officer, first in the Tuscarora War and then in the Yamasee War, were evident in his tough-looking stare and stern face. His hair was black and streaked with grey, and it was an open joke that he looked like an actual bull, with his temper, stubbornness, and brute strength of personality to go with the nickname. Bull's nostrils flared as Evans handed him back his shoe, and he was in the foulest of moods.

Evans responded carefully, "We were down in the basement inspecting the servants' quarters, making sure everything was shipshape," he lied convincingly, "What do you need at this time of the evening, sir?"

Bull responded, "Sit down over there. I need you to send a couple of urgent letters. I'll dictate them to you." The Acting Governor pointed to Evans to sit in the governor's chair. It was familiar enough for Evans to sit at Bull's desk transcribing his letters.

Bull paced the office dictating to him while sucking on his pipe and quaffing port. "The first letter needs to go to Colonel Palmer; he is out on the frontier with his men and needs to return to Charles Town to await further instructions. The next letter is for Colonel Vanderdussen. I need him to begin arrangements to raise the militia. I doubt we'll need them yet, but I want them drilled and ready. War with the Spanish can't be far off. Also, you can tell him that Governor de Montiano left Cádiz with three Spanish galleons and around six hundred men. He'll be halfway to Cuba by now and will be reinforcing St. Augustine soon."

Bull stopped and looked at Evans quizzically, then continued, "You know everything we discuss is sensitive, Evans? Some things more than others."

"Yes, sir," Evans answered, knowing Bull's signal that what he was about to say was top secret.

Bull continued, "I always make it clear when discussing ultra-sensitive things?"

"Yes, sir."

"Well, this is one of those moments, Evans. Not a word to anyone, not even to your chum Williams. Add this to Colonel

Vanderdussen's letter and quote me directly. We have learned from one of our spies in St. Augustine that the Spanish have agents skulking around South Carolina, fomenting rebellion amongst our slaves. They have offered freedom to any fugitives who convert to Catholicism and volunteer for a period of service in the Spanish militia. This is Montiano's work. He isn't even there yet and has dreamed up this scheme. It is pretty clever, really. Evans, you don't have to quote that part! Our spies tell us that he plans to turn St. Augustine's slave town into a fort and enlist all the men into his militia. No doubt to further strengthen their defenses. Tell Vanderdussen to ready the militia should there be a revolt and to keep his beady eyes on those Portuguese slaves from the Kongo. They're already popists."

Evans looked up from the letter. This revelation was quite a shock, and he wondered who the spy was that Bull depended on for his information. "Right, last letter. I suppose we're going to have to send a letter to Oglethorpe to congratulate him on his generalship! It'll have to go to Savannah; he should depart from London soon. We're going to need those fresh troops he has with him that's for sure."

Evans leaned over the table, head in hands in despair. He knew how this was going to go. He readied himself for Bull's anger and histrionics, pulled a stack of defensive books towards himself, and grabbed a pile of writing paper. This was going to be a long and dangerous night for Evans.

It went exactly as he'd expected. The first attempt at the letter was cordial, contrite even, but ended up flying out of the window on fire. The next one was sarcastic but subtle. That one ended up with a port all over it. Evans had tipped it over as he threw himself to one side to avoid a heavy paperweight that sailed suddenly in his direction and just past his head. The third was downright caustic, the fourth held little of Bull's disgust in the decision back, and the fifth let all of Bull's anger rip in the full-on language of the worst kind. It was eventually getting late into the middle of the night, and Bull was tired. They finalized a short missive, the general gist was: "Congratulations, come visit when you're back. We need to talk."

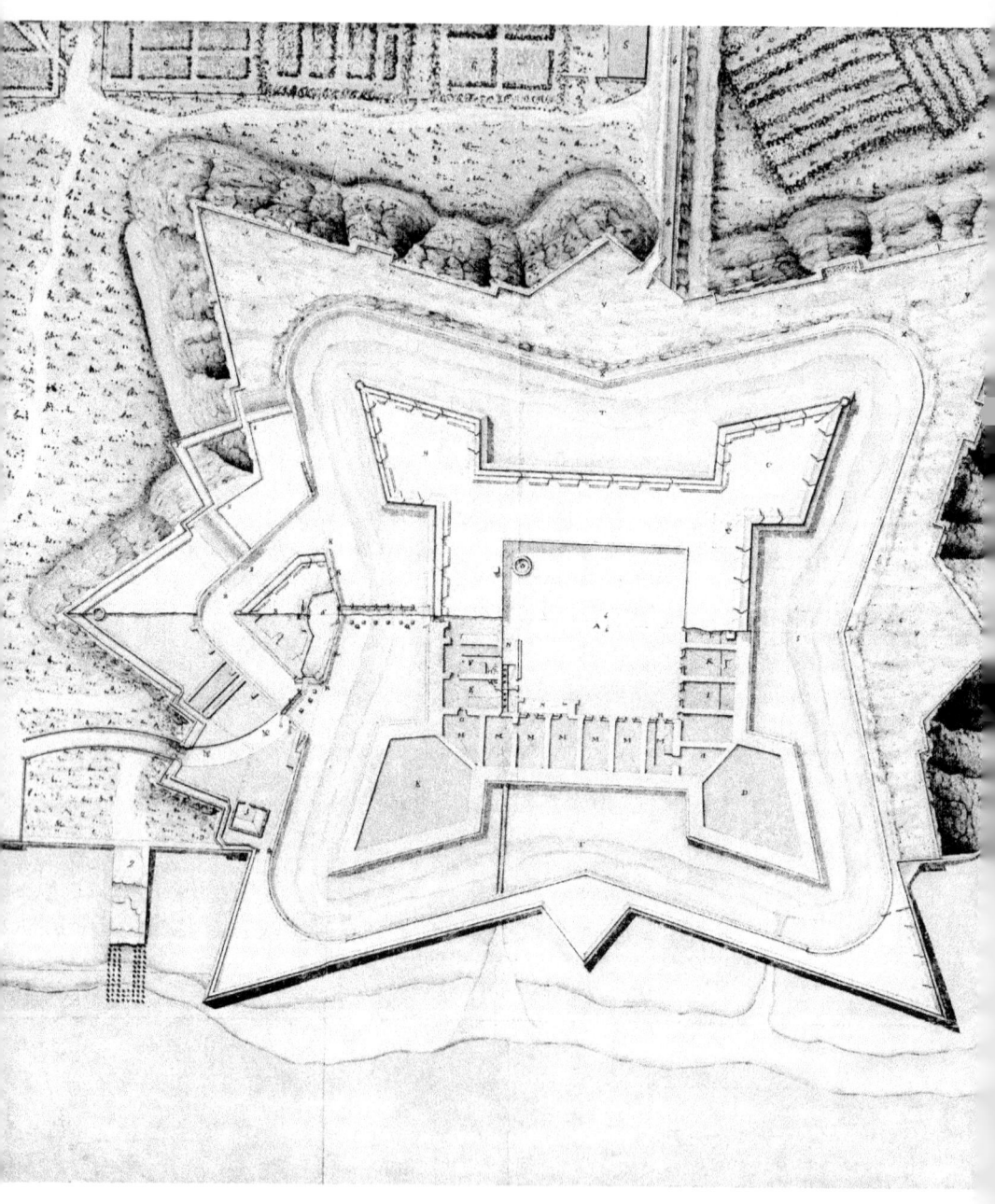

Castillo de San Marcos, map from 1763

Chapter 5: Gracia Real de Santa Teresa de Mose

Lamine Ndiaye couldn't see himself as an agent provocateur, yet that's what he'd become. As an occupation, it was a long way away from his former service as a translator for Prince Ayuba Suleiman Diallo. Job Jalla, as he'd been known to his companions, was a prince of the Fulani, an educated man, and a scholar. They'd both been captured by their erstwhile enemies, the Mandingo, sold into slavery and transported to the New World.

His experience of slavery wasn't something he wished to revisit, especially now that he was a fugitive from South Carolina and a freeman. It had been a strange turn of events. He'd been sold to a new owner in Georgia. He met his friend Chioke, and only a few days later, they were released and led to their freedom by some Yamacraw Indians.

They had taken different paths. Chioke preferred the native ways and sought out the Yamasees in Pensacola. In contrast, he preferred the more civilized company of the Spanish and relocated to St. Augustine. Yet, now here he was, planning to head back into that nest of vipers in South Carolina to risk being enslaved again. It shouldn't have surprised him that they'd sought him out. Lamine was an educated and skilled linguist; he could speak English, French, Spanish, and, importantly for this work, Portuguese and several West African languages.

As a former slave who knew the region, he was an obvious choice. Though he sported the distinctive rusty briar-like tattoos of his tribe, which were laced across his face, he didn't particularly stand out from other Africans, which was necessary for the intended clandestine efforts. He was also hardy, intelligent, and an experienced tribesman who could live off the land if needed while looking docile and pliant when required. His play-acting skills might come in handy. Yes, he had the ideal combination of skills for the task.

The residents were only just starting to get used to the new name for their town. Formerly Freetown, it was to be known as Gracia Real de Santa Teresa de Mose. Some had already taken to calling it Mose for short. The new governor had sent an immediate decree on his appointment. Lamine considered this new man, Manuel de Montiano, a clever choice. He hadn't even arrived, and he'd already strengthened the colony of Florida by formalizing the existence of the black freetown, beginning its fortification, and inviting its residents to join the militia.

The town was a couple of miles north of St. Augustine along the coast, so this action strengthened the northern approaches to St. Augustine and the Castillo. Lamine loved the township. Though now formally a Spanish municipality, the settlement had been here for a long time and had hosted fugitive Africans for years. On first appearance, it looked like a shanty town, though its looks could be deceiving. The residents had used the materials at hand; to an experienced eye, the buildings betrayed the stunning diversity of the population.

Lamine could literally pick them out as he walked past. There's an Igbo house, that one's Fulani, probably Fon, definitely

Yoruba, maybe Abron or Wolof, surely Chamba, and so on. The varying house construction wasn't the only representation of this mixture of African tribes. Lamine greeted those he knew in multiple dialects and languages, though often the residents defaulted to English. As the tongue of their oppressor, this habit annoyed him enormously.

To Lamine, the wonder of the place was never-ending. Former enemies were now neighbors, Fulani with Mandinka and Igbo with Yoruba. The food, though limited by access to native plants and animals, was a smorgasbord fusion of African cuisine. Meals took on new qualities as the Yorba's smoked fish and bean soups fused with the Fulani's grilled meats and yogurt.

The religions likewise compressed an entire continent into one town. The Fulani Muslims alongside the Bakongo Catholics, those practicing Hoodoo alongside others who preferred Minkisi. It was a true melting pot of the greatness of Africa, and Lamine considered it a minor miracle that the town worked at all. Perhaps it was their shared loss of their tribes, of their homes, and a consequence of their shared experiences being enslaved that made this community work.

Lamine was heading south to his meeting. He carried all he needed for his enterprise, a small bag with spare clothes, some minor personal possessions, and a sharp knife wrapped up and hidden within. Dressed in modest threadbare pants and top, walking barefoot, he looked the part he was destined to play. Slaves didn't have much, so there was little point in taking more than he had. The little knife was the only luxury he allowed himself in case things took a nasty turn or he needed to live off the land for a while. A knife made both circumstances easier. He had all he needed: his intelligence and linguistic skills.

As he reached the edge of Mose, he looked back, bidding the small town a fond farewell. Construction crews could be seen on the edge of town digging defensive ditches and raising the palisade, aiming to turn the village into Fort Mose, not just Gracia Real de Santa Teresa de Mose. His journey was just starting, and he hoped he would get back here and not end up returning to slavery in South Carolina.

Just south of town was his rendezvous on a beach, just off the Mose to St. Augustine path. The Irish agent was waiting for him. Lamine stumbled over the dunes, navigating between the clumps of seagrass. It was a long, flat beach, and the Atlantic waves crashed onto it heavily. The skiff was there, rolling up and down as the waves hurtled ashore. Richard O'Sullivan was waiting on the beach in front of the boat. The man looked his part - of a South Carolinian slave owner. O'Sullivan didn't stand out. He likely could disappear into the background in any situation.

Despite being Irish, he looked like most other Englishmen Lamine had met. Brown hair, brown eyebrows, brown eyes, and eyelashes. Totally nondescript. He had a short, thin nose, a knowing, sarcastic smile, and a chunky jaw. The only noticeable variation from type was a slightly darker tan than most, likely caused by the Florida sun. He wore what Lamine expected; tanned breeches, long black boots, a light grey breast coat, and a brown tunic. He held his brown tricorne hat under his arm while holding on to the skiff's anchor rope with his other hand.

Like Lamine, O'Sullivan was a skilled linguist, but he applied his trade differently. O'Sullivan's great talent was switching between British accents at the drop of a hat. One moment, he was Welsh from the southern valleys. Next, he was Cornish, and then a moment later, he was from Essex. There was only a hint of an Irish accent if he chose to offer it.

The skill came at a cost. O'Sullivan occasionally lost his voice, so he didn't talk much unless necessary, or during some subterfuge, he was enacting. O'Sullivan had another trait that made him ideal for this mission. He was a proud Catholic and one who hated the Protestant English and Scots. Acting against his supposed country didn't worry him; he was genuinely aligned with the Catholic Spanish and willing to engage in any act supporting the Catholic cause.

"Good to see you, Lamine. The ship is waiting. Are you ready?" O'Sullivan asked. Lamine was as ready as he was going to be.

"Well, I'm here, aren't I? So, I guess I'm ready. You must give me more information before we scull that thing over those waves. What exactly are we doing?" asked Lamine.

O'Sullivan didn't waste words and told it as it was. They were to take the boat and row to a Port Royal fishing vessel waiting for them just off the beach. The fishermen would take them up the Broad River and drop them at Shell Point in South Carolina. From there they were to travel across land to the Stono River. During this journey, O'Sullivan was to feign being a slave owner, and Lamine would be placed in irons and would have to pretend to be his slave. They were to make an acquaintance there, a Kongolese slave called Jemmy, who was orchestrating a rebellion, and they were to assist him in accomplishing his goals in whatever way they deemed necessary.

Lamine interrupted, "O'Sullivan, you do understand that I'm Fulani Muslim? I'm not sure how much credibility I'll have with the Kongolese Catholics."

O'Sullivan continued, "Yes, I do understand that. You'll let me do the talking when it comes to the role religion plays in this effort. You're here because you speak Portuguese. You are a former slave with firsthand Mose experience that you can tell

Jemmy about. They need to know there is something better for them if they are to shrug off the bonds of slavery. You can tell them about the town, about freedom for fugitives, and about the opportunity to serve in the Spanish militia. They will be able to fight the British and exact revenge for how they have been treated."

Lamine understood his role was to convince the rebels that there was a life worth having in Spanish Florida if they were willing to take it. As an intelligent man, he knew why the Spanish might seek such a rebellion. In doing so, they could distract the South Carolinians and the other British colonies from helping Georgia. Following which, General de Montiano might be able to take back the disputed lands from the thieving British through force of arms.

It was clear that war was coming, and they might be the first pawns on the board. O'Sullivan was done talking. He returned to his muteness and indicated it was time to go. They grabbed the skiff and, with immense exertion, got it over the waves. They got stuck on the sandbar for a few moments. O'Sullivan dipped his foot into the water and pushed, releasing them from their predicament. Lamine could see the fishing boat on the horizon, and they rowed hard towards it. His new life as an agent provocateur had truly begun.

Chapter 6: Wedding Gifts

Clang, clang, the bell tolled. Tom Ellis listened intently. Something didn't sound right with that bell; its peal had a clack somewhere within the clang; perhaps a crack had appeared someplace in the bell? Tom considered that a flaw would be typical since it was only recently installed in Christ Church. Tom had been there for its construction and witnessed the final clapboard strut being hammered to the roof. He missed Minister Herbert and his boring sermons. The original minister had joined them on their journey to Georgia on the Anne. Like so many others in those first two years, he had died of the pox and been laid to rest in the small graveyard nearby. It was a beautiful little church, but it had already outlived its usefulness as Savannah had expanded rapidly during the last few years.

The congregation had grown to where the church couldn't cope, and there were now consecutive services on a Sunday, much to the elation of the current minister, John Wesley. He was cut from a different cloth to Herbert, educated in Oxford, and brought to Georgia by Oglethorpe; he was intense, passionate, and articulate. His sermons were poetic affairs with deep religious understanding. A High Churchman who wished to revive primitive Christianity in Georgia, he was intrigued by and spent time with Georgia's Moravian settlers. He was a popular figure for those who shared his beliefs, but his revivalism was too much for many colonists. Tom had heard the rumors as well. Wesley had fallen in love with Sophy Hockey, had been spurned, and then had refused her Communion. Now, there was a lawsuit. Tom didn't think Wesley would be staying in Georgia too much longer, but he was glad of his presence today. Wesley stood, dressed in his minister's robes, just before the altar, waiting for the bride.

They all waited for the bride, but she was late. Tom idly looked about the congregation, hoping that Mary Hicks had not left him at the altar as Sophy had rebuffed Wesley. To his immediate right sat Uga. Tom's adopted son, Duke, and his fourteen-year-old pal, Noble Wimberly Jones, kept the bulldog amused and quiet. Uga slavered everywhere he went, and the church couldn't escape; there was a small pool of spit splattered around where he sat. The boys had grown up. Duke Cannon was the taller of the pair. The spitting image of his recently deceased father, he already had a solid looking physique with a particularly muscular upper body. Like his father, he had blonde curly hair, a snub nose, large ears, and a constant generous smile. Wimberly was the counterweight, a tall, skinny lad but a bright kid who learned whatever was presented to him quickly. Where Duke was blonde, Wimberly was dark brown, and his deep brown eyes sparkled with intelligence and an element of wildness.

Time ticked along and Tom wondered where Mary was; he hoped she was coming. He nodded at his best men. It had been a novel decision to have two best men, but his choice had really raised eyebrows. Stood close by were his friends Hillispilli and Sinlouchi, the Yamacraw Indians from the local village, or Hilli and Sin as they were known to Tom. They had been his close friends since his arrival in Georgia. They showed him the ways of the Indians, how to hunt in a foreign land, and how to fight the Indian way. He had hunted with them, fought beside them, and saved the colony because of them. How could he not choose them to stand beside him on his wedding day? They were bedecked in their most splendid outfits. An array of dazzling feathers protruded from the crown of their heads, thick bead necklaces tightly encircled their collars, and complex-colored shawls enwrapped their upper bodies and were fastened with deer hide belts. They wore their best-tanned leggings and moccasin long boots. True friends dressed to impress for Tom's big day.

Tom was getting worried. Where was she? He looked at the back of the church. The congregation was likewise fidgeting, chatting quietly, and waiting. It was quite a congregation, and he was happy to share his day with them. Noble Jones and the rest of his family sat in the pew behind him. While he was an indentured servant, his surrogate family had become close, and it was appropriate that they sat in the first pew on the bridegroom's side of the church.

Mary Musgrove sat with them. The small mixed-race woman was a stalwart of the community, an essential link to the Creek Indians, and a noteworthy trader and translator. Without her leadership, the community would never have come into being. She had aged quickly in the past two years after the death of her first husband, John. The stress of his long illness and death had been further exacerbated by her need to secure her lands and possessions, which were at risk if she hadn't remarried. Mary Musgrove's marriage to her new husband, Jacob Matthews, was

53

next up at Christ Church, and he stood proudly next to her in the pew.

Gordon, the bailiff and leader of the militia, waved at him. Wilson, the sawyer and reformed fool, yawned exaggeratedly as if to say where is she? In the church pews back to the narthex, Tom saw the community, including many of the original settlers who arrived aboard the Anne. It was also noticeable how many were missing. Except for Duke, the Cannons were all dead, likewise the Goddards, the Littles, and the Warrens. Entire families had been wiped out by the pox, and most families had suffered loss. The graveyard was nearly full. Like the church, it had outlived its usefulness and would have to be enlarged or moved. The colony's dead had been continually replaced by new settlers, and Savannah had remained a bustling and successful venture. Much thanks to Oglethorpe for that, thought Tom. A shame he couldn't be here for my wedding, still on his way back from Britain. Assuming there is going to be a wedding, of course. Where is she! Tom was getting anxious and hoped she wasn't having second thoughts.

Tom needn't have worried. There was a noticeable sign from Minister Wesley, and the small church choir began to recite an appropriate psalm for the bride's procession, which the congregation repeated. Nobody could help themselves, and the congregation craned around to watch the bride enter the church and walk along the nave. What they saw surprised and delighted them. Tom was awestruck. Mary Hicks didn't have much money. She'd recently been an indentured servant and had only just been released from her servitude because of John Cannon's death. So, it was even more surprising. Mary was a tiny woman, he often called her his shrew, but she enraptured the church and its congregation as she glided down the nave towards the altar.

There were several reasons for this captivation. Mary Hicks was outstandingly beautiful in her simple white dress that hugged her shape perfectly, both simultaneously demure and alluring. Her bouquet of local forest flowers had been carefully gathered by the Yamacraws, and it was a profusion of bright colors that were offset by the white of her gown. She floated along, almost as if on air. As she did so, a strange light entered the church through its windows. It was a peculiar diffusion that separated into individual beams, basking her in an aura of spellbinding rays. Each ray was precise and gleaming as it lit up the air, appearing to be individual sparkling specks like pixie dust. The timing of that light was auspicious as far as Tom was concerned. It was a sign of love and a sign of a providential future.

If the crowd weren't mesmerized enough, they had only to cast their eye towards Mary's escort. It had been an open question, who would give Mary away? She had no family in Georgia, and the family she'd served had been decimated by the pox. Only Mary Musgrove could've solved that problem in this way. Nobody had told Tom what solution had been agreed.

Escorting his bride was Tomochichi, the local Yamacraw Mico. Age is indeterminate for the Yamacraws, and nobody knew exactly how old he was. Still, it was known that he was in his nineties. He was still a tall, splendid figure of dignity and wisdom. All the etchings of a well-lived life were carved into the contours and crags in the lines crisscrossing his face. His distended earlobes were bejeweled for this occasion, and his hair was dressed in a traditional and outlandish headdress made of beads, shells, and feathers. His hair was cropped on top, long down one side, and grey flecks finally began to show. He wore the ceremonial gowns of the Creek Indian leader. Tomochichi's traditional bear fur was slung over his shoulders, a green silk scarf around his neck, and his deer skin shirt, breeches, and moccasin boots were tight fitting and of outstanding quality. The crowd was excited that this local leader was in church to give Mary away, and Tom was delighted to see him.

Minister Wesley welcomed Mary and Tomochichi to the altar and began the wedding rites. Tom and Mary glanced at each other and smiled in mutual satisfaction for this moment in their lives. Despite his tendency for intellectual discourses, Wesley kept the service simple—beautiful and simple like Mary's dress: "Dearly beloved, we are gathered together here in the sight of God, and in the face of this Congregation, to join together this Man and this Woman in Holy Matrimony."

For Tom, the service seemed to fly by. More psalms were chanted and recited. Minister Wesley asked, "Wilt thou have this man to thy wedded husband, to live together after God's ordinance, in the holy estate of matrimony? Wilt thou obey him, serve him, love, honor and keep him in sickness and health, and forsaking all other, keep thee only unto him, so long as ye both shall live?"

Mary answered that she would, and Tom responded, "With this ring I thee wed, with my body I thee worship, and with all my worldly goods I thee endow." Hilli passed him the ring, and he slipped it on Mary's finger. Before he knew it, they were married, kissing, and on their way down the nave and out of the church. Another psalm was chanted and repeated by the congregation as they left.

⏳ ⏳ ⏳

The after-wedding party was hosted at Noble Jones's house. It was ably organized by Sarah Jones in her usual professional fashion. Only a small group of close friends and family attended.

The dining room table had been decorated with white paper chains, and much of the fare was white. Laid on the table were bread, buns, assorted candied fruit, milk, and various foods. Sarah had baked two white cakes, one for the bridegroom and one for the bride. The party ate the bridegroom's cake but saved Mary's so the couple could celebrate anniversaries after it was preserved in alcohol. Uga ran off with the remainder of the first cake firmly between his jowly jaws while Duke and Wimberly chased after him, giggling.

Tomochichi began the toasts. He honored Tom for his bravery and being a true native, learning the Creek way, and befriending the Yamacraw. He thanked Mary for putting up with Tom. Hilli and Sin put on a quick show that had the guests in fits of laughter at Tom's expense. Mary Musgrove thanked the couple for their friendship and Tom for his willingness to protect the village from the more scurrilous folk.

It was finally Noble Jones's turn to toast the couple. He started with the usual platitudes about marriage, life, and his hopes for them and their future kin. Noble was an accomplished speaker, though, and he soon charmed his listeners with stories of their past, their fight for better prospects as indentured servants, and their yet-to-be-realized contribution to this land they all called Georgia. At the height of his oratory, the audience was spellbound, and he flourished two letters at this moment. As Noble put it, "A gift from our founder, the father of the colony, the Protector of the Southern Frontier and now General, James Edward Oglethorpe." He handed the letters to Tom.

Tom tentatively took the letters from Noble and inspected them. Sure enough, they were Oglethorpe's letters, addressed to him in his usual scrawl and sealed with wax using his stamp and coat of arms. He wondered what words they might contain.

He carefully opened the first letter and glanced at Mary as he did. The anticipation of their gathered friends and family was palpable. The first letter contained an inconceivable gift.

Oglethorpe had personally given the couple sixty acres of land near the new city of Frederica on St. Simons Island. As Oglethorpe put it, "Tom, you are a free man now, and all men must have land to protect, to farm, and to build upon. With this gift, I invite you to join me in building the next frontier city in Georgia. Build with me the city and fort of Frederica. I have surveyed this land along the river. It will be productive and valuable land where the river straightens to the north of the new settlement. It will be where you and Mary can start your true adventure as free citizens and begin your family." It was a generous gift, and it would have taken Tom years to accomplish it with his carpenter's salary.

What could the following letter contain? Tom wondered. He broke the seal. The next gift offered a strangely mixed blessing. Oglethorpe's scribble had not improved any, "On the recommendation of Captain McPherson for your service at the battle of Fort Argyle and for your recent actions to protect the colony from subversion and smuggling you are to be promoted to corporal in the Georgia rangers." This part was the true gift and included a salary to go with the commission.

Tom was shocked by the following sentence, though. "You will report to the mounted division of the rangers following receipt of this letter." Setting aside their plans for a honeymoon, this part truly horrified Tom. He'd always been attached to the foot and boat divisions of the rangers; he'd never really learned to ride a horse, so this was an unwelcome development. How could he lead mounted soldiers if he couldn't even sit on a horse? Hilli immediately read his expression and slapped him on the back, breaking him out of his undiplomatic response to these lavish gifts. He smiled and thanked Noble Jones profusely for being the bearer of these beautiful letters.

Sin whispered, "Don't worry, my foot sore friend. You will learn, and your feet will become soft like the rest of these slow-running fat men." Tom couldn't help himself and laughed, breaking him away from his anxiousness about horse riding. Oglethorpe had probably assumed without thought that he could ride as most freemen could. The after-wedding party continued late into the night with much dancing and drinking. Noble even broke open a bottle of his best whiskey.

Chapter 7: Not Jenkins' Ear

Hernando Perez was sick. Sick of the cramped quarters onboard the San Luis that constantly stank of stagnant sweat, an overflowing latrine, and human bodies packed too close together. He was sick of the ocean, the constant movement, the waves, and the storms. Above all, he was sick of throwing up his guts. Would his seasickness never end? He peered down at the waves as they lapped the side of the ship, making a slapping noise as they smashed into the oak timbers of the hull. His head poked out of a gap in the gunwale as he readied himself for another bout of vomiting.

Antonio, the butcher, whacked him on the back suddenly, so unintentionally hard that Hernando feared for a moment that he might fall overboard. "How are you doing?" he asked.

The distraction caught Hernando as the bile was on the way up his throat, and he gagged, coughed, and swallowed it back down. It would've been better if it had come out. He paused for a moment to catch his breath. "Not good, I'm clearly meant to be a soldier, not a sailor. That last storm was a beast. Any sign of the other ships?"

The last storm had indeed been severe. The San Luis and her two accompanying galleons had left Santa Cruz de Tenerife. When the storm hit, they were crossing the Atlantic on their journey to Cuba. The ship had been thrown about, and their small squad had been terrified while confined in their quarters. Even the hardiest veterans among them were scared the ship might go down, and the two youngsters had been deathly white with terror for days afterward.

By all accounts, it was a vicious storm. The sailors confessed that they'd not experienced anything like it for years. It had scattered their small squadron of vessels, and now the San Luis was alone and more vulnerable. Worse still, the ship was damaged during the tempest. Several sails on the mizzen mast had been ripped, rigging connected to the lower stay had failed, and the topgallant mast had taken a beating and appeared damaged. The sailors were now fixing her, but she was limping along while the repairs were being carried out. She was a big ship with sixty-two guns, fifteen hundred sailors, and a combined force of three hundred marines and soldiers. Limping along damaged and without her escort nonetheless made her vulnerable to British privateers. The San Luis's captain and the General de Montiano kept a wary eye out for the enemy as they scanned the waters.

"No sign of the other ships yet. The sailors tell me we are heading into Caribbean waters and will be in Havana in days. The going should be fairer; maybe you'll stop chucking up by the time we get there!" With that ditty, Antonio left Hernando to continue his shipside contemplation. At least he was allowed to be deck-side; seasickness in the cabin was horrid. The stench, the inability to throw away the remains, the lack of ability to clean the space due to the overcrowding. Better out here on the deck with the wind in his face.

As Hernando continued his vigil, between episodes of illness, he looked out across the expanse of the ocean. It was endless. The sky had cleared of the intense dark clouds, which was a stunning sight. It was a deep turquoise, with the odd wisp of streaky white clouds. The sky offset the darker hues of the ocean, and the waves sparkled as they rose and crested, catching the sunlight as they peaked before tumbling back into the darker blue of the trough. At the horizon, the two divergent blues met and merged in a symbiotic curve that was juxtaposed one against the other.

Hernando gazed out across this pleasing horizon and noticed three dark dots. He watched them. They looked strange and out of place. After some time, they grew and appeared to be headed in San Luis' direction. After another interval, he noticed they were ships, smaller than the San Luis but fast-looking. The speed with which they grew accelerated, and they cut through the water at an astonishing pace. He couldn't see any colors; perhaps they were pirates.

Hernando suddenly became aware of the hustle and bustle around the San Luis. The captain and his sailors had spotted the encroaching vessels as well. Gunners had been dispatched to ready the guns; the marines and General de Montiano's soldiers had been called on deck. The sailors were up in the masts and rigging, trying to coax as much speed out of the San Luis as possible. Hernando realized that he must report for duty and join his squad. He picked up his equipment and went looking for Sergeant Moreno-Rodriguez. The Marines were formed up in the ship's main deck and forecastle while the soldiers had been placed in the poop and quarter decks.

As he sought out his squad, Hernando saw the general and captain talking; both held extended field glasses and carefully observed the ships heading in their direction. They were clearly debating who these adversaries might be and where they'd sailed from. Close by, he found his squad forming up in the front section of the quarter-deck near the main mast. The sergeant was geeing them along and slapped Hernando on the shoulder when he arrived, "You should've been quicker getting here. Stop carrying that kit around and get dressed!" Hernando obeyed immediately, fastened his breastplate, put on his helmet, and began to load his long musket. Miguel and Rodrigo were formed up to his right, while Alvaro and Benito were to his left.

The attacking ships were moving fast. Hernando heard a sailor shout, "Looks like they're out of the Caribbean. Currently heading to engage on the larboard!" He took a quick look. The three ships weren't dots anymore. They were sloops, smaller vessels with two masts, slim hulls, and bristling with eighteen guns along one deck. What they lost in size and firepower, they gained in speed and maneuverability. Even though the San Luis was one of the most formidable galleons in the Spanish Navy, there was no guarantee it would see off these three smaller sloops. Gun for gun, the three vessels were nearly evenly matched with the San Luis.

In retrospect, Hernando reflected that it was odd that the ships weren't a hive of activity like the San Luis. Surely, if they had meant to engage, their crews would have been running about readying for battle and preparing their guns. Instead, they concentrated on catching up with the San Luis. That should've been the clue to what happened next.

They noticeably slowed and hoisted their ensigns as they gained to within cannon distance. It was the standard of the Spanish Navy: red, white, and yellow stripes with the emblematic golden crescent, black crown, and black-winged griffin. These were Guarda Costa's sloops designed to enforce the trading rules in the colonies. They were there to intercept and govern British slaving ships and prevent them from smuggling contraband merchandise into Spanish Cuba.

The San Luis was ordered to slow and the gunners to stand down. The sloops quickly maneuvered to different positions to create a defensive formation around the San Luis. One went to the starboard; another went to the larboard, and the last one followed behind the stern. The lead sloop, La Isabela, hailed the San Luis and sent over a small boat containing a few sailors and the captain. They were hoisted aboard and greeted by the San Luis's captain and the General de Montiano. With the danger over, the soldiers and marines stood down, and the sailors returned to their regular duties.

Hernando still had his leave to be deckside, so he lingered nearby, no longer feeling sick but not wanting to return to his confined quarters until he absolutely had to. Sergeant Moreno-Rodriguez and Antonio stayed with him, curious about their new escort of coastguards. The rest of the squad drifted away, many returning to their bunk beds since they hadn't been given leave to be on deck.

As they surreptitiously observed the greeting on the San Luis, they realized it was a historic affair about which they would tell stories for years. Not only were they closer to Montiano than they had ever been, but the man welcomed aboard was none other than Juan de León Fandiño. He was the legendary Guarda Costa who'd taken Jenkins' ear. This controversy was central to the current Spanish and British dispute. A dispute that was likely going to lead to war.

The sailors that had rowed Fandiño across from the sloop immediately captured Hernando's and Antonio's attention. Antonio was quicker to remark, "Look at the sailors. Have you ever seen such a bunch of crooks?" Hernando eyed them carefully; he didn't want to be obvious. They were a brutal-looking gang, hardy, weather-beaten, and battle-hardened. Antonio's gibe, though, had been more subtle and directed at something else. Unlike the galleon's white Spanish sailors, these men were part of an assorted group of colonials. Black former slaves, mixed-race servants who had escaped servitude, and Indians who had somehow been enlisted into the Spanish coastguard. He didn't feel the same way about it. Hernando was thankful to have men like this on the Spanish side. He'd rather fight beside them than against them, for sure.

General de Montiano and Fandiño were talking amiably. They couldn't quite hear the conversation. Montiano wore his black tricorn hat, black tunic and pantaloons, white cravat, golden woven waistcoat, and long leather boots. Montiano's gold-incrusted sword hung by his side. He was animated as he spoke, his face creasing as he smiled, his long prominent nose and closely cut beard noticeable features.

Fandiño was of a different ilk altogether. The contrast couldn't have been greater. Stout, slightly overweight but in an overbearing way that suggested fortitude. He didn't look like he'd ever washed; his clothes were basic, brown, and laden with dirt. Hanging by his side was a wicked-looking cleaver of a cutlass etched as if it had been well used. Like his crew, Fandiño appeared to know his way around a sloop and had lived a long and dangerous life harassing the British. His eyes were sharp, deep brown, almost vindictive in their penetrative gaze as he spoke. A notable lack of blinking was unsettling. As were the deep scars that crossed his cheeks, arms, and hands. His long hair was black and greasy, as was his beard. Whenever Hernando imagined a pirate, this would be the man he would picture.

Then Hernando saw it. A black, shriveled, grisly ear hung from a leather band around Fandiño's neck. Was that it? Was that Jenkins' actual ear? The one that was causing all the trouble. The one that had led Hernando and his squad to be posted to the Castillo de San Marcos. He turned to Moreno-Rodriguez, "Look, he's still wearing it. He's still got Jenkins' ear!"

The sergeant laughed, "You know nothing, Hernando. Jenkins still has his ear. Yes, Fandiño chopped it off, but Jenkins presented his mutilated ear to the British Parliament. So he must still have it. That's what started all this in the first place. I'd reckon that was some other poor blighter's ear. Fandiño probably keeps it to remind everybody who he is!"

The welcome for Fandiño was short. He joined the captain of the San Luis and General de Montiano in the captain's quarters for a meal. Later that afternoon, he returned with his sailors to the La Isabela. The three coastguard sloops escorted the San Luis to the Havana port in Cuba. Other vessels were sent out to look for the two missing Spanish galleons, which were later found and brought into port. Hernando wasn't seasick again and was grateful when the San Luis reached its dock in Havana. A break from a close and uncomfortable cabin and a chance to see Havana would be welcome relief from their journey.

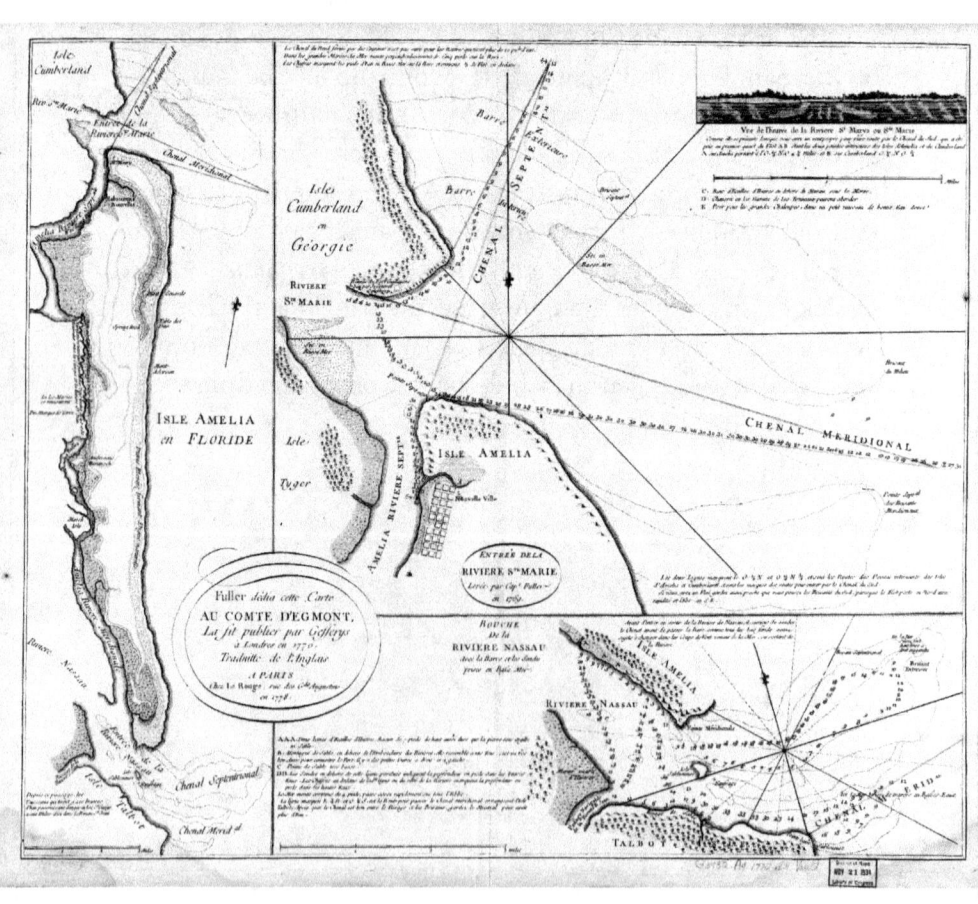

Chapter 8: Shell Point

The stench was atrocious. Odors of all varieties. The fish guts stank of offal. The saltwater smelled of brine. The sailors reeked of perspiration and grime while the boat combined them into some sort of perfumer's hell. Lamine was not taken with the fishing boat. Even worse, he disliked being at sea again. It gave him bad memories of a slaver's ship crossing the Atlantic.

It was a small fishing boat with one mast, two small cabins, and a crew of six. There was not enough room for the masses of fish they were landing, piling up in the deck hold, overspilling it, and adding to the pong aboard. Though the boat had been sent to ferry them to Shell Point, the crew carried on with their primary business of fishing, and it was proving to be a successful trip. Lamine was unfamiliar with the variety of fish hereabouts, but it was a productive bounty. There were sizable silver-blue fish, strange-looking bonefish, and red-colored small fish, along with others Lamine had never seen before.

Standing at the bow, Lamine looked out across the water. At least it was calm. He never wanted to experience storms aboard a ship again. The waves lapped gently against the hull, and the boat moved through the water, rolling up over the small crests and down into the slight troughs. Occasional spray flecks burst over the side, misting him lightly with salty wetness. He appreciated it.

The gentle wind out of the northeast and the spray allowed him to momentarily escape the intense heat. The boat was headed northwards, urgently seeking South Carolina's Broad River headwaters. A crowd of gulls followed the boat constantly. Their incessant squawking was a further irritation that made sleep difficult.

During the journey, his Irish companion was his usual tight-lipped self, rarely saying a word, let alone engaging in a conversation. He often sat at the stern of the boat, hunched up and covered by his cloak. O'Sullivan was a strange fellow. He seemed to meditate continuously throughout the trip, concentrating almost solely on his boots—in another world entirely.

As their northern route progressed, they began to pass the barrier islands that dot the coastline. The boat's captain pointed out Amelia Island, "That's where the real Spanish control ends and the disputed lands start."

To Lamine, the island appeared covered in a mango-like forest but with strange moss. It had long sandy beaches. The next island was much larger, covered in the same style of forest, and had long beaches like Amelia.

As they reached the third island, O'Sullivan seemed to have returned from his stupor. It was almost as if he'd been reserving his energy for this moment. O'Sullivan stood and carefully left the stern to where Lamine sat in the bow. He trod carefully, not to slip on a briny, slippery spot, and stepped over several fish that had somehow escaped the deck's hold. As he reached Lamine, he smiled broadly and sat beside him. The sudden change of demeanor surprised Lamine. It was almost as if O'Sullivan were two people. One reserved, quiet, and sullen. The other was generous, open, and friendly.

O'Sullivan looked out over the bow and towards the north, not caring to disguise his Northern Irish accent, "Here's the craic. We're off in enemy territory now. Be two islands; once past, we'll be at St. Simons. It's still Spanish. The Sassenach are building a town and fort, calling it Frederica. Time to start acting, mo cara."

O'Sullivan took a thick rope and fastened it around Lamine's neck, not too tightly. He secured Lamine's wrists with a slaver's manacles and chains; again, he was careful not to make them uncomfortable. If they were spotted here, it would be from a distance. No sense making it worse than it needed to be that would come later when they made landfall. They were to look like a slaver who'd recovered his escaped property. The image was complete when O'Sullivan pulled out his wicked-looking crop. A thick cord of interwoven lines of twine. A short, heavy whip that would be used to control his charge brutally.

Now, they were acting the part of slaveowner and slave. Lamine spent all his time sitting by, talking to, and sleeping near O'Sullivan. Though he remained uncommunicative, Lamine learned much about him over the next two days. He pieced together fragments of conversation and learned most one evening while drinking rum. O'Sullivan's guard dropped, and Lamine had all the pieces to fill the jigsaw.

O'Sullivan had grown up on a farm in Fermanagh. His father and grandfather had been significant landowners. They'd lost everything, including their lives, because of their support of the Jacobites during the Williamite War. The Anglo-Irish had taken control of the land, setting up plantations, and O'Sullivan's family farm was taken along with all his family's possessions. As a young man without a family, as well as landless and destitute, he nearly starved. His sense of injustice, a deep hate for his Protestant overlords, and his craving to fight for the Roman Catholic cause had kept him alive.

Somehow, he'd survived by pretending to be other people and using this skill to beg, borrow, and steal anything he needed. He found his way south to the port of Cork. Using one of his English dialects, he posed as a sailor and joined one of the trading ships as part of the crew. The ship was loaded with beef, pork, butter, and cheese headed to the West Indies. His hate for the British deepened when he saw the enormous abundance of food that was shipped out, raped from Ireland while the people starved.

As soon as he reached the West Indies, he absconded. It took him time to get out of Jamacia. Still, eventually, he bought himself a berth on a trader going to Cuba. Once in Havana, he immediately sought out the Spanish garrison and offered his services. It took more time for him to be trusted and a further spell to prove himself. Eventually, his value was accepted by the Spanish. He was enlisted into their network of spies and deployed against the British in North America. It was some tale. Lamine reflected that it was almost as convoluted and complex as his own story.

Before long, they passed the Savannah River, leaving Georgia's waters and entering South Carolina's. Lamine could sense O'Sullivan becoming tenser and more alert as they went deeper into enemy territory. He also became harsher, recognizing their need to fully adopt their roles. On one occasion, O'Sullivan suddenly lashed out at Lamine with his slaver's whip, leaving a great welt on Lamine's upper arm. Later, he told Lamine that he would have to be ready to receive such treatment when they were landside, and some might expect to see such injuries. Lamine knew; he'd been a slave after all, and if he was to look the part, this mistreatment had to occur. O'Sullivan tightened the rope around Lamine's neck and restricted his manacles so that they chafed at his wrists more and made clear red gouges in his skin. They were ready.

At last, they arrived at the mouth of the Broad River. As its name described, it was broad. The land on either side was low-lying and marshy. Not much in the way of trees or scrub could be seen. It was inaccessible, and lots of small creeks and inlets snaked into the river from across the marshland. The small fishing boat didn't seem out of place coming inland and going up the river. Lamine saw an occasional farmhouse of typical South Carolinian construction, small log cabins with attached gardens, surrounded by open fields. He saw one or two slaves working the land as they passed. Those small farms reminded him of his former life, and unexpected shivers shot down his spine. He hoped this affair wouldn't end up with him back in chains permanently.

The river was lightly populated, and they saw very few settlements after a while. It was an ideal location for smugglers to land or, indeed, for provocateurs to infiltrate. After a short way, the captain signaled the crew to tack to starboard, and they headed into one of the larger streams. They pulled in the mainsail and rowed carefully up the stream. It seemed like they'd arrived at Shell Point. The land continued to be pocked with many streams, creeks, and inlets, and Lamine considered it would be easy to get lost in this marshy landscape. Traversing this land would be challenging if you were unfamiliar with it.

They continued up the stream for about three hundred yards when the crew began to slow their rowing. A small wooden dock, perfectly designed for the fishing boat, appeared at their port. The crew carefully brought the boat up alongside the pier. Two crew members jumped out and tied the boat securely. This was it. They would finally leave this stench and be done with the strange combination of smells that had lived with them for five days since their departure from Mose. Lamine didn't think he would ever get rid of the smell. It would be deeply woven into the fabric of his few possessions for longer than he cared to imagine. O'Sullivan grabbed the rope around Lamine's neck and led him off the fishing boat, pulling constantly. They carefully tottered across the wooden boards that separated the boat from its wharf, careful not to slip and land in the creek. Lamine's chains rattled, and his manacles scraped his wrists; every move seemed to remind him of the pain of his former existence.

The captain and crew were quick to leave. They were headed for Port Royal with a significant catch and couldn't afford for it to spoil. All said their goodbyes, and Lamine watched the boat move tentatively back down the small Shell Point stream. He wasn't sad to see it go.

There was a camp area with a well-used fire, a gazebo-style overhang, and a dry mound-like area that had clearly been used before. They set up camp and waited while eating dried tack and deer jerky. Lamine reflected that some of the worst food could be the best when all you've eaten for five days is fish, fish stews, and fish soups. He was grateful for the change.

O'Sullivan explained their pause, in a perfect home counties accent, "We're waiting for my contact to arrive with a horse. From Shell Point, we head overland to join the Port Royal to Charles Town road. Our greatest danger may occur on that road if our characters and story aren't believable. We will pass all manner of folk and can't afford to be queried. If a slaver is walking and not on horseback, that could raise some questions, so we wait." He continued, "As we get closer to Charles Town, the risks of our subterfuge being discovered are much higher. So, at an arranged point, we drop off the horse and head across the land to our rendezvous with Jemmy. He's on a plantation near the Stono River. This route was much safer than getting the fishing boat to drop us off up the coast nearer to our destination."

The afternoon ticked by, and there was no sign of O'Sullivan's contact. He began to look furtive and muttered to himself, "Where on earth is he? It should be here by now. Damn the boy, he's only coming from Port Royal." That afternoon disappeared, and the early evening moved in. Then, the boy and O'Sullivan's horse turned up. Lamine was as astute as ever and heard it first. The boy was trotting the horse along the path towards the camp and dock where they were. When he broke through the foliage into the clearing, it was evident he was a young kid, barely twelve years old. Despite all his muttering, when the boy arrived and dismounted from the horse, O'Sullivan gave him a fatherly hug. Lamine thought there was an interesting story here somewhere. He didn't dare ask, though, because now he was playing the role of a slave and it would have been inappropriate for him to address his slaveowner. He needed to be docile and didn't know who he could trust. It was time to play his role to the full.

As it was late into the evening, the boy stayed, and they ate dinner around the campfire. O'Sullivan tied Lamine's neck rope and chains firmly to a post near the fire. It was designed for a specific purpose. He was given scraps from their meal and treated as any slave would be. Overhearing the conversation, it was clear the boy was giving O'Sullivan a report about the comings and goings at Port Royal, about the gossip and the latest news. O'Sullivan was as focused and intense as Lamine had ever seen him. Seeking to remember everything. Gathering intelligence for his Spanish masters, it seemed.

The following morning, they set out back up the track the boy had used. The youth sat behind O'Sullivan on the horse, and Lamine trudged behind, trying not to trip as he was tugged along by his neck rope. When they hit the main road from Port Royal, the lad bid O'Sullivan a fond farewell and ran at some pace up the road towards Port Royal. O'Sullivan watched him run and smiled. He then turned the horse toward Charles Town and set off. The road was no more than a dirt track, wide enough for a horse and cart. Lamine began his long hike to the Stono River. O'Sullivan had warned him to expect at least four days of walking.

Chapter 9: Three More Letters

Cheese on toast, or Welsh rarebit, as he preferred to call it, was Evans's breakfast. He was sat at the small table in the scullery, just off the kitchen, chomping at his food. He'd added some brown sauce, which seemed to improve the flavor. As he cleaned his plate and wiped his mouth with his handkerchief, a summons came to attend Acting Governor Bull. While there were many benefits to his role as aide to Bull, lazing about doing nothing wasn't one of them. It was a constant flow of work from sunrise to dusk and sometimes even late into the night. Even dice was out as Williams had been sent to help the Acting Lieutenant Governor, who was adjusting to his new role.

As he moved through the kitchen, he dropped off his plate and thanked the staff for the meal. They were quick to whip up food when he needed it between his constant errands. Evans made his way up the back stairs to Bull's office. It was interesting to compare the rudimentary, dusty, scuffed stairwell that the servants used to the opulent polished stairwell at the front of the house. One was designed for utility, while the other portrayed grandeur and status. Bull's house was certainly taking on the appropriate image expected of an influential colonial leader. Few other houses in Charles Town could rival it.

As he reached the top of the stairs, he noticed Bull's office door was open, waiting for his arrival. That was the first unusual thing of the day. Then, as he tentatively entered the office and instinctively ducked, nothing was hurled in his direction. Very odd. Then Evans saw Bull. He was sitting behind the desk, writing letters with an enormous grin almost spread from ear to ear. His pipe sat on the desk. Wisps of smoke slowly drifted from it as if it had been left unattended and gone out.

Evans couldn't recall when he'd seen Bull sit down or smile. He was a man of action, a colonel who had successfully defended the colony in several Indian wars. Bull usually paced the office like a caged animal; he never sat at the desk and rarely wrote his own letters. And yet here he was, sitting and scribbling away. Evans knew Bull to be a severe and combustible man who lost his temper quickly. He wasn't an ungrateful or unjust man, just not a happy, joyful type. And yet here he was, beaming with joy like a child who had just been given candy. Evans was perplexed. What a strange day.

Bull looked up, "Evans, I have some important errands for you. It'll mean leaving the house for a bit, so you'll need to pack a few things to take with you. I have three letters for you to deliver by hand. We have received critical intelligence from our St. Augustine spy. I need the information to get to Vanderdussen, Palmer, and the militia at Port Royal." As he talked, Bull closed the last letter and began to seal all three with wax and his stamp displaying the Governor's insignia. Evans thought immediately that the information must be of the utmost secrecy if Bull had avoided dictating the letters for him to write. He'd written them and sealed them himself. That was an obvious clue as far as Evans was concerned.

After sealing the letters, Bull continued, "Vanderdussen is drilling the militia in Charles Town, so you must go to him first. Then, next, find Palmer and the Rangers. They're out west. They recently crossed the Congaree River and are headed back to Charles Town. Then, go to Port Royal and give the final letter to Kingston, the militia leader there. That is the least important of the three and should be delivered last. Now, this is critical, Evans; I'm trusting you. Take these letters there as quickly as you can. Do not - and I emphasize this! - do not give the letters to aides. These letters should be delivered to Vanderdussen, Palmer, and Kingston in person. The letters should be destroyed immediately after they've read them. Understand?" Evans understood and confirmed it. Obviously, the letters must contain critical intelligence. Then, another odd thing happened. As Bull passed the letters to Evans, he whistled a merry tune. Evans was flabbergasted as he'd never heard Bull whistle before. Whatever news he'd received must be valuable and helpful for Bull and South Carolina. Given Bull's penchant for throwing things, Evans earnestly hoped the Acting Governor received more news from this spy in St. Augustine. As he left the office with three of the most essential letters he'd ever held clasped tightly in his hand, he considered it a very unusual day.

Evans secured the letters carefully. It was clear it would mean serious trouble for him if he lost any of these letters. They were stashed in his leather case, which would sit securely in his saddle bag. He quickly prepared to leave, gathered a few spare clothes and obtained hard tack and other food from the kitchen. He changed into his riding gear and then went out to the stables. Bull must have sent prior notice to the stable boys as Evans's bay colt Llewelyn was fully tacked. He checked the saddle, stirrups, and girth strap; everything seemed in order. The stable lads rarely made a mistake, but Evans always checked to be sure. He mounted the colt and set off at a fast walk, moving quickly into a trot along Meeting Street as he headed across town.

Colonel Vanderdussen's letter was the first of his deliveries and the easiest. It was a simple trot across town to the parade grounds where Vanderdussen was drilling the militia. He'd been doing this for many weeks. Rotating different groups of citizens through their paces. With everybody switching between their regular duties as citizens and militia training. One day, the baker would be baking bread, and the next day, he'd be stripping and cleaning a musket. The sawyer would alternate between the hard graft of sawing wood and conducting musket drills, with its complex loading, presenting, and firing exercises. The day after, it would be the tailor's turn to stab straw dummies with his gun and bayonet; attention, squat, thrust, stab, withdraw, and then repeat. Then, the brewer's turn to practice with the singlestick. Man against a man with a broad stick in bouts that only ended when one man had drawn blood from the other's head.

As Evans arrived at the wide-open area of the parade ground, he could see that Vanderdussen was putting several groups through their exercises. One was strung out along the end of a shooting range, being drilled with their muskets, with the captain shouting at them for some error. Another group was conducting bayonet drills. The colonel stood back with this second group, watching his captain lead the drill. Evans slowed Llewelyn to a walk and crossed the parade ground to where the colonel stood. He dismounted and guided his horse by the reins the last few yards.

Colonel Vanderdussen, like all the militia, was a citizen. He was a prominent merchant and a plantation owner, but more relevant as far as Bull was concerned was his role as a member of the Commons House. Despite his non-military background, he immediately appeared to have a military bearing. Vanderdussen was prim and straight-backed, almost as if he were constantly standing in attention. He looked like a colonel, and it wouldn't have surprised Evans to see him among the British regulars. His militia uniform was spotless, and it looked starched. The lines in his trousers were perfect. His boots were impeccable. This aura of military correctness transitioned into his face. A short pencil mustache was immaculate, sharp hazel eyes that looked stiff with attention to detail, and a thin, precise nose lacking flaws. Evans concluded instantly that this was a parade ground colonel in every aspect of his appearance and manner.

As Evans approached, the colonel's attention shifted from the bayonet drills. He acknowledged his visitor, "Good morning, Evans. No doubt here on formal business? Look at these boys." He pointed at the group trying to stab the straw dummies, saying, "Wouldn't stand a chance against regulars. Let's hope it never comes to that!"

Evans replied, "Indeed, Sir. And yes, Sir, here on Acting Governor Bull's business. May we find somewhere a little more private? I have a letter that must be delivered by hand and destroyed afterward."

Colonel Vanderdussen was immediately alert to the implication, "Yes, of course. Over there, my office. Follow me." A small cabin sat alongside the parade ground. It was the only visible structure beyond a storage shed used for drill equipment. The colonel led Evans to the cabin. Llewelyn was secured. Evans fetched his leather case from Llewelyn's saddle bag, and they entered the colonial's office. It was an austere cabin. It is virtually empty but contains the essentials: a small desk and chair, some writing materials, a reading chair, and a small conference table. It was neat, proper, and organized, very like the colonel himself.

"Take a seat, Evans. Let's see this letter then." Evans fished Vanderdussen's dispatch out of his satchel, passed it to him, and sat at the conference table. The colonel also sat and inspected the Governor's wax seal as if it might have come from somebody else. He slowly opened it in a tedious, almost fastidious way that Evans found irritating. As the colonel read the letter, Evans keenly observed his facial expressions for clues about the contents. There was horror. There was anger and then sternness. Then, there was a shift to surprise; his eyes almost bulged out of his head. Then, the same bizarre glee and satisfaction that had stunned Evans this morning when he'd seen Bull. Whatever was in that letter certainly hit all the emotions.

Evans asked, "Sir, I must insist that you now destroy the letter in my presence." Still somewhat dumbfounded, the colonel stood and crossed over to his desk, where a stone block lay ready for destroying such orders. He ripped the paper into shreds, placed it on the stone, and set it alight. Evans waited until it was destroyed. Flicks wafted into the air momentarily, and there was uncomfortable smoke in the small cabin that made Evans cough. Vanderdussen gave no hint about the contents of the letter. Evans made his exit. He untied and mounted Llewelyn and headed west out of Charles Town. The first and most accessible part of his dispatch deliveries had been completed.

His next delivery would take him west towards the Congaree River, searching for Colonel Palmer and his rangers. This task would be much more challenging, as Evans had yet to learn precisely where Palmer would be. Some settlements were on the east side of the river, and a small dusty track connected the settlements through the wilderness to Charles Town.

Presumably, if Evans took that road, he would eventually meet the Rangers heading in the other direction. This would require that he travel a short distance along the central Charles Town to Port Royal road before taking a westerly fork toward the river settlements. He'd traveled the route before and knew where he was headed. It was also safe. There were no dangers in this part of South Carolina until you crossed the river into the disputed lands that Palmer had recently been patrolling.

Evans knew it might take a few days to reach Palmer, so as he reached the outskirts of Charles Town, he moved Llewelyn into a trot and then a canter. As it was the main road between two key South Carolina settlements, many travelers were going in both directions, and he soon found that he had to slow down to a walk more regularly than he cared for. It was during one of these moments that more oddity entered his day.

Coming toward Charles Town, astride his horse, plodded a slave owner. The man was going slow because he held a rope attached to the neck of what appeared to be a runaway slave. The slave was no different from any other black man that Evans had seen, other than a strange briar-like tattoo running down the side of his face. The man on horseback seemed familiar, though as far as Evans was aware, that man wasn't a slave owner.

Evans greeted him as if he knew him: "Afternoon, it's good to see you, Rhodri Edwards. I didn't know you were in the slave business."

The man looked at him stunned and responded, "My apologies, Sir. I'm not Rhodri Edwards. My name's John Price. I'm a slaver returning this slave to his rightful owners nearby, down along the Stono River." Evans knew Rhodri, and he was Welsh and from the Vales. This man had a clear home counties accent, but the resemblance was extraordinary. Evans apologized for the mistaken identity and bid the slaver goodbye as they proceeded towards their destination. It was a very peculiar experience and added to an already unorthodox day.

The afternoon wore on, and Evans arrived at the westerly fork on the road he sought. He started along this path and was beginning to think about setting up camp for the night when the forest broke, and he came into a clearing that seemed perfect for his campsite. This was as good as he would get and had been used before. A flat, dry area could accommodate many campers, trees nearby for securing horses, a usable firepit, and a crystal-clear stream nearby. So he stopped, dismounted, and set up his campsite in the clearing.

He'd barely been there an hour when he heard a group of horses approaching from the west. For Evans, it was fortuitously Colonel Palmer and his remaining group of twenty rangers. This good fortune would undoubtedly make the delivery of his dispatches easier than he'd expected. The rangers were very different from the militia. They were seasoned professionals who spent much of their time patrolling the western reaches of South Carolina. They were all clad in green uniforms, but there was a lot of variety in their accouterments and weapons.

Some wore hats made from racoon or beaver fur, while others preferred their traditional green flat cap. Some wore European leather boots, while others adopted Indian moccasins, both moccasin shoes and boots. A few rangers had cross belts, while others preferred a thick cummerbund wrapped around their waists with a leather belt underneath it.

Likewise, their choice of weapons varied. They all seemed to sport the American rifle, but a couple had pistols. Their choice of steel crossed the gamut of options. There were hatchets, tomahawks, Scottish cutlasses, short swords, and the occasional cavalry sword. A few of them had multiple blades and visibly bristled like hedgehogs. At least one had a cavalry sword, a tomahawk, a short sword, and numerous small knives arranged in careful proximity for fighting purposes. Evans missed being a ranger sometimes, and this was one of those times.

As the rangers reached the clearing, they began to dismount. It was clear that they also intended to camp in the clearing. Evans welcomed them as they reached his location. He couldn't tell which one was Colonel Palmer. He could discern no symbol of rank, which was unusual. Usually, an officer would have a red plumb in his hat. After a couple of quick questions, Evans identified Palmer.

Typically, he was the one with the most weapons. A solid, hard-looking man who was clearly a veteran of Indian warfare and the frontier. He was the antithesis of Colonel Vanderdussen. Where Vanderdussen was straight-backed and constantly standing to attention, Palmer was agile and free-moving. Where Vanderdussen was formal, Palmer was jovial and friendly. Where Vanderdussen sported clean-cut lines and a fastidious attire, Palmer was filthy from travel and wore practical clothes necessary for the job. Palmer's face was chunky, with a broad jaw and nose, chubby cheeks, and a prominent forehead. While Vanderdussen looked like a fox, Palmer looked like a bear. It was a stunning difference. Colonel Palmer was the field officer, whereas Vanderdussen was the parade ground officer. The contrast couldn't have been starker.

Once the rangers set up camp, Evans got Colonel Palmer alone and shared his mission: "Sir, I have a dispatch from Acting Governor Bull for you. He said I am to give it to you in person, and you're to destroy it in front of me once you've read it." Like Vanderdussen before him, Palmer was aware immediately of the letter's significance as these were unusual requirements.

"Evans, step over here. Let's do this away from the squad. Perhaps over here." They stepped into a small covert of trees, where some brush shielded them from the others. Evans handed the letter to Palmer. No inspection of the seal, he ripped it open and read it. Many of the same emotions crossed his face. There is not as much horror and anger, but a lot more determination and stoniness and far less joy at the end. A bit of tiredness and concern contrasted subtly with Bull's and Vanderdussen's closing expressions.

Colonel Palmer was about to hand the letter back to Evans. Though his curiosity was undoubtedly getting the better of him, he held up his hand, "Sir, you're supposed to destroy it. I don't know anything about the contents of the letter. I can't burn it for you."

"I see. Sorry, Evans. Bring me a burning stick from the fire, will you?" Evans returned to the clearing, picked up a burning stick from the firepit, and returned to the colonel. Palmer burned the letter then and there.

Evans camped that night with the Rangers. He enjoyed it. The camaraderie, the fire, and the camp food reminded him of his time as a ranger. He hoped he would get another opportunity to be back in the field. That could come if there was war with Spain. For now, he had an important job serving the Acting Governor, Colonel Bull.

The following morning, he set out early, back toward the fork, and then headed toward Port Royal to deliver his final dispatch to the militia's leader, Captain Kingston. He continued to wonder at the contents of the three letters, which had led to such compelling emotions in their reader's faces.

Chapter 10: Tallahassee

The Yamasee tribe was a hive of activity. They broke camp slowly, deconstructing the temporary bivouacs, packing possessions, and loading up the few horses they had captured. Unlike the Europeans, the Yamasee rarely rode the beasts. They found them helpful when moving sites and for eating when short on options.

Chioke watched his favorite women help. Over by the stream collecting water for the journey was Catori. A muscular, tight-framed woman who fought beside the men as if she were one of them. She had a true warrior spirit. Then, there was Luyu, who helped pack one of the horses. A shorter woman with an hourglass figure and pronounced childbearing hips, she was much younger than Catori. Luyu had a wildness that the tribe had learned to accept. She would disappear into the woods for days and reappear suddenly possessed and unkempt, almost as if in a trance. Folks thought she would become a spirit woman, and her medicinal herbs and concoctions promised much. His favorite, though, was Pakuna. She helped parcel up the nuts, dried berries, and jerky for individuals to carry. Pakuna was a big girl, tall, heavy-set, and corpulent like an Igbo woman. She had large breasts, very sizeable buttocks, and amble curves everywhere that mattered. She also had a sunny disposition. Always singing, smiling, and laughing wholeheartedly. If Chioke had to choose one, it would be Pakuna.

⏳ ⏳ ⏳

Before long, the tribe embarked on their journey, heading from Pensacola to Tallahassee. It would take about seven days. Chioke took up his position at the vanguard of the column, along with Catori and half of the fiercest warriors in the tribe. Another group of the best fighters guarded the rear while chiefs, lesser warriors, and scouts positioned themselves along the flanks. The center of the column contained the pack horses, the younger women, and the children. Luyu and Pakuna led the horses in the center. The pace was fast. The entire tribe alternated between fast walking and trotting at double pace. The track was well-worn and easygoing.

Their route skirted along the coast for three days, then headed inland on a north-easterly path. Though the signs differed from Chioke's home, he had learned to read them and was adept at navigating through the forest. The paths made it easy, and it was a well-known route. The journey was uneventful. They stopped regularly to fill up waterskins, and sleep came quickly when they stopped for the night. To pass the time, as they walked and ran, they sang. Chioke enjoyed the Yamasee's fondness for singing. It reminded him of his own tribe. The songs spanned the tribe's history. There were chants for the brave warriors who'd fought and lost the Yamasee War. Some ballads celebrated the birth of the tribe. There were love songs, fighting songs, and songs to venerate the Yamasee's gods.

When they stopped for the night, they built fires, ate, and sang lullabies to coax the children to sleep.

⏳ ⏳ ⏳

They had good fortune on the fifth day, somewhat short of their destination. The vanguard of the column ran straight into a large flock of wild turkeys. It was hundreds strong and sitting in the middle of their trail. The loud gaggle the flock made provided an ample warning for the approaching Yamasee. Chioke and the others stopped running instantly and began to step forward stealthily. Like a poised cat ready for the kill, he saw Catori's muscles tighten and her instincts sharpen. Chioke hoped he appeared poised and dangerous in case she looked his way.

They moved in on the turkeys. Their blue-grey heads and red necks seemed to bob in and out of the massed multitude of brown bodies. Hundreds of grey legs jutted out from under the brown throng. It was impossible to tell which legs belonged to which bird.

The assault was coordinated, instantaneous, and over in moments. Chioke swung his staff in two beautiful sweeps and took down two turkeys. All the Yamasee warriors acted with swiftness. Arrows flew and struck home, deep into the bird's hearts from yards away. Tomahawks swept and decapitated suddenly. Muskets fired, taking down birds as they fled. The gun's retorts were the last act of the attack, echoing through the forest.

Catori grinned at him, satisfied and as competitive as ever. She had taken four turkeys to his two. One with a quick bow shot, two beheaded with her tomahawk, and the fourth she caught fleeing with her throwing knife. He would surely hear about that tonight while she lay in his bed. He suspected he might also be hearing about it for a while afterward. While they had killed plenty, the mass of the flock had escaped, running away in that odd scuttling fashion, and it would recover to provide food again. As the column moved up to the killing ground, the dead birds were gathered, and a suitable site was found for their evening feast. There would be much plucking, eating, and singing as they roasted and dried the meat. They would have a plentiful supply that would feed the tribe for many days.

The following two days flew by as they made their final approach to Tallahassee. Here, they were to stay until the conference with the Spanish, who were en route from St. Augustine. The Yamasee hoped to forge an alliance, and the negotiations would take place in this old Apalachee territory. It was a large open expanse of land that had visibly been several Apalachee towns. A series of burial mounds dotted the landscape. Fields surrounded the site, which had been cleared and previously used for agriculture.

As Chioke patrolled the old Apalachee land with his small band, he could see the evidence of these prior settlements everywhere. Several towns, with prominent earthworks surrounding many ruins, could have housed hundreds of people. Then there were occasional smaller ruins that looked like they might have been villages and even an odd individual homestead dotted across the fields. Often, the ruins were alongside lakes or close to the bay, which was named after the Apalachee. Chioke reflected that by native standards, this must have been a large society. Perhaps not as big as Igboland, but nevertheless, it must have been a significant undertaking.

There were other newer settlements on this land, mostly Seminole but also Spanish settlers. Hence, the Yamasee were careful not to offend the current inhabitants they wished to ally with. They kept away from the villages and homesteads. They were careful not to hunt or gather produce on territory that was close by.

The Yamasee chiefs picked an old Apalachee town for their conference with the Spanish. It was located just south of a large horseshoe lake and within the southern curve of the lake. They were careful to situate their camp outside of the former Apalachee town, conscious not to awaken the ghosts of the former occupants. It was a good site, with excellent access to water, fertile land, and productive hunting. This would have been a great spot if the Yamasee had been the settling-down type.

Where the Apalachee had gone was a mystery that caused much debate in the councils of the Yamasee. Chioke thought they were just wasting time with idle chatter while they waited for the Spanish. Still, it was an intense debate with many theories. Some argued that the Spanish had killed them. This view was sternly turned down by the wiser chiefs who recognized its political ramifications for their upcoming treaty talks. Others insisted that the Apalachee had died out during the great disease that had swamped the land and which had decimated other tribes. The more optimistic suggested they had survived but moved west to escape the Europeans. The final thesis was that they still lived here and were, in fact, the forefathers of the Seminoles and the Creeks. Like all conversations in the councils, the debates were never-ending and circular. Chioke became bored and went looking for Pakuna. He hoped to ingratiate himself into her attention for the night.

$$\text{⧗} \quad \text{⧗} \quad \text{⧗}$$

Days grew into weeks, and the Yamasee began to get concerned. Where were the Spanish negotiators? Was the alliance dead before it had even started? They needn't have worried. The reason for the delay became apparent once the negotiators arrived. The Spanish had hauled overland from St. Augustine two ox carts full of gifts for the Yamasee. It seemed that the Spanish might be even keener on the alliance than the Yamasee's were.

Chioke carefully observed the arrivals. The two ox carts were solid-looking wooden contraptions covered by canvas awnings. Each was pulled along by two massive oxen. These were white, muscular beasts with shaven horns designed to protect their handlers, and their halters were securely fastened to the carts. They reminded Chioke of the water buffalo he'd often hunted back home. The oxen and carts were led by two white men dressed in drab, dull clothes who seemed inconsequential—servants or something similar.

Sixteen Spanish soldiers accompanied the carts. To Chioke, they looked like all other Europeans he'd seen. A little darker tanned than the British. All of them had black or brown hair, and there were no redheads or blondes dotted in amongst the group, as there so often were amongst the British. The uniforms were almost identical to British soldiers, but instead of red, they were blue. The same material, the same fashion, the same cut. Similar cross belts. Blue hats instead of red but of an identical design. White leggings and strappings over black boots.

The only difference Chioke could discern was that a few wore traditional breastplates that the British had long discarded, and their muskets were longer. Also, the uniforms were more flamboyant. An extra dash of red here and a bit of white there. Slightly more ornate buttons and a ribbon or two attached to a belt. More drawn-back cuffs and puffy shoulders on the coats. Chioke could see no reason for these extra accessories, and he felt that they were as superfluous in a fight as the Yamasee's goose feather headdresses. Their leader stood out only because he was decked out in the most unnecessary gaudiness of them all. Chioke had once seen a peacock, and if this man had been reincarnated, it was a sure thing that he would come back as one of those birds.

The Spanish soldiers were all mounted, which was a lazy way to travel. The ponies were solid, sturdy animals but smaller than their British counterparts. As they heaved the carts into the campground prepared for them, they looked tired despite their slow, ponderous journey. Chioke wondered about these men and what sort of allies they would make. Slow ones, for sure, and even lazy ones. Perhaps allies that weren't worth having. His Yamasee brethren seemed to think differently. An ally was only as good as the gifts he bore, and the Spanish had just arrived bearing the most significant payload of gifts the Yamasees had ever seen. This alliance negotiation would be a serious business.

The conference started in the tedious way Chioke had expected, with long speeches and the smoking of peace pipes. He knew enough about the culture to know the negotiation would be drawn out over many days despite both sides' apparent desire and intent to seal an alliance. It was a full council, and all were welcome and expected. Chioke sat as he often had, trying to understand whatever he could despite his language constraints.

Both sides talked about their hate for their enemies. The Spanish seemed most perturbed by a man called Oglethorpe and by the new settlements he had founded in a land called Guale. Chioke assumed this was Savannah, the city from which he had escaped. The Spanish leader talked long and mournfully about these transcreations. He clearly understood the nature of the conference, but Chioke hadn't known Europeans to be so longwinded. The Yamasee poured their scorn on the South Carolinians and decried the desecrators of their ancestral lands. Each chief spoke at length and told long stories of lost relatives who had been attacked and killed in the Yamasee War. They invited individual warriors to tell their stories until the crowd angrily wept.

As smoke from the pipes wafted over the delegates, the hatred moved on to different enemies. The lead Yamasee chief started by pointing to Apalachee lands and accusing the Creeks of obliterating the Apalachee. To Chioke, that stretched the truth beyond breaking point. It was an opening gambit that worked. Others talked at length about the Creek incursions into Florida, their raiding of the Seminoles, and their untrustworthiness. The Spanish leader pitched in and accused the Creeks of being allied to the British, sending the delegates into an outraged frenzy.

As the evening drifted in, esoteric abstractions about the Creeks entered the conversation. What was the difference between the Upper and Lower Creek positions in their alliances with the British? Would the red sticks, seeking war, win the debate against the whites who sought peace? What bearing would these internal Creek positions have on their commitment to the upcoming war? At this point in the evening, Chioke zoned out and went to look for Luyu. She had whispered some fine words into his ear earlier, and he hoped to find her before nightfall.

⌛ ⌛ ⌛

The next day, the conference was filled with debates about the other players. Where did the French stand? Would they ally with the British? This was a concern for the Yamasee, as the French were close to their present location. The French position would definitely impact the engagement of the Seminoles. The Spanish leader assured the delegates that the French would stay neutral at the very worst and might join the fray on the side of their fledgling alliance.

The debate drifted on to the Seminoles; where did they stand? The Spanish promised that the Seminoles had agreed to join their alliance. With the French neutral, the Seminoles would be free to fight. The Seminoles had smoked the peace pipes, accepted gifts, and made their allegiance pledges. This led to a detailed conversation between the chiefs and the Spanish leader about how many warriors the Seminoles could bring and what value they might add. Several of the Yamasee chiefs were brutal, in their opinion. Several hundred warriors at most and little use. These chiefs reasoned that they were a small agricultural nation spread over many leagues in small settlements. As farmers, they weren't well suited to warfare. The Spanish leader delicately conceded to this opinion but pointed out the success of the Seminoles in repelling both the Creeks and the French when they'd raided the Panhandle. No small feat for a small agricultural nation was his closing argument. Well-made point, thought Chioke. It was settled that the Seminoles would fight alongside the Spanish and the Yamasee and that their Indian cousins would bring several hundred seasoned warriors to the field.

⧗ ⧗ ⧗

The following day was spent debating the other Indian nations in the region. Where would the Choctaws and Chickasaws stand if a great war occurred in the region? The Spanish leader had to concede that he didn't know. The Spanish had little contact with these tribes and no information. He'd hoped that the Yamasee chiefs would provide some insights. Never missing an opportunity to talk, the chiefs discussed their somewhat contradictory opinions about these other nations at length.

Chioke was confused, primarily because he had never heard of these tribes. According to one group of chiefs, both nations were allied to the French and would do what the French would do. Another set of chiefs disagreed; the Choctaws and Chickasaws were charlatans who would work for whichever master paid the most. Chioke thought this ironic, given that the Yamasee's level of interest in alliances was motivated by the size of the gifts offered.

One chief mentioned Mary Musgrove and was convinced she'd coaxed the Chickasaws to the side of the British and Creeks. The chief felt that the Choctaws were likely to stay neutral. He was also convinced that the Upper Creeks would remain neutral and wouldn't join the war alongside the Lower Creeks. The thesis was that the Upper Creeks would fear an attack by the Choctaws while their best men were off helping the British.

After much debate, a consensus emerged that the conference really didn't know where the Choctaws and Chickasaws stood, should there be war. Chioke was shocked and indignant. It had taken all day to reach this conclusion, and it had been evident after the first speech in the morning that nobody knew where the two tribes stood on the coming war. Sometimes, he yearned for the ways of his old tribe, the Igbo. Leaders should lead! Why talk so much when you can act?

The night descended, and the conference adjourned but closed out with a feast, dancing, singing, and drinking. The Spanish soldiers must have wondered what was happening to their leader as he ate the Yamasee food, drank their strange hallucinogenic cocktails, and danced joyously with their women. Chioke thought the man was a fast learner. He'd understood the Yamasee culture and was closing the deal. Undoubtedly, the alliance would be sealed tomorrow.

⧗ ⧗ ⧗

The conference started a little later the following day. The revelers needed to recover. It was as Chioke had expected. The Spanish leader's patience and cultural aptitude had paid off. The chiefs declared their intent that the Yamasees would join the alliance. Still, before pledging their allegiance, they must assess the costs and the gifts. A lengthy debate ensued regarding how many fighters each partner could commit. The Spanish officer clarified that General de Montiano was now in Cuba with three galleons and hundreds of soldiers and would be heading to St. Augustine imminently. The free blacks at Fort Mose had joined the militia, amounting to over fifty motivated fighters, and the Seminoles could field around three to four hundred warriors. Each galleon had a combined force of fifteen hundred sailors and marines, and these ships could be backed up by three coastguard sloops, each containing eighteen guns. Not to mention the Castillo at St. Augustine, one of the most formidable fortresses on this side of the Atlantic.

The chiefs listened and accepted these numbers. Chioke considered them optimistic. Who could say the ships and their formidable forces would stay near St. Augustine? They might be needed elsewhere. Realistically, they would field around a thousand, still a large force, but was it enough to see off the British and their allies?

It didn't take long before the chiefs discussed the force they could bring into play. They argued that the total fighting force of the Yamasee was about five hundred. Chioke thought the chiefs were playing the same game as the Spanish. We'd be lucky to bring two hundred real fighters to the war. Some of these fighters, though, would be dispersed across a vast region and couldn't be brought to bear all simultaneously in one place. There we go, thought Chioke, pushing up the cost while avoiding the consequences. The commitment was two hundred in one place at one time, but five hundred was the cost. A nice bargaining maneuver, if ever he'd seen one.

All that was left for the conference was to finalize the Spanish gifts. Chioke hoped they hadn't driven two empty ox carts halfway across Florida, or the negotiation might end in a bloodbath. Catori was by his side for the revealing of the gifts. Her warm hand was in his, and her enthusiasm was contagious.

The Spanish offered everything the Yamasees could possibly have wanted. As far as the tribe was concerned, it was wealth beyond their wildest dreams. There were all manner of weapons. Muskets, pistols, cleavers, axes, swords, knives, and a sufficient supply of gunpowder. Clothing materials that were sorely required. Cotton, wool, leather, ribbons, beads, and shells. All the things the Yamasee needed to make new clothes. Then there were the household goods that rarely made it to the New World, let alone the wilderness. Simple things like frying pans, spades, knives, pickaxes, needles, and nails were all things that wrought iron could make. These things were like gold dust and changed lives but weren't typically made by the Spanish. These were British goods, so that raised new questions for Chioke. How did they come to be gifts from the Spanish to the Yamasee?

The crowd around the wagons only saw the riches and gave no thought to their origin. Chioke saw it then and there. The entire tribe had been bought, but for what purpose and to what end? Could this alliance avenge their losses, and could it protect them from further British incursions? Was it going to stop warfare with the Creeks? None of this seemed evident despite the lengthy debates and long-drawn-out conference.

The Spanish leader and his troops left with fond goodbyes and final pledges to confirm the alliance. Several warriors left with the Spanish to act as scouts and to ensure swift communication between the allies. The empty carts were drawn by much lighter-footed oxen. Chioke wondered about this. These goods they'd been given were heavy, and wrought iron offered many benefits, but it would slow the tribe down. What would they do? Stay here and never move again? If they did leave, could they travel at their usual speed? Many questions arose that were unsettling.

He had similar concerns about the muskets. It would be great if you could fire them at speed, but they lacked accuracy and were cumbersome. The gunpowder was heavy and dangerous if stored incorrectly. Again, the gifts appeared more troublesome than his Yamasee brethren had realized.

Chioke was thankful to be relieved of these questions and concerns. The chiefs had arranged with their new Spanish allies to send bands of Yamasee into the disputed lands. Chioke was to join one of these small groups. To his delight, he would accompany Catori and four other Yamasee warriors. Their task was simple. They were to head up the Chattahoochee River towards Coweta and the Lower Creek territories. They were to avoid interactions with the Creeks; it was purely a scouting mission. They were to skirt to the south of the Lower Creek lands and head across to the Ocmulgee River, where they were to find an excellent location to observe the river.

They were watching for a delegation from the Georgians going up the river to meet the Creeks. Observation was required, but if they could disrupt the delegates, they were allowed to do so. Similar small bands were sent throughout the disputed lands to the Okefenokee swamps, the St. Mary's River, the Satilla River, the Altamaha River, and other locations. They all had a simple job, to observe and to disrupt. If the Yamasee could prevent the establishment of an alliance between the British and the Creeks, it would be worth ten times the gifts the Spanish had endowed.

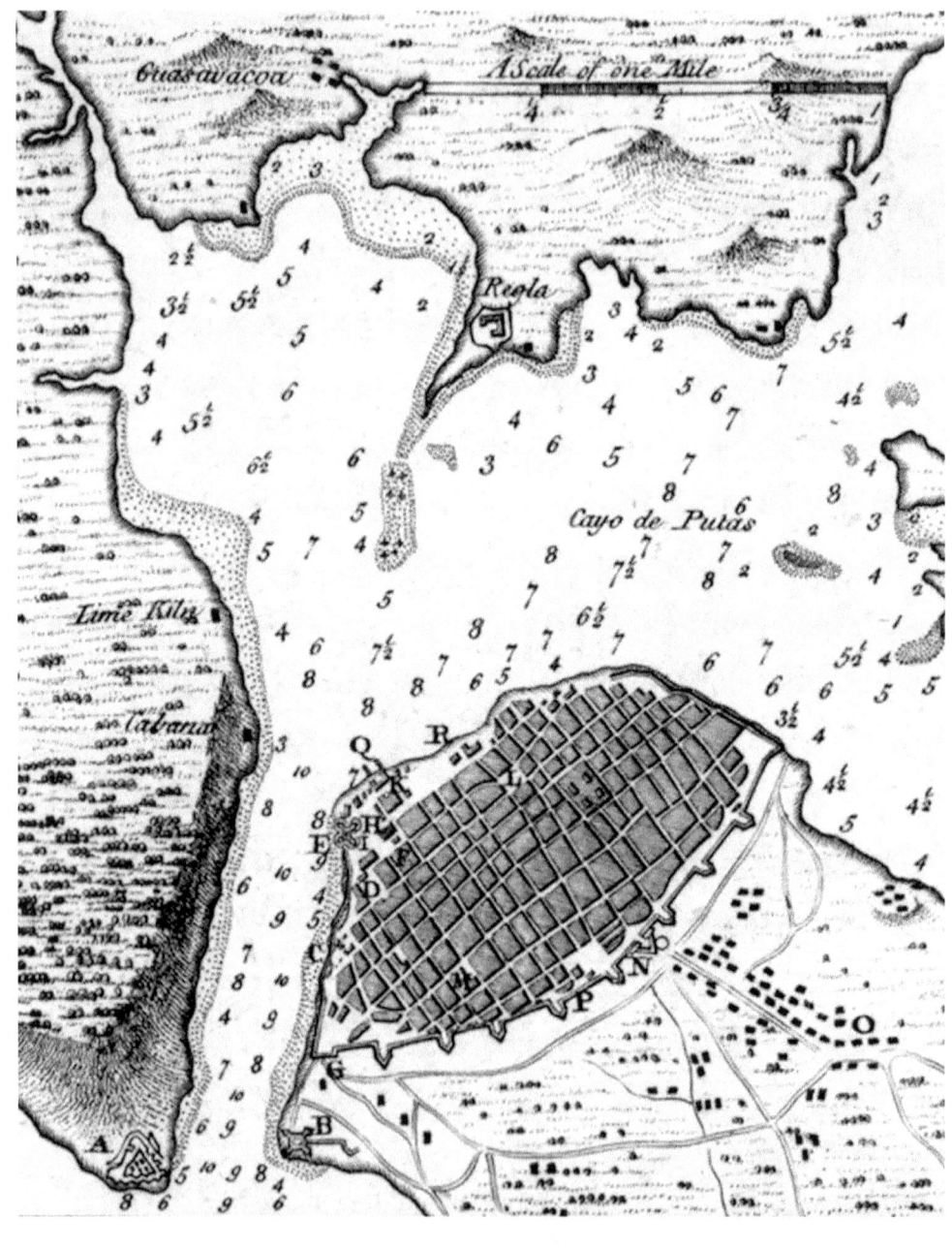

Guasavacoa

A Scale of one Mile

Regla

Cayo de Putas

Lime Kiln

Labana

Q R

H

E

D

C

A

B

G

P N

O

Chapter 11: Havana Knights

The punch came suddenly and out of nowhere. When the fight began, Hernando Perez was simply sitting there enjoying his wine in the Havana hostelry. Of course, it had been Miguel and Rodrigo who'd caused it. They'd been playing cards, working the joint together, and cheating unabashedly. Someone eventually took exception to their uncharacteristic losses and blamed the brothers. Nobody accuses Miguel and Rodrigo of chicanery and gets away with it. So the man was now lying spreadeagled on the floor of the tavern in a pool of his own blood. The locals were angry with the man's treatment, and now they were all involved in a drunken brawl. Unwisely, the locals had set themselves against several squads of visiting soldiers.

Fortunately for Hernando, he'd hardly drunk anything. The man swinging at him was inebriated, and with a slight dodge, Hernando avoided taking a smash to the cheek. As the swing careened by, he used his attacker's momentum and weight to pitch him to the floor. Then he set about him, kicking the man in the balls and then the head. Blood spurted as his foot connected, and there was a distinct snap of a broken nose. The man stayed down in agony, writhing about, holding his face.

Hernando's squad was a brutal group of seasoned professional soldiers, so a tavern brawl offered little danger. Antonio the Butcher was the most dangerous, and he took no prisoners. One man was lying on the floor, stabbed through the eye, lifeless. The sudden butchery kept other would-be aggressors at bay. They were visibly giving the big man a wide berth.

Sergeant Moreno-Rodriguez had two men in headlocks and was bashing their skulls against the solid oak bar. Miguel and Rodrigo fought side by side. Though the target of the bar's fury, they were faring well and were winning a fistfight with three assailants. Their boxing skills came to the fore as they ducked, shimmied, and pounded their opponents.

Gonzalo, Francisco, and Hernán fought near the door and hunted like a pack. As silent killers, they were often as deadly as Antonio. On this occasion, they simply laughed at the others and took out the odd local, keeping the door clear for the squad's impending exit.

As he observed the scene of the bar's destruction, soldiers and locals fought across the entire setting. The tables were upended. Men were at each other's throats, rolling around wrestling. Stools were being thrown and chairs broken. Two men lay dead, and at least one appeared mortally wounded. It was time to leave.

With concern, Hernando looked for Alvaro and Benito, the least experienced of the group and virtually boys. He spotted Alvaro. Lying on the floor with another man on top of him. He was being pummeled with both of his assaulter's fists. Taking three quick paces, Hernando picked up a stool and whacked it across the man's back. The guy fell sideways, and moments later, Alvaro was on his feet, looking slightly bruised and bloodied but in one piece. Antonio had spotted the same problem and had gone to rescue Benito. Antonio's arrival was enough to save Benito as his assailants scurried away, scared to death. Hernando and Antonio bundled the two young men to the door and safety.

Hernando shouted at Moreno-Rodriguez, "Sergeant, it's time to go!"

The sergeant released the two men he'd thoroughly beaten and relayed the message in his strongest tipsy sergeant's tone, "Squad retreat! Get out! Miguel, Rodrigo, let's go before we have more company!" Miguel dished out one more precision thump, and the entire squad bustled out the door as Gonzalo, Francisco, and Hernán covered their retreat.

Their stay in Havana had been like this most of the time, but this was their last night, so they were making the most of it. The squad had nicknamed themselves the Havana Knights for the number of barfights they'd become involved in. Havana was, after all, a frontier town where the Spanish soldiers and sailors mixed with the Cuban locals and South American colonials. It was a true melting pot. Large numbers of taverns, cafes, and restaurants lined the harbor. Enough for General de Montiano's soldiers to get themselves into constant trouble. The general had stopped in Cuba to discuss martial matters with the Cuban governor and replenish supplies. But they'd outstayed their welcome, and it was time for the fleet to leave for St. Augustine.

As Hernando wasn't a heavy drinker and disliked the squad's constant fighting, he'd managed to find the city attractive in other ways. Though a frontier city, it was well-developed. Many wooden buildings lining the streets spread in a criss-cross fashion away from the harbor. These houses reminded him of Cádiz, with noticeable Iberian influences but with a slight colonial twist. The streetscapes were older and cleaner than he'd expected. Beautiful gardens could be found dotted amongst the houses in little backyards.

There were charming civic buildings like the two convents, a monastery, the chapel of the Humilladero, and the Castillo El Morro. The city had been endowed with a golden key to symbolize its importance as the key to the Gulf of Mexico and had been fortified accordingly. Hernando had taken some time to tour these defenses, and they were formidable. City walls were under construction around the entire municipality, and three castles guarded critical positions. Hernando concluded from his observations that capturing Havana would take a colossal undertaking. He didn't think the whole British navy could manage it. The city was as safe as Cádiz, and he'd resolved to move his family here if things didn't work out in St. Augustine.

⧗ ⧗ ⧗

The following morning, the fleet sailed. The San Luis had been fixed up in the Havana port. The mizzen canvass had been sewn, the stay had been secured, and the damage to the topgallant mast was patched up until a more permanent replacement could be found. The San Luis had been reunited with its two fellow galleons. Fandiño's three sloops escorted the ships out of Cuba's coastal waters. It was an impressive sight. This flotilla would strengthen the Spanish position at the Castillo de San Marcos in St. Augustine. Fandiño had assured de Montiano that he would come and support his mission if needed.

Hernando's troop returned to their cramped quarters, with their stacked bunkbeds and horrendous living conditions.

Fleeting thoughts of the toca crossed his mind as he drifted off to sleep the first night. Despite his fears of drowning, he enjoyed the remainder of the voyage. The waters between Cuba and St. Augustine were blissfully quiet. The seasickness didn't return, and his moments of deck leave were breathtaking. The galleons painted an awe-inspiring picture of power and majesty as they slid through the still waters of the Caribbean. Each with their striking insignias fluttering in the breeze. The profusion of masts and rigging of three enormous ships felt like a small forest in the middle of a desert to Hernando.

Despite the splendor of the galleons, it was the Caribbean itself that was truly breathtaking. Hernando had only ever known the waters of the Atlantic. In Cádiz, these waters lapped the beaches and flooded the coastal inlets. They weren't severe but were constantly churning, a dark blue hue, a mass of waves full of debris and silt. These seawaters had taken on a whole new complexion in the middle of the Atlantic and during the storms. Vast waves had soared above the ship they sailed in and crashed with overwhelming power. Then there were the deep, dark, and endless depths that reached into the bottom of the world itself.

The Caribbean was different. It was a graceful sea, translucent and aquamarine. Where the Atlantic was dark and foreboding, the Caribbean was gentle and inviting. He almost wished he'd learned to swim. As they left Cuba, he witnessed gorgeous coral reefs, resplendent in vivid colors and swarming with sea life. As he peered over the gunwale, there appeared to be no end to the variety of fish. The sheer magnificence of the colors, the range of shapes, and the complex diversity surrounding the reef stunned him.

On another occasion, they passed a series of remarkable islands. Like Havana, which was thought to be the key to the

Gulf of Mexico, the sailors described these islands as the keys to Florida. The flora was unique and different from Cádiz or even Havana. Small trees with red roots grew along the coastline and seemed to flourish in the salty, brackish water of the swamps. Then there were the stumpy strange cabbage-like palmettos and the tall palms, with their interlaced trunks and profusion of spiky branches poking out the top.

The fauna was also distinctive. Hernando saw unusual white birds with long white legs, long curved necks, and odd red dashes on the beak and knees. These birds waded through the rushes in the deep coastal areas, seemingly sifting through the saltwater. Closer inland, he saw smaller white birds with shorter legs that pecked constantly at the mud. Then, there was a strange bird of prey with fawn feathers, a white head, and white legs. This bird smashed into the water quickly and emerged with a fish in its talons. It was like paradise, untouched and exquisite in every detail.

As they moved up the eastern coastline of Florida, Hernando's opportunities to come up on deck were limited. When they did come out of their billets, it was for drill duty. Moreno-Rodriguez explained it, "This means we're getting closer. The general wants the men ready, and when we go ashore, he wants the populace to be impressed. We are the reinforcements, after all. It motivates the locals, we're told."

The drills were as usual. They cleaned their equipment, and muskets were inspected. They practiced loading and firing from the poop deck. The officers and sergeants bawled at them, enough to coax an extra second or two from their loading and firing speed. They practiced with bayonets. They fought mock skirmishes. The exercises were constant, and the troops were exhausted when the evening came. Even Antonio dropped into his bunkbed each night shattered, cursing loudly that he wanted to arrive at St. Augustine and be done with the drills. Hernando had little chance to see Florida's coastline. What glimpses he got excited him. While the flora and fauna had changed noticeably from the Keys, these long untouched beaches were dotted with sand dunes and grasses behind which stood intriguing forests. He saw no inhabitants; it was genuinely untouched.

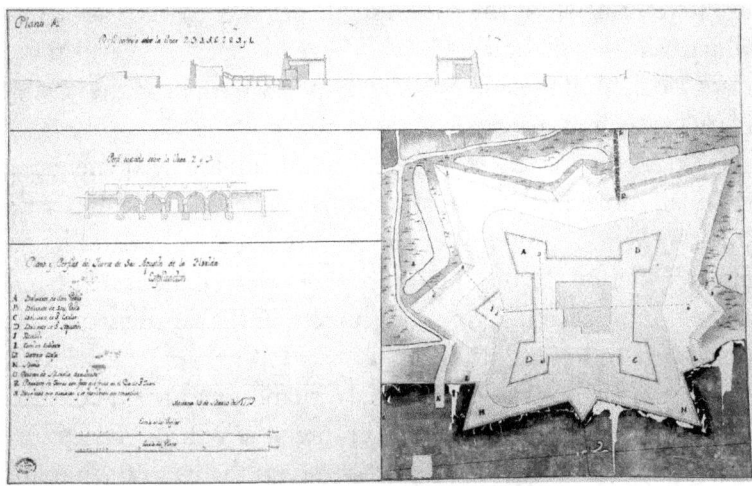

After a long journey, they finally arrived at St. Augustine. The general presented the display of power that he hoped would motivate the garrison's soldiers and populace. The entire battalion was formed up on the decks of the three galleons, all standing to attention in their best, spotless uniforms. Somewhat disingenuously, the general used the marines to bolster the numbers formed on the decks. Who could say whether the ships and their marines would stay? They would likely have other duties, but it was an impressive display nonetheless. The galleon's captains had bought into General de Montiano's display of muscle. The ships approached the Castillo de San

Marcos in a formidable-looking battleline as if they were going to engage the castle in broadsides, one after the other. As they cut through the waves, they deftly shifted into the more conventional and less threatening V-shaped formation. It was a remarkable display of seamanship that was bound to impress. Each vessel fired one gun to announce its arrival. The Castillo de San Marcos shot three guns to answer each individually.

It took a while for the pilot to get out to the San Luis, which infuriated the general, and even longer to get all three ships docked alongside St. Augustine's wharf near the castle. Hernando's first impression of his new posting was optimistic. They passed a beach with a few small, idyllic settlements as they had moved up the coast towards the castle. Near the castle stood a town. Many of the houses were like Havana and had a distinct Iberian flavor. Their occupants clearly emigrated from his region of Spain, giving him hope that his family would be welcomed and could fit in.

The castle itself was striking. Hernando hadn't expected to see such a well-constructed fort in the New World. Perhaps his prejudices had misguided him? Sitting on the western shore of the Matanzas Bay, it appeared impregnable. It was star-shaped and made of masonry construction that seemed unusual. Hernando later learned it was made of coquina, ancient shells bonded in limestone rock. The stone had been extracted from the island across the bay. A bastion with a sally port was on the edge of each star tip. The fort appeared to be constructed on an artificial mound surrounded by a dry moat. Embrasures were built along the walls and in the bastions, and cannons were protruding from these holes. Below the cannon embrasures smaller holes for the defender's muskets were visible, offering enfilading fire for both canons and muskets. It was not a prospect attackers would welcome.

It was an impressive fortress, and Hernando immediately felt more confident after seeing the Castillo de San Marcos. This wasn't a bad place to live—it was defended, Iberian-looking, and had the added benefit of a beach community. He could see Juana and his kids, Isbel and María, settling in here, and the things he'd seen along the way convinced him of the possibilities for life in Florida.

Chapter 12: Spartacus, Not Cato

Lamine had never seen O'Sullivan look scared. Ashen-faced, his eyes almost bulging out of their sockets, he was noticeably sweating with fear. His accent lapsed as he glanced back at the young gentleman on the fine horse trotting in the opposite direction: "Jaysus, that was close!"

Lamine knew not to reply, but his raised eyebrows betrayed the query. Half talking to himself, O'Sullivan continued as he corrected his enunciation, "Well, would ye believe that! Acting governor's aide, that's all he is! I've been warming him up over a few beers and cards at the local. A lot of wasted effort. It's a hard graft being a Welsh settler from Bridgend. I was hoping to get some real value out of him. It's dead in the water now and not an ounce of useful information! Rhodri Edwards will have to go west or something."

They continued to trudge slowly along their path. Dense forest enclosed either side of the byway; the path was dusty, dry, and well-used. Lamine's wrists were sore. The chaffing from many days of wearing shackles had caused an oozing mess of raw flesh under and around the irons. His neck was little better. It was stiff from being towed behind O'Sullivan as the rope dragged him along. It felt like it, too, was tender. The rope had shifted constantly like a noose before a hanging. It was a cost he was willing to accept as part of their subterfuge.

Before long, they reached their rendezvous. A small clearing in the forest just before they reached the open fields that skirted Charles Town. These fields were dotted across the landscape, small but productive. Lamine mainly saw corn, some wheat, and the occasional cotton field. The lush green stalks stood tall, to attention alongside the smaller wheat grasses and cotton bushes, with their white fuzzy buds. The corn kernels were ready to be picked. The crops swayed in the light breeze. As Lamine and O'Sullivan reached the clearing, they disturbed two young bucks. The deer raced away. Their white tails swished as they bounced into the undergrowth. It was an idyllic scene. A bountiful land full of rich promise that was being realized by the locals. It stood in stark contrast to the wilderness they had recently passed through.

From the main road, a narrow path split southward, "Once we meet our contact and offload the horse, we will head down that path." O'Sullivan pointed to the path; it was concealed and overgrown. Then he continued, "It's about three miles, and then we head overland to the north bank of the Stono River. We'll make camp there. Then you'll need to get into the plantation to talk with Jemmy and find out how far along he is with our plot."

Lamine nodded his agreement. This was their prearranged plan, that he would leave O'Sullivan at camp, would pose as a local slave, and liaise with Jemmy on O'Sullivan's behalf. Obviously, it would be extremely odd if a white slaver was caught trying to meet up with a slave on another man's plantation. Inevitably, such a situation would raise questions. So Lamine's role was as a go-between, to share with O'Sullivan Jemmy's preparation, tactics, and overall scheme. To give Jemmy the go-ahead for the rebellion on behalf of Spain's principal agent in the colony.

This time, they didn't have to wait long for O'Sullivan's associate to arrive. It was another young man who trotted up the road from Charles Town. He was mounted on a stout chestnut pony with a huge bulbous stomach. Though a young man, he was clearly too big for the pony. The image of his feet dangling near the ground was comical and almost made Lamine laugh, nearly breaking his ruse. He caught himself just in time but couldn't hold back a thin smile. O'Sullivan noticed and yanked the rope harshly, bringing Lamine's humor to an abrupt end.

The associate dismounted and welcomed O'Sullivan with a stiff, manly handshake. Though only just a man, he looked solid and muscular, like he'd been a blacksmith's apprentice. Lamine couldn't help but wonder at this new associate's appearance. There was a definite likeness to O'Sullivan. Another son, perhaps, but living in a different part of South Carolina? O'Sullivan's story grew more complicated by the day, thought Lamine. O'Sullivan and the young man privately conversed while unloading the saddle bags. Then, the associate stepped into the right stirrup, mounted O'Sullivan's horse, and set off towards Charles Town. The short, fat pony ambled along behind.

O'Sullivan packed his few possessions into two rucksacks, slung one over his back and the other over Lamine's. They set off briskly along the overgrown path, south towards the Stono River. After a couple of miles, O'Sullivan stopped them. They sat, drank water, and ate, taking a brief spell of rest. Lamine watched tiny blue birds flitting amongst the brambles as they ate quietly. Before setting off again, O'Sullivan removed

Lamine's neck rope and manacles. "We wouldn't need these now. We shouldn't see anybody along this route, and you'll now pose as a local slave, not a runaway. Just a minute, I need to change. There is no call for a slave trader in these parts." He disappeared into the thicket. Lamine rubbed his sore wrists and neck, relieved to have the slaver's restrictions removed.

After a few moments, O'Sullivan reappeared, looking like a completely different person. He'd removed his hat and expensive clothing and replaced them with rags and worn shoes. His face was dirty, his hair unkempt. His shirt was tattered, his pants were torn, and both were stained and grimy. His shoes were almost worn out. Several toes poked out of holes and the soles looked like they might fall off. In a new broad Devonshire accent, O'Sullivan explained that he aimed to appear like a local indentured servant or a weary traveler looking for work. Lamine immediately gained more appreciation of O'Sullivan's skills; the change in appearance was dramatic.

O'Sullivan stashed some of his possessions in the coppice, and they set off again along the path, continuing to head south. After another two miles, they left the trail and headed southeast across open fields. These fields were also full of crops, but the land was hillier, undulating somewhat. As they reached the Stono River, the landscape noticeably flattened and opened into a floodplain, covered with small streams that filtered into the river. Marshland surrounded the river, and bullrushes, cord grasses, and spartina spread across the vista, dominating the vegetation, which was almost treeless. The river itself was wide. It meandered gently towards the Atlantic, heading northeast from their location.

As O'Sullivan and Lamine crossed the marsh looking for a suitable campsite, they saw all manner of birds. It was a scene dominated by an enormous profusion and diversity of fowl.

Freshwater and saltwater varieties were intermingled. Gulls, ducks, herons, pelicans, terns, finches, and skimmers were joined by vultures and red-shouldered hawks, looking for an easy meal. It was clamorous, with chirps, caws, twits, twerks, and all types of sounds proliferating around them. The sheer number of birds and the variety were awe-inspiring.

Eventually, they found what O'Sullivan was looking for. There was a previously occupied camp just before the Wallace River's juncture with the Stono. A wooded area enclosed the region, but a small site had been cleared within the covert. It was secluded and private, with old huts and carefully constructed hearths designed to limit the escape of smoke from the little settlement's fires. It seemed like a secretive place, well-hidden and well-used. As O'Sullivan wordlessly settled in, Lamine assumed the huts would be their headquarters for a while. He took one as his sleeping quarters, was given blankets and a food supply, and left to his own devices for the evening. O'Sullivan's distant snores could soon be heard alongside the occasional hoot of an owl's call.

⧗ ⧗ ⧗

The following morning, the plot began. O'Sullivan briefed Lamine. His first task was to contact Jemmy and determine his plans. Then, he was to bring Jemmy to meet O'Sullivan so that the Spanish commitments to the rebels could be confirmed. When the rebellion started, Lamine was to join the rebels and act as the eyes and ears of the Spanish. Lamine hadn't anticipated this part of the scheme, nor had O'Sullivan shared it. He knew that the risks for him personally had just increased significantly, and he wasn't pleased to have such an unpleasant surprise at such a late stage in their gambit.

O'Sullivan drew a crude map in the campsite's dust. From their location, the Stono River headed northeast. Lamine would canoe along the river until the eighth creek, called Wappoo. O'Sullivan had marked it earlier, so he couldn't miss it. He just had to look for a white cross on a boulder. When Lamine found this creek, he would stash the canoe and walk, following the creek inland. Once Lamine was at its end, he would be on Cato's plantation, and the first hut he would find would be Jemmy's. This was a route they'd used before, and it would be perfectly safe, provided he went up the correct creek. If he took the incorrect one, he would reach the wrong plantation and likely be taken for a runaway slave.

Once briefed, Lamine set off. The canoe was an old native one but was well made and cut through the water well. Lamine was an experienced canoeist and he found the going easy. Though the paddle was strange and the canoe was balanced differently from those he'd used before, he adjusted quickly. The river was wide, so he kept tightly to the northern bank to limit his chances of being seen. He saw little evidence of humans alongside the river. Just the same complex marshland with its profusion of wildfowl crisscrossed with streams. It took a lot of work to assess the major from the minor streams, and soon, he grew concerned about whether he'd miscounted. Was he on three or four? Was that little stream too small to be counted? As he emerged from the marshland, there were some small fields and evidence of settlers. Throughout the day that gnats had been a constant irritation. Wishing to escape the swarm and avoid the unnecessary risk of passing small settlements, he landed, hid the canoe, and waited until dusk.

As Lamine watched, the moon's luminescence began to dominate the sky, and the multivarious colors of the sunset declined. He recovered his canoe and slipped it back into the river. Though it was night, the full moon provided plenty of light, and he could continue unimpeded. The stars sparkled throughout the sky, and the dark river water lapped gently against the canoe. It was cooler; a moderate breeze brushed against him. He worked hard with the oar and made swift but silent progress along the river.

He'd canoed most of the night before arriving at Wappoo Creek. His concerns about finding it had been misplaced. The creek was well-marked; the boulder with its white cross was clearly visible in the moonlight. Lamine punted the canoe up the shallow creek for several yards and then jumped out. He pulled the canoe out of the creek, dragged it under a thicket, and camouflaged it with branches and dead leaves. It was adequately hidden once he'd finished. There were a few hours left before daylight, so he took some time to rest.

When the morning came, it was another spectacular day. A brilliant sunrise of contrasting reds and yellows that almost outshone the previous day's sunset. Having slept, Lamine was rested but weary. He moved around carefully to avoid making a noise as he prepared to depart. The walk along Wappoo Creek was challenging. A narrow stream that fed into the Stono was overgrown and difficult to follow. After incurring excessive scratches from the bushes and losing the stream twice, Lamine concluded it was easier to wade up the stream. This proved to be a good decision. Though knee-deep in some places, it was generally shallow, and solid granite under the water provided a firm footpath. He slipped several times, but the water was cold and refreshing, which was welcome as the morning began to heat up. The stream even provided some respite from the constant swarm of gnats that seemed to follow him everywhere.

After a few hours of walking, the stream connected to another river. This seemed to be the end, as O'Sullivan had described it. Across a clearing, he saw a small, somewhat dilapidated hut. Like the huts in Mose, it had a unique African feel, and Lamine could tell immediately that the hut had been constructed by a Kongolese. This must be Jemmy's hut, for sure. It was just after midday and Lamine knew that Jemmy would be in the fields working. So, he found a spot to lie down and nap for the rest of the afternoon to catch up on his lost sleep.

⧖ ⧖ ⧖

Early in the evening, Lamine heard movement across the small field in the hut, and he knew that Jemmy must have returned. He ambled across the field, stretching as he did, aiming to remove the remainder of his tightness following his long afternoon wait. He called out to Jemmy in Portuguese using their prearranged code, "Os corvos estão prontos para voar?" Lamine heard Jemmy stop and saw the door to the hut open cautiously.

Jemmy was a tall, thin man with a shaved head. It appeared almost waxed as the sun sheened off it. His forehead was pronounced angular, and his nose was wide. Lamine immediately noticed the man's eyes. They were big, deep brown, and shone with intelligence. Though thin, his body had the tautness that only a poor diet and constant farm work provided. His muscles were lean but simultaneously powerful-looking. Though dressed modestly, the same as Lamine, there was no disguising that this man had been a chief, a warrior, and a leader amongst his people. An aura of significance appeared to be cast by the man's very shadow. He'd met such men before but not since leaving Africa, and the moment reminded Lamine of the Prince he'd once served, Ayuba Suleiman Diallo.

Jemmy's greeting was warm, and his smile contagious. Lamine knew immediately why O'Sullivan and the Spanish would pick such a man to start a rebellion. Where he led, others would follow. Jemmy welcomed Lamine into his hut and gave him a small cup of soup before they began proceedings. Thankfully, it wasn't fish soup. It was customary for the host to ask after Lamine's kin. So, they discussed irrelevant topics in Portuguese for a while. Both knew why they were meeting but couldn't set aside their customs.

Eventually, they closed on the topic at hand. "O'Sullivan has sent me to gather intelligence about your operation. We're here to help if you need it," Lamine stated bluntly.

"My friend, you are a Fulani. You are a Muslim. How does O'Sullivan expect me to trust you?" responded Jemmy equally bluntly, "Our cause is a Catholic one. What place do the Fulani Muslims have at the table?"

It was a fair question and one that had been anticipated: "We are no longer simply Kongolese Catholics and Fulani Muslims. We are the enslaved, the damaged, those who must be set free. My friend, I come with stories about freedom and Gracia Real de Santa Teresa de Mose. So you know that what you fight for is worthwhile, worth having, should you seek it."

They talked for some time about the free blacks, the town of Mose, and the new freedoms the Spanish had given. How Fulani, Igbo, Kongolese, Fon, Yoruba, and others lived side by side. They were no longer enemies, but friends united to defend their freedoms and fight the slavers, the British. Lamine described the new militia, how proud he was of it, and how it had been formed to defend these newfound rights. It was a profound case, and Jemmy was compelled to see an unrealized future for his people. Jemmy saw another literate, educated man in Lamine who could intelligently lead the people out of their predicament. Setting aside his natural distrust of the Fulani, Jemmy chose to trust. To trust in a future beyond slavery. A future in which the free blacks defended their own rights and fought alongside the Spanish. He chose to trust in the ascendancy of the Catholic faith and to accept this Muslim man, who'd brought communications from his allies.

Having gained Jemmy's trust, it was Lamine's turn to listen. Jemmy explained that the rebellion followed a simple plan: "Have you ever heard of Cato the Younger?" Lamine scratched his head. He'd heard about a Roman called Cato, but surely there was no relevance. Jemmy carried on, "Cato was a great man who opposed tyranny. He ultimately failed but spent much of his life opposing the dictator, Caesar. Few people know that Cato also fought against Spartacus, the leader of the Roman slave rebellion. I find it ironic that my overlords have the same name, Cato, and that people call me Cato. I think I would prefer to be Spartacus to their Cato."

Lamine only partially followed but let Jemmy continue anyway. "We have a simple plan. There are twenty-one of us, all former Kongolese warriors. We will do what Spartacus did. We will march on Hutchinson's store by the Stono River bridge, we will seize their weapons and ammunition, and then we will march south towards Florida. As we go, we will do as Spartacus did. We will free and arm the slaves as we pass through the country, destroying the plantations and seizing weapons. By the time we reach Florida, we will be a great horde, an army of freed slaves, ready to help you fight the British. It is simple, and it almost worked for Spartacus."

Lamine agreed; it was a simple and audacious stratagem. Only a small force would be required to start a gigantic ball rolling down the hill. The ball would roll south away from South Carolina's rangers and militia, crushing small resistance in its wake and acquiring weight of numbers and weapons as it gained momentum. An added benefit was that it would destroy many productive plantations, strike a brutal blow to South Carolina's food supply, and undermine their ability to defend Georgia when the Spanish attacked. If successful, the free black militia would swell to enormous numbers and become an army to be reckoned with. It might grow to four or five hundred men, more significant than the Spanish garrison.

He realized he must get word back to O'Sullivan. They needed to secure the Spanish contracts for the rebellion and support this man with some cast iron promises. Jemmy might become the new Spartacus, establishing an era free of slavery. He told Jemmy that the plan was superb in every respect. He immediately departed towards Wappoo Creek to recover his canoe and head to the Stono River to share the plot with O'Sullivan.

Chapter 13: Darien

Uga didn't look happy. His eyes were sad, and his jowls reverberated almost as if he was set to cry. Dribble, dripping off his chin, was more pronounced than usual. Tom preferred to leave him in Savannah while he took his squad south to Frederica, as the dog's stout little legs wouldn't keep up with the horses. Perhaps he should have got a different breed, one with longer legs. Uga would have to stay with Mary and Duke. Mary had gradually become accustomed to the mess the dog made; she just about tolerated him. On the other hand, Duke had become the dog's shadow; he took Uga for walks and played with him when he wasn't with Noble Wimberly. Tom knew the dog would be in safe hands.

The few weeks following the wedding were challenging. Now, a corporal in the mounted rangers, Tom had new responsibilities: a small squad of men to lead and he had to care for his horse, which was a beauty. A black gelding named Noir, just above average height at fourteen hands, his muscular frame often glistened handsomely in the morning sun. He was a feisty horse that was difficult to ride, even for an accomplished horseman. Tom was convinced the lieutenant was joking when he gave him the most challenging animal they had. It had been a painful couple of weeks.

Tom had taken more time than he cared to acknowledge to learn the basics. The tack all seemed so complex at first. The pad and saddle were straightforward, but he kept twisting the girth strap and had been useless when adjusting the breeching and bridle straps. He couldn't determine the correct length for the reins or the stirrups. A young lad in his squad, George Hill, took pity on him and showed him how to prepare the horse. After a few days, he'd mastered it. Then, with trepidation, he had to get up onto Noir's back.

Learning the basics of riding had proven to be a troublesome and dangerous affair. Tom almost fell off immediately the first time around but jumped from the saddle and landed safely on his feet. It rattled him, and he was overly cautious. Noir sensed it and played up more than usual. His efforts were laughable but aided his small squad's bonding. Hill was joined by the other two, John Coleman and Andrew Sanders, and they all watched him, amused, giving constant and sometimes contradictory advice. It took a couple of weeks, during which Tom was constantly bruised and embarrassed. Just before they departed, he reached a passable level of competence, much to the relief of the entire squad.

⧖ ⧖ ⧖

Tom's squad followed in the rear while the lieutenant led the small troop south along the road between Savannah and Frederica. Tom sat astride Noir. His ornate exquisite rifle, another gift from Oglethorpe, was slung over his shoulder, and his tomahawk, a gift from Hilli, hung at his belt. The road was nothing more than a dirt track, just wide enough for an ox cart to pass by. It was hot and sticky, as always at this time of year, and the swarm of gnats was joined by a multitude of horseflies, which had made Noir skittish. Tom was riding adequately, though struggling with the reins while trying to prevent the gnats from flying into ears and up his nostrils. Occasionally, a gnat got stuck in one of his eyes and he had to blink continuously to remove it.

As they moved south and chatted, Tom assessed his men. Hill was the talkative one, a friendly man of average height who was just a bit younger than Tom. As was typical, he wore his coffee-colored hair long, almost down to his shoulders, though it was tied tightly in a ponytail at the back. He had a thick, wiry beard and mustache that were closely cropped. His hazel eyes often blazed with an intensity that suggested intelligence, and he had a long, straight nose. A good-looking man with a solid physique who likely attracted much attention from the girls. Dressed in the all-green garb of a ranger, with his well-oiled rifle and short sword, he would certainly stand out.

Then there was Coleman. A taller man who was equally handsome, probably slightly older than Tom. His hair was a light auburn with flecks of blonde that curled uncontrollably. He had an angular jawline, a small gold earring in his left earlobe, and an infectious smile that caught a person's notice. His eyes were a deep luminous green that betrayed thoughtfulness and sometimes shyness. Like Hill, his build suggested much physical work as a laborer. His rifle was less well-kept and was older than Hill's, but he bristled with blades. It appeared he liked to fight with a knife and had several stashed about his body, in his cummerbund, his boot, and in his webbing. His sword was more of a cutlass with a wider curved blade; it was spotless and sharp. It was clear which weapons gained his care and attention.

Last in Tom's squad of men was Sanders. He was prematurely bald, an older man who'd not progressed far in the rangers. He had an egotistical streak that Tom was wary of; everything seemed to have to revolve around him. Of the three, Tom was least sure about Sanders. He had several unexplained scars, one from his right earlobe to the base of his neck. Another slashed across his forehead from his left temple to just above the center of his eyebrows. The third scar appeared white and indented just underneath his right eye, digging deeply into his cheek. His eyes were often furtive. He was fastidious. His ranger's uniform was almost always spotless, as were his rifle and short sword. Sanders hardly engaged in conversation, and when he did, he always turned the subject around to himself, which irritated his colleagues. His physique was wiry, and despite himself, Tom compared Sanders to a super clean weasel.

These were his men now; he would do everything to protect them and lead them well. His first formal command, and he was determined to prove himself. As they headed south, he gauged their qualities. It was clear that Hill was their marksman; like Tom, he was a proficient sniper and an excellent shot with his rifle, which explained the care and diligence he applied to the weapon. Coleman was their streetfighter. The man you'd want next to you in hand-to-hand combat. Rapid as a viper, Coleman could fight well with his hands, knives, and sword and would be deadly at short range when throwing a dagger. Despite his personality, or perhaps because of it, Sanders was their expert scout. The man could disappear into the undergrowth undetected and reappear in another location without so much as a branch moving in the undergrowth. He would be deadly sneaking up on a lookout and highly competent at investigating an enemy position. Each had qualities that melded into a team, and Tom was proud to lead them.

⧗ ⧗ ⧗

The trip to Frederica was tedious and without event. Tom had moments of concern when he thought he might lose control of Noir or simply just fall off. These fears proved unfounded, and he survived his first significant journey on horseback. It helped that they had walked and trotted most of it. Tom didn't think he was ready for cantering or galloping and was glad he didn't have to find out. Not having ridden much, he was tired of the effort. He was also sore and chapped where the saddle had rubbed the insides of his legs. It was an unpleasant type of pain that had him waddling like a duck, much to the amusement of the others.

This was his first outing to Frederica, and he was intrigued to see the colonial outpost for the first time. Situated on St. Simon's Island, Frederica was inland alongside a river given the same name. It guarded the northern river course from a Spanish incursion into Georgia and was a fortified town with a garrison. As Tom understood it, the town now had about thirty houses, a palisade, and a small blockhouse, which was to be strengthened by their troops. Tom couldn't wait to see the town, the fort, and, more importantly, the land north of the fort that Oglethorpe had gifted him and Mary on their wedding day. As soon as he could build a dwelling and work the land, he planned to bring Mary and Duke down from Savannah to their new home.

Before they could reach Frederica, the regiment had to pass through Darien, the Scottish Highlanders' settlement. At Darien, their lieutenant was to report to Captain Mackay, the leader of the Scots. It appeared that the Scottish Highlanders at Darien oversaw the building, supply, and defense of Fort Frederica.

As they approached Darien, the land they crossed perceptibly changed. Their route so far had been dominated by Georgia's pine forest on one side and the barrier islands' marshland on the other. There was little evidence of habitation, though they did see the occasional smallholding. As they reached Darien, the forest had been cleared, and broad pasture fields could be seen. These looked productive and were full of highland cattle. There was little evidence of arable farming, though as they entered the outskirts of town, they saw modest fields of wheat and small vegetable gardens.

As with elsewhere in Georgia, Tom could tell the residents' origins from the design of their houses. Clapboard houses in Savannah looked like those from the English South. Log houses in Port Royal had northern English and Scandinavian roots. Ebenezer had a Germanic-Salzburg feel. Here, the houses were unmistakably built by the Highland Scots. These houses were low-lying, timber-framed, and thatched with long overhanging rooftops. Some houses had mottle and daub bricks encasing the walls, while others had constructed walls of roughhewn stone.

It was an impressive town, with many such buildings and accompanying small gardens that looked well-tended and productive. Darien appeared like a fortress, and Tom could tell the Scots had built it, assuming that the Yamasees or the Spanish might attack them at any time. Tom wouldn't have fancied trying to mount such an assault. Defending the southern approaches, a battery housed four cannons; nearby was a formidable-looking guardhouse. Closer to the center were a storehouse and a chapel; both looked sturdy like the guardhouse and could easily be used as defensive positions if assaulted. The entire town was encircled with a ditch and a fence. Though there was no protection against cannonades, these fortifications would certainly impede an Yamasee attack or infantry assault.

What impressed Tom most, though, were the people. These were clearly settler-soldiers. No soft underbelly of traders, artisans, and administrators like Savannah. Tom couldn't help but recall Job Jalla's description of the pit fighter Old Donald McBane. Every single one of the men in the town could fit his description. A very tall man, thick with muscles, a strong-looking hardened face, moving a massive frame with agility, clearly capable of fighting hard if needed. Each of these men dressed similarly in tartan leggings and a tartan shawl, secured with a thick waist cummerbund or wide leather belt. Most sported muskets and Scottish Claymores. Tom saw a small contingent of Scottish rangers with rifles. There wasn't a short one amongst them. Tom was a tall man who didn't feel out of place in this town of giants. There were also many more men than women and children, at least a four-to-one ratio. It was clear why Darien existed as far as Georgia was concerned. It was more akin to a barracks than a town.

Another surprise was the dialect. At least Tom thought it was a dialect until Hill pointed out it was a different language. Everybody in Darien spoke Gaelic. It was a melodic language, but unlike Irish, it had harder edges. Tom learned quickly that most of the settlers had come from Inverness. They had brought the language with them when they fled Scotland after the Jacobite rebellion. Jacobites or not, these men were welcome here. Tom wasn't surprised that Oglethorpe had accepted them, given his family's history with the Jacobite cause. More importantly, these men were soldiers. Who better to have on the edge of Georgia's frontier than these hardened veterans?

Tom and his squad settled into their quarters and enjoyed a night in Darien, drinking beer, dancing, and singing with the locals. Their lieutenant meanwhile made plans with Captain Mackay for the troop's deployment. There were no surprises. They were to join the garrison at Fort Frederica and help strengthen its defenses. There would be work to do. They would help finish the construction of the palisade and the blockhouse. Tom's squad would patrol the region to check for roving bands of Yamasee, which were said to be more active than usual. Tom was excited by his mission. They were to regularly journey down to Amelia Island, on the border with Spanish Florida, to communicate with the highlander outpost and keep it supplied. The lieutenant promised that there would be time for him to visit his new land and begin constructing his dwelling.

Chapter 14: Oglethorpe's Return

The Frederica River meandered gently around an acute narrow bend and flowed leisurely across an expansive flat landscape. Tom spotted a wood stork wading in the shallows. Its bald, coarse head looked like a wise old man's, while its slightly curved beak rested on its chest. The stork was standing still, to attention, a sentinel of stone waiting half asleep. Tom noticed many other birds, egrets, herons, and ibises. He took their prevalence as a sign that the river offered a productive bounty.

This was Tom's land, the acres that Oglethorpe had gifted him. It was as the general had described it in his letter. Oglethorpe had a surveyor's eye and picked Tom's parcel well. While there were small coppices of Georgia pines, they didn't dominate the land like they did inland. There were tracts of marshland, but they didn't overwhelm the plot like they tended to on the coast. That wetland would provide a safety valve when the river flooded. Open grassland constituted the bulk of the property, perfect for a house, garden, and farm. Tom had surveyed the site to choose the house's location and placed it on a slight rise where the river looped to the east. He'd had time to build the foundations, fell the trees, and prepared the timber for the frame. His squad of men had helped him build and often visited, camping onsite. They all agreed it was a lovely property that would become an idyllic home for Tom and his family.

Tom's land was north of Fort Frederica and its small settlement. Captain Hugh Mackay had overseen the building of Frederica, and the highland Scots from Darien had supplied much of the labor. It was consequently well built. Named after the Prince of Wales, the fort had a star-shaped palisade within which sat a large barracks, officer's quarters, and magazine. These were stone-built using the Scots' building techniques. Many embrasures punctuated the wooden walls through which cannons poked. Holes were cut into the fortifications, which enhanced the defender's musketry firepower. Along the fort's interior were stairs and gantries devised for shooting from the parapets. Similar forts had been built across the region. The star-shaped Fort St. Andrew had been constructed on the north end of Cumberland Island and aimed to guard Terrapin Point. The smaller Fort St. Simons had been raised at the southern tip of St. Simons Island, designed to protect the entrance to Jekyll Sound. The smaller garrison at Fort. St. Simon was also built to warn the more significant force at Fort Frederica if an enemy tried to approach up the river. It was an excellent defensive arrangement.

Tom's squad alternated between Fort Frederica's barracks and their assignment supplying Amelia Island's outpost. Occasionally, they stayed in the small Frederica settlement and enjoyed its tavern. The fort sat beside the river, guarding its northern path while the settlement sat behind it. The town of Frederica had been growing and now had many houses, a store, a church, and a pub. There were over five hundred residents of the town. Unlike Darien, the houses were of a clapboard style, like those in Savannah, and the church was a rustic affair, crude and basic but sufficient for the community. The bar didn't offer the quality of ale he could get on the riverside in Savannah, but it wasn't bad; it just lacked a unique flavor. The owner was said to be developing his style, but Tom had not seen any sign of success.

His squad's duties had been light. They'd be drawn into the occasional drill when they were in the garrison. Often, it was basic training, loading, and firing practice, bayonet practice, and so forth. Occasionally, the drills were more advanced, designed to prepare the defenders to protect the fort and rout an attack. Cannons would be fired. The garrison would test fire muskets from the embrasures and scaffolding. Invariably, Tom's rangers would be called upon to shoot their rifles long distances from the parapets. The aim of the exercise was to test the killing zone between the forest and the fort. After these checks, the garrison was sent out to clear a line of trees or burn a section of scrub.

Tom's squad was sent with supplies to resupply the outpost on Amelia Island every week. They usually took food and beer, but sometimes they delivered gunpowder and musket balls. It was a trek that took up to two days on horseback. They soon worked out that it was more accessible by boat. After requisitioning a skiff, their supply duties eased. It required just over a day to arrive, and they began to take more provisions. Their course took them down the Frederica River, past Fort St. Simons, and into the Jekyll Sound. They'd navigate past Jekyll Island and down to the tip of Cumberland Island. Occasionally, they'd stop at Fort St. Andrews for the night and reach the outpost the following morning.

The Amelia Island base was nothing more than a hut. Two highlanders were stationed there. The cabin was of a log-style construction, solid but hardly defensible. It was surrounded by a small, practical garden filled with a small crop of corn, potatoes, other root vegetables, and legumes. The lookouts hunted across the island, so they needed a resupply of gunpowder and shot. It was only an observation post to watch the Spanish fort set on the island's northern tip. Tom considered it an intensely boring duty, and the two highlanders, Connor MacDonald and James McKinnon, were always pleased to see them. Sometimes, his troops idled there longer than they should, playing cards. Despite the prohibition on hard liquor, they'd smuggle rum down to the island and engage in a night of drinking. The two men had become friends, and Tom's squad enjoyed their company.

⧗   ⧗   ⧗

As Tom watched the wood stork, it suddenly became more alert. The stork raised its beak and leaned forward. Its whole body seemed to tighten, and then it placed its beak into the water, patiently trying to lure a fish into its trap. Tom reflected on the past few weeks. Their routine of garrison drills followed by supply runs to Amelia had been upended by Oglethorpe's return. The general's frigate had arrived and sailed into Jekyll Sound. Due to his appointment as a general, Oglethorpe had arrived with an entire regiment of British regulars, the 42nd Foot. Tom had seen British troops before, and they were usually impressive. These men were different from what he expected, and he reckoned the general would have his work cut out to prepare them for conflict. The regiment had been pulled out of the garrison in Gibraltar and was full of all sorts of rogues who'd gotten used to a comfortable life. Worse, there was a large contingent of Irish Catholics whose allegiance to the Crown seemed questionable.

Despite his obvious qualities, Tom was surprised that Oglethorpe had been named Commander in Chief of the

Military Forces of South Carolina and Georgia. He'd met the new Acting Governor of South Carolina, Colonel Bull when they'd sited Savannah, and he didn't think the man would take the snub well. Georgia's defense would depend on collaboration with its neighbor. They'd need South Carolina's professional rangers and militia, so the decision offered a troubling start to a significant relationship. War with Spain was closing in, and it might be a matter of months before it started.

The first change occurred quickly. The regulars had to be billeted somewhere. Tom's squad was turned out of the garrison and into the town, and the 42nd Foot was stationed at Fort Frederica and Fort St. Andrews. With Oglethorpe's return, they had to curtail the rum-running to the Amelia outpost, much to the chagrin of all concerned. Instead, they had to suffice with the local beer, which still needed to be improved.

The trouble started rapidly. Recognizing the need to keep the new regiment happy, the general recruited a large group of single women from England and transported them to Frederica. Tom didn't think Mary would like these women. Harlots was the term Tom used, but others preferred cruder terms like prostitute and ladies of the night. A few were respectable, but most weren't.

Frederica rapidly became one of the worst frontier towns in Georgia. While the 42nd Foot fought constantly with the locals and highlanders, the new women caused their own problems. Insidious rumors began to circulate about many prominent citizens. Captain Mackay was said to like large women even though he was happily married. It was rumored that Oglethorpe liked to have two women in a bed and that he'd had an affair with Mary Musgrove. Tom knew the general well and recognized that the gossip aimed to deliberately undermine Oglethorpe's and Captain Mackay's leadership. Though a good-looking single man, Oglethorpe was undoubtedly a gentleman who behaved accordingly. Tom knew Mary Musgrove well and understood such tittle-tattle to be beyond laughable.

With less garrison training, Tom sent his men out into the town to root out the cause of the gossip. Hill and Coleman were young, handsome, and thus well suited to the work. They made their way through the increasing number of disreputable houses in the town and spoke to the new womenfolk. Tom thought they might have brought too much enthusiasm to their task, but they took little time to identify the sources. Two women who'd recently moved from South Carolina were identified as the source of the rumors. Reflecting on it now, he thought it odd that these women hadn't arrived on the frigate with the 42nd Foot and the other women. It was a simple fix. They packed them up and sent them back to South Carolina on a fishing boat and the rumors stopped.

Tom's musings were momentarily interrupted by a splash. The stork had caught something. It gulped the fish down quickly and returned to its pose, its bill stuck in the water, seeking to catch another fish by touch. It was an impressive fishing technique. He returned to his thoughts. The real trouble had started after they'd sent the women away. It was a mutiny; there was no other word for it.

On the face of it, the mutiny had complex causes. The 42nd Foot had been garrisoned in Gibraltar too long; they hadn't seen active service for years, and their former commander hadn't drilled them well. Consequently, they'd grown soft and lazy. Finding themselves posted into a wilderness appeared to be a punishment duty to many. Their pay and provisions had been slow to arrive from the far side of the Atlantic, and they were supposed to receive hazard pay, which had yet to be confirmed.

Tom saw it himself. The soldiers were poorly fed, inadequately armed, and hadn't been paid in months.

His squad had just arrived at Fort St. Andrews, stopping for their regular night layover to Amelia. Twenty-five men posted there tried to assassinate the general. To Tom, its origins appeared dubious. Of course, there were complaints, but the mutineers were led by one of the Irish Catholics and were dominated by anti-protestant sentiments. The more he considered it, the more suspicious the two events seemed. It was a close call, though. The general could easily have died.

Tom had just visited Oglethorpe. It was his first opportunity to thank him for his wedding gifts. They'd had a pleasant few moments, and Tom was leaving the tent as Oglethorpe moved on to his other business with Captain Mackay. The men were gathering on the parade ground. Oglethorpe and the captain were due to inspect them.

Suddenly, the mutineers surrounded the tent. The leader took up his musket and fired into the tent at close range, aiming at Oglethorpe's head. Tom heard a whoosh as the ball fizzed past him. The distance was near, impossible to miss, and Tom had no chance to react. Oglethorpe looked stunned by this sudden, unexpected violence and didn't move. Miraculously, the ball grazed his cheek. They found out later it had passed between his wig and collar, damaging both but not inflicting the intended damage on its target.

Another man tried to fire a second shot. His musket misfired. Somehow, his powder had gotten damp. Tom jumped the man, wrestled him to the ground, and smashed his hand away from the gun with the blunt edge of his tomahawk. The man cried out in agony but had enough sense not to struggle further.

A third man drew his short sword and rushed into the tent, looking to finish off the general. Tom saw immediately that this was a mistake. Now, Oglethorpe was alert. He drew his sword, jumped forward, past encumbering furniture, and parried the man's initial blow. As Tom knew, Oglethorpe was no fool with his weapon. They exchanged several blows. Thrust followed parry, followed by counter-parry. Then counterthrust followed by a deft sidestep. In moments, Oglethorpe's assailant was lying in his own blood at the front of the tent. He was clearly dead. Oglethorpe's novel Balestra, the short jump and lunge, had surprised the man and finished the bout.

Another mutineer had then run-in with his sword drawn and inflicted a deep cut across the general's arm. Oglethorpe dropped his weapon and was exposed. Still sitting on one attacker, Tom launched his tomahawk at this latest assailant. The axe arched through the air haft over bit, and struck the man firmly in the back. It cleaved in deeply, a killing blow. The mutineer tried to grasp the weapon, crying in pain, and then fell into a crumpled heap on top of the other dead man. Tom threw the misfired weapon to Oglethorpe. Favoring his good arm, the general used the gun as a club to prevent further attack. By this point, he was in a rage, and nobody else dared come close.

Now alert to the danger, Captain Mackay, other loyalists, and the highlanders stepped into the breach to defend their commander and arrest the remaining men. Oglethorpe, aiming to defuse the standoff, declared that anybody giving up the mutiny would be pardoned immediately while anyone continuing would be shot. This did the trick. The remaining 42nd Foot, recognizing their commanding officer's good fortune and courage, gave up the assassination attempt.

The loyalists searched the regiment's barracks. They turned up twenty-five loaded muskets, ready for use. Rather than ordering floggings and firing squads, the general talked privately with each mutineer. Listening to their complaints, he made up their pay out of pocket. It seemed that the ringleaders had died in the attempt, so no further retribution was needed.

Tom was flabbergasted at Oglethorpe's actions. Instead of shooting twenty-five regulars, squandering men, and losing credibility with the regiment, he'd gained loyalty because of his munificence. He'd won the confidence and trust of the entire 42nd Foot, and many of the problems they'd caused began to go away. It was a surprising decision but effective. Remarkably, the general had survived three assassination attempts. A musket ball had gouged his cheek; he had a nasty wound in his arm, but otherwise, he was untouched. It was astonishing luck.

Sitting here now, watching the stork and thinking about the two incidents, Tom conjectured deeply. Both aimed to undermine the general's leadership. Though less direct, the gossip was no less dangerous, and it had some strange aspects. For example, why was there a peculiar attempt to scandalize Mary Musgrove's relationship with the general? Irish Catholics in the regiment had clearly led the assassination attempt. Was that a coincidence? Or could there be something more sinister behind it? Was it just about the pay, or was there a more concerted, conspiratorial effort somewhere in it? A guiding hand behind the scenes. The more Tom ruminated, the more suspicious it all appeared. They'd be without their Commander in Chief moments before a probable war with Spain if it had been successful. What a convenient gain for the Spanish.

The wood stork gave up fishing, languidly lifted itself into the air, and flew away. Tom ended his birdwatching and resumed his property tour. He would have to get back to building the house soon.

Chapter 15: Call Out the Militia

Last night's storms had been intense, some of the worst Evans had seen. Lightning had cascaded across the sky horizontally in great webs of electricity. The thunder had boomed as if fifty canons had fired simultaneously. The rain lashed sideways, like cold razorblades flying diagonally, smashing into the sides of buildings. Rainwater ran everywhere and pooled into deep gullies; so much fell it had nowhere to run to, and the Ashley River overflowed its banks. The gale that arrived with the storm whistled as it circled in vortexes with a power that downed trees and uplifted roofs from their moorings. Many took the storm as a harbinger of ill, an omen of some unknown deceit. The damage it left behind was significant, and the city would take many months to fully recover.

The morning that followed the storm was unnaturally quiet. As the morning heated up, a thick mist enveloped the city, and it was hard to see from one street to another. It was in this mist that Evans now ran. Something had rattled Bull. With a roar of command, he sent Evans to the stables to get their entire contingent of horses ready for departure. All the able-bodied men in Bull's household had been commanded to join him on a sortie out of town to the south. Though a ride into the countryside wasn't unusual, the suddenness and urgency with which Bull had commanded it was. Evans wondered if he, too, had taken the storm to be a portent of something terrible.

The household was a hive of activity. All the stableboys rushed around, gathering horse tack and preparing the horses. The men hurriedly dressed and gathered their weapons. Those that were set, assembled in the courtyard. Bull was one of the first to arrive. A commanding presence, he bellowed at the laggards. As a colonel in the rangers, he dressed in his green uniform and bristled with his weapons of war. He was a man of action. The transition from an elderly statesman relaxing in his study, puffing his pipe, to a model commander assembling his troops was instant. Evans quickly assumed his natural role as Bull's aide-de-camp. There were six of them, including Bull, Evans, and Williams.

Once convened, Bull led the small squad of mounted men out of the courtyard. They were all officers, or former officers, and rode their mounts swiftly along the misty city streets. Williams led the way and called out regularly to warn passersby to make way as the men gathered speed, passing from a trot to a canter. As they reached the outskirts, they began to move into a fast gallop. They rode through pools of water, and flecks of mud were thrown up in all directions as the horses' hooves splashed thunderously along the road. They were now moving quickly, a mass of armed men on warhorses. A cavalry looking for an enemy. Evans moved up alongside Williams, reins tight. He concentrated on his horse's path as they sped along, keeping pace with Williams's grey mare.

What had spooked Bull into this sudden martial action remained a mystery to all, including Evans. Bull had them going southwards along the Port Royal road. His determined face was etched with concentration and tenacity. He moved up to the other side of Williams so that the three of them could form the vanguard of the men. As suddenly as they had started their gallop, Bull raised a fist and brought them all to an abrupt halt. He addressed the men directly, "We've just heard that Hutchinson's store on the Stono River has been raided. They killed two storekeepers and stole weapons and ammunition. It looks like a group of runaways, but it's likely to be much more dangerous. We've been expecting a slave rebellion fostered by the Spanish, and if I'm a betting man, I'd bet good odds that this is the start of it. We need to head south across the open farmland from here. Right now, we need to know how many they are. Stay close and don't engage them until I give the say-so. I need to know what we are dealing with!"

Not waiting for any questions, Bull wheeled his horse, jumped a ditch, and headed across the fields. He was several furlongs ahead of them before they could react. Evans was the first to pull his horse around and follow. Williams was half a furlough behind him. The rest of the squad soon circled and chased behind at the rear. Bull returned to a gallop but a slower one, more conscious of the divots and ruts that peppered the tracks beside the fields along which they raced. The sudden action pumped Evans with adrenaline. He felt like he was hunting on horseback again, racing across fields, jumping gullies and hedges in pursuit of some quarry. He knew though this situation might be a serious business. He recalled the three odd letters and the St. Augustine spy. Bull knew what was happening, and his response suggested that it endangered South Carolina's sovereignty. As he charged along, Evans checked his weapons. Before this day was out he might need them. His rifle was secure in its padded gun holder, his sword hung ready at his belt, and his pistol was safe and at hand, fastened just below his saddle. If he needed them, they were there, and he'd had the good sense to load them before they'd left.

Their going was swift. Fields drifted past at pace. They cleared overflowing ditches, muddy gullies, culverts that had turned into streams with heavy rainwater, low-lying hedges, and small bushes. The horses worked up a sweat and began to blow hard as they sprinted. Clods of mud from the heavily wet mud flew as they flew. Their haste almost proved to be their undoing.

Suddenly, Bull pulled hard at the reins of his horse. It abruptly slowed and stopped, almost rearing as it did. Having fought alongside Bull often enough, Evans and Williams quickly followed suit. Their three escorting colleagues were slower and nearly ran full tilt into their enemy. Thankfully, the slowing vanguard got in the way of the rearguard's horses and slowed them enough to stop them from plowing into the mass of armed rebels that were marching across the fields almost directly in their path. It was a close shave. A couple of shots sounded, and a musket ball or two whizzed through the wheat field nearby.

It was shocking to see. In front of Bull's small squad were more than eighty escaped slaves; many men were armed with muskets, pitchforks, scythes, machetes, and all manner of weapons they had taken from their plantations. They maneuvered into a defensive formation as they saw the small group of horsemen. They shouted in unison, "Liberty from slavery! Liberty for all!" Some began to load their muskets. Evans pulled his pistol and fired into the heaving mass, unaware if he'd hit a target or not. Other members of their small unit drew weapons as if readying to attack.

Bull took immediate charge. An excellent military leader knows when to retreat, and Bull was a veteran. He bawled,

"Get back. Move, get out of here!". A few more shots were flying in both directions. One of Bull's men grunted in pain as a musket ball shattered his left wrist. He swore loudly. Blood flicked up the side of Evans's horse.

The next thing he knew, the entire unit was dashing back across the fields, following Bull away from the enemy and the danger they'd nearly blundered into. Their foe was on foot, so Bull's men weren't followed. The rebels continued to move south along the trail away from the Stono River.

Bull headed for a small hillock from which he could view the fields and watch the small slave army as it resumed its march. He took stock of their situation, "Well, that was close! I didn't expect them to be this far south yet or that big. This could get out of hand quickly. Evans, Williams, to me! How's Collins?" Collins was the injured man. He'd survive, but his wrist was a bloody mess, and the bone poked out dreadfully; it looked broken in several places. One of the men was binding it, stemming the blood flow. Collins grimaced in agony. Bull pulled out a hipflask and forced Collins to drink his best whiskey. "It will help with the pain," he explained.

Evans pulled his horse to the top of the hillock beside Bull's horse and looked down the slope towards the slave army. "That's already a formidable force, sir! I guess they're rolling across the plantations and gathering more rebels as they go. Give them two more days, and their little army will be bigger than anything we are likely to be able to handle?" It was posed as a question but was really an astute observation.

Bull eyed Evans sharply, "Evans, we'll make a leader out of you yet! Of course, you're right. This will get out of our hands completely in two days. What do you think they're doing to the plantations, though? I would suggest we'll find a lot of dead friends burned in their homes when we have time to look. We can't worry about them now. We need to get this thing under control and quickly. Evans, you take Collins back to Charles Town, find Colonel Vanderdussen, and have him call out the Charles Town militia. They are to track this host south along the trail. Once you've done that, find Colonel Palmer and his rangers. Have them come overland to this hillock; you'll come back with Palmer, and both of you will meet me here before dusk. Williams, you got the most important job!"

Williams led his horse further up the hillock, "Yes sir, ready and willing!"

Bull carefully explained his instructions, "Williams, you will need to move fast and avoid getting into trouble. If you fail, our plan will likely collapse. You're going to Port Royal to meet with Kingston. Have him call out the Port Royal militia. They're to come north and stop the slave rebels before they cross the Edisto River. His job is not to engage them. I repeat, he is not to engage. He is to make it impossible for them to safely cross the river. The crossings wouldn't be easy after these storms we've had."

Bull drew a crude map on the ground. A snake resembled the Edisto, and he pointed to a spot along the snake and sketched three arrows. The first arrow, across the river, indicated Kingston's Port Royal militia and their blocking motion. Here, Bull drew a horizontal block. The second arrow, to the flank, depicted Palmer and his rangers. Seemingly they were to provide a diversion and covering fire. The final arrow indicated the arrival of Vanderdussen and the Charles Town militia, who were to hit the rebel army's rear. It seemed like a neat plan if it worked.

"This hillock will serve as our HQ until tonight," Bull commanded, pointing to the remaining two men. You two have just become scouts. I need you to track the whereabouts of this force and regularly report back to me. I need to know if they head in another direction other than south. If they stop and make camp, I want to know exactly where they are."

Bull sat astride his horse, looking imperious as he pulled out his telescope and scanned the fields to the south, now steely with his silence. The men understood that orders had been given, and they all set about their business. Evans wished Williams good luck with his task and set off to the north with Collins. Williams headed southeast to avoid the marauders. Given the storms and heavy flooding, he had yet to entirely work out where he would cross the Edisto or his best route.

Evans looked back at the figure of Bull sitting alone on his hillock, now his HQ. It was just like him dispatching his entire entourage and giving no thought to his own protection. If the rebels knew that the Acting Governor and military head of South Carolina sat on his own, on a little hillock nearby, surely they would send out a small group of men to attack him. It was an incredible risk but a calculated one. He needed all the men he had available to bring his plans together. And without his plans coming to fruition perfectly, the rebellion would swing a brutal and devasting blow. South Carolina might struggle to recover from such a setback. Its economy was too dependent on its enslaved people and plantations. Destroy either, and the consequences might be dire. Destroy both, and Evans had no idea what could follow. Perhaps a Spanish invasion.

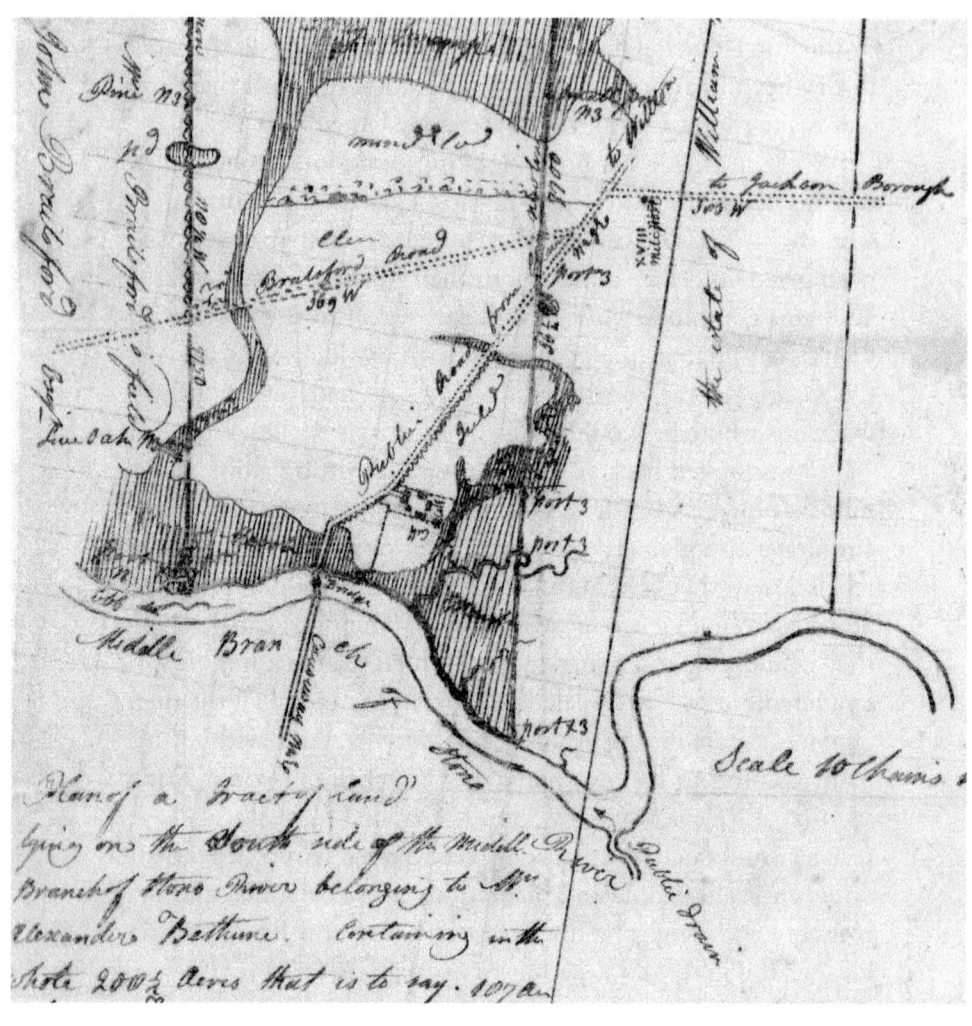

Detail from a 1780s plat showing Wallace Bridge over the 'Middle Branch of the Stono River,' and a nearby cluster of buildings representing the site of Thomas Wallace's Tavern. North is at the bottom of the image. Source: https://www.ccpl.org/charleston-time-machine/stono-rebellion-1739-where-did-it-begin

Chapter 16: Stono Rebels

Everything had progressed quickly. Lamine had reported back to O'Sullivan, who'd immediately seen the genius in Jemmy's plans. They'd met, and the Spanish spy provided the rebels with needed assurances. Now, here was Lamine ensconced in a rebel slave army heading south. The rebels were destroying, sacking, and killing everything in their wake. They slew their masters, stole weapons, burnt houses, destroyed crops where they could, and slaughtered the animals. It was a scorched earth tactic that was both devastating and effective, a horrific undertaking, but this was war and the business of war.

The plot began as expected. Jemmy and Lamine were joined at the hut by twenty Kongolese warriors, some of whom violently left their plantations that morning, killing the families they'd served. They were veterans; like Jemmy, they were tall, lean, and muscular. They had fought in the Kongo's civil wars and knew how to handle their weapons. Their incarceration, first on slave ships and then on plantations, had hardened and strengthened them further. These men were all soldiers who just happened to be enslaved. Most spoke Portuguese, and it was easy for Lamine to understand them when they discussed the plan. They were armed with weapons available on the plantations. Many had axes; some held scythes, and others clenched machetes. All looked warlike, were composed, and ready to act.

The rebellion was as much a religious revolt as it was an insurrection. They'd deliberately chosen the day after the Feast of the Nativity of Mary for its opening. Many of the men held up religious banners and wore symbols. As a Muslim, Lamine didn't understand the implication of the symbols, but he knew they were Catholic. There was no mistaking the meaning of their chants, though, as they set off for the Stono bridge. They switched from Portuguese to English and chanted "Liberty!" repeatedly, as well as some variations on their theme, "Liberty from slavery!" and "Liberty for all!"

When the rebels reached Hutchinson's store, they stormed it en masse. The storekeepers, forewarned by the chanting, fired several ineffective shots and were butchered brutally. Lamine was at the rear, but he would never forget the blood that oozed across the store, tacky underfoot. One of the storekeepers had been beheaded, and the other had his guts hanging out. Both were the victims of axe wounds wielded by proven warriors set on retribution for their mistreatment.

The rebels quickly set about arming themselves with muskets and ammunition from the supplies. Other useful weapons and spare muskets were loaded onto a handcart, which was dragged away by three men. Another cart was laden with as much food as it could hold and was hauled off into the nearby wood. The speed with which the store had been captured and plundered impressed Lamine. The core group of rebels acted concertedly, betraying their military experience. Only minutes had passed, two men were dead, and a small group of rebel soldiers were headed south, fully armed and supplied, ready to cause havoc across the countryside.

The mayhem followed instantaneously. It was ruthless but efficient. The plan was simple, and the men were trained to follow it perfectly. They fanned out across the countryside in small groups. They raided every plantation they came across as they followed the river south. Every white person was killed with no exception. Men were shot, women were stabbed, and children were bludgeoned. The rebels inflicted their carnage quickly. Few survived the onslaught. By chance, some lived to tell the tale, but only because they were left for dead or were somehow missed in the onslaught.

Plantation slaves were freed to join the rebellion. In some cases, they did so happily. Others were coerced, while some were forced against their will. Everything was stolen or destroyed. Weapons were taken. Food was captured and added to the rebels' growing supplies. Houses were set alight and burnt to the ground, often with their dead occupants inside. Animals were butchered, and fields were set afire. Nothing was left that would be useful. Jemmy's plan seemed to unfold perfectly... until it didn't.

⏳ ⏳ ⏳

The first sense that something was wrong came when Lamine saw the horsemen. They'd amassed quite a troop of freed slaves, primarily men and all armed, about eighty in total. Most of the plantations were behind them, on fire, and they were situated south, approximately halfway between the Stono and Edisto rivers. The track along which they marched was slightly elevated. The six horsemen were racing across the fields at a gallop and seemed to be heading towards the rebels. It was evident to Lamine that they were in a dip in the fields and couldn't see the rebel force. He pointed this out to Jemmy.

Jemmy was an astute, accomplished military leader who was alert to danger. These horsemen were about to career straight into them. He tried to form up the men so that they were ready to fire at these madmen as they rode up the crest of the dip. As he commanded loudly, the men maneuvered haphazardly. For Lamine, it was clear that adding large numbers of untrained people to their numbers had negatively impacted their fighting competence. Several of Jemmy's Kongolese warriors loaded their muskets, and Lamine hoped it would be enough. They had to kill these men, or they might raise the alarm and call out the militia.

When the first horse hit the cusp of the ridge, it pulled up suddenly. The rider was clearly an expert horseman; such a move in the circumstances was impressive. Most riders would have carried on. They would have been too slow or too inexperienced to stop in time and inadvertently plowed into the killing zone. The horse momentarily reared up. The following two horsemen accomplished the same feat. The following horses might have blundered on but were barred from proceeding by their van.

The horses didn't enter the effective musket range, so Jemmy paused. Not all the men were as disciplined. There was a sudden report of three muskets, but the shots went wide and missed. One of the horsemen pulled a pistol and aimlessly fired at the crowd. Lamine felt a man drop next to him. He looked down. The pistol shot had taken his associate in the stomach, and blood began to seep through his fingers as he grasped at the wound. He cried out in pain. It was a taut, knowing cry. He'd been hit in the gut and would be dead in hours, and the man knew it.

Though the distance was still too long, Jemmy ordered them to fire. Lamine pulled up his musket and discharged it. Balls flecked towards the horsemen, but muskets were almost useless at that range. One of the horsemen was hit by a random bullet. He wheeled away and grabbed his wrist. The leader shouted a command, and the squad was gone as quickly as they'd appeared.

Jemmy looked concerned and swiftly spoke to his leading men, including Lamine: "That's unlucky. I'd hoped we might have the whole day before discovery. They'll head back to call out the militia. We need to quicken our pace. If we can make it across the Edisto River before nightfall, that will help us get away. Then we can destroy the plantations and free people further south."

Lamine, Jemmy, and the original rebels set about moving the gathered mass more quickly. That proved to be another oversight. They'd picked up some women, children, and some reluctant stragglers. Moving these people at speed proved challenging. The undisciplined, who didn't grasp their predicament, just got in the way of the Kongolese, who were trying to get the column moving. Worse still, heavy rains the night before had made the track heavy underfoot, bogging down their progress and severely hampering their ability to move the carts. They could have abandoned them and moved more quickly, but they needed the food, weapons, and ammunition the carts carried. It became evident they wouldn't make the Edisto River before the evening and couldn't hope to ford it before the following day.

Eventually, after much cajoling, the file began to move more quickly. The carts were sent to the rear and were escorted by a contingent of Jemmy's most trusted men. Jemmy and Lamine led from the front and set a swift rate. The remainder of the

Kongolese were strategically placed along the line to ensure everybody else moved in tempo with the vanguard. While the column stretched out more than advisable, it was a risk they were willing to take. It seemed unlikely that the militia, or any of South Carolina's military, would catch up with them yet. Their main job was to get to the Edisto as quickly as possible and ensure they forded it before the Charles Town militia engaged fully in pursuit.

Though they made better progress, it wasn't enough. Jemmy and Lamine arrived at the Edisto ford just as dusk was setting in, and it would be many hours before the rest of the column would join them. The carts probably wouldn't get there until the middle of the night. Jemmy was morose, and Lamine shared his sentiment. The next unplanned obstacle faced them and it wouldn't help their progress. The storms the night before had caused a swell in the river, and the ford was flooded. What should have been an easily fordable spot was now dangerously swirling with the dirtiest, ugliest-looking floodwater they'd ever seen. Large branches and stumps of trees swept past in the heavy current. Somebody trying to ford would either drown in the strong currents or get bashed into smithereens by the heavy debris shooting along in the eddies.

Given the situation, their choices were all bad. They could stay put and wait for the floodwaters to recede, but likely, they would get caught by Charles Town's militia before they had the chance to cross. It might take days for the floods to abate before they could use the ford. So, it was unquestionably a poor option. One option was to follow the river to the southeast and hope to cross nearer the ocean. This, too, was an awful choice. As the river widened, it was even less likely to be fordable. That direction would bring them closer to Port Royal and its militia. They could follow Edisto to the northwest, hoping to find a more favorable ford. That took them in the wrong direction, and they would lose momentum and followers.

After much discussion, their only real option became clear. In the morning, they must march northwest a few miles to capture the Parkers' ferry at Jacksonboro. Capturing the ferry might not be straightforward. There were always armed guards, but not enough to defend against their force. Taking everything across would take time, and that was a risk. With these floods, the ferry might not be usable, which made it a risky option. But those were the risks they had to face since this was the only option left, and it was Jemmy's choice.

Lamine privately mused over the options. It wasn't the only option remaining; he could see another. They could find a defensible position and fight. Their force was not inconsequential and properly arrayed; it might beat a militia. However, the day had convinced him that Jemmy had made the right choice. The real fighters were the Kongolese, and there were only twenty or so of them. There were definitely a few others amongst the rebels that could be reliable, men who'd been warriors. Still, most were unblooded farmhands with little aptitude for fighting. Others were reluctant participants who'd likely melt away once the action started. The day had shown that they would likely need a more significant force in a real battle.

As the night closed in, the column assembled at the ford. Jemmy posted sentries, and Lamine took up duties along the riverside near the flooded ford. It was a close call. Had the ford been usable, they would already be across and, by tomorrow, halfway to Georgia. Now, their situation was uncertain, and it became more dangerous for them as the hours passed. Late into the middle of the night, the carts and the rearguard finally arrived.

The following day produced another surprise. The water in the ford had started to recede far more quickly than expected, and it might be passable in a few hours. Their morning optimism was soon derailed. The distant report of a rifle gave them their first warning sign. Moments later, there was another echoing crack from a rifle shot. One of the Kongolese warriors guarding the ford fell, instantly dead from the distant shot. It was a mortal wound that took him fully in the chest. Blood gushed out of the hole that punched a gaping chasm in his back. Eyes wide open, his face was set with surprise. His death occurred so quickly that no other emotions registered, not even pain. It must have been a rifleman, likely a highly competent sniper.

Lamine looked for the source and quickly discovered its origin. Across the ford, a militia was arriving. Two men had fired rifles and taken down the Kongolese guard. Most of the militia had muskets and posed little danger from a distance, but the riflemen were slowly reloading. They worked hard, ramming the cartridges and bullets into the grooved gun barrels.

The real jeopardy was subtler. The arriving militia had taken away their newly acquired optimism. There was no way they could cross now. If they tried, they would be attacked piecemeal and die before they reached the other side. If they reached the other side, they would die when they were charged by the militia, bayonets affixed. Or they could be captured and hung. On top of opposing the crossing, if Jemmy wasn't careful, these men might block his intended escape using Parkers' ferry. Their situation looked more problematic by the minute as more militia arrived and took up defensive positions across the river. Jemmy shouted for everybody to take cover. Before the riflemen could reload, he intended to starve them of targets. Some subterfuge might be needed to capture and use the ferry. They'd need skill and a bit of luck if they were to avoid becoming stuck on their side of the river and annihilated.

Chapter 17: Edisto Battle – Part I

Too slow. Evans knew they were going too slow. Collins's injury wasn't deadly but hindered his ability to ride fast. He'd lost a lot of blood, and his bandage was soaked in it. Collins understood the danger the rebellion posed, and he pushed himself hard. It had been this effort that had nearly caused his blackout. Collins slid from his horse and almost fell. Now, they were going slower, cantering rather than galloping, but it was too sluggish. Evans needed to raise the alarm and call out the militia and do it quickly.

That day seemed to be full of good fortune. When they hit the Port Royal road, they instantly encountered a local merchant heading into the city. Evans hurriedly explained the situation and left the merchant to escort Collins to the surgeon. He could then continue up the highway at the fastest gallop he could muster. Time was of the essence, and now Evans was unhindered. Evans crossed the city streets as fast as he dared, carefully avoiding pedestrians and the occasional carriage.

Thankfully, he found Colonel Vanderdussen where he'd expected: at the parade ground. His primness and efficiency suddenly seemed welcome as Evans gave Colonel Bull's orders.

"How long will it take to call out the militia and get them down to the Edisto River?" Evans asked.

The colonel paused for a moment while considering the question, "I reckon it will take an hour to get them out and on the road. It'll be a large group, maybe sixty or more. Probably two to three hours on top of that to get us down to the Edisto. There is no way of us getting there before nightfall."

Evans replied, "Acting Governor Bull requests that you march all night if necessary. The militia must be ready to engage the rebels along the north bank of the Edisto tomorrow morning. Acting Governor Bull asks that you follow their trail and engage them in the rear. He has scouts out and has his HQ to the northeast, about half an hour from the river. The colonel requests that you send a runner to contact him as soon as you are closing in on your position. Colonel Palmer's rangers have been ordered to meet us there. They will begin the engagement from a distance, hitting the enemy flank. That will be the sign to start your own action. The Port Royal militia have been called out, and they will block the advance of the slaves, stopping them from crossing the river. The aim is to engage them in the rear and the flank while they are stuck there trying to ford the river."

The plan was straightforward. Vanderdussen acknowledged his orders and set about calling out the militia. Evans headed off across town to find Colonel Palmer and the rangers. First, he went to their quarters. It was getting late in the afternoon, and naturally, they weren't there. After a few urgent queries, he found them in a nearby tavern. Fortunately, they were only on their first pint and reacted instantaneously. Though a small squad of twenty men, these were the professionals, the seasoned veterans. Their sharpshooting and experience in Indian warfare might prove essential. After sharing with Palmer his orders, the colonel had his men kit up and form up in double time. Given their setting, relaxing in a bar, the speed with which the squad acted impressed Evans. They were ready to go and were on the road within twenty minutes.

Evans led Palmer and his rangers back along the trail he had already traversed twice. They went along the Port Royal road for several miles. Then, they cut across the fields, retracing Evans's route earlier in the morning. It was nearly dusk when they arrived at the small hillock that served as Bull's headquarters. The Acting Governor was there waiting for them along with Johnson, one of the other men from his household. It seemed that Smith was still out keeping tabs on the rebels. Evans was relieved to see his leader untouched; it had been a risk, but it had paid off. The small rebel army would find it challenging to assault the site now that it was fortified with Palmer's seasoned veterans.

Bull welcomed them, slapped Evans on the back, and gave Palmer a firm handshake: "You made good time, Evans. Well done! I trust Collins made it back okay? Good to see you, Colonel Palmer. What news do you have of Vanderdussen and the militia?" The questions were shot at Evans. It was clear that Bull had not enjoyed the wait for his plan's wheels to turn.

Evans reported, "Collins will be fine; he's at the surgeon now. Colonel Vanderdussen called out the militia late in the afternoon. They should be halfway to their position now. He estimated their arrival to be around midnight."

"Very good, son, nice work." Bull directed his attention towards Colonel Palmer, saying, "We need to relieve Smith and Johnson. They've been out there all afternoon and need some rest. Can you send three of your men out scouting for the night and replace them? They can do alternating duties during the night. It doesn't look like our enemy intends to move. They stopped and made camp at the ford. We got lucky; it's impassable, and it's slowed down their movement. These storms have given us a lucky break. The rebellion would have spiraled out of our control if they'd got across that ford today. Can you also post a picket? I don't think we are at risk here now, but let's not take any chances. Everybody else should get some sleep. We have a hard fight tomorrow, so there's no question there'll be some type of battle. Let's hope it goes according to our designs for South Carolina's sake!"

Palmer responded, "Yes, sir!" and went off to organize his men for the night. Evans dismounted, took care of his horse, and found a dry bit of grass on which to sleep. He was exhausted. It had been a hard day of riding, and he had covered many miles at speed across open farmland. His legs throbbed, and his feet had been rubbed raw by the stirrups. Perhaps he needed to buy some new boots. As he rested, he wondered how Williams was doing. He had the more arduous task of getting to Port Royal and raising the militia there. The distance was further, and Evans had no idea how Williams would get across the Edisto River while the river was flooding. Later in the morning, he learned that his friend had been courageous and had taken a significant risk. He'd swum across the flooded river using his horse as a shield. It was a miracle that they'd made it and avoided being swept away by the torrents. Another stroke of good fortune had shone its light on their endeavors. They were having a lucky day.

⧗ ⧗ ⧗

They all rose early the following day. The Acting Governor was in great spirits. He'd heard that the Port Royal militia were arriving on the south bank of the Edisto, and he was delighted with the news. Runners had also arrived from Colonel Vanderdussen. The militia had appeared later than expected due to the heavily mudded and churned-up tracks. Still, they'd had some respite and would be ready. Bull clasped Evans tightly around the shoulders, "Your friend Williams is in my good books. After this, you two can play dice in my basement to your heart's content!" Evans rolled his eyes but was secretly grateful for the praise and that they'd both served their leader well. Bull was a man who was easy to respect.

Bull led from the front. They mounted, and the entire party moved southwest to rejoin the rangers' scouts and seek out their foe. The plan was for the action to start with a flanking rifle assault led by the rangers. The initial attack aimed to draw the rebel army in their direction, at which point Vanderdussen and the militia were to engage their enemy's rear. One controlled musket blast was to be followed by a bayonet charge. It was expected that the defenders would then run and could be picked off individually by rifle fire or by mounted rangers.

It was at that point that Evans heard the first two shots. He listened carefully. The sounds echoed across the valley. The shots came from the south and were clearly rifles. It must be the Port Royal militia, but either that meant they'd engaged their foe when they weren't supposed to, or the rebels were somehow crossing the river. Bull looked across at Colonel Palmer. Not a word passed between them. They appeared to have a common perception of what the shots meant. Bull ordered the mounted rangers to move forward at the canter. Clumps of grass were torn up as they descended into the valley and up the other side to join the scouting party. Evans felt the initial gut-wrenching fear that bubbles up inside when battle nears. An acidic pain shot up from his stomach, up his chest, and into his throat. He knew what that physical reaction meant. He'd be fighting soon.

The battlefield lay before them when they reached the top of the hill. On a typical day, it would have been a beautiful panorama. Mist covered the landscape. The residual storm water had steamed up under the sultry morning sun. The Edisto River snaked along to their left, heading northwest. A low fog wisped along its course, masking the flooding ford. They could see in the distance Parker's ferry. The valley was flat, barring a small knoll close by the ford. Ditches, dykes, and gullies were strewn across the fields. Some appeared to be manmade and encircled the little hill. The knoll itself might have been from some lost civilization. Evans had seen similar mounds elsewhere. Small thickets and coverts dotted the valley. The scrub was sparse but enough to provide cover for a defending force.

As they arrived, the battle was taking hold. Yesterday, their luck had been advantageous, but today, it looked like it had turned and now favored their enemy. All of Bull's carefully constructed tactics were unraveling. The rifle fire from the Port Royal militia had been the first mistake. It warned the rebel slaves, and they took cover. Evans could see that they had chosen their camp well. They'd used the knoll to benefit the defender during an attack. The ditches, dykes, and gullies gave them natural protection against sniping. The small, wooded areas gave them a degree of protection from Vanderdussen's muskets. Having been warned, the enemy hunkered down in a solid defensive position.

Worse errors had occurred. Colonel Vanderdussen had taken the rifle fire from Palmer's rangers as his signal to attack. He had launched his rearguard action precipitously. He'd lost Palmer's diversion and, consequently, the element of surprise. Evans saw with horror that the situation was degenerating. The mist was hiding the battlefield damaging Vanderdussen's sight of the rebel's defenses. Consequently, the militia's first volley, which was supposed to devastate and demoralize the defenders, had been fired too early. As the defenders had taken cover, it went high. A couple of the rebels fell, but the volley didn't cause anywhere near the damage intended. Following his commands to the letter, which was inadvisable in the circumstances, Vanderdussen and the militia charged the defensive positions, bayonets fixed. As the rebel army hadn't been displaced, they fired their own musket volley, and the South Carolinians took casualties as they rushed forward. Already, the entire Charles Town militia was fighting hand-to-hand combat against rebel slaves on the north side of the mound. More ruinous still, the rebel leader was reinforcing that side of the mound with defenders from the south and southeast of the mound. Those defenders could stand back and shoot into the attacking force as they fought in melee. They could use the height of the mound to shoot over their own men and into their foes. It was a desperate situation.

There was nothing left for Bull to do but to attack. He took command accordingly, "Colonel Palmer, have your men fire one round. They must take out those men there," he pointed at the men gathering on the mound above the militia who were about to cause severe damage with their musket fire. Continuing, Bull commanded all the rangers in his most demanding way, "Men, we have to become cavalry, or the battle will be lost. We will charge our horses down the hill, across the valley, and hit the southeast side of the mound. Use the horses to do as much damage as possible, but don't try to take your horses up the mound. Go round it. Try to stick together. Good luck, Godspeed, and remember fortune honors the brave! The militia needs you, they are your brethren, your citizens, and your friends. Save them now, they need you! For South Carolina. Go!"

The rangers were ready and responded in unison, "For South Carolina!" Every man on the hill was an expert marksman with a rifle, and they were prepared to fire. Colonel Palmer signaled, and they discharged a volley. There were twenty-three shots. A peel of blasts rang out. A smell of cordite and a waft of smoke momentarily concealed the scene. Then Evans could see each man had hit a target. One moment, there was a group of rebels pointing muskets at the militia, and a moment later, they were gone. It was a pivotal moment in the battle that protected those fighting hand-to-hand and turned the tide against the rebels defending the mound.

Then, the rangers mounted and charged. It was a strange thing for them to do; each man knew it. Rangers fought in the forest against native enemies. They fought on foot, hidden by trees. They adopted the Indian methods, no silly lines and no daft fighting in the open with muskets. They did not fight on horseback. They did not charge down hills like cavalry into opposing infantry. The day would undoubtedly be one they would remember. That is, if they lived. Each of them drew their blades and kicked their mounts into a gallop. Those with short swords and cutlasses wished they'd followed the advice of their friends and donned a cavalry sword, but it was too late.

For Evans, time slowed. Unlike most of the rangers, at least he was trained to conduct cavalry assaults. There was a swish as he heard his sword drawn from its scabbard. He tightened his left hand's grip on the reins. Evans maneuvered his sword into the correct position for the cavalry charge, point facing forward. He noticed almost subconsciously that his heels dug deeply into the haunches of his horse. And then he was traveling down the hill at speed, leaning forwards, his body close to the neck of the horse. As the aide-de-camp, he positioned himself to Bull's left. Palmer was on Bull's right, and they were flanked on either side by ten galloping rangers, creating an arrow-like formation with Bull at the tip. The entire squad hurtled down the hill at full tilt. The pounding of the hooves was almost deafening as they thundered towards their foe.

Next thing Evans knew, he was in the thick of the fight. Musket balls flew past, and an eerie whoosh accompanied the gun's bang. The discharge odor wafted past as the horse dodged a large bush. Evans jumped a ditch and went up and over a dyke. One ranger's horse tripped and fell. The man and horse quickly disappeared from sight as they tumbled. Then, there were enemies in front of him. One angled twist with his sword and a man's forehead seemed to come apart from his skull. Blood flecked horizontally and gushed down the sword to his guard. Then, a man launched himself towards the horse, trying to unseat him. Evans tightened the reins and swerved the horse slightly. His assailant bounced unceremoniously away, flailing and landing in a crumpled heap.

He saw Bull take a man's head clean off with a perfect sweep of his sword. Palmer was using a tomahawk, unconventionally battering the enemy as he went. Then, there was another foe stabbing his musket and bayonet upwards towards Evans. A forward swing cleaved the man's shoulder apart. He screamed, dropped the musket, and faded away. Before they had time to think, the charge reached the defender's mound. Bull led the left flank around the south face of the mound, and Palmer led the right flank around the north face. Evans followed Bull. They slaughtered their enemy and used the horses as weapons of terror. It was a devastating assault, and it saved the militia from defeat.

Just as the battle looked like it was won, a tall, lean, muscular man launched himself from the mound. He swung his axe in an overhead motion as he jumped. The timing was perfect, and Evans knew the man was an experienced warrior. He hadn't worried about the rider but aimed to take down the horse. Evans swept his sword upwards at this new danger, but his blade was deflected by the heavy axe. After sweeping through the parry, the warrior's axe cut deeply into his horse's neck. There was a strained whinny, followed by a sharp guttural cry. The horse died and fell, its labored breaths fading to a whimper as it hit the ground.

Evans had little time to register it. He'd been galloping, and the horse's legs suddenly gave way at full pace. The horse seemed to disappear from under Evans, and it felt like he was flying through the air alone. The ground suddenly appeared, and he hit it face-first. Dirt got in his mouth, his lips were scratched, his eyes got gouged, and his right ear split. Evans head smashed into the ground dazing him. Immediately, he felt a heavy force smash into his body from above. There were a few moments of pain and then blackness.

Chapter 18: Edisto Battle – Part II

After the rifle shots, the rebels were forewarned of imminent danger. Jemmy's army took cover to avoid taking more casualties from the snipers. Their camp had been well chosen. It was on a small hillock surrounded by culverts. The ditches, trees, and bushes were sufficient to provide some cover. The mound provided difficulties for an attacker. It had steep sides that would be challenging to storm. Mist stretched across the valley and drifted over the river, restricting visibility. It was the mist that caused them to miss the approaching militia.

The attacking force had advanced towards them quietly; the fog had disguised their movements. Few expected the militia to arrive from Charles Town so promptly, and the sentries hadn't raised the alarm. Lamine assumed that they were dead now. Perhaps a knife stuck in the back or a throat slit. The rifle fire from over the river, though unlucky for the dead Kongolese warrior, had proven to be a lucky break for the defenders. However, the mist also provided cover and had disguised their dug-in position on and around the small hill. The militia attacked unexpectedly. It would have destroyed them but for their good fortune.

Lamine had jumped into one of the ditches. He was joined by four Kongolese and several freed slaves. He was armed with a musket and was diligently loading it. The channel was full of muddy, murky water, and his boots were soaked instantly. Lamine was grateful for the cover the ditch afforded, and so ignored his discomfort. There was a small scrub to their right, and several other fighters had taken cover around it. The hillock was behind them.

The first sense they had of an assault was a sharp metallic clank. Some poorly trained citizen soldier had accidentally bashed his musket against a blade. Lamine instinctively ducked behind the gully. There was no good reason for him to do it; it was just a sudden intuition. Then all hell broke loose. There was a sudden deafening blast of a hundred muskets firing simultaneously. A thunderous sound broke the peacefulness of the quiet, misty morning. It echoed across the valley, signaling the start of a terrible day. Musket balls seemed to whistle through the air, thudding into the ground around them. Mud was flicked up over their position from the impacts. One of the men who'd been hiding behind the bushes took a hit and was pitched into the ditch, falling on top of another man. His thigh had a huge gash that spurted blood in gushes. Those around him quickly applied a tourniquet, and the bleeding was checked.

Lamine looked over the edge and examined the scene. A few men were down, injured, or dead, but the massive musket volley hadn't inflicted the intended damage. Lamine couldn't tell whether it was because of the mist or the shelter their forces had taken. A volley of this nature was designed to be destructive, especially if the defenders were surprised, as they had been. He didn't have time to think about it. A sudden cacophony of a hundred voices shouting and screaming followed as the militia charged their position with bayonets fixed.

Before Lamine could react to the noise, the militia appeared from nowhere out of the fog. There were at least a hundred men. It was an incredible sight, and despite himself, Lamine nearly ran. He saw that a few of the coerced slaves, who had little interest in fighting, scampered. Though the losses weakened their defenses, most of the men stayed put. Lamine pulled up his musket, aimed it at an attacker, and fired. He wasn't alone, and a second musket volley echoed across the valley. If they'd been regular soldiers, that counterfire would have obliterated their attackers and ended the battle. As they were untrained rebels, many shots went high or low, entirely missing their targets. Their one opportunity to inflict real damage was lost. Lamine saw, though, that the loss had still been significant. At least twenty of the charging militia had gone down, either injured or dead. Bodies were strewn across the landscape, heaped in strange, contorted shapes. The wounded cried for help while the dead twitched in dying convulsions.

Lesser-trained militia might have broken and fled. These men had been drilled well. After a few moments of shock and pause, they continued to charge. The defenders had no time to reload their muskets. They met the charge with their own bayonets and with the axes, scythes, and blades they had taken from the plantations. The battle became a moment-by-moment affair typical of man-to-man combat.

Six of the militia charged the position that Lamine and the Kongolese held. They screamed and shouted abuse as they raced in, their bayonets leveled at the defenders. Lamine held the barrel of his musket and used the gun as if it were a club, wielding it harshly against his opponent's gun, trying to deflect the aim of the man's stab. It was a close call. Lamine's swing missed, and the militiaman stabbed him with the bayonet. Inches to the right, and he would have died. The bayonet sliced through his shirt and scoured the inside of his left arm and the side of his chest. A wave of pain hit him, but it was a superficial wound. Lamine didn't miss with his second swing and hit the man square on the side of the head with the butt of his weapon. The militiaman fell and was dragged away by another man before Lamine could administer a killing blow.

Lamine saw that one of his Kongolese squad was down. He'd been taken out by the first bayonet charge. Two of the squad had inflicted their own killing blows. The axes they wielded deflected the bayonets and dug deeply into their assailants. One was pulling an axe out of the dead man's head, while the other had cleaved off his attacker's gun-wielding arm. Blood was everywhere. Nearby, two men were wrestling in the mud of the ditch, each trying to get a better purchase so that they could strangle the other. One of the Kongolese went to help. He swung his axe into the militiaman's back. The man arched in pain and flopped dead into the bottom of the waterlogged culvert. The defender was pulled to his feet. A foot was placed on the dead man's back, and the axe was leveraged out of its deeply embedded spot.

The rebel fighters were gradually giving up ground to the attacking militia. The weight of numbers was taking a toll. Jemmy's men had been arrayed around the entire hillock while the charging militia concentrated to the north. Lamine picked up a dead man's axe and dropped his musket. It was no use to him in close quarters. The fighting was now desperate, and behind the vanguard, militiamen were reloading their muskets. They would soon be exposed.

Jemmy took command of the battlefield. He cajoled men who had fled into the fight and moved men from other locations around the mound to the site of the fighting. The hill suddenly became an asset as the militia started to fight up its steep sides. They struggled to push the rebels back, and the extra height gave the defenders added reach. A significant advantage turning the tide against the attacking militia. Jemmy's reinforcements hadn't discharged their muskets yet, so he instructed them to fire at the reloading soldiers. The retort of musket fire was again deafening as the rebels removed the threat. Several militiamen fell to the ground, multiple shots killing them instantly.

As the battle started to turn in their favor, Jemmy made a decisive move. He corralled ten of his best men from the melee to the top of the mound, where they started to reload their muskets. The intent was clear. To fire volleys from the top of the mound over the heads of the defenders and into the ranks of the attackers. It would indeed be decisive and end the fight. At least, it might have. Just as they reloaded, there was a new noise; rifle fire. It came at them from the east. Whoever they were, the riflemen had a devastating impact. All the men who stood at the top of the mound died. Some had multiple wounds. The wounds were all exact, some headshots, some chest shots. Worse still, these had been Jemmy's best warriors, ten of the original Kongolese. It was a heavy price for the defenders to pay.

Then, Lamine saw the horses descending into the valley like attacking cavalry. There were only twenty men, but the two simultaneous incidents had a massive psychological blow. Some of the defenders fled. Stupidly, they ran in all directions, some towards the horses. These men were cut down by the horsemen using their long cavalry swords. Lamine grasped that they were professionals. They moved their horses with ease while swinging their sabers in a deadly fashion. It took them little time to cross the valley. The dead bodies of fleeing rebels were scattered behind them. As they reached the mound, they split into two troops and swept around the hill's edge. One went clockwise and the other counterclockwise. As they rode around, they cleared the slopes and gullies of defenders. The militia gained new enthusiasm and were pressing the remaining defenders hard. Moments later, everybody was running, and the battle was lost.

Lamine couldn't tell whether it was a brave last stand or the act of a desperate man, but it was one of the most courageous things he'd ever seen. Jemmy picked up a long axe from one of the dead Kongolese warriors. He ran across the mound's precipice and launched at one of the horses. It was a beautiful horse moving at a gallop, and the young man on its back wielded a long sword. Jemmy raised the axe and jumped at full speed as the horse ran alongside the mound. The young man tried to parry, but Jemmy's momentum and the axe's weight were too great. As Jemmy flew, he brought the axe down, smashed the lad's sword away, and stuck the cleaver deeply into the throat of the horse. There was a vast gaping slash across the horse's neck, and it went down instantly, whinnying as it fell. The rider was tossed from the horse, and both tumbled, their motion smashing them into the ground. Jemmy landed on his feet, axe in hand, but was immediately surrounded by the other horsemen. It looked like they planned to take him alive. It was the last desperate act of a desperate battle.

It was time to leave, and Lamine hoped to escape during the chaos and aftermath. Rebels were fleeing all over the valley and being pursued assiduously. A few horsemen were heading west, exacting a terrible revenge on the defeated. He needed to get south, back to Florida, and clear of the horses. The militia was a spent force. They were slowly starting to round up the fighters who had surrendered and were trying to cut down those who hadn't.

Lamine led the remaining three Kongolese warriors south towards Parker's ferry. They could follow the original plan, capture the ferry, and escape. If they were lucky, the Port Royal militia were still sitting at the ford and hadn't considered defending the ferry. As they went south away from the militia and the horsemen, they picked up more stragglers, those who had fled early and gone south. By the time they reached the ferry, they had acquired a small contingent of the original army, which consisted of nearly twenty mostly armed men. Capturing the ferry proved a simple task. The guards had heard the battle, and as soon as they saw the small group of rebels, they fled. Lamine ushered his force across the Edisto River via the ferry. If they'd had more time, Jemmy's plan would have worked, and the entire army could have escaped that way. The Port Royal militia remained in their defensive positions across the river near the ford and hadn't barred the route. Lamine's troop of survivors escaped southwards. They were exhausted and hungry but still armed and dangerous.

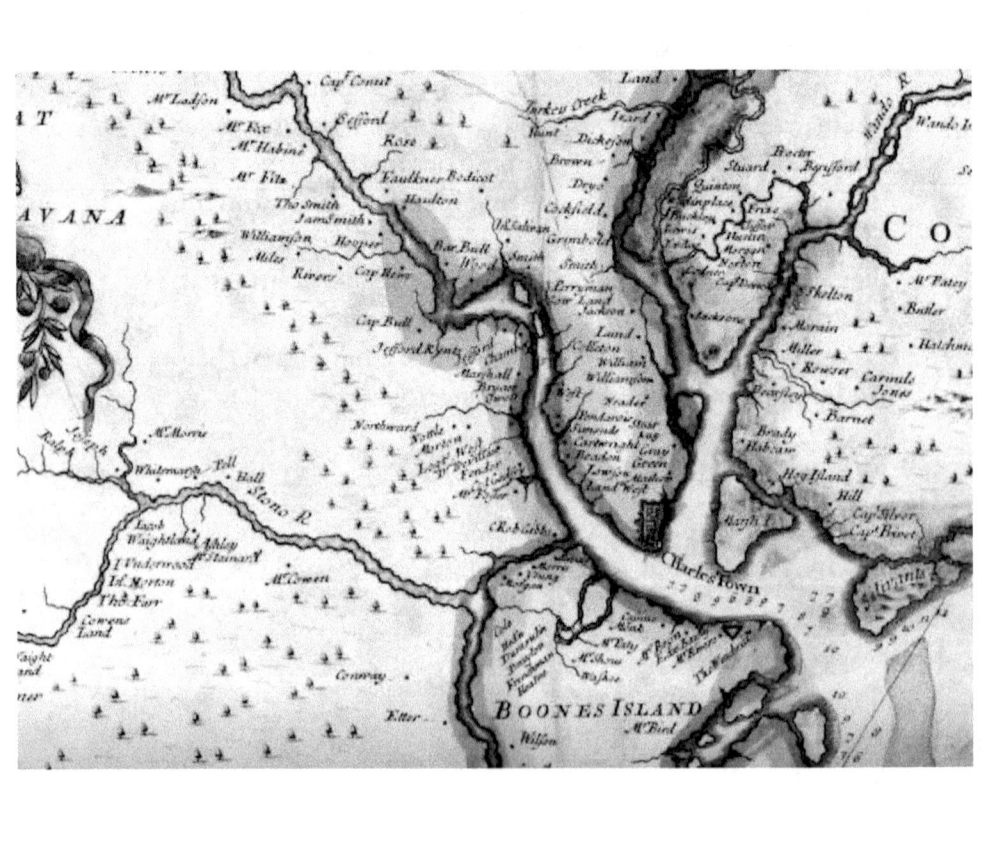

Chapter 19: Battlefield Dead

Williams stared across the Edisto River. The floods had finally lowered enough for the ford to be navigable. It had taken most of the day. The entire valley was masked in fog when the Port Royal militia arrived. It had been a long night and day for Williams. He'd left Bull's headquarters late into the afternoon and had headed southeast. Eventually, he realized that his only way across the river was to swim with his horse, which he used as a shield against the heavy flooding. It was a risk. There'd been a couple of moments when he thought all might be lost. The horse's head ducked under a wave at one point, and he nearly lost his grip as they reached the far side. No question, he'd been lucky to pull it off. Once he'd made it across, he galloped across the fields to the road, got to Port Royal, and raised the alarm. It was some distance for the militia to cover, and they'd ridden all night, only just reaching the ford in time.

The maneuvers had been near perfect until two scouts had spotted the rebels across the other side of the ford. They'd acted against orders, fired, and shot one of the defenders. Surprise had been lost, and Williams heard the battle begin from a distance.

He thought it a curious experience. From their defensive position, they could see almost nothing. The fog enveloped the far side of the river and the battleground. While they could see nothing, they heard everything. The initial musket volley of the militia and its charge. The counter volleys. Yells and screams of men fighting and dying as they battled hand-to-hand. Then, there was a sudden report of rangers' rifles fired from a distance and the thundering charge of cavalry. It would have felt like forever for those fighting the battle, but for those listening, it started and ended quickly. No more than an hour at most.

It was a shocking sight as the mist dissolved and the battlefield became visible. In that short time, many men had died, and many more were injured. The bodies were strewn across the valley and almost piled up in heaps to the north of a small mound. Horses continued moving to the west, capturing and killing the fleeing enemy. Men were drifting through the dead bodies, looking for a friend or helping the injured. Occasionally a soldier would pull a body to onside, presumably a dead friend they had just found. A few rangers and militia had rounded up and guarded the enemy survivors. Officers Bull, Palmer, and Vanderdussen were with this group, so he led the vanguard of the Port Royal militia across the ford and headed in their direction.

The aftermath of the battle was atrocious. There was blood everywhere. Contorted shapes were splayed in odd configurations as if they were children's dolls just thrown down in a heap. He saw a leg lying on its own, its owner nowhere to be seen, and a body with no head. Men were sitting and crying as they held their hands over an open wound that they knew meant a certain but slow death. Others were getting help. The Port Royal militia dispersed as they crossed to help the injured and move the dead. Williams saw some dead that he knew. The baker's body. The best brewer in town lying on his back in a ditch, his sightless eyes staring at the sky. The tailor, with half his chest missing, lay across the bodies of two of his opponents. Despite the victory, the costs of the battle were significant.

As he approached the officers, Bull spotted him, "Williams! What the bloody hell happened? The orders were clear! The Port Royal militia wasn't supposed to engage the enemy; they were meant to block the ford. This fiasco is down to those two riflemen. Where is Colonel Kingston anyway? Before I forget, well done Williams, outstanding work getting the militia from Port Royal here in time!"

Williams wasn't about to take the fall for two wayward scouts. "Thank you, sir; it's most appreciated. The orders were clear. I heard the colonel give them himself, sir. Two of our scouts were a bit over-enthusiastic when they saw the enemy. Colonel Kingston is on his way. He is coming across the ford with the main body of the militia, sir."

"Thank you. Williams, I need you to serve as my aide-de-camp now. Your friend Evans is down; he's over there. You'd better go take a look. Be quick, though; I'll need you back. We don't have time to be sentimental right now. Too much to do!"

Aghast at the news, Williams simply replied, "Yes, sir!" Despite the shoe dodging, he'd always secretly coveted Evans' job, but not under these circumstances. He trudged over to where Bull had pointed. A couple of the militia were pulling the body across the ground to add it to a pile of broken men. The bodies were to be transported back to loved ones and burial. Evans' corpse was a limp mess.

He got the story from the militiamen dragging the carcass across to the heap. The rebel leader had attacked Evans's horse, cut a massive gash in its neck, and the horse threw the rider. As they fell, the horse smashed into Evans and crushed him. His skull was smashed in, and almost every bone in his body was broken. It was a horrendous way to die but at least instantaneous.

Williams examined the body. It was strange to see a young man so full of life reduced to a lifeless piece of flesh. His eyes were dull, and despite the beginning of rigor mortis, so much was broken that his body appeared like jelly, wobbling in unnatural ways. Williams closed his friend's eyelids, said a short prayer, and wished his friend well in heaven. He'd miss their banter, as well as their card and dice games. He didn't have time to mourn his friend correctly now; that would have to follow. There was a battlefield to clear, captured rebel slaves to deal with, and escapees to track down.

As he returned to the officers, he cast an eye over the captured rebels. The leader stood out, tall and thin but muscular, clearly a Kongolese. Despite being herded by angry guards, he was dignified and controlled. He even called out the rebel's slogan, "Liberty, from slavery! Liberty for all!" Until one of the guards, fed up with hearing it, cracked him in the mouth with the butt of his musket. The leader spat blood and teeth onto the floor and stopped his sloganeering. His eyes, though, were sharp and angry. They'd rounded up over twenty survivors, many of them wounded from the fight.

The officers discussed what to do next, and Bull led the conversation. Williams came up alongside the Acting Governor in case he was needed to convey orders. Colonel Palmer expressed some reservations, but Bull asserted his authority, "Colonel Palmer, it's my decision. I understand your concerns, but we must stamp this thing out; otherwise, we will have to deal with more rebellions. A sign must be given that we wouldn't tolerate it. Besides, these men have ransacked half the countryside, pillaged and burnt plantations, and killed their occupants. Not to mention the toll from this battle. We've lost two rangers and well over twenty militiamen plus my aide-de-camp. There must be at least fifty dead slaves, property that wouldn't be easily replaced. I'll hear no more talk about it. We hang the survivors. I want every dead slave decapitated and their heads mounted on pikes a mile apart along the roads surrounding Charles Town. They think they were led by a modern-day Spartacus; let's give them a Roman ending. Heads on pikes will remind our slaves how rebellions end."

The decision was made. Colonel Palmer took his rangers off to arrange for the hanging of the captured. At the same time, he instructed the militia to begin the decapitation of the dead rebels. Bull turned to Vanderdussen, "Do you have any scouts?"

"Yes, sir. We have two Catawba and a Chickasaw," replied the colonel.

"Good. Have these scouts return to their tribes. We'll set a bounty on every escaped slave they recover, dead or alive. I don't want any of the rebels getting away. I want Catawba and Chickasaw scouts out across the entire region. Nobody gets away from justice!" Colonel Vanderdussen set off to find his scouts and send them to mobilize South Carolina's friendly tribes.

Bull's face was getting redder. Williams could tell that the battle fatigue had passed, and now he was angry. "Where the bloody hell is Colonel Kingston!" The colonel's timing couldn't have been any worse. As he arrived, Bull grabbed him by the scruff of his collar and pulled him to one side out of everybody else's earshot. There was no mistaking the dressing down that was being given. The Port Royal militia had failed. They hadn't followed commands, and Bull ensured the colonel knew he was culpable for the following disaster. Kingston wasn't easily intimidated. Still, he quailed in front of Bull's onslaught. Clearly, the two blundering scouts were in some serious trouble. They were lucky they were militiamen, not rangers or regulars; otherwise, it might have been a flogging offense. Now Kingston had a red face, perhaps from embarrassment rather than anger. He was sent packing. Directed to go and find the two scouts and to discipline them.

With that off his chest, Bull seemed to calm down. He turned to Williams, "I'm sorry about Evans. He was a good lad. Terrible way to go. I've seen a man crushed by his horse before; it makes a real mess of a man's body, but at least it's quick."

"Yes, sir. He'll be missed. I'll need a few drinks to celebrate his life and toast the loss of a good friend later, sir," Williams responded morosely.

Bull continued, "I don't know something, Williams. Did he have a woman?"

"No, sir. Just an occasional girlfriend, nothing serious."

"Good to know; we'll have to get his body back to his family then. Williams, I'm afraid you will get the butcher's duty. I want you to work with Colonels Vanderdussen and Kingston and have the militiamen clear up this battlefield. Take those two carts the slaves had and use them to take our men's bodies back to Charles Town so they can have proper services and be buried fittingly. You probably passed a couple of mortally wounded men. They're going to die, but it'll take hours. Find some of their friends and have them sit with them. If we can get a pastor, that would help ease their way into the afterlife. Send somebody back to town to see if we can get one in time. A few men need surgeons; have them go on the first cart back. The other injured can wait and make sure they get help with their wounds onsite. Once Palmer's finished hanging the captives and decapitating them, you'll need to burn the bodies. Get some men together and set up a pyre over there. As soon as you can, have those bodies burned. It stinks to high heaven around here already!" Pointing to the sky, Bull resumed, "Look, the damn vultures are here already."

Williams looked up and noticed the increasing number of vultures circulating above them. Both turkey and black vultures hovered, ready for a feast. Turkey vultures with their distinct redheads sat in trees nearby, patiently waiting to get down to the battlefield to rip flesh from the carcasses. The landscape was thick with crows; occasionally, one would dart towards a target, peck quickly, and then fly away. He even heard the howl of a coyote, which was unusual at this time of day. The thick, sickly smell of blood had brought them all to the killing ground.

He set about his tasks quickly. All he could think about was the body of his friend being eaten by the vultures. Nobody should be sent to their maker in pieces. It was bad enough that poor Evans had been crushed by his horse. They gathered the injured who needed a surgeon and lifted them into the first cart. A squad of men hitched two horses to makeshift halters and set off towards town. He found a militia officer with a horse and sent him to go and get a pastor. They arrived back several hours later, but it was too late for one of the critically injured men. Williams formed squads and allocated them different tasks. Two groups looked after the militiamen with minor injuries. One larger group built a bonfire. Another one picked up the debris of the battle. Guns, blades, and other implements strewn across the scene were stacked for later transportation.

The pyre was lit, and they were soon piling the headless corpses of the rebels onto the fire. The smell of burning flesh was pungent and disgusting, like hundreds of pigs roasting on hundreds of spits simultaneously. The cracking and spitting from an enormous fire full of the dead was hard to stomach.

Though many of the rebels were Catholics, nobody cared whether the slaves were buried appropriately or had had the last sacraments. These men were enemies who'd inflicted damage across the countryside and who had killed friends. Nobody cared when Palmer's rangers dragged the recently hung and headless bodies of the captured men to the fire. They simply picked them up and threw them on top. And nobody cared when the last body was finally heaved up with the rest. It was the leader's body, a man called Jemmy. It was a brawny, black, lean, long cadaver, but now it was headless just like the others.

Chapter 20: A Last Stand

Foolishness, pure foolishness, and no chance to recover from it. As his small contingent loped southeast, Lamine realized they'd abandoned too many weapons and provisions. It was a natural inclination to drop annoying hindrances quickly after a battle so that you could run away, but now the pursuit had begun, and they would need those discarded weapons and food.

Nineteen of them escaped after the battle. Lamine and the three Kongolese were the most experienced warriors among them. The remainder were the stragglers and coerced slaves, those who had fled at the first sight of the enemy and who couldn't be relied upon. Lamine was the nominal leader, and he knew their best option was to flee. If they had to fight, they couldn't possibly win, and bolting wouldn't be easy either; their pursuers were sure to employ natives to track them. So, they had to move quickly. Abandoning weapons, though, had been a bad idea. They had five muskets left, a few long knives, and a couple of axes. It wouldn't help much if they were caught. Worse still, they had little food and only a few skins for water. Their situation was desperate, and Lamine knew it.

They made it across Parkers' Ferry and away from the Port Royal militia. The militia had been guarding the ford and had yet to think to post a sentry at the ferry. Lamine had observed the militia arriving and knew it was a significant force that needed to be avoided. Consequently, their band had headed east away from the militia when they crossed the Edisto River. It was easygoing, open farmland with a clear track to follow. Unfortunately, there was no way they could disguise their route, so they hurried, intermittently jogging and sprinting. They were all fit from farm work and could keep up the tempo. Occasionally, they stopped to get a breather and a swig of water, and then they would set off running again.

After a few hours, they came to another river known to one of the slaves, the Ashepoo River. The river was narrow, shallow, and, despite the recent floods, was easily crossed. They understood their pursuers would be mounted, so they ran again as the early evening set in. It was a hard night. They wanted to use the darkness to put as much distance between themselves and their pursuers as possible, but they were all fatigued. It was a dark night, cloudy and overcast. Weariness and poor light slowed them down to a fast walk. Even then, they tripped over roots and other debris that littered the track. Eventually, the exhaustion from fighting a battle and running all day made them halt. Even Lamine and the Kongolese warriors were spent. They set up camp in a nearby field, ate a small ration, and slept. They tried to gain whatever rest they could for another day of flight that would start the following morning.

☒　☒　☒

The dawn came suddenly. It felt to Lamine like they'd only just fallen asleep when the sun rose and beckoned them into another day of running. They were all sapped, and the weaker amongst them began to waiver. After an hour of intermittent jogging and sprinting, the band of men stretched out over a long distance. Their group was starting to lose its unity. Lamine could tell they couldn't keep this pace going for much longer. Alongside him, the Kongolese looked refreshed and capable, but the others looked worn out. He reckoned they had most of the day before they would need to find shelter for a proper rest. He stopped them for a short period so the laggards could catch up.

A small group of white-tailed deer were disturbed as they set off again. The youngest of the deer darted zigzagging while the older bounced off over the bushes. Their white tails stuck up to attention, swaying. The deer were alert to the danger that the men posed as they raced away. Some of the men took this to be a positive omen. Their positivity spilled over to the others, and the squad brought more enthusiasm to their flight. In the next few hours, unity was recovered, and they made better progress as they jogged steadily to the southeast.

Eventually, they came to a small, abandoned settlement near the Salkehatchie River. It appeared as if it was an old Yamasee village. A few tiny houses, ramshackle and overgrown, long ago deserted. One of the houses was quite sturdy and made of ancient timber logs. Half of its roof had collapsed, but it offered comfortable shelter. The village was on old Yamasee lands, the small native town of Yemasee was nearby, and the site was secluded and off the beaten track.

There was much debate amongst the fleeing rebels. Some felt they should keep running, while most thought it an ideal hiding place. Lamine couldn't convince them to keep going.

He knew this would eventually be a death trap if they stayed, but most were tired and acting irrationally. He thought about taking the Kongolese and leaving, but they were adamant. They wanted to keep to the spirit of Jemmy's plan and wouldn't leave the escapees to fend for themselves. Lamine decided to stay but scouted the village to ensure he had an exit once the inevitable happened and the militia caught up with them.

⧗　⧗　⧗

Almost a week passed before they were discovered. It was only about a three-day hike from the Edisto River, so it surprised Lamine that it took so long for the scouts to find their secluded hideaway. When they'd forded the Ashepoo River, they'd waded up the river some distance before leaving the ford, and perhaps that had put the scouts off their trail for a bit.

During the intervening period, the group had spent their time productively. The old log cabin had been cleaned up and repaired. Several portholes had been cut into the side of the walls to help fortify the cabin's defense so their muskets could be fired from within. The circumference of the settlement had been fenced in with barricades of trees, brambles, and bushes. The wrecked houses had been reconstituted as sallyports from which the defenders could rush at the attackers. Pits, holes, and gullies had been dug across the site. Many had been built with wicked-looking pine pikes and spikes and covered up to act as unexpected traps. Spring-loaded wooden spikes had been erected across the position, and these could be triggered by a defender or set off by trip vines. They had hunted nearby and stockpiled food. They'd built storage containers and had plenty of water. The meat had been smoked. Nuts, berries, and roots had been gathered and stored.

Lamine contemplated. A week was a long time to prepare a defensive position, and they had been afforded more time than expected. Of course, they would still lose, but their defense would be epic. They wouldn't allow the militia to simply walk in and take them. They'd have to fight for every inch, and the attack would be ponderous and painful for the attackers.

⌛ ⌛ ⌛

Something was different the morning of the assault. Lamine couldn't place his finger on it. Perhaps it was the smell, a distant whiff of horse sweat. Maybe it was the sudden influx of new flies, the large, agile bloodsuckers that accompany horses. Perhaps it was the lack of sound, of quiet intensity, when birds fall silent before a clash of opposing forces. He was immediately alert, as were the Kongolese warriors. They'd fought too often to ignore the signs of impending danger. Then they heard it. A slight clang of metal on metal. The militia had once again betrayed their presence through a lack of discipline. It took only one man to make this basic mistake, and an astute defender was forewarned. Lamine acted immediately.

The militia were sneaking in from the northwest. Lamine sent three runners towards the barricade on this section of their position. They were highly visible and sent deliberately as a lure. As they reached the barricade, they jumped into one of the prepared ditches. Seeing the runners, the approaching militia fired their muskets rashly, hitting nothing but the branches and bushes in the hedge. Immediately, five defenders, including the three Kongolese, rushed from one of the sallyport houses and fired a deliberate volley straight into the massed rank of attackers. Through the smoke of the two volleys, it was difficult to see if they had caused casualties.

Still, the surprise attack was halted, and the militia retreated to regroup.

The next attack was more cautious. Too cautious. The militia spread out around the northern periphery of the settlement and took occasional potshots at the defenders. It went on for hours with no noticeable effect. One of the rebels gained an injured hand from some flying fragments thrown up by a musket ball, but that was the only injury. The defenders had prepared their positions well and simply hunkered out of sight. The muskets needed more accuracy, and the defenders didn't offer any targets. Lamine was grateful that their foes didn't appear to have any rangers with them firing their deadly rifles. They stayed where they were, chewed on dry venison, and sipped water. Lamine was careful to ensure they didn't fire back, which would have wasted their limited supplies of gunpowder and shot. Let the attackers waste their ammunition had been his suggestion.

Having failed at a sneak attack and then a sniper attack, the militia commander went to his next tactic. He aimed to storm their position with a breaching attack. To Lamine, it appeared the opposing leader was working through ploys listed in a training manual. First, you do this, then that, and so on. There wasn't much subtlety to it, and it was predictable. Lamine could see the militia preparing for their effort to breach the outer rim of their position. They'd moved away from their extended line and massed at one point. It appeared as if a small force would attack the barricade while a more considerable force gave covering fire. Of course, while predictable, the tactic still presented much danger for the defenders, and it was likely to inflict more losses than the prior attempts.

When the assault came, it was brutal. A contingent of militia rushed the barricade with axes and chopped at it quickly to clear it out of the attacker's path. The defenders popped up from one of the pits to fire their muskets into the breaching party. Two of the militia went down. The cover fire was prompt and well-aimed. A barrage of musket balls hit the pit. Much of the fire missed, flecking mud all over the place, but three of the defenders were shot; one was dead from a head wound. Brains seemed to fly from a deep cavity at the back of his head.

The Kongolese, knowing they were safe from the muskets, took the opportunity to lead a party out of the prepared sallyport house into a melee with the breaching party. Using axes and long knives, they tried to stab and cut at each other across the barrier. It was another nondescript engagement. Neither party was able to inflict much damage with the barricade in the way. Both groups sensed their danger as muskets were reloaded and thus retreated to their prior positions. A couple of the Kongolese gained superficial wounds but nothing serious.

The stalemate went on for hours. The defenders were dug in and challenging to dislodge, unless the attackers were willing to accept the inevitable losses they would take when storming the position. Given the situation, the obvious thing to do would have been to wait, simply surround the small force, and starve it into surrender. Lacking the good sense to do the obvious, the militia commander lost patience and sent all his men to them in one big assault. There was no way they could defeat it, but they would inflict their share of damage. It was a last stand and a heroic way for the rebellion to end.

The entire militia force formed up and marched up to the makeshift barrier. The few muskets the rebels had were fired, and a couple of militiamen went down, but the impact was minimal. Then the militia fired a large volley over the barricade, perhaps forty or fifty muskets. The entire settlement was flecked with musket balls, and several of the defenders were hit randomly despite their careful defensive fortifications. At least two were instantly killed, while several others were severely injured. As the breaching party removed the barrier, the remaining militiamen reloaded. There was no hope for the small defending force to rush such a large mass of attackers, so they retreated gradually to the log cabin and the other prepared positions. Once the barrier was removed, the attacking force came forward, ready with a second large volley. The second volley was momentous. Now, at close quarters, it destroyed the smaller huts in the settlement. Most of the defenders died in that volley. Few men in the huts survived it.

Lamine, the Kongolese, and several others who had retreated to the log cabin endured that devastating fire. The cabin was sturdier, the logs thicker, and few balls made it through. As the militia came forward, they started to be hit by Lamine's crude traps. A couple of men fell into a deadly pit and were impaled. A young man tripped over one of the trip-vines and had a sudden wooden spear shot into his thigh. Having never seen such booby traps before, the attack stalled. It was then that the defenders fired from the cabin's portholes. There were only a few muskets left, but the militia were exposed, and the fire was deadly. Several men fell, and it caused a sudden, panicked retreat. The militia fell back behind the barriers erected at the outer circumference of the northern part of the village.

The next attack would be the rebellion's end. It was time for Lamine to leave. The Kongolese decided to fight to the finish, but Lamine had other duties. He was responsible for serving the free black militia in St. Augustine and defending Fort Mose. The remaining men recognized this and understood that he was an agent of the Spanish who ought to escape when the conclusion came. They said their goodbyes before the South

Carolina militia reformed to launch their final assault on the little cabin and its few rebel survivors. The Stono Rebellion was over.

Lamine left the cabin and headed south along his prepared exit route. His aim was simple. He was going to escape down the Salkehatchie River. He'd prepared a raft, and it was a gentle river. The raft would take him down the river several miles, which would help him lose any remaining scouts. Lamine would then work his way south along streams in the marshes, back to Shell Point. Nobody lived in the marshes, so if he lost the scouts, there was no chance anybody would see him and think he was an escaped slave. He knew he could wait for O'Sullivan's fishermen to return or reunite with O'Sullivan himself. He wondered about the Irishman; where was he now? Then Lamine heard it. The last volley. The last rebel deaths. The last stand of a brave but failed rebellion.

Chapter 21: Heads Everywhere

Tongues lolled out through blackened teeth. Flesh hung off sunken cheeks. Lanks of hair, curly and unkempt, skinned off in chunks, dangled over foreheads and down necks. White translucent, sightless eyes stared opaquely; long lost consciousness gone. Skin crinkled taut in the hot South Carolina sun. The heads were awful, true horrors for the ogling passersby as they viewed them mounted on spikes. Yet this wasn't the worst of it. The stench of death was everywhere, a sweet, putrid reek accompanied by a musty tinge that was hard to forget. The flies that hovered constantly around the heads were only outdone by the carrion crows and vultures, who swooped down and pecked some morsel or other away from the skulls.

There was no questioning the statement. These heads were spiked onto wooden spears every mile on the roads outside Charles Town. This was all that was left of the slaves who'd rebelled, asking for liberty. A few, captured later, had been resold into slavery and sent to the Caribbean.

O'Sullivan walked these roads and understood the statement it made to the remaining enslaved and the populace.

Slavery was here to stay, and the authorities wouldn't tolerate any pity towards these people. The institution was too valuable for the plantations and for the broader economy. No freedom and no mercy.

Then, O'Sullivan saw the last head before he entered the city. It was Jemmy's. He remembered their final meeting. The man was a genuine leader who was educated, intelligent, and strategically aware. The plan was viable, and the rebellion might have worked; it was simple and efficient. Alas, it was not to be. Now Jemmy's head sat here on the last spike, impaled like the others, and was gradually stripped of flesh by the sunlight and the scavengers. His eyes were ghost-like, white without irises. The penetrating stare seemed to peer deeply into O'Sullivan's very soul. O'Sullivan shuddered slightly. The end was nasty, but despite the outcome, the rebellion had accomplished its goal for the Spanish. When the war began, the South Carolinians would think twice before sending their militia south to help the Georgians. O'Sullivan had put them up to this, knowing that success or failure didn't matter. It was the future threat and the second thoughts that mattered. He had moments of regret, but O'Sullivan put these aside quickly. The greater Catholic cause was far more critical. A few dead slaves didn't count in the grand scheme of things.

The Spanish conspiring was getting mixed results, though. If the Stono Rebellion had been successful, South Carolina would have experienced severe damage to its plantation system and economy. Florida, in contrast, would have gained a large free-black militia, further fortifying the Spanish colony. Ultimately, the damage was less pronounced, even though it would make South Carolina more cautious.

Other efforts were seeing even less success. The two female provocateurs that O'Sullivan had sent to Frederica had been quickly uncovered and sent back. Their efforts to undermine General Oglethorpe's reputation had been a miserable failure. It was a long shot, anyway. He'd wanted to damage Oglethorpe's chances of an alliance with the Creeks and undermine his relationship with Mary Musgrove. Nothing had come from that effort as it had been discovered too quickly.

Then there was the assassination attempt. O'Sullivan had heard about it. He'd played no part in the plot, but he didn't doubt that it had been led by his St. Augustine spymasters. It was too organized, too convenient, to be purely a mutiny. Miraculously, Oglethorpe had escaped unscathed. O'Sullivan thought the man must have a guardian angel or something. Two shots and two sword assaults, yet he'd survived and continued to command Georgia's defense.

They'd had too many failures, and it was time to quit. O'Sullivan knew it in his bones. Acting Governor Bull was no fool. Evidently, Bull had his own spy network and must have known about the rebellion. How convenient for his party to stumble across the revolt at precisely the right time. It was suspicious that the militia were at a heightened drill level just before the rebellion. Likewise, O'Sullivan wondered why Bull had called Palmer's rangers back from the frontier. He was a spy, and he didn't believe in coincidences. Bull was using his own network and must have known about the uprising in advance. It was also clear that the authorities were digging around looking for an agent. Countless questions were asked, and many of his people were getting scared. The authorities grasped that the Spanish had somehow encouraged the slaves and were now looking under the rocks for the source. It would only be a matter of time before someone gave him away and his network was rolled up. Yes, it's time to leave. Time to become someone else again.

As O'Sullivan wandered along Charles Town's streets aimlessly. He made the decision instantly. He wouldn't go home. He would abandon everything and everyone once again. Live off his wits and use only what he carried now. O'Sullivan ruminated on it as he roamed the avenues, scarcely conscious of the comings and goings around him. Where should he go? Who should he become? As he passed the docks, the answer became obvious.

Every tavern and shop on the boulevard lining the quay was full of sailors and fishermen. Tough-looking men who traveled up and down the Atlantic coast. Ships traded goods between the British colonies and occasionally sneaked off on smuggling trips to Florida. He'd become a sailor again. It had worked for him before, and he knew the trade. He might learn important intelligence information in the other British colonies. And if he was lucky, he might get a chance to jump ship in Florida. So, he would hang out on the quayside and become a sailor for a second time, but who should he become?

⏳ ⏳ ⏳

O'Sullivan took time to work it out. He'd a stash of gold coins sewn into his clothing. This was his contingency money; O'Sullivan would draw on it now while planning an escape. He rented an apartment in one of the taverns. It was the roughest sailor's tavern along the quayside, not an obvious place to look for a spy. O'Sullivan stayed here for many nights, blending in and becoming anonymous. He drank with the clientele, played dice, and listened. During the day, he reconnoitered the docks. Seeking knowledge. Which ships went where? Which captains were decent and treated men well? Who was rumored to smuggle, and where did they go? As his snooping progressed, he homed in on a particular ship and captain. Captain Drayton and his merchant ship Freedom became O'Sullivan's most promising prospect.

Drayton was an interesting man. He seemed to favor a French crew, tended to sail much further distances than his contemporaries, and was rumored to smuggle to Spanish Florida and the French city of New Orleans. The Freedom was a sound ocean-going merchantman, larger than most, with a broad, deep hull perfect for smuggling. The ship appeared well cared for. Its crew cleaned it regularly, and those sailors looked well-paid and provisioned. Whatever Captain Drayton was trading in was a reliable living, and the crew benefitted from it.

As O'Sullivan learned more about Drayton, he discovered he was generous and fun-loving. He liked to play dice, as well as laugh and joke incessantly. One night, O'Sullivan sat across from the captain and watched him carefully. In some ways, he looked like most merchant captains. Stout, stocky, and resilient, Drayton had the typical hallmarks of a life at sea. He was suntanned; the saltwater had etched harsh lines and creases into his face. His clothes were practical. Leather pants tucked into long leather boots underneath a leather overcoat. All had been waxed with goose fat to make them waterproof. What stood out about Drayton, though, was his hair and his warmness. The man was a redhead. He had intense, long, shaggy, bright hair, a wiry bush of a beard, and thick, unkempt eyebrows. It was a stunning look. When added to his voracious appetite, colossal stomach, and infectious chuckle, the captain came across as likable.

O'Sullivan made the decision. This was the captain, and the Freedom was the ship. Following Jemmy's efforts to gain liberty for the slaves, the ship's name seemed auspicious. It took O'Sullivan a week during which he feared the Freedom might sail. He started by sitting near the sailors when they visited the tavern and listened intently. Some of them spoke French, others spoke English with a French accent. Sprinkled in amongst them were locals from Charles Town, with their South Carolinian dialect. O'Sullivan now knew who he'd become. He would be an immigrant: A French mother and English father, they had lived in the wilderness in Louisiana. She died early, so he had a French accent but remembered just a few words of the language and spoke mainly English. His father had fought with their French neighbors and been killed, and so he'd left Louisiana for a sailor's life. He'd once visited New Orleans and had enough knowledge to make the deception work. It was a risk, but he thought he could pull it off.

O'Sullivan's next task was to perfect his French accent. He was an accomplished mimic, but his skill was in English accents, so it took him longer than expected. He listened constantly, sat close when the sailors visited the tavern, and hung out near the Freedom during the day. He was careful not to raise any suspicions. He practiced for many hours at night. Once he'd mastered the accent, he began to befriend the sailors, buying them drinks and playing dice. It took a few more days, but eventually, he ingratiated himself with Captain Drayton. Soon, O'Sullivan had the offer he'd sought all along, a chance to become one of them and join the ship. He was now a French immigrant sailor. O'Sullivan would soon escape South Carolina and avoid the repercussions that would surely come from the uncovering of his spy network. His people would be hung, but once again, he'd survive. O'Sullivan would be dead as far as his Spanish overlords were concerned. At least he would until he decided to reveal himself if he chose to do so.

⧗ ⧗ ⧗

Before long, the Freedom set sail. Its main cargo was rice and tobacco, set to be shipped to New York and then Britain. Stashed carefully underneath the cargo and within the holds were illicit manufactured goods destined for the Spanish and French colonies. It was a common enough ruse. The trade goods would be welcomed by the French and Spanish settlers. Still, the authorities policed the smuggling intensely and sometimes violently. After all, this was why Jenkins lost his ear, and the region was about to get embroiled in war. In New York, the ship would offload its cargo of rice and tobacco. It would pick up more manufactured goods and carefully hide them along with the current stash. Then, the Freedom would head to the Bahamas, where slaves would be bought. The slaves would be shipped to Cuba under the guise of the Asiento de Negros contract held by the British and they would be used to hide the smuggled goods. The Freedom would try to sneak past the coastguard. If it was caught, they'd hope their hidden compartments would survive the inspection, as they'd done before. Once into the Spanish docks, they'd work with their co-conspirators to offload their legitimate shipment of slaves and their illicit shipment of trade goods. Then, they would head to New Orleans for a cargo of lumber. It was a supply route Captain Drayton had successfully navigated many times, hence the captain's and crew's affluence.

Part Two: The Siege of Castillo de San Marcos

Chapter 22: Homing Pigeons

White alabaster stones, erratic spider cracks, and black blotchy mold that crept up from the cobblestones. The wall facing Hernando was becoming as familiar as the door he once guarded in the Castillo de Santa Catalina. Blessedly, there were no sounds of torture or inquisitors to trouble his nightmares here. Occasionally, though, in his boredom, he hallucinated and once more heard the agonizing screams of the inquisitor's victims. It seemed he would never forget the desperate cries of the garrucha, toca and potro. He stood guard again, but now his duties were more mundane. He was the regular sentry for General de Montiano's quarters in the Castillo de San Marcos. There were worse duties, but there were also better ones. His squad was spread out all over the castle and its environs. The veterans Sergeant Moreno-Rodriguez and Antonio had been given plum jobs, securing the castle's gateway, checking passersby, and confiscating illicit goods, which had a habit of ending up in their haversacks. Miguel and Rodrigo were stationed in the towers on lookout duty, and Gonzalo, Francisco, and Hernán were being used as scouts, protecting the roads towards the Castillo. The poor rookies

Alvaro and Benito hadn't been so lucky. Placed on duty near the garderobe, they constantly suffered the stink of the moat as the soldiers' excrement was deposited into it. Though they'd become immune to the smell, the rest of the squad hadn't, and it seemed to follow the young men everywhere. Nicknames were soon agreed upon, Alvaro became Apestar, and Benito turned into Caca.

Many months had passed following their arrival in St. Augustine, and Hernando had been able to explore their new garrison thoroughly. He liked it. The beach near St. Augustine was pristine and beautiful beyond words. It lay south of the castle along the coastline of the nearby barrier island. Sand dunes were dotted near the beach, salt-tolerant grasses dominated the mounds, and they constantly swayed as winds swept in from the Atlantic. Gulls, terns, and black skimmers teemed across the landscape, keeping a wary eye out for the occasional eagle that soared above, scoping out the beach for an easy kill. A small village had become established behind the dunes. Its Andalusian architecture is evident in the vaulted ceilings, pebbled courtyards and stone walls that dominated the design of the little houses, with their bright colors and painted tiles. Reached via boat, the village was pretty, quaint, and designed to appeal to local tastes and aspirations to experience a home away from home. A couple of cafes had opened, benefiting from the constant traffic of settlers trying to escape St. Augustine and their duties.

St. Augustine itself was not without its attractions. The town was situated south of the castle along the channel between the coast and the barrier island. Many more houses of varied Spanish styles and colors were flanking the narrow-cobbled streets. The site of the Catholic church of Basilica sat demolished, timbers charred and sticking out of the remains.

It was continually under construction, an unpleasant reminder of the last time the British tried to capture the Castillo de San Marcos. Hernando did not expect it to be rebuilt soon, so a Sunday mass for the community was held in the hospital and apothecary. The wharf sat near the town and close to the castle and was a constant hubbub of activity. It was the trading center of the city and where many of the town's restaurants and drinking houses were located.

Hernando had even visited Gracia Real de Santa Teresa de Mose, the free black town north of St. Augustine, to help inspect its fortifications. The new Fort Mose, as the locals had named it, was a large and strange collection of houses of African-like design. It was alien to Hernando, but he considered it a robust community critical to the colony's defense. The fences and dykes that had been raised around the town had turned it into a small fortress that would buttress the northern approaches should there be an attack on the castle. He was impressed with the battlements. The free black militia was a hardworking force that had moved from constructing the town's defenses to constant drill and practice. Hernando thought they would be a fighting force to be reckoned with if the British attacked the garrison.

The garrison of Castillo de San Marcos itself impressed Hernando. His former garrison was a castle of crude stone-built construction, lying by the sea, a prison for the poor souls who met the inquisitor. San Marcos, in contrast, was constructed of a strange stone, a cement of limestone and shells called coquina. When Hernando looked closely, he could see all manner of shells embedded in the stone, like cockles, sea snails, and limpets. The walls were also much thicker than he had seen elsewhere. Other Spanish castles had not always held up under siege; poorly constructed and inadequately maintained, a few well-positioned cannons sometimes caused trouble, brought down walls, and created breaches through which the attackers stormed. Not so this castle. Nearly thirty years ago, when the British last attacked, it was said that the cannon balls had bounced off the coquina walls, fortuitously proven to be made of more rigid materials than those used for traditional Spanish castles.

As he'd toured the garrison, it was clear that the architect had been inspired by Italy's bastion system. A deep moat was followed by steep, slightly inclined walls, topped by battlements on top of which sat many cannons and mortars. Embrasures were well positioned, ideal for sharpshooters and some for large bore cannons. The four-pointed star shape of the design made internal movement swift along the castle's passageways and up the wooden gantries. Each star contained a lookout, a bastion, and a sallyport. Now that General de Montiano's force had strengthened the garrison, a robust and well-trained corps would defend fiercely if attacked, and the castle seemed impregnable.

The general himself inspired confidence. He was a leader that the garrison believed in, battle-hardened, wise, and tactically astute. Many of his decisions had already strengthened the colony. He mobilized the free black militia and gave them a purpose to fight. Montiano had built alliances with the natives, including bringing the ferocious Yamasees into the Spanish camp and committing the peace-loving Seminoles to fight. It instilled confidence in Hernando, and he was convinced they would defeat any attack by the British even if they sat a squadron of frigates in the channel next to the castle and battered it with everything they had.

Hernando's thoughts about the garrison were interrupted. He tightened up and clenched his musket firmer. The cause of the squad's long wait materialized. Sergeant Moreno-Rodriguez and Antonio were at the gate; they'd be watching for her to pass the gatehouse on her way back to town. Gonzalo, Francisco, and Hernán were stationed at the woman's house; they'd searched it extensively and already found the evidence. It was his job to follow from behind at a good distance to ensure there could be no escape.

It had been unfathomable; he had not believed it at first. Yet, here they were, ready to arrest an old maid for treasonable conduct. The maid emerged from the general's quarters, just as she'd done for thirty years, for as long as anyone could remember. She had served many of Florida's governors. Her ancient, creased face was leathery and blotched, hidden slightly by her shawl. She'd wrapped her ancient dirty cloak tightly around her petite frame and scrapped her rough, worn leather shoes on the floor as she edged through the doorway. She moved slowly. Hunched over, her deformed back was damaged from years of scrubbing floors and cleaning latrines. Her legs were bowed uncharacteristically, warped out of shape, giving her an odd gait as she dragged her feet down the cobblestone corridor. Hernando watched her go; he didn't move not wanting to alert her.

They'd finally uncovered the British spy. After all these years, a chance event led to her undoing. The maid had been so indistinguishable and irrelevant that her work and the danger it posed went unnoticed. Nobody expected a maid to read and write. To be intently listening to the governor's conversations through peepholes and long ago hidden compartments. Nobody expected a maid to collect and keep homing pigeons delivered to her by smugglers from South Carolina. The sheer subtly had evaded the garrison, even when they'd suspected a spy was betraying their secrets. Hernando continued to muse over it while he waited a little longer. The maid's detection had been pure happenstance. Hernán had been skulking around as usual, probably up to no good, trying to steal something. Near the maid's house was a small covert, where he'd found a dilapidated shed. Hernando couldn't understand why he'd even bothered to look in it; the shed was so decrepit, but he did. It was a good job because he'd found five caged pigeons, parchment paper, wax, and a strange letter sealer with an odd symbol. It's not something you'd expect to find in an ordinary shed. After observing the hut, the squad tracked it back to the maid. A bit more digging and they'd discovered some savory titbits about a romance with a British soldier during the last siege, and it all began to add up. They all expected a reward when they arrested her. Sergeant Moreno-Rodriguez was ecstatic, and he'd promised to buy them all dinner, even the squad's smelly youngsters, and constantly slapped their backs in satisfaction, beaming with joy.

Hernando realized it was time to move, time to follow his quarry. He shouldered his gun and strode along the corridor, tracking the maid. Hernando knew where she was headed, so there was little urgency, and her afflictions led her to move slowly. As he marched, the sound of his boots echoed. The corridor was damp, and mold occasionally grew in the corners and recesses. White alabaster peeled back in spots, revealing the coquina limestone underneath. He caught glimpses of the maid as she turned corners, heading for the exit. Before long, he was leaving the castle and treading through the muddy grass that led up to the gatehouse. He saw the maid approach the gate and stop to talk to the guard. Hernando loitered momentarily. She was soon through the gate, the soldiers more accustomed to checking arrivals than departures. Hernando reached the gate with its tall stone columns and thick circular outer walls.

He saw Antonio's huge bulk and his sergeant standing nearby, grinning intensely. Moreno-Rodriguez slapped him on the back again, unable to contain his glee. The three of them tailed her as she walked into town, keeping their distance, knowing where she was headed.

They shadowed her along the beaten tracks from the castle to the town. The paths were worn by the constant foot traffic. Occasionally, they lost sight of her and quickened their pace correspondingly. The route took them past the blackened remains of the Catholic church, the garrison's hospital, and the outer stretches of the town, heading south adjacent to the barrier island. The old maid moved sluggishly but doggedly and stopped to exchange words with a passerby she knew. They nearly overtook her at one point as she paused to talk to the baker and bought a loaf of bread. Soldiers were common in St. Augustine, so their presence at the fruit stall inspecting the produce did not attract any attention. The maid resumed her journey, and after a short gap, Hernando and his colleagues restarted their pursuit. Before long, she arrived at her dwelling. A small hovel, old and dilapidated. The lintel bowed precariously, and the roof appeared to lean perilously—a strange metaphor for the woman herself. A small herb and vegetable garden lined the front yard, while pretty flower gardens circled the sides and rear. The property was dotted with established oak and elm trees. Though tired, old, and decaying, the house somehow remained lovely, with its bright colors and beautiful setting.

The maid entered her cottage, and the pursuers lingered, finding secluded spots to hide and observe. It had been agreed with Hernán that they would wait nearby while his unit waited hidden around the hut. They had enough information and could arrest her at any time, but they wanted the pleasure of capturing her in an act of espionage. It seemed like an age, but it couldn't have been more than half an hour before the maid returned. The transformation was unbelievable; the woman was almost unrecognizable. Rather than bent over, with crippled bowed legs, she stood straight and walked normally. There was no more threadbare cloak and damaged shoes. Her garments were of quality cotton that hugged her curved body tightly, and her boots were fine leather. Hernando almost gasped aloud. She suddenly looked much younger, attractive even. What was this? A type of witchcraft? She strode towards the coppice, with its hidden hut and concealed soldiers.

He followed slowly, seeing her drag the hut door open and enter. Once she was inside, their movement was quick. They ran to block the door and any possible escape. Everything happened quickly. Hernán rushed out of his hiding spot when a pigeon emerged from the hut's side window and flung his knife deftly. There was a fluster of feathers as the pigeon rose and then plummeted suddenly as the knife's blade struck it in the chest. It bowled onto the grass, rolling dramatically to a stop. The pigeon's message was tied to one foot. Simultaneously, Antonio barged open the hut's door. Already weakened, the door collapsed under his weight, and he fell forward into the modest space, unbalanced. Unceremoniously, Antonio hit the floor and swore loudly. The woman was now alert to the danger and moved quicker than any of them could have expected. Knife in hand, she immediately slashed her own throat straight across the trachea. The scene fell into instant chaos. Moreno-Rodriguez tripped over Antonio and ended up sprawling on top of him while the maid died in front of them. Blood spurting out of her wound sprayed everywhere in the confines of the small shed, and she slumped to the ground in a heap, her beautiful clothes rapidly ruined by the sticky and sudden flow of her lifeblood as it spread everywhere. It was not a pretty end. Not a good way to die. A terrible finale to their attempted arrest.

Chapter 23: Enemy Territory

Chioke watched the bead of sweat trickle along Catori's thigh and then flick into the air. It happened in slow motion despite the speed at which they ran. He fondly recalled their recent night together; those muscular thighs were one of many things he found attractive about Catori. As Chioke raced behind her, he couldn't conceal his admiration. She was their leader, a passionate lover, a most competent warrior, and an outstanding hunter. Igbo women were strong, but never this way. Chioke enjoyed many aspects of his new Yamasee tribe, and he'd learned to appreciate the acceptance of women into the warrior class. Many of the female warriors were equal to their male counterparts, and in Catori's case, she exceeded all. She was the leader of their small band, and Chioke followed willingly, knowing that as a formerly enslaved person adopted into the tribe, he must follow and not lead.

Catori led them through the thick pine forest, her every move a testament to her leadership. As they raced along the forest floor, they jumped over debris that littered their path. Tall pine trees towered above them; their branches swayed in the wind. The dense foliage constricted their way. A sickly citrus, resinous scent overwhelmed Chioke's senses, and the fragrance fused with the earthy musk of damp soil and decaying pine needles. They were not alone. Chioke followed Catori closely; he felt the reassuring presence of Maikoh and Alo behind him and two others behind them. They were a band of warriors, united in their mission, and Chioke drew strength from their company as the group raced at full pace along the trail.

Their mission had been straightforward. They were to head up the Chattahoochee River and skirt across the lower reaches of Creek lands, aiming to find a spot to observe the Ocmulgee River and disrupt the British delegation heading to Coweta. They aimed to get through enemy territory undetected. Like all plans everywhere, it had failed almost upon commencement, and now they improvised.

Catori's warriors had swiftly canoed up the Chattahoochee River and experienced little impediment. The moment they landed their plans went awry. They hadn't noticed a small child swimming in the river nearby, and invariably, the child had seen the headdresses of her sworn enemies, the Yamasees, and soon raised the alarm. Now, they raced along the forest floor. A small insignificant band of warriors, without much protection, trying to escape the clutches of their pursuing Creek enemies. Speed and endurance would be their only protectors, along with serendipity and subterfuge.

Chioke tried to estimate the number of their Creek adversaries. Initially, he'd thought maybe twenty warriors pursued them. It was becoming increasingly clear that it was many more, perhaps sixty. Each time they turned along a new path, another troop of Creeks blocked it. They'd taken an abrupt junction in the trail, hoping to throw off the pursuit of their trackers, only to race straight into a new enemy pack.

Only Catori's senses and the enemy's disturbance of a small clutch of wood pigeons had prevented disaster. The cooing of the pigeons as they'd been flushed from the bush had alerted her, and she'd led them swiftly along a new route. At another juncture, they'd traversed a stream and then traveled within the stream for many leagues, hoping to disguise their path. It had proved fruitless. Another band of Creeks had picked up their spoor, and now that group was close behind. That is how it had gone for many hours. Catori's Yamasee had taken evasive action, running through the forest only for the Creeks to thwart the maneuver. The Creeks were master trackers, so escape depended almost entirely upon the Yamasee group's endurance and luck. Chioke's confidence lay solely with Catori; if anybody else had led them, they likely would be dead already.

Catori's powerful frame suddenly became taut, and she took another sudden turn while simultaneously hurdling a dead tree. Chioke followed and leaped high over the tree trunk, only to get an abrupt smack across the face from a stray branch that whiplashed into him. A new and challenging trail lay ahead. Though the thick forest disguised it, the trail undulated downward, down a steep hill. The path was covered with the forest's old debris, and the going became tougher. Chioke heard a grunt as Alo fell heavily behind him. Alo was lifted and pushed forward by Maikoh. The two Yamasee warriors following them shoved them both and swore, encouraging Alo and Maikoh into a sprint. It occurred to Chioke that his comrades at the back were getting worried. Their Creek hunters must be gaining ground in their pursuit. In confirmation of his suspicions, an arrow swished past his ear and plunked into a nearby oak. Then he heard the retort of musket fire and the telltale swoosh of musket balls as they flecked through the undergrowth. He trusted Catori but wondered if they might make it; the Creeks were close.

The hillside track became even steeper and more dangerous. Their skill at running, zigzagging, and jumping kept them alive. It was hard going, and Chioke began to breathe unevenly and perspire excessively as he sped downhill. He tripped, stumbled, and recovered. Chioke cursed at himself for his weakness. Alo fell again, and this time, he was left behind. They heard his screams as the Creek warriors encircled him, butchered him with tomahawks, and scalped him. Chioke hoped to die a more honorable death. Alo's screams betrayed his weakness, already demonstrated by his two stumbles.

The path became sheer, almost impossible to navigate. Catori's pace quickened. Chioke had never seen anybody run so swiftly and certainly not faced with such obstacles on a downward trajectory. It was wild, and yet he followed her. Their small squad knew that life and death depended upon this impractical route; they sensed Catori's determination and certainty and followed her instinctively.

Suddenly, the dense foliage of the forest opened into a bright blue, cloudless horizon. After the pine forest's closeness and gloominess, the intense glare was blinding. Chioke raised his hand to shield his eyes. Catori disappeared; she seemed to fly and then plummet. It was too late to stop. Chioke realized that the trail led straight off a cliff. It was too late, so he sped up and jumped. Legs and arms flailing, he saw that the path led along a cliff next to a waterfall, and Catori had jumped right out into the middle of the mist and disappeared into the vapor, dropping into the waterfall's depths. It was too late to stop; Chioke saw the mist envelop him, its sudden dampness chilling his sweaty stickiness as he fell. He prayed; he had not prayed for a long time, but in those few moments of descent, he prayed that Catori knew what lay below. The fall was harshly interrupted as he hit the water. It was a brutal impact that knocked the wind out of him. Before he had time to react, he was submerged and swept away by the current. The intensity of the flow held him under the water. He fought it, seeking air as soon as possible. Yet, he could not break free from the water's embrace. A darkness began to descend, and Chioke knew he must get air soon. Just as he thought his end was near, a hand grabbed his wrist and pulled him out of the intense swell. He gasped, spluttered, and spat out water; he'd been on the verge of drowning. It was Catori; she had pulled him free of the tributary and saved him.

Catori and Chioke had found safety from the tumultuous flood by hefting themselves onto a gigantic granite outcrop. It jutted out into the middle of the river, in a perfect position following their jump. Either they'd had incredible luck, or it was brilliant decision-making by Catori. She yelled over the din of the torrent surrounding them, "Chioke, get ready to catch the others!" Almost as soon as she spoke, Maikoh's head bobbed toward them in the swell. Chioke missed his arm but grabbed Maikoh by his soggy hair. As Chioke dragged him onto the rock, Maikoh bellowed in agony. It was an unceremonious rescue, but a rescue nonetheless. Maikoh spluttered and swore as large chunks of his hair came away in Chioke's clenched fist. Catori successfully rescued another Yamasee warrior, hauling him onto their boulder. There was no hope for the last man, though. He sped rapidly past them, submerged under the water; he was sucked into the current as it flowed haphazardly and urgently downstream. They'd lost another of their squad, and likely he'd drown. Not a warrior's death nor a pleasant way to go, reflected Chioke, but at least the warrior didn't scream like Alo.

As they were on the outcrop, they had little time to recover their wits. Knowing the area, their trackers did not follow them over the cliff into the waterfall; it was too risky. Instead, they opted to pick off the Yamasee with musket fire from the edge of the precipice. The first blast echoed astonishingly noisily within the confines of the narrow gorge. Chioke again heard the whizz of musket balls hurtling in his direction. He instinctively ducked and was fortunate. One of the missiles flew just inches above his head. Chioke heard it whistle by. Other sounds reverberated around them. Musket balls slapped into the water, and he heard thwacks as they ricocheted off boulders. A bloody thump and crack rang out in contrast. Chioke watched, horrified, as a giant cavity blasted out the back of Maikoh; blood and bone were sent flying in all directions. It was a lethal wound. Maikoh was pitched back into the river and was likely dead before his body splashed into the deluge.

Given the chance of escape, Catori took charge immediately. The Creeks were reloading, so the remaining Yamasee had time to race along the outcrop and throw themselves into the deep cover of the valley. The Creeks followed along the gorge's edge for as long as they could, firing sporadically. It had little effect. Catori used the shelter available well and led their small band away from further trouble. Their flight, however, had come at a terrible cost. Both Alo and Maikoh were dead, and another warrior was lost, likely drowned. Catori and Chioke managed to hang on to their weapons, but their remaining colleague lost a musket while jumping over the cliff. Many of their provisions were waterlogged and likely ruined. At least they had lost the Creeks, but their joy of escaping soured when they found the corpse of their drowned associate. His mangled body lay further downstream; it was bruised and mud-covered. The man's mouth gaped open, and a strange foam bubbled out of the nostrils. His skin was white, almost translucent. The body was already bloating in the oppressive heat, and flies congregated in earnest. They had no time to care for him and immediately carried on, aware that the Creeks might still follow. Catori, Chioke, and their remaining colleague talked little as they traveled along the tributary and eventually reached their destination on the Ocmulgee River.

⧗　⧗　⧗

Catori led them to a carefully disguised campsite beside the Ocmulgee River. It was a perfect spot. They could easily spy up or down the river from their location atop a hill. The three of them made camp and set out to spend a tedious spell observing the river. There was plenty of game, so Chioke replenished their provisions while the others built a bivouac. Catori barely spoke; she was angry, and the rage Chioke sensed inside her never dissipated. He knew the source. Catori was furious with herself for losing half of her squad to the Creeks. Chioke sensed that she might not forgive herself. After many days, she crept into his arms one night. Though she was too brave and proud to cry, he consoled her quietly. The following morning, she spent more time with Chioke and spoke openly about their losses. The conversation quelled her demons, and she began to recover; after all, they still had an important task to complete. Catori explained, "We stay here until the British go up the Ocmulgee River to Coweta for their conference with the Creeks. We were to try to disrupt them, but that might be difficult after our losses. Our job will now be to send word back to the Yamasee chiefs and our Spanish allies. Once the alliance is sealed between the British and the Creeks, we'll know the war is close, and it'll be time for our tribe to go to St. Augustine." Chioke was disappointed; watching events happen wasn't part of his nature. Perhaps there was hope yet, he could kill a British soldier or two.

General James Oglethorpe (from a portrait by Ravenet)

Chapter 24: Ocmulgee River

The four skiffs sat alongside the Altamaha River. Tom's squad had requisitioned the best boats in St. Simons Island for this journey. He had sent Hill and Coleman, knowing he could trust them with the task. They had found two anchored off Fort Frederica. It took much scurrying around the settlement, but Hill and Coleman eventually found the final two skiffs near Egg Island, in the Altamaha Sound. These were two excellent craft; convincing the owners to part with them took a while. Eventually, paying over the odds and threatening the owners with incarceration in the fort's prison worked. The four skiffs were now assembled. Meanwhile, Tom and Sanders had secured the provisions for the trek up the Altamaha River. Their journey was straightforward. They would canoe up the Altamaha until they reached the Ocmulgee River, then go up the Ocmulgee, finally traveling over land until they arrived at the Creek city of Coweta. The trip would take three to four days of challenging canoeing, punting against the river's flow, and more days on foot. Tom's squad of rangers were now waiting for Oglethorpe's party to arrive, following which the entire company was due to depart.

Tom was relieved to be back in a boat. Though he loved his horse Noir, he remained a novice rider and continued to suffer from rider's sores.

Feeling a mix of excitement and apprehension, Tom would lead the first boat, while General Oglethorpe led the expedition. Oglethorpe had clarified that he needed skilled rangers who appreciated and understood the Creek Indian culture. Their presence in Coweta was an essential step in an alliance between the British and the Creeks, and they couldn't afford any mishaps or misunderstandings. Tom was delighted to learn that his friend Mary Musgrove would join the delegation along with several Yamacraw warriors. Tom expected Tomochichi's nephew, Toonahowi, to represent Yamacraw's interests, especially now that Tomochichi was too old to travel long distances.

General Oglethorpe's delegation soon arrived. Tom always smiled when he saw his friend James—splendidly attired as usual in his new general's uniform, with his precious tricorne hat. Oglethorpe's red coat, sleeves, and epaulets were covered in gold braid and black bands. The red jacket covered a golden interlaced waistcoat. Spotless long black leather boots and white pants completed his ensemble. General Oglethorpe beamed quickly at Tom, "Good morning, Corporal Ellis. Are we set for departure?"

"Yes, sir. We have four of the best skiffs in the garrison, have secured all the provisions required, and await your orders," Tom replied, his voice filled with pride and excitement. The mission to Coweta was a welcome break from his squad's monotonous duties at Amelia Island's outpost. Tom, who had never visited the Creek lands, was thrilled at the prospect. He was eager to be part of this important expedition, even if it was likely uneventful. The anticipation of what lay ahead filled him with a sense of adventure.

As Oglethorpe admired and then boarded the second craft, he said, "Excellent work, corporal, let's get everybody onboard. I want to push off as soon as possible." Close behind the general followed Mary Musgrove. As Oglethorpe helped her into the boat, Tom welcomed her. Tom hadn't seen her since the wedding, and she somehow looked younger. Tom speculated that she must be happy following her betrothal. She acknowledged his welcome with a fond smile and nod. Her long black hair, with its streaks of grey, was tied back in a tight ponytail. She wore her usual attire: tanned leggings, moccasin boots, and a beaded leather overcoat. Shell necklaces, indicating her prestige among the Creeks, adorned her neck. Tom knew that Mary's presence would be essential to their success. She held much sway among the Creeks, had many relatives in important leadership roles, and her language skills would be critical during the complex, nuanced negotiations that would precede the alliance.

Toonahowi's band of Yamacraw Indians soon arrived to help guard Mary Musgrove and General Oglethorpe during their negotiations with the Creeks. Tom hadn't seen Toonahowi since he was a boy, on his way to England nearly six years ago. He'd changed a lot and now Tom saw why Tomochichi had placed Yamacraw leadership into his nephew's hands. The boy had grown into one of the tallest warriors in the tribe. Though lean, Toonahowi's muscles bulged subtly as he moved, revealing an underlying hardiness gained from habitual training and much physical work. Slightly extended earlobes adorned with small gold loops and crosshatch tattoos along one side of his chest marked him as Tomochichi's heir. The Yamacraw mico had short, black-cropped hair on one side and, on the other side, a long dangling braid festooned with several eagle feathers. A red scarf was tied around his neck. Moccasins, a deer hide shawl, tanned leggings, and a shirt completed Toonahowi's outfit. Tom noted an impressive sense of command from Toonahowi and an aura of respect from the Yamacraw warriors who followed. For a long time, Toonahowi had been groomed for leadership by his uncle, and it showed.

Toonahowi was accompanied by a large troop of Yamacraws, perhaps twenty warriors. As Toonahowi got onboard the third boat his men began to separate into groups and board the four boats. Though Tom and his men provided the vanguard for the delegation, the Yamacraw Indians would provide the escort and protection. As the groups split to join the skiffs, Tom was overjoyed to see his Yamacraw friends Hilli, Sin, and Umphichi. They quickly made their way to Tom's boat, though a tight fit, they joined his squad of rangers in the front boat. Tom hadn't seen them since his wedding, so there were fond embraces and brief exchanges before they heaved ho. Tom was ecstatic to be on another adventure with his Yamacraw companions. He remembered warmly their last outing to build Fort Argyle, how Sin and Hilli had taught him to hunt, the Indian way of warfare, and how Umphichi's knowledge of forest medicine had earned Tom's respect. The memory was tinged with sadness, though. Umphichi endured a limp from an old wound inflicted by a Yuchi arrow, and Tom still had nightmares about his first kill, an assassination of the Yuchi leader.

The old friends had little opportunity to catch up. It was time for the British delegation to the Creek Nation to leave. Sin sat alongside Tom at the front, while Hilli and Umphichi sat behind them. Tom's squad, Hill, Coleman, and Sanders occupied the rear of their boat. Tom stashed his precious rifle and tomahawk within the confines of the skiff, and all followed his lead. It was agreed that Sin would assist Tom in spotting the river course while Coleman would steer, and the others rowed.

Following General Oglethorpe's order, Tom pushed the boat away from the riverbank, and they set off. He looked backward to check that the other boats in their entourage had set off in unison without issue. All were now heading into the Altamaha River while Tom and Sin observed the current and spotted their course. General Oglethorpe's delegation to the Creeks had begun its voyage inland to Coweta, hoping for an alliance to counter shared foes, the Spanish, and the Yamasee.

⧗ ⧗ ⧗

The mouth of the Altamaha River was wide, and the going was easy. As they were relatively safe near Fort Frederica, all available were occupied, rowing the boats upriver. Only General Oglethorpe and Mary Musgrove were spared the effort. They were conversing about the upcoming negotiations with the Creeks. Tom heard occasional sentences and noted that they spoke both English and Muscogee. Tom assumed Mary was continuing Oglethorpe's linguistic training before arrival in Coweta. Tom loved moments like this, on an open river, headed into the wilderness. Other than Oglethorpe and Mary, few spoke. There was an occasional groan as they all focused their efforts on the oars and aimed to make good progress while they were fresh and there was little danger.

Once Tom was relieved of his spotting duties by Hilli and pulling an oar himself, he could study the landscape more closely. The mouth of the Altamaha River was broad; it meandered constantly, was dotted with small tributaries, and was surrounded by marsh. Occasionally, Tom saw an alligator sunning itself on a rock or by the side of the river on a mudflat. Tom had an unhappy flashback to the last time he was on an adventure with his Yamacraw friends, and one of the rangers had an arm snapped off by one of those beasts. Tom shivered; he hoped never to come up against one of those animals alone. It was an irrational thought, as they generally avoided human contact. Along with the alligators, Tom noticed turtles, the occasional heron, and many wetland gulls, storks, and terns.

As they moved upriver the landscape began to change. The river narrowed. Though it continued to meander there were fewer tributaries. Marshland gave way to woodlands of hardwoods, pines, and palmettos. Along the forest wild irises blossomed and painted the forest floor purple. Cypress and tupelo branches started to litter the waterway. The occasional mudbank and sandbar jutted out, requiring careful navigation. Steering became more complex, and Tom gave the task to the Yamacraw scouts, who were familiar with the river.

The paddling, in contrast, was as easy as Tom had ever experienced. It was a sluggish river that was slow-moving. Some of the bends in the river were frustrating; Tom noted many times when the river almost completed an oxbow lake. If the forest hadn't been so dense, carrying boats across the land might have been easier than paddling around the large bends. Their first day was uneventful and they made excellent progress up the river. They made valuable headway on their second day. By the end of the third day, they reached the Ocmulgee River just before nightfall. Sin and Hilli estimated they had at least another two days of rowing before arriving in Coweta.

⧖ ⧖ ⧖

They took more precautions as the delegation began to row up the Ocmulgee River. Two guards with guns loaded were posted in each boat, leaving fewer rowers and slowing their movement. General Oglethorpe and Toonahowi were resolute;

if they were to be attacked, it would be between Creek lands and the growing influence of the Frederica towns and forts. Likewise, Tom noted the narrowing of the river and the increasing number of small hills that dotted the landscape. Several small bluffs overlooked the river, and these offered adventitious attacking positions. Their exposure became increasingly obvious and led to a heightened sense of awareness. The entire company was on high alert. Rowers cast a wary eye up at the hillocks, feeling their vulnerability, and guards were twitchy, seeing things that didn't exist and reacting to shadows as they danced across the landscape.

When the anticipated attack came, it was swift but less daunting and more damaging than expected. Three arrows shot suddenly out from a bushy covert. They were aimed at the second boat and clearly directed at General Oglethorpe. Tom cursed out aloud. He'd begged James privately many times to stop wearing the damned redcoat. In the wilderness, the general stood out like a sore thumb, an easy target. So, it proved today. Tom wished Oglethorpe would adopt the green uniform of the rangers and blend into the forest more, but the general wouldn't have it. He'd earned his generalship and would wear the uniform. General Oglethorpe had no intention of becoming a naturalized colonial like Colonel Bull; Oglethorpe was British through and through. Tom thought it an odd point of view for a founder, a man called the 'father' of the colony of Georgia. As these thoughts raced through Tom's mind, the arrows arched, fell, and landed. Tom was accustomed to the swoosh of arrows as they sped downward, gathering pace. These three came in fast and accurate. Somehow, General Oglethorpe's prestigious luck saved him again. The first two hit an inch too low and reverberated with a loud twang, embedding themselves into the skiff's side. The third arrow sailed between Oglethorpe's left arm and torso, scraping his arm, tearing his precious redcoat, and drawing blood. The arrow hit the inside of the boat and stuck fast. He was scratched but otherwise unharmed.

A larger attacking force may have caused serious damage, but they were not at war yet, and this was evidently a small Yamasee raiding party trying to disrupt their mission. With the element of surprise gone their assailants were now exposed. The guards fired into the coppice hiding the attackers. Eight guns banged, and echoes reverberated across the valley. As the guards began to load, the rowers scrambled for their weapons, picked them up, and shot. Constant sporadic gunfire ensued as warriors and rangers reloaded and discharged their weapons. It was hard to tell if the defenders inflicted damage; the forest was so dense. They had no sense that they'd hit anything of consequence. On this occasion, Tom's rifle hadn't offered any advantage over the muskets. Reloading speed and blind shooting took precedence since their quarry was close but well hidden. No further attacks were tried, and the delegation continued rowing up the Ocmulgee River.

When they made camp that night Umphichi dressed the general's wound. It was a simple scratch, but Umphichi was suspicious, and much to Oglethorpe's dismay, he began to sniff the cut. Unable to contain his embarrassment, Oglethorpe demanded that Umphichi stop, and the bandaging was completed. Tom wondered about this, knowing Umphichi's expertise with Indian medicines. He watched the Yamacraw closely. Umphichi disappeared down to the riverside where the boats were moored. He soon returned with the arrow responsible, carefully handling it and sniffing its tip. Umphichi's brow was furrowed in confusion and thought. He was both perplexed and concerned. Tom didn't like it at all. He trusted Umphichi, and all the Yamacraw's actions suggested something more sinister than a simple scratch. It didn't take long for the entire party to become concerned. Though it wasn't a particularly hot and humid evening, General Oglethorpe began sweating profusely, and then he complained of a fever, chills, and a headache. Then nausea set in, and he vomited. Oglethorpe wasn't well and all feared the arrow had poisoned him.

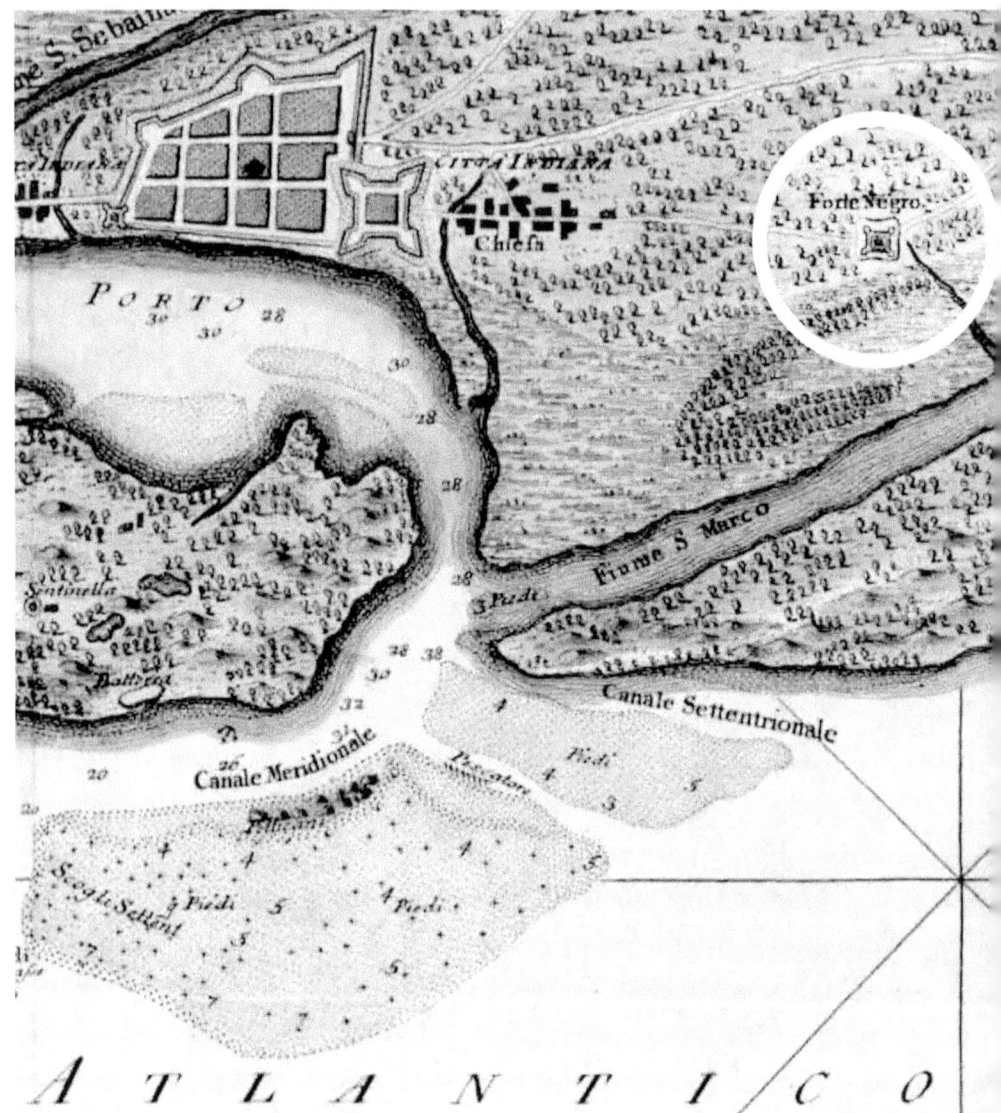

The white circle shows the location of Fort Mose (here called Forte Negro) just north of St. Augustine (north is to the right); map from 1763. Source: https://tampabayhistorycenter.org/exhibit/florida-front-and-center/fort-mose-forte-negro/#gallery

Chapter 25: The Free Black Militia

Stunning moonlight shone brightly across the stream. A full moon lit the night sky, and Lamine saw a swarm of glimmering stars. It was an incredible sight, transfixing despite his sleeplessness. As he enjoyed the panoramic view above, the landscape below hummed with busyness. Bullfrogs croaked sonorously, and a violin concerto of crickets chirped. The hum was interlaced with occasional hoots, whistles, and coos of marsh owls. Lamine sat on the dock, his legs overhanging the edge, swinging aimlessly. He shifted and gazed at the everglade; a swarm of fireflies danced across the brook, blinking like little stars falling from heaven. They seemed to join the concerto, shifting in tune to the nighttime chorus. It was a beautiful scene and one that was becoming familiar.

Lamine had spent many such wakeful nights of late. He was unable to sleep. The battle beside the Edisto River remained a fresh ordeal. Dreams about Jemmy followed many unsettling nightmares, reliving fatalities. Lamine feared he was cursed. It was O'Sullivan's fault for using him as a tool to encourage the rebellion. An uprising that had led to the death of so many of his brethren. He no longer believed the Kongolese to be an alien tribe, with their Portuguese and Catholicism, but considered them free blacks, like himself. As Lamine reflected, he knew it was an intellectual shift brought on by the violence. All the Africans enslaved by the whites were one people, his people. They came from many tribes across diverse African regions and had various languages and contrasting religions. Yet, they were one, all sharing the oppression of slavery. He concluded that the Spanish were little better, using the rebels as pawns in a larger game—a game which Jemmy and his followers had lost.

Despite his thoughts, Lamine aimed to head back to St. Augustine and the Spanish. The lesser of two evils was his reasoning. At least the Spanish allowed freedom. Following his escape, he'd returned to Shell Point, hoping to reunite with O'Sullivan. After weeks of waiting, it was clear that O'Sullivan wasn't coming. Either the man had been captured or given his wily ways, abandoned all to save his skin. So, Lamine waited until the fishermen returned. He understood that they must return at some point. Meanwhile, he hunted, gathered nuts, berries, and roots, and spent nights awake enjoying the vista.

⏳ ⏳ ⏳

Lamine's patience was eventually rewarded. One morning, the fishing vessel returned as the sunrise blanketed the horizon with colorful hues. It was a welcome sight, silhouetted against the dawn sky, bobbing on the gentle waves as it made its way up the river. He hid in the brush on one side of the campsite to be safe. The fishing boat docked, and the fishermen disembarked. They went about their business, settling into the campsite. Lamine observed carefully. Once sure nothing was amiss and it was the same crew, he scrambled out of his hiding place and sought out the captain. They welcomed him as if he were an old friend and immediately asked about O'Sullivan. Though the crew were paid by the Spanish, Lamine was unsure how much to share. The captain was adamant, and that night, around the fire, he shared parts of the story about the rebellion and the battle by the Edisto River. The company of the crew was welcome; they hung onto every word, and telling the tale eased some ghosts. For the first time in a while, sleep came naturally.

They arose early the following morning and left Shell Point onboard the fishing boat. As the vessel eased away from the dock, Lamine studied Shell Point one last time. Despite the cause of a long sojourn here, he'd keep fond memories of restless nights watching the moon, stars, and fireflies and listening to the nighttime melodies of nature. A many-day trip lay ahead. They would be buffeted by the constant swell, sprayed with saltwater, and would need to maneuver carefully through marshland and past barrier islands. It was a long coastline from South Carolina to Florida, so the crew settled into their usual routine of trawling for fish.

⏳   ⏳   ⏳

Lamine's voyage was long, and he was again sick of eating fish stew. The journey was nearing its end, in any case. Standing up at the bow, one of the crew hollered, "There it be, South Ponte Vedra – we've nearly arrived in St. Augustine." Lamine was relieved. The constant churning and undulation of the vessel had begun to irritate. The crew was friendly, but their conversation was simple and often repetitive. They told the same stories, asked identical questions, and relived jokes. Lamine yearned for more educated company or just new people and, above all else, a diet change. He was itching to get home, back to Fort Mose. See the shanty town again and eat Fulani food, especially grilled meats with yogurt. Saliva wet his mouth at the thought, and his belly rumbled.

The fishing boat continued to make its way along the Ponte Vedra beach. Occasional waves splashed against the hull as it rolled across the breakers. Spray wet the side of Lamine's face. Gulls swooped towards the craft, hoping to steal its catch, wailing and squawking as they descended. As the vessel turned inland, he remembered his drab, dirty clothing. The disguise required threadbare garments, which were almost falling off now. Not to mention the horrible stains that lived on as constant reminders of the fighting and failed rebellion. Lamine vowed to burn them; the sooner, the better. The boat headed up the Tolomato River and berthed beside Fort Mose. Thankful for his safe arrival, Lamine bid farewell to the captain and crew while secretly appreciating the end of circular conversations and bland fare.

As he disembarked and entered Fort Mose, Lamine was stunned by the changes. The houses remained where they stood, with their eclectic mix of styles, but many fortifications had been added. Gracia Real de Santa Teresa de Mose could genuinely be called a fort. The nomenclature of Fort Mose now made sense. The township was surrounded by a palisade, a crude moat had been dug around its base, and fortified gates marked the entrances to the town. Many loopholes were cut into the wooden walls, designed for defensive musket fire. Striding through the open gateway, he noted that the fortifications inside had many wooden platforms and ladders. These enabled defenders to shoot over the top of the palisade. Though there were no cannons, Fort Mose had become defensible, and it would have taken a significant force to capture it. He liked what he saw, and his confidence in General Manuel de Montiano's leadership was further enhanced. It was still made of wood, though, and wouldn't bear a significant artillery assault.

In the hours that followed, there were many things to do. Lamine checked that his small hut was still standing and enjoyed the welcome of his friends and neighbors. He found clean clothes, burned his old ones, visited Bello, and gorged on her famous Fulani meat and yogurt dish. Before long, word of his return had gotten out, and he was summoned to the Castillo to report on the mission and its outcomes. As he trudged reluctantly to the Castillo, he noted the heightened preparations. The fortress and population would be ready if war came to St. Augustine and the Castillo de San Marcos. Produce from across the countryside had been brought to the castle and was in the process of being stockpiled. Wafts of pungent smoke from smoking racks filled the air. Venison, beef, pork, and chicken smoke stands leaned against the fortress walls, and the aromas were mouthwatering. An enormous volume of meat was being smoked for storage in the castle's storehouses. Alongside the meat lay many drying shelves for fish. Freshwater trout, bass, black crappie, and bluegill sat beside saltwater varieties like redfish, snook and blackdrum. All had been fileted, seasoned, and set out to dry in the heat of the Florida sun. Other foods were dried: mushrooms, onions, herbs, forest fruits, and roots. Carts full of agricultural produce bustled along the road outside the fortress, carrying grain, rice, corn, and vegetables. It was as clear as the light of day that the Castillo prepared for a possible siege. The evidence was everywhere. Masons were busy fixing weak spots in the castle walls and buttresses. Sawyers were working in pits, sawing planks to mend the castle's internal platforms and walkways. Soldiers practiced with bayonets and swords, sweating in the warmth of full uniforms and clashing with purpose. Unlike his predecessor, General Manuel de Montiano took no chances, and the fortress was plainly preparing for war with the British.

Lamine entered the castle through the main gate and headed along many corridors in search of the spymaster's quarters, which were located near the general's lodgings. A Spanish soldier stood guard outside. Lamine addressed him formally, "Sir, I am here to meet Colonel Ramos. I have been called to report to him."

The guard exuded calmness and friendliness, immediately setting any concern at rest, "I assume you're Lamine? He's expecting you. I'm Hernando." The man saluted; it was an unexpected gesture that made Lamine smile. He chatted about the castle's preparations while waiting nervously for an audience with the colonel. It didn't take long. After an audible order, Hernando dragged the oak-paneled door open, and Lamine entered the colonel's office. Colonel Ramos was seated at a large oak desk. It was ancient, pocked with the marks of an old woodworm infestation, and covered in dents and scratches. Papers, wax, seals, pens, and ink were strewn across the desk. The room itself was austere, with a few discrete furnishings, a leather chair, a shabby rug, and modest oak shelves stuffed with timeworn, dusty books. The chamber was cold, dark, and unhospitable. A tallow candle burned in a copper candlestick. It felt like a priest's or teacher's cubicle.

Colonel Ramos could have been a priest, he looked just like one. He looked up from some paperwork as Lamine entered. He squinted as if his eyes were adjusting. The colonel was a tiny man, probably under five feet tall, but it was hard to tell while seated. He had black-trimmed hair, a pug-like nose, a pointy mustache, and a goatee beard. His uniform was worn and poorly cleaned, and his hands were soft-looking, almost feminine. Despite appearances Lamine immediately noted the man's intelligence. As the colonel's dark-brown eyes adjusted, they became sharp, observant, and knowledgeable. The spymaster's worth to General Manuel de Montiano became visible then, but only if one looked carefully at those eyes.

Colonel Ramos did not invite Lamine to sit. Instead, he began to interrogate him on all aspects of his recent adventure to South Carolina with O'Sullivan. It was a debriefing, and Lamine steeled himself for many hours of questioning. So, it proved to be. Lamine was never asked to sit, but he recounted every aspect of his voyage, from his disgust of fish stew aboard the fishing boat to the moment he fled the Edisto battle and the rebellion's last stand. Eventually, the colonel relaxed, "Such a shame. It was a good plan, if I must say so myself! It should have worked; it nearly worked. Such a shame for a plan so audacious to unravel simply because of awful weather." The colonel audibly sighed. "So, where's O'Sullivan?" Lamine answered as best as he could but had no idea what had happened to the Irishman.

The interrogation was over, and Colonel Ramos lightened up, "I recall that you were a translator for a Prince. You speak multiple languages, including the vast array of dialects spoken by the free blacks. You demonstrate much intelligence, a skill our Lord does not give out generously. Your account shows that you can fight, have a tactical and strategic awareness in a battle, and people follow you." As far as the colonel was concerned, it was a statement of fact; no response was invited. "This is why we are commissioning you, Captain Lamine. We need educated men to lead the free black militia. The militia must be molded into an effective fighting force that can help defend St. Augustine. Our garrison requires you to take on this captaincy. All your skills will be used to guide these men, and we cannot take no for an answer!" It was evident that refusal wasn't an option. Lamine would become a captain in the free black militia. Now, he understood Hernando's salute. Captain Lamine was elated; he knew the quality of the men who lived in Fort Mose, and it would be an honor to lead them. Besides, he was beginning to get a sense of a new people, of African tribes melded into one nation in this new and strange land of Spanish Florida.

Chapter 26: Choctaws

Mary was getting accustomed to her new surname, Ellis. It took time; neighbors still addressed her as Miss Hicks and not Mrs. Ellis and then corrected themselves. Mary was overjoyed to be married. Tom was a decent man, and she was deeply in love. They'd been fortunate to find each other, survive the pox that had decimated Savannah, and buy themselves out of their indenture. She was grateful for the life they were leading. Now, they had inherited this fine house following the passing of the Cannons, and Oglethorpe had gifted them a farm outside of Frederica. They could consider themselves wealthy. Tom was away more than she'd like, but her husband had responsibilities as a corporal in Georgia's rangers. Mary's thankfulness was often tinged by sadness. The Cannons, who she'd emigrated with, were all gone, except for the son, Duke. Dead from the journey, pox, and murder. Undeniably, the flashbacks of Clemmie's murder still haunted them all.

She had more reason to be joyful, though. Mary knew she was pregnant; the signs were obvious. A missed period, followed by morning sickness, cramps, irritability, and fatigue.

It can't have been more than a few weeks since Tom was last home. Her thoughts were rudely interrupted by a flash of white as Uga raced past her, his little stumpy legs carrying his chubby body at speed. His paws almost skated across the wooden floor as he ran, claws scratched, and jowls quivered. Despite herself, she giggled girlishly. The dog was a menace, chewing the furniture, drooling everywhere, and scoring everything with his long nails. They loved him even though he was in trouble most of the time. As Uga skittered past, he began to bark, the loud defensive woof he rarely used. Now, that was strange. The dog came to a skidding halt at the front door and growled aggressively. Again, odd and unlike him.

Duke came hurtling down the stairs, intuitively aware that something was bothering Uga. The boy was fourteen and growing rapidly. His arms and legs had suddenly grown long, lean, and lanky, though muscle was already starting to build. He had that delicate, feathery fuzz on his lip and chin, so often associated with teenage boys. Duke's voice had recently broken, his sweet boy's vocals displaced by a peculiar low-pitched basso. To top it all, at least as far as Duke was concerned, he'd broken out with dreadful acne. Mary watched him as he launched himself down the steps, two at a time. Their adopted son would surely turn out to be a sturdy and dependable man.

Duke raced across the entrance room and grabbed Uga's collar. Mary put down some plates she was drying and left the kitchen, heading toward the front door to find out what all the commotion was about. As Duke kept a firm grip on Uga, Mary opened the door. It was an extraordinary surprise. Stood on their doorstep was a peculiar-looking Indian holding a flail and a warming pan. His arms were full. The man was utterly terrified of Uga and took several steps backward. Mary was familiar with the local Yamacraws and years ago had seen the

Lower Creeks. This man was dressed entirely differently and was evidently of another tribe. He tied his long black hair back with a bright red bandana. A blue patterned and embroidered cane kilt encircled his lower body, down to the knees, and a copper collar ringing his neck held a profusion of red feathers. Leather sandals and an ornate belt completed his attire. His sharp nose led to intelligent, friendly eyes that were currently alight with terror.

It was a perplexing sight to experience in the middle of Savannah, but Mary, Duke, and Uga were in no danger. In fact, the Indian looked as if he'd seen a ghost and couldn't stop gazing at Uga. The man took several more steps backward. Taking one last look at the dog, he turned and rushed off carrying his stash. Without thinking about her well-being, Mary sent Duke and Uga back into the house and set off to find out what was happening. The morning continued its wonders. All around Savannah, there were similarly clad Indians helping themselves to household goods from the residents' properties. Though there was an occasional shout of anger and even a scream, there was no violence; the populace was too stunned to react. Thankfully, a minor miracle had transpired, and the situation had not descended into bloodshed. As Mary studied the mysterious Indians emerging from numerous doorways in Savannah, she noted the items they'd pilfered. Plates, bowls, small cauldrons, wine bottles, candles, trenchers – all manner of household items had been picked up and carried off. She also noticed that none of the warriors were armed. Not a single tomahawk, long knife, bow, or musket could be seen. Despite its oddness, whatever was occurring wasn't intended to be an assault on the city.

As Mary turned the corner of Broughton Street, she saw that Noble Jones and William Spencer had called out the militia and brought some order to the abnormal events. Many armed militiamen were carefully coaxing the Indians into the central square. Muskets loaded were pointed and prodded. Gradually, the warriors were corralled, sat down or squatted, and dumped their various stashes of manufactured possessions beside them. The Indians were smiling pleasantly and talking incessantly in a Muskogean dialect nobody had heard before. None of them spoke English. They just sat with their takings and waited. The militia already surrounded about thirty warriors and another ten stragglers were being encouraged to join the crowd. The residents of Savannah were confused, and there were many bewildered onlookers. There appeared to be no ill will or intent, yet around forty Indians had walked into multiple residences across the city and helped themselves to property. It was a day steeped in peculiarity.

Mary spotted Noble Jones directing the militia and strolled up to him, asking, "What's going on, Mister Jones?"

Noble was as puzzled as everybody else, and deep creases furrowed across his brow as he spoke, "Honestly, Mary, I don't know. They're Choctaws. The whole band just turned up this morning outside Savannah. They were looking for Oglethorpe, as they kept asking for him. Beyond that, I don't know why they came into the city, went into houses, and took whatever they wanted. It might not have been a problem, but all our Muskogean speakers are with General Oglethorpe and Mary Musgrove on their way to Coweta and the Creek negotiations. Thank God Tomochichi is still in the Yamacraw village. We've sent for him, and hopefully, he can unravel this mess for us."

Mary could see that it was indeed a mess. While the Choctaws sat contentedly chatting, the militia appeared angry. Many hazardous moments of unnecessary aggressiveness

260

occurred as the militia pushed the final Choctaws into the square. Some militiamen were twitchy, shouting obscenities, and Mary could sense the tension. One man used the butt of his musket to smash a Choctaw in the stomach, while another kicked a warrior as he pushed him to join the throng. It might take just one error of judgment to cause a massacre.

Jones and Spencer were unusually commanding and aware of the dangers of a potential slaughter. They were directing and compelling individuals to desist hostile behaviors with their threats. They knew General Oglethorpe would want to avoid tipping the Choctaw Nation into an alliance with the Spanish, and if the situation got out of control, that would surely be the outcome. The pressure rose further as the ring of captors encircling the Choctaws tightened, and the residents began shouting, demanding the return of stolen items. One act and the situation could descend into chaos. Fortunately, the Choctaws remained friendly and did not react to the incitement.

Mary watched, appalled. It was shocking to see so many friends and neighbors become furious to the point where they might commit an atrocity. She hoped Tomochichi would arrive quickly before the affair spiraled out of control. As a crescendo of outrage began to build, Spencer nipped it in the bud. It was a skillful act. He was commander of the militia, and he commanded them to disperse Savannah's populace. The decision simultaneously released the stress on the militia that might lead to a mistake and stopped the crowd from their shouts of rage. The tightening ring of armed men surrounding the Choctaws redirected their efforts to disperse the mob, and the immediate crisis was averted. As the mob disbanded, the militiamen stayed to guard the Choctaws and took up positions around the square and streets nearby. The Choctaws continued to wait in the square, chatting affably, almost unaware of the circumstances that could have led to their deaths.

As Jones and Spencer gained control of events, Mary recalled a conversation between Tom and Sin, his Yamacraw friend. It had been a rare occurrence. Sin and Hilli visited them at their house in Savannah after the wedding. The Yamacraws rarely visited Savannah, and the evening was special. It had been a chance for them to spend time together before Tom's posting to Fort Frederica. Early into the night, Mary joined them in the backyard, and they debated the variations between Georgian and Creek culture. It was a profound conversation, encouraged by a little too much wine. She wasn't even sure if Tom remembered it the following morning, especially with the hangover. Since Mary had been busy and didn't drink anyway, she remembered parts. Several bits seemed relevant to their current circumstances. It was about ideas of land and property and how these differed between the settlers and their native friends.

As Mary recalled, Sin had become spiritual about Creek concepts of land. He'd tried to explain in his pidgin English, "You settlers, when you move in somewhere, you think you own the land. Little do you know that the land owns you."

Tom had been perplexed and asked, "I don't understand. How can the land own me?"

Sin chuckled, "Tom, my friend, we must teach you more than how to fight like a Yamacraw. Can't you see it? The land is alive; the truth is everywhere. If only you had the sense to look. The tree grows from the land; it's an extension of the soil. The squirrel lives off the tree and provides food for the hawk. The hawk dies at the hand of the Indian, a spiritual offering to honor the warrior's power. The warrior perishes under the wrath of his enemy, and all return to the earth. How can you own something that is the root of everything and to which all return?" Mary remembered the point. The Yamacraw's land was not owned individually; it existed independently, was on loan to the community, and the tribe acted as its stewards.

As Mary recalled, the next part seemed critical to their current predicament. Tom had asked, "What about private property? Do you own anything individually?"

The question had made Sin chortle again, and Hilli had giggled his usual girly laugh that seemed inappropriate for a man of his size. Sin answered, "Of course we do. My house is my house. Hilli's tomahawk is his, and your rifle is yours. If we didn't own property, how could Hilli honor you by gifting you his tomahawk? Not all the tribes are the same. Take the Choctaws; their views on property differ from the Creeks. They own their own houses, weapons, and slaves, but they share communal goods. Items useful to all are owned by all, including storage, cooking, gardening, and farming tools. I often think it's a way to use what you have most, and I wish the Creeks had the same customs. The Chickasaws share this Choctaw belief."

Though the conversation had been months ago and shot through Mary's thoughts in moments, she realized it was vital. The Choctaws had taken what they believed to be communal goods. They wouldn't recognize that the residents of Savannah would think their acts were theft. Knowing the import of this knowledge, she quickly shared it with Jones and Spencer. Questions remained: Why had the Choctaws come to Savannah looking for Oglethorpe, and why had they entered the city to collect all these hardware goods?

With the new insight, Jones and Spencer were able to remove the final onlookers and placate the angrier militiamen. Although the events had nearly led to an unfortunate calamity, they were now entirely under control. Then Tomochichi arrived with a small entourage of young Yamacraw warriors. Mary was glad to see him and welcomed him fondly. Since the wedding, he had noticeably aged. He was no longer walking unaided and was showing his full ninety years. Once a leader of Tomochichi's stature was present and conversing in Muskogean with the Choctaws, the situation became more apparent.

They had visited Savannah expecting to have a conference with General Oglethorpe, intending to seal a friendly alliance. The Eastern Choctaws would agree to stay neutral if the British waged war with the Spanish. The Western Choctaws would remain allied with the French. In return for their neutrality, the Choctaws were expecting some gifts. With no Oglethorpe present, they took it upon themselves to collect their gifts and misunderstood the British culture of ownership. It didn't take long for Tomochichi to unravel the impasse. The Choctaws were to keep the items they'd collected from households, while the residents of Savannah would be compensated from the Trustee's stores. Jones and Spencer agreed on the outcome of these negotiations on Oglethorpe's behalf. Within a few hours, the Choctaws departed, arms laden with valuable manufactured goods, and the colony of Georgia had bought itself the cheapest alliance of the impending war. Mary knew about the distant lands of the Choctaws, far to the west of the Creeks, and never stopped wondering about the challenges of hauling those gifts over such a distance.

Chapter 27: Coweta

Tom was elated. Coweta was only a few miles away; he was filled with anticipation and wondered what the Creek town would be like. It reminded him of his feelings, seeing the bluff above the Savannah River for the first time—a mixture of anxiety, joy, and curiosity. Tom's enthusiasm had spilled over to his squad of rangers. They all hiked with renewed energy now that the destination was near. The going had been taxing. They'd followed a threadbare track from the Ocmulgee River overland towards Coweta. Though used occasionally, the path had been overgrown and had wound through a dense jungle. Tom spotted many trees that were rare by the coast: alders, cypresses, cottonwoods, and maples. Umphichi pointed out new ones: Catawba, Copalm, Chinquapin, and Dahoon.

At points, the trail had become so overgrown they had to hack their way through thickets of undergrowth. Branches grew across their way and had to be chopped down. Dense patches of scrub had grown, often laced with brambles; these had to be carefully removed. It was grueling, sweaty work. The rangers and Yamacraws had been separated into smaller parties and took turns hewing through these obstacles. The sweltering, stifling, muggy heat had made the work demanding. The constant attention of gnats, mosquitoes, and horseflies had rendered it virtually unbearable. Tom and his squad were relieved their efforts were nearly over and were excited to see Coweta for the first time. Should the need arise, the outcome of their labor was a more passable route between Fort Frederica and Coweta.

General Oglethorpe's condition had further slowed their progress. It had taken them far longer than expected. Oglethorpe endured prolonged fevers, headaches, and chills, and the affliction had advanced somewhat with more symptoms, including diarrhea and extreme fatigue. He'd only been able to walk a mile or two before resting. As they slowly advanced, Umphichi ruminated on the general's symptoms. There had been no evidence of infection at the site of the wound. This seemed unusual; a poisoned arrow would undoubtedly have led to some corruption. After investigating the arrow tip's scent, Umphichi detected a compound of water hemlock combined with resin and barks from poisonwood and manchineel trees. If the arrow had penetrated, it would have been deadly, but he doubted that a scratch would have triggered Oglethorpe's illness. The symptoms were wrong. Death from such a toxin would have been sudden, an instantaneous collapse of the victim's nervous system and heart.

Umphichi persuaded Tom that Oglethorpe's illness was something else. He'd seen the symptoms before, especially among settlers who'd traveled inland. It was a common ague that led to intermittent fevers and chills that came for a while, dissipated, and then returned. Umphichi once discussed the malady with Noble Jones, who concluded it was caused by unhealthy air. He thought Oglethorpe would recover but suffer relapses.

Nightfall approached as they emerged from the forest. It was a remarkably panoramic scene. The sun had just begun to set. A warm glow enveloped the open countryside between the forest and the town. Magnificent reds, oranges, and purples produced a cascade of color that shimmered vibrantly across the horizon. Small, enclosed fields dotted the landscape. Tom spotted one full of legumes; next door were some unidentified tubers and sweet potatoes. There were several fields of corn, with hardy, erect stalks crisscrossing the ground. They had begun to reach skyward. The multi-colored baby ears and tiny tassels were becoming visible. Cultivated blackberry and raspberry hedgerows surrounded each field. Along the hedgerows lay beds planted with strawberries, Cherokee rose, and wild onions. Cultivated orchards of persimmons, pawpaw, and wild plums were dotted around the fields. Surrounding these were expansive woods of black walnut and hickory.

Beyond this cornucopia lay abundant rolling meadows. Sprinkled among the long grasses were a plethora of colors and types of wildflowers. Tom glimpsed a profusion of white-tailed deer, turkeys, and pigeons occupying the grasslands. Assorted ducks flew overhead between the many ponds, surrounded by bullrushes and packed with swarms of red-winged blackbirds. The abundance of sweet aromas assaulted Tom's senses, and the songs of the evening entranced him. As the sun set further, brilliant colors swept further into the heavens. Paradise, there was no other word for it. A land bursting with life, tendered with careful hands over generations, offering a permanent bounty for the future.

In the far distance, Tom could see Coweta. It stood on a hill beyond the meadows, orchards, woods, and ponds. Dams appeared to encircle the settlement. Creek dwellings and community structures were densely distributed throughout the knoll. This was no town; it was a city that was at least as big as Savannah. Tom was captivated by a land of richness, serving a noteworthy nation, and this was only one of the many communities in the Lower Creek region. Then there were the Upper Creeks, and beyond lay the Eastern Choctaws, Western Choctaws, and Chickasaws. It was awe-inspiring, and a profound sense of respect struck Tom's soul. The Georgia colony was just a small undertaking compared to these native civilizations.

By Tom's estimates, the journey had been over two hundred miles, and every step had been worth it. Every branch that had been cut away with his tomahawk. Every scratch lacerating his arms from thorns and thickets fought against. Every bite from the irritating mosquitoes. It was all worth it to experience this moment. When Tom was incarcerated in the dungeons of the Fleet prison, it would have been impossible to imagine this vista. He glanced at Coleman and the other men and saw they, too, were impressed. Despite his infirmity, Oglethorpe was likewise stunned by the scene and mesmerized by the sight of Coweta.

Their reverie was disturbed by a party who set out to meet them. It took a while for the two delegations to merge as both crossed Coweta's farmlands. The Creek delegation comprised of Mary Musgrove's kin was the welcome party. Traditional greetings were attended to between family members. Mary and Oglethorpe were escorted to dedicated quarters provided by Mary's family, while Toonahowi's Yamacraws were disbursed to their respective clan houses. Disappointingly, Tom and his men were commanded to bivouac on the edge of the meadows outside Coweta. They would have no chance to enter the city itself.

After such a long journey, this was a letdown. Tom wanted to see the town. Sin and Hilli took pity on the rangers and set up a camp nearby, recognizing the lack of hospitality implied by the positioning of the ranger's encampment. It was clear that the Yamacraws were here to protect Oglethorpe and Mary during their negotiations with the Creeks. The rangers joined the trip to provide extra protection during travel and were likely no longer needed. Tom sensed they'd have a boring stretch ahead. Given the sensitivities of their mission, he'd need to keep a close eye on his men. Boredom often led to mistakes, and they couldn't afford any here.

⧗ ⧗ ⧗

The conference began the following morning. General Oglethorpe, Mary Musgrove, and Toonahowi would be smoking peace pipes and starting the lengthy deliberations that accompanied treaty talks. Though curious, Tom had no interest in attending the tedious conversations that would probably span many days. Fortunately, the rangers were allowed to hunt in the woodlands and restock the delegation's supplies for the return trip. Sin and Hilli joined them, eager to witness Tom's shooting prowess. They were forever fascinated with Tom's rifle and ability to shoot a buck over extreme distances. The squad and Yamacraws crossed the meadows, skirted the ponds, and entered the woods. They experienced the abundance of the Creek lands firsthand. Wildlife flitted throughout the meadows; every step seemed to disturb flocks of turkeys. The birds appeared to be almost domesticated and rarely ran far. The white-tailed deer were more skittish and took flight once the squad entered the meadows, heading straight into the woodland. The ponds were likewise carefully maintained to boost the natural habitat and attract game. The number of duck species was notable. Mallards, wood, hooded, pintail, and teal ducks were all in plentiful supply. Tom saw several varieties of geese and lots of moorhens. The squad moved past the ponds.

Their permission was for a couple of deer, and so they continued. Entering the woodlands, they saw that these, too, had been cultivated. Predominantly, nut-bearing trees had been planted, and over many years, they had been maintained to maximize the harvest. The trees seemed to have been purposefully pruned and conserved. Evidence of bountiful nut production was everywhere. Squirrels, chipmunks, and deer also appeared to be enjoying the benefits, along with the native Creeks. They chose to set up a den rather than stalk their prey. Coleman and Sanders gathered dead branches to set up the camouflage while Sin and Hilli assessed the trail and determined where best to site it. After building the hide-out, they settled down and waited in the heat for nature to return. It didn't take long; the abundance of animals repopulated the forest floor soon after, and they had bagged two deer within a couple of hours. The party hauled the carcasses back to their encampment, butchered them swiftly, and started smoking the meat before the morning was done.

With the rangers busy, Hilli and Sin headed into Coweta to see what tidbits they could collect about the conference. They'd agreed to report back to Tom if they learned anything. Tom begged them to see if they could get him into Coweta; he yearned to see inside the settlement. It would be a shame to travel so far and miss out. He envisioned himself as an older man, sitting by a future campfire, regaling stories about the Creeks and Coweta. Sin promised to try. All concerned felt it advisable that the rangers stay outside the city.

Hilli and Sin returned later with Umphichi. The rangers had built an adequate fire, and the venison was being smoked. An earthy, gamey odor wafted across the meadow, mingling with hickory wood's sweet, robust fragrance. Tom and the rangers had kept some steaks and roasted enough for all. They squatted nearby and devoured a welcome treat. Sin shared what he knew about the talks, "Well, they've started. The peace pipe has been passed around. Customary grievances about the Yamasees, the Seminoles, and the Spanish were shared. I learned that a band of Yamasee passed through Creek lands recently. They killed some. There isn't much else from what I hear."

Tom appeared interested, and he leaned forward slightly. "I wonder if that was the same group that attacked us? The Spanish probably have Yamasee scouting parties all over the region by now. We might run into more on the way back to Frederica." He turned to Umphichi, "How's General Oglethorpe doing? Is there any sign of a recovery yet?"

Umphichi replied, "Well, he's still ill, but he has attended everything and seems to have improved. He's not running to the toilet every two minutes, and his fatigue is lessened." Unable to contain himself, Hilli laughed with one of his compulsive guffaws. In front of the other rangers, it was neither the time nor the place, though Coleman smiled. Tom gave Hilli a telling stare, and he stopped. They continued to munch down their steaks in silence. The venison was delicious but a messy eat. Grease dripped down their fingers onto the grass, and Sanders kept wiping his mouth with his sleeve. Tom could tell the act irritated Umphichi. When they'd finished, Tom thanked his Yamacraw friends. He pulled them to one side out of earshot of his men, "Umphichi, can you keep an eye on Oglethorpe? I don't like this affliction he has. Everything will unravel if he dies. Sin, Hilli, keep gathering as much information as possible on the treaty talks. It'll be helpful to know what's happening. If you can get me into Coweta, you know I'll be in your debt. Yes, it's selfish, but I don't want to come all this way and sit outside town and see nothing. I swear the beers are on me when we return if you can make it happen." Sin, Hilli, and Umphichi had insatiable appetites for Savannah's beer, and this was a promise they planned to take advantage of. They smiled broadly and patted Tom on the back as they departed toward Coweta. As if to say, "That's a deal."

⧗   ⧗   ⧗

The following days rolled by sluggishly. The conference seemed to move in slow motion. Tom received regular reports from his Yamacraw friends, but they didn't amount to much. There had been an impasse between the red sticks, seeking war, and the white sticks, wanting peace. The British needed Creek allies in the battle to come; neutrality would be a failure. General Oglethorpe had skillfully won the debate and convinced the delegates to favor war and an alliance with the British. It had taken many days to achieve this outcome. The effort had taken a toll, and Oglethorpe experienced a relapse of his illness. The conference was suspended for a few days while he recovered. Mary and Toonahowi acted as intermediaries between the general and the delegates for a few days, and then he returned to the conference.

Next, the general had to navigate a split between the Lower and Upper Creeks. The Lower Creeks were happy to send warriors to join the fight, but the Upper Creeks were nervous about the Chickasaws and the French. They didn't want to weaken the defense of their homeland by sending warriors south to Florida. Ultimately, it was resolved that only the Lower

Creeks would supply warriors for the fight. For Oglethorpe, this was a minor defeat but not disastrous.

Many days had passed, and the conference had begun to focus on the gifts the British must provide to the Creeks to seal an alliance. Tom was getting frustrated. It looked like the alliance might be concluded before he'd have a chance to get into town. Then, the moment he'd hoped for arrived. Hilli and Sin virtually ran from Coweta to the ranger's encampment in the meadow. They had news. Tom was to be adopted into their clan, the alligator clan. The ceremony will start tomorrow. It had taken days of persuasion, but the clan had accepted Tom. The crux of the decision revolved around his actions to save Hilli's life and Hilli's subsequent gift of a sacred tomahawk. The tipping point, though, had come when they'd shared Tom's presence during the revered alligator rites. Tom was elated. Finally, he'd get the chance to go into Coweta. His enthusiasm was tinged by apprehension. What would being a member of the Creek's alligator clan mean? What would the ceremony involve? Well, he mused, he'd sure find out.

Chapter 28: Missing in Action

As Williams strolled along the path, the sight of the hydrangeas in full bloom stirred a mix of emotions within him. The summer heat and stickiness were in stark contrast to the delicate beauty of the flowers. The whites of the hydrangeas were accompanied by buttery tickseed dotted around the base of the shrubs. At the same time, varieties of Black-eyed Susans added a profusion of mahogany, orange, and deep-red flowers. The Congregationalists had established an appealing and peaceful oasis surrounding their circular church. Williams spotted goldfinches and cardinals flitting busily among the bushes. Occasionally, he could hear coos from wood pigeons sitting somewhere on the church's roof. The path meandered past older graves. Williams was in no hurry. He read several headstones; the dates suggested they commemorated the lives of early Charles Town residents. Williams had come to visit Evans' burial place and think. It was always quiet here, and he cherished the moments away from Acting Governor Bull's household.

The track eventually took Williams to the outer loop of the churchyard, where the newer graves were placed. There were numerous new burials. Recently, dug earth was turned over in piles along two lines, and several bunches of fresh mourning flowers were lying on them. One or two had brand-new pristine gravestones. The many recent burials were a consequence of the Edisto River battle. It was a picture that was replicated across the graveyards of Charles Town. The city had paid a heavy price despite the militia's defeat of the rebels. Williams found the grave he was looking for. He'd added a dedication plaque and some flowers during an earlier visit. Bull had promised to pay for a proper headstone, but they were waiting for the mason to carve it; the man had a backlog of jobs to do. Evans would have laughed at the irony. There had been plenty of work for the undertakers and masons following the battle.

Williams sat in front of his friend's grave, careful to sit on dry grass rather than newly dug mud. He often came to pay his respects; it was becoming a habit. At first, he genuinely grieved at the loss of Evans. They'd been close; Evans' sudden death and the manner of it had shocked Williams. As time passed, he began to find the solitude and break from the Governor's house a welcome respite from his duties. So, while he mourned Evans less as time went by, he continued to come and sit by the graveside. It was a significant opportunity for him to think. To reflect on the rapid flow of information, decisions, and events that swirled through the Governor's office, a burden he now carried alone. With Evans' demise, he'd inherited the full weight of dodging angrily thrown shoes and managing Bull's affairs as chief clerk. In theory, he'd been promoted to Lieutenant, but it didn't mean much while he ran errands and wrote letters. These visits to the grave were a bittersweet reminder of the past and a source of solace in the present.

Williams had wanted to get out of the Governor's mansion. So, he'd made his excuses and taken the long way to the congregational churchyard. Many things vexed him. Bull had always been an explosive man, quick to anger but swift to recover. Of late, the governor had become unbearable. The man's fury appeared particularly elevated, and he was wrathful for extended periods, much longer than usual. Deep bouts of sadness punctuated these moments. Both emotional states were unusual for the man, and Williams feared that some sickness had taken hold. The turmoil had set the entire staff on edge, and there was gossip about the cause. It had taken Williams some time to ferret out the reason; the governor's prize asset in St. Augustine had gone quiet. She was missing in action. The spy had been crucial to Bull's success in anticipating the rebellion, and now he felt blind. They'd since heard news that a spy had been detected in St. Augustine and killed herself during the arrest. Bull took the information badly, and his emotional condition deteriorated. Williams could not fathom what the woman meant to Bull, but he could swear the man was grieving her loss. Perhaps there was more to the story, but Bull wasn't telling.

On top of the loss of the spy, the governor was reeling from the number of deaths inflicted on the militia and the populace by the Stono Rebellion. Notable citizens and their families had been slaughtered, and economically valuable plantations had been burnt to the ground. Though the rebels had received no quarter, they'd given none either. They had butchered whole families, smashed children's heads with spades, and attacked women. The failure of the battle plan had led to more losses than the militia could take, severely depleting it as a fighting force. The Stono Rebellion had weakened South Carolina significantly, and the governor wasn't sure how long it would take for the colony to recover. Everybody was on a heightened state of alert, keenly aware that another revolt could be catastrophic.

As Williams ruminated on these issues, he watched as a red-tailed hawk circled above screeching. Some squirrels dashed for cover, jumping up nearby trees and launching into the foliage. South Carolina's weakened position had been a deliberate stratagem employed by the Spanish. Bull knew it, and Williams saw the telltale signs as well. After the battle, they rolled up a network of spies. Some had been tortured, and others executed. They'd all been minor participants, working for a spymaster and unconnected with each other. The architect of it all, though, seemed to have disappeared. There were traces and odd rumors, but nothing concrete. They'd reached a dead end and would likely never find the person who'd pulled the strings. What they'd learned had been enough. The Spanish had offered freedom, had agitated and enabled the Catholic Kongolese, who'd led the revolt, surely an opening gambit before the war started intended to weaken one of their adversaries.

Williams gazed at the hawk one last time as it gave up the hunt and left to look for better prey. The Spanish plan had worked, that's what Williams had concluded, and he suspected it was a key reason for Bull's temperament. War would be declared soon, yet South Carolina had been critically weakened. General Oglethorpe had already requested that South Carolina's rangers be moved to Fort Frederica, and it was clear he'd soon request a contingent of South Carolina's militia. The general was gathering an invasion force to attack Florida and lay siege to St. Augustine. Williams knew that Governor Bull would have to comply with the request, but he was delaying. Bull could hardly dispatch his best troops to the disputed territories, with the militia currently depleted and the community anxious about further rebellions. They were needed at home to solidify the colony's defenses.

Yamasee raids were increasing across the west, and farms were being attacked and destroyed. Likewise, the militia had just taken an enormous hit; how would the governor call the men up so soon after the Edisto battle and send them to General Oglethorpe for his invasion force? Stuck between a rock and a hard place, the governor had chosen to slow-walk Oglethorpe's request and keep his troops in South Carolina as long as possible. Bull was a man of action; Williams concluded that this decision was likely eating away at him. He'd generally be the first to get on a horse and launch himself into a battle. So, this caution, though necessary, didn't come naturally.

The squirrels, noticing the absence of the hawk, returned to gather food among the headstones. Two goldfinches flew nearby and rested on the burial next to Evans' grave. Williams realized his time was up, and he needed to return to his duties. The moments of cogitation had been helpful. They put into perspective the governor's disposition. Bull agonized over events critical to the colony's future and was naturally worried. He was worried about more slave rebellions. He was troubled by lost spies and aggressive spy networks and bothered about the depletion of the militia. He was nervous to send forces south to strengthen General Oglethorpe. And above all else, Bull was apprehensive that South Carolina might not be ready to contribute to the war. Williams knew such worries would upset a man like Bull.

Williams stood, bowed his head briefly, and said a short prayer, "Well, boyo, what a fine mess South Carolina's in! I pray you are up there enjoying some dice games and always winning. Put in a good word for your Welsh friend when you can. I might need it!"

Later that afternoon, Williams returned to his obligations in the governor's mansion. He was nestled in Bull's office, completing correspondence. As usual, the room was strewn with discarded papers, and books were piled up randomly across the shelves. He'd cleared a space on the oak-panelled desk and was scribbling out replies to letters sent to the governor. The quill pen scratched incessantly as he wrote. It was all trivial stuff:complaints about militia call-ups; veterans were requesting government help; letters from farmers desperate about Yamasee raids. Bull had no time for it. As was often the case, Williams responded on the governor's behalf. Bull, in contrast, was trying to do something about the problems South Carolina faced. He was downstairs meeting Colonels Palmer and Vanderdussen, discussing responses to the Yamasee attacks out west.

Williams heard a strange sound as he scrawled his answers to the letters. It was off in the distance, almost like the remote sound of multiple bees' hives buzzing relentlessly. The irritating noise was off-putting, and he stopped writing. Williams wondered what it could be. As he listened more intently, the sound grew in intensity as if it were moving toward him. Individual voices could now be vaguely heard within the tumult. It sounded like a great crowd headed in his direction. Williams rose quickly, knocking over the office chair, and raced to the window. Peering out of the tobacco-stained window, he saw that there was indeed a great horde of Charles Town's inhabitants moving toward the governor's mansion. The chitter-chatter was loud but not intimidating. It was almost a party atmosphere; they seemed curious and excited. The mass of people was proceeding into town from the docks.

Ahead of the crowd walked two British soldiers, a color sergeant decked in his dress uniform and an officer, equally resplendent. They strode into town carrying a British flag and a dispatch box. The flag fluttered in the scorching summer day, caught by a mild wind that had brought a British frigate into the harbor. Williams could see the ship in the distance, its three masts towering over the other boats and harborside warehouses. British soldiers marching into town holding a Union Jack flag and a dispatch box could only mean one thing. As Williams knew, the populace understood what this meant and were following. They didn't want to miss history in the making. The commotion grew louder as the crowd entered the streets and continued toward the governor's house. Williams turned, ran across the study, and vaulted down the stairs, taking two or three steps at a time. He wanted to be by Bull's side for this momentous occasion.

Governor Bull and colonels Palmer and Vanderdussen had heard the furor. They'd already moved from the meeting room to the front steps of the residence and were surrounded by the household staff. Williams didn't hesitate. He elbowed his way through the throng on the steps of the mansion until he stood just behind the three men. A few nasty looks were cast in his direction as toes were stepped on and ribs bruised. All knew his status in the household, though, and begrudgingly let him through. Nobody wanted to miss the announcement.

Williams could see that half the population of Charles Town had turned out. News traveled fast in their community, and this dispatch had a weighty consequence. Houses and businesses were emptied of people, and all followed the soldiers to their destination. The sergeant carrying the flag stopped marching and stood to attention in front of Governor Bull's group. The multitude following quickly became still, and a sudden hush descended over the scene. Everybody wanted to hear what happened next. There were a few whispers and a few shouts to be quiet, and then utter silence descended.

The officer marched forward, up the entrance steps of the governor's house, and asked the three colonial officers, "Which of you is Acting Governor Bull?" Bull strode forward and acknowledged the presence of the British colonel with a salute. It was a formal occasion, and the man returned the salute. His tricorn hat, periwig, red uniform, white pantaloons, and black boots had been meticulously cleaned. The officer knew when history demanded attention to detail. "Sir, I have a dispatch for you from King George II!" The officer pulled open his leatherbound dispatch box and handed a pink-red dispatch to Bull. Williams had never seen a letter of that color before. The King's wax seal was visible. Governor Bull momentarily stared at the seal before breaking it open. It took moments for him to read it. Nobody breathed, and time dragged on for an eternity.

Acting Governor Bull invited the officer into the residence and then addressed the gathered populace, "King George II, Britain, and all her territories have declared war with Spain. Ladies and gentlemen, South Carolina is at war!" Bull gave a short speech. Williams later remembered some of it, about sacrifices and the colony's future. Many of the details were blank; he'd been distracted by the event's importance. War had been declared. South Carolina would join Georgia and attempt to throw the Spanish out of Florida.

As the crowd dispersed and Bull's entourage turned and headed back into the mansion, the Governor handed the war dispatch to Williams: "Lieutenant Williams, this is an important historical document. Make sure it is carefully stored in the Governor's archives."

"Yes, sir!" replied Williams. As he sauntered back to the office, Williams couldn't help but browse the text of the pink letter, which read:

By His Majesty's Command,
From the Admiralty Office, London.
The Twenty Second Day of October, In the Year of Our Lord One Thousand Seven Hundred and Thirty-Nine.
To His Excellency the Acting Governor of His Majesty's Colony of South Carolina,
Whereas the insolence and provocations of the Spanish Crown hath long vexed the Honour and Commerce of His Majesty's Subjects upon the American Coasts, and whereas grievous Affronts hath been committed against Persons and Properties of the British Nation. His Majesty, GEORGE THE SECOND, of Great Britain, France, and Ireland, King, Defender of the Faith, hath ordered hostilities be commenced against the Kingdom of Spain.
His Majesty hath commanded that the Fleet of His Royal Navy and the British Army be immediately employed against the Spanish, and that reprisals be taken to avenge the Outrages suffered by our People, chief amongst them being the Barbarous Mutilation of Captain Robert Jenkins, whose severed Ear remains a Testament to the Savage Injuries inflicted upon British Subjects.
His Majesty doth direct all Colonial Governors to lend

their utmost Aid to His Forces by provision of men,
material, and such resources as may be requisite for
success. His Majesty and the Fortunes of Empire are
at stake, and His Majesty doth rely upon the Zeal and
Fidelity of his Subjects in these distant regions.
God Save the King
By Order of His Majesty's Most Honourable Privy
Council

Williams reflected on the letter's contents. So, Britain was going to war over Jenkins' severed ear. He'd heard it had been paraded around Parliament, causing quite a sensation and much consternation. However, Williams had never believed the incident could trigger a war between empires. Shaking his head, he wondered, had the world gone utterly mad?

Chapter 29: Alligator Clan

Tom had gotten a lot more than he'd bargained for. Adoption into the alligator clan was bound to have some sacred rites. Stripping off his ranger's uniform and donning a Creek warrior's outfit wasn't something he'd anticipated. It had begun seriously as a ceremony with some import. Sin and Hilli had collected the garments and had been sure to secure quality tans and hides. They'd brought them to the ranger's encampment to help Tom prepare before entering Coweta on his way to the clan house. He'd undressed and pulled on tanned leggings and moccasin boots. A band of alligator skin encircled his midriff. It was a rugged leather belt with a red loin cloth attached to it. Hilli dressed and braided Tom's long black hair with white feathers. An ornate necklace with rows of alligator teeth was fastened around his neck. Sin and Hilli used a deep, muddy dye to paint dark green undulating stripes across his arms, legs, and torso. They'd added dark brown hues in the style of gnarled, knobby alligator skin. All had gone well. Tom felt he looked like a Creek warrior. Examining his friends' attire, he was sure he looked like the part of a Creek alligator clansman.

As Tom stepped out of the tent, the reality dawned that he might not appear as impressive as he'd hoped. Gazing at their corporal Coleman, Sanders and Hill immediately repressed grins. Their grins rapidly became suppressed chuckles and then descended into open laughter. Tom was concerned that their humor might offend Hilli and Sin, but as he turned, Tom saw that they were both in fits. Hilli, never one to hold back, could barely contain himself and hooted with joy at Tom's expense. The laughter was infectious. Looking at his arms, legs, and torso, Tom realized that he looked very odd indeed. The dark green painted streaks didn't conceal the pale white, almost pallid, parts of his body that had not been bronzed by the hot Georgia sun. The bits exposed to the sunlight were a russet tan, quite a deep suntan. The combination of green stripes and fair and tanned skin appeared ludicrous. Despite himself, Tom smiled and then joined the merriment, chuckling loudly.

The fun was cut short. Sin pointed toward Coweta. They stopped laughing and watched as a sizable troop of Creek warriors trotted out of the town's entrance and across the glen toward their modest encampment. It was an impressive-looking group. Jogging in double file, the warriors were decked out in the same garb that Tom now wore. Nobody laughed. The Creeks appeared menacing as they traversed the fields between Coweta and the camp. Not a pallid blanched piece of skin between them; they were all dark, tanned, and muscled. They moved in unison, aware of each other's steps. The clan's alligator skins and paintwork appeared intimidating, even at a distance. The troops were fully armed, bristling with tomahawks, long knives, bows and muskets. They carried their weapons comfortably, and the long hours of practice were evident in their movements.

Tom's squad reacted as if they were about to be attacked. They began to load their weapons and ready bayonets. Tom stopped them immediately. Despite their threatening appearance, the band were friendly allies, arriving to escort Tom to the clan lodge. While Tom commanded his men to cease and withdraw, Hilli rushed to fetch Tom's tomahawk and ornate rifle. The alligator clan rites required the consecration of his weapons as well as himself. Tom gratefully received the tomahawk and rifle from Hilli; he fastened the tomahawk to his new alligator belt and slung his rifle over his shoulder. As Tom's squad withdrew, Hilli and Sin led Tom out to meet the Creek troop. They left the ranger's camp behind and hurried across the open meadow. A group of wood pigeons were disturbed by their movement. Each bird flew vigorously, flapping while skirting the meadow's grasses.

Sin had briefed Tom. From then on, all his movements and actions were to be observed, and he was to earn the right to join the clan. Consequently, he was careful to follow what his Yamacraw friends had taught him during their long hunting outings together. Tom conserved his energy as he paced behind Sin and positioned his weapons to be available immediately. The two detachments of alligator clansmen met in the middle of the field. Sin and Hilli greeted the Creek leader with a traditional gesture of welcome, a "Hesci," and introduced Tom in Muscogee. Tom's language knowledge had advanced somewhat, but he found the Creek dialect more challenging and different from the vernacular spoken by his Yamacraw friends. He picked up some of the conversation. Tom understood that he was to be offered as a novice and was to be initiated into the clan. Sin confirmed proper preparation for the initiation process had been completed and that the recruit was ready for the ceremony.

Tom was excited and simultaneously anxious. He knew that many challenges lay ahead and that his performance during these trials would be judged. Only if he passed muster would he be allowed to become a clan member. As they talked, Tom observed the Creek band of warriors. There was nothing average about them. The tribesmen were fit, taut, and lean muscles bulged with every movement. The leader and several others wore full alligator skins. The roof of the alligator's head covered the men's mohawks and protruded over their faces. The elongated snout, sharp teeth, and beady eyes had been carefully preserved so the alligator appeared alive and ready to fight. The men's faces were hidden so that an enemy would only see the fearsome animal's head. The armored black bony plates of the skin hung behind the warriors' backs while the skin's arms tightened the pelt across the naked chest. The other warriors had distinctive alligator accessories, including leather belts, shields, headdresses, and leg guards. The clan's dress was unique and unlike traditional Creek clothing. The addition of dark green paint, instead of customary red, marked the clan as unusual amongst the Creeks. It was instantly evident that they were an elite warrior clan. Tom's pride and trepidation grew. To be accepted into such a clan as an equal would be a considerable honor, and he hoped not to fail his friends.

With the initial greetings completed, the troop pivoted and jogged back toward Coweta, maintaining a disciplined and synchronized effort. Tom joined the back of the group and ran alongside Hilli. Finally, he was to get his wish and see the Creek town of Coweta. As the group raced across the meadow, they disturbed more birds. Two meadowlarks scattered suddenly. Circling above them, a northern harrier noted the larks' movements with several sharp keks. It dived abruptly and caught one of the larks in midair. Hilli noted the positive omen to Tom via a hand signal. Maybe this was an auspicious start for his initiation. They made quick progress back across the valley. Coweta's gateway loomed ahead. Though the town wasn't walled, Coweta sat on a steep hill. The troop's tempo didn't slow, and Tom felt the extra exertion as they climbed. This was the moment he'd waited for. It reminded him of when he'd first seen Yamacraw Bluff beside the Savannah River. A seminal instant in his life that he was destined to remember, forever.

Coweta was a sizable town. It sat on a tabletop hill with sheer sides and a level top. The town spread across the entire hill, perhaps two miles wide. Many residences were dotted across the hillside. The house construction varied. There were many permanent log cabins, horizontally stacked logs with gabled roofs. To Tom, these appeared like those he'd seen in Port Royal. They tended to be the larger houses on the outskirts, offering some defensive value to safeguard the community if attacked. Tom noted arrowslits along the walls of these fortifications that might be used for protective musket fire. Other small buildings were scattered amongst these larger structures. A few Chickees, open-sided and on stilts with thatched roofs, seemed to provide shade. These appeared to be the hub of activities; meetings, cooking, and trading were all visible within various Chickees. A few appeared to host more casual activities like drinking, talking, and gaming. Alongside these buildings were many smaller wattle-and-daub houses. Family dwellings that were both circular and square. These were constructed from frameworks of wooden poles with thatched roofs supported by daubed clay and straw walls. Many of these minor houses were colorful; deep orange or burnt yellow was typical, though there was occasionally deeper crimson and lighter beige. The town reminded Tom of some of the more vibrant villages he'd seen in Southern England.

The track became hard underfoot as the clan climbed the incline toward the gate. It was well worn; many feet had compacted it so that it was rounded and smooth. Two log cabins with their profusion of arrow slits marked the entrance to Coweta. Though it lacked a portcullis, Tom imagined the combination of the steep ascent and the two guard houses would make the entrance arduous to assault. As they reached the entrance, a group of children waited for them. The departure of the alligator clan from Coweta had caused a stir of interest and rumor. Many of the children were curious to see what was happening and had heard a new, strange inductee was to be tested. They'd gathered at the gate to watch Tom's arrival. There was an electric air of wonder; much giggling and nattering could be heard as they approached. There were toddlers held by sisters, little boys shoving each other, and young teenage boys trying to look like men. Most had long, braided dark black or brown hair. Dark brown, round eyes inquisitively stared at Tom. Many of the girls wore vivid gowns woven with bright lattices of beads. The boys were practically naked, wearing tight leather belts, loincloths, bead necklaces, and small headdresses with one or two feathers attached. All were dusty as if they'd been playing in the baked soil for hours. As Tom's squad passed, the chatter intensified, and the youngsters began to scurry behind, following the alligator clansmen. The anticipation and interest were stirring, and no one laughed at Tom regardless of his strange paleness and odd look.

As the alligator troop made their way through Coweta and to the clan house, Tom had time to glimpse the town's features. The small, richly colored wattle and daub structures were undoubtedly family houses. He passed several and saw women of various ages weaving, preparing food, cooking, and chatting. Like the children, they wore vibrant gowns of animal hide laced with beads and arrayed in complex designs. Many sported exquisite moccasin slippers, intricately patterned belts, and striking shell necklaces. As Tom's squad loped past, a few women glanced at them, but most carried on with their labor, seemingly oblivious.

The town's men congregated around the Chickees and log cabins, engaged in trading, debating, and lounging. Their dress was like the Yamacraw's. Varied hairstyles and headdresses, mohawks, buns, knots, and braids. A few ostentatious headdresses adorned with various feathers and beads, many more understated and subtle, feathers hanging from long cords down the back. All wore practical moccasin boots, tanned leggings, and loin clothes attached to leather belts. Occasional complex necklaces, blue tattoos, or earrings denoted a man of rank. While a few donned furs across the shoulders despite the summer heat and humidity. As the alligator clan hurried by, groups of men made strange clucking, hooting, or whistling sounds. Tom saw that the clan always responded with the same harmonized hiss, and he began to join them in the retort. He supposed these were inter-clan rivalries. Tom had heard alligators hiss when protecting their young and thought the clan's response mimicked the animal.

Eventually, they reached the town center. The pace began to slow somewhat, and Hilli used a hand signal to indicate they had reached their destination. The structures in the town center were much more significant than elsewhere. It contained many clan lodges and a large meeting house. The squad slowed to walk and began to approach one of the lodges. The clan lodges were large rectangular buildings supported by thick poles almost two feet wide, open on one side. The closed sides were mounted with cross-poles and thick, substantial wattle and daub mud walls. Each lodge was a unique color, representative of its clan. Naturally, the alligator clan house had olive tones and streaks of darker jade. The roofs were more substantial than other buildings and had been assembled using cypress-bark shingles. The gables were left open, and white smoke billowed from the gaps. These lodges surrounded the center, while the meeting house dominated the town center itself. Although it was of the same construction, it was vast, circular, much taller, and broader than the others. This was the heart of the community, the meeting house and clan houses. Tom knew Oglethorpe and Mary Musgrove must be hosted nearby and would have discussed their alliance with the clan chiefs and matriarchs in the meeting house.

As the clan entered the lodge, Tom was invited to sit. He wondered what would be next; his initiation into the clan must start soon. Hilli sat to his left and Sin to his right. The other alligator clan members convened in a large sphere surrounding the lodge's central hearth. A large pot stood in the center of an open fire. Flames licked the sides of the pot, and it was evident it had been cooking for some time. The inside of the lodge was gloomy, and the shadows of the flames danced on the rear wall. The internal poles securing the lodge's structure were adorned with intricate carvings of alligators, while a complex mat of interwoven reeds covered the floor. It, too, was decorated with paintings of alligators in a wide range of poses.

To Tom's surprise, the ceremony started with a meal. Sin whispered briefly in English, cautioning, "Do not reject anything." Several wooden dishes were fetched, and the large pot was opened. Steam poured out in a sudden hiss, and the assembled clan hissed back in a common reaction. The clan's leader began to scoop the scalding stew into the dishes and passed them around. A warrior took a hot sip, tentatively picked a piece of meat from the stew, and passed the bowl to the next man. Each took a turn, and as the bowl emptied, it was refilled. To Tom, it seemed like a ceremonial meal with religious importance. Each man seemed to meditate for a moment before consuming the food.

When it was Tom's turn, Sin murmured again, "Halpadalgi." It was like a light went on. Of course, they would start with a ceremonial meal of alligator stew. Taking in the beast's strength for the benefit of the hunt was a part of the ritual that Tom already understood. He'd eaten alligator before and knew what to expect: a fishy chicken flavor that wasn't distasteful. When it was Tom's turn to eat, he prayed briefly for a positive outcome and acceptance into the alligator clan and then ate in the same manner as the others.

The bowls continued to circulate amongst the clansmen until the pot was emptied. Once the ceremonial meal was finished, the clansmen began to sing. Tom thought of it as a song, but really, it was a strange combination of noises that had a musical quality. Many types of hisses, sudden bellows, rumblings, grumbles, and roars, interspersed with coughs and chumpfs. It wasn't random; there was a rhythm, and several of the clansmen stood and danced to the beat. Hilli and Sin arose at this juncture and moved to the middle of the ring. The chief crouched in the hub of the lodge and pulled his full alligator skin over his head. Gradually, he began to move like an alligator. In the dark gloom, with the shadows playing in the background, it was deceptively realistic. Tom's Yamacraw friends approached the chief, who handed them a small copper cup embossed with alligator motifs. It was full of liquid. On behalf of Tom's sponsors, Sin accepted the cup. They turned and returned; concern was etched across their faces.

Sin handed the cup to Tom. He sniffed it briefly, not wanting to offend. The liquid smelt earthy, woody, slightly sweet and pungent. The song's tempo had peaked, and the dancers whirled and jumped. Tom knew that he must drink. He raised the cup and drank it, downing it in one swallow. Like the smell, the taste was earthy and sweet, not unpleasant, but perhaps a bit like chewing a piece of wood. He sensed a change come over himself immediately. There was a sudden slowing of time. As the dancers twirled, they appeared to stop in midair and only advance at a slower speed. The music began to take on a new cadence as if he were surrounded by approaching alligators ready to eat him alive. The chief disappeared, and only the alligator survived, swaying aggressively and fearfully.

Yet, Tom wasn't scared. He looked up into the roof of the lodge. There, he saw the spirit of an alligator, translucent, spiraling in a universe lost in time. Stars surrounded the vision, glinting, marking the sky, and the constellation grew to a boundless mass of stars and cosmic clouds. Shooting stars shot through the constellation, embedding gigantic arrows in a glowing alligator mirage. The spirit arrows drew power inward; stars were sucked from the cosmos into the shafts, and a bright blaze of light burst outward, enveloping the ceiling of the lodge house. The dazzling, intense illumination suddenly reversed and shrank rapidly backward into a pin light. Then, it exploded into many tiny lights, drifting randomly like a host of fireflies. The fireflies then appeared to float above the heads of each warrior and drill slowly, in a spiral, deep into their foreheads. It was as if each was receiving a part of the alligator's spirit life. Tom felt a firefly piercing his skull. His eyes were on fire; the heat concentrated as the insect burnt through his cranium into his brain.

Collapsing, Tom entered a dream world. Spiraling backward, he was in Yorkshire, images of his brother Mark playing in a stream. Then, crying as they were separated for Tom's apprenticeship. Then torture, relived pain at the hands of his carpentry master, and the argument before he fled. Time sped up. Oglethorpe was there, a fight in a bar. Mud and offal in a London street. Wet, cloudy skies and constant rain. Trauma and death in debtors' prison. Cannons firing and bouncing off; why do the cannon balls bounce? Heads rolling, the poor Scottish Highlanders, what can he do? Mary on the Anne, beautiful Mary, his beloved. How much he misses her. Uga is running through the house; who is the strange man at the door? Mary, be careful! A sudden surprise, is my horse dead? Time stands still as the marsh goes red. Sweat, tears, more sweat, and blood. Finally, a blissful sleep, a bottomless sleep, oblivion.

Chapter 30: Return to Florida

Igboland is a paradise of rainforests, hillocks, and mangrove swamps. As it often did, Chioke's dream had drifted back to his homeland. He was navigating the lush rainforest in search of bushbucks. The antelope was shy and likely well-hidden. The narrow trail passed several groves of Iroko trees. Chioke sensed their spiritual presence. Suddenly, the scene changed. Kolanut trees were now in front of him, and his family was there, gathering up the nuts. He missed them so much. Chioke's dreams shifted to another setting. Now he canoed along the Niger River accompanied by other warriors. The river's great expanse made him feel tiny and insignificant. Egrets, herons, and hammerkops fished along the verges and scurried across the mudbanks. A purple heron emerged from the brackish water nearby with its striking purple and chestnut plumage. The Igbo sang as they rowed, and Chioke joined in the familiar song.

Then, a new image forced itself into his imagination. Chioke was alone now. He was stuck in one of Igboland's many mangrove swamps, a child, lost in an unidentified creek deep within the swamps. Scared, he may never be found or ever get out. The mangroves are dense and impenetrable; roots grow aggressively everywhere, grasping his legs and pulling him into the soft mud. Knee deep, mud sucking him in, and the roots dragging him down. Chest deep, his father's hands trying to grab him and pull him to safety. Suddenly, Chioke's dreamscape is abruptly disturbed and he wakes.

Catori nudged Chioke and woke him up. He'd been snoring, disturbing her. Both needed sleep desperately. He was grateful not to bother her anymore; she appeared blissful and started to doze again. Catori rolled over and resumed breathing gently. Chioke stared aimlessly at the top of their bivouac. It had been a long and arduous mission. Deep in enemy territory, they had lost their entire squad. Butchered, shot and drowned. Three Yamasee warriors lost to their Creek enemies. Catori blamed herself, but it was a high-risk assignment. Chioke knew that she had led them well despite the losses. A band of warriors going through an enemy's territory was always dangerous, so it had been proven almost from the outset.

Their last squad member had been lost to a fusillade of musket fire. Another high-risk but necessary task. They'd waited a long time by the river. Eventually, the British delegation had passed them. If only they'd had more warriors. Catori's selection for the ambush had been perfect. The river narrowed, and the hillock she'd selected overlooked the gorge. The arrogant British general in his redcoat stood out, but somehow, they'd missed—a lucky leader, maybe, but maybe not. Chioke had seen his arrow skin the man's inner arm; perhaps the poison had done its work. He knew that if you cut off the head of the snake, the creature offered little peril. Maybe they'd been successful at cutting the British snake's head off.

They'd talked about it for hours and hoped it would be so. Perhaps the general had already died. The resultant musket fire, though, had taken their last squad member. He was blasted into smithereens by the fearsome weapons. Chioke and Catori were fortunate to escape. As the British fired randomly, the balls flicked past but did not harm either of them. Now, they journeyed south to St. Augustine to reunite with the Yamasee tribe.

They'd already traveled six days from the site of their ambush alongside the Ocmulgee River. It had been a hard slog over land, following old Yamasee raiding trails. Much of the way had been overgrown. Dense thickets had blocked the route; they had lost track several times. They found their way back onto the trails only by reading the forest and following the stars at night. Eventually, they reached Okefenokee, the wild swamps of the mysterious immortals. This was a land lost in time, untouched by habitation. A vast expanse of water wilderness, thick with cypress trees and the stench of peat bogs. They'd reached the upper tip of the swamps, where they were now encamped. They knew a canoe was stashed nearby, but they had looked for it for a whole day without success. Catori had no intention of going through the swamps; they were to avoid the land of the immortals. Though Chioke didn't subscribe to the Yamasee beliefs about Okefenokee, his dream had been warning enough. He could tell that Okefenokee was a complex web of small lakes, atolls, streams, and bogs. They seemed destined to get lost. When they found the canoe, they would use an old Yamasee route that skirted the edge of the wetlands, and Chioke was relieved when Catori proposed it.

⧗ ⧗ ⧗

In the morning, the fog rolled across their encampment. It enveloped their world, creeping in, blanketing the swamps and cypress trees. Each breath tasted of dank peat. Shadows danced within dreamlike haze, and the mist swirled in the light wind. It was easy for Chioke to imagine that the immortals were reaching out from Okefenokee to take their souls. As he awakened Catori, dew droplets glistened like jewels on the underside of their shelter. One dripped and landed on his cheek. It was light and fresh, promising a new day and, hopefully, the canoe's discovery. As Catori stirred, Chioke kissed her gently on the head. Catori's almond-shaped brown eyes opened and gazed at him with gentle affection. It took her a while to fully awaken. Slowly, she began to stir; her eyelids fluttered as she dozed momentarily. A contented sigh escaped her lips as she stretched fully and turned onto her back. Chioke watched intently as Catori's muscles became firm and pronounced. She had a powerful yet lovely body. They embraced briefly and then discussed the day's plan. Chioke was to trace backward along the path and revisit previously searched places where the canoe might be concealed. Catori would move forward along the trail and explore new places. Meanwhile, they would have to wait for the fog to lift. They used the time productively, building up an appetite for breakfast by passionately making love.

After a breakfast of cornbread, the mist began to lift, and the work of finding the hidden canoe recommenced. As agreed, Chioke retraced their path and searched places they'd already examined while Catori moved in the opposite direction, exploring new hiding places. Occasionally, they would whoop loudly, maintaining contact to avoid getting lost in the swamps. After Chioke's dream, he waited apprehensively for each contact with Catori. Though he didn't believe the stories about the immortals, he was fearful, nevertheless. After several hours of searching, they eventually found what they were hunting for. Secreted into a thicket further along the path, Catori found it— an old weather-beaten canoe with a rugged wooden frame and a skin of birch bark. Though well built, sewn, and caulked with spruce gum, it had sat unattended for a long time. Slimy moss had grown inside the deck, and a thick layer of hardened gunk coated the keel. They spent the remainder of the day cleaning it, rebuilding segments, and checking it was waterproof.

⌛ ⌛ ⌛

The following day, they set off navigating along the fringes of the Okefenokee wetlands. The terrain was flat. There was little water current and occasional patches of dry land to camp. The streams meandered haphazardly. Though an expert tracker, Chioke was amazed that Catori could know where they were headed. Each paddle stroke inched the canoe through a dense cypress forest. Branches and entire trees littered their path, making their progress slow. Paddling was sluggish and strenuous. The water was often too shallow, and they had to drag the canoe through the mud. The mosquitoes, gnats, and dragonflies were ever-present nuisances.

Occasionally, the impenetrable jungle of cypress trees would break, and they would cross open prairies dominated by grasses, ferns, and rushes. Water lilies, pickerel weed, yellow-eyed grass, and golden club proliferated in some wetter places. In these sites, Chioke saw many herons, egrets, and ibises. On one occasion, Chioke saw a wise and cunning tortoise. He did not expect to see one here so far away from Igboland. Like the stories of his childhood, the tortoise had a bulky shell, elephantine hind feet, and shovel-like forefeet. It had a yellowish undershell and seemed intensely burrowing as they passed. Alligators and snakes were everywhere. The alligators kept their distance, sunning themselves, but the water and rat snakes seemed oblivious and regularly swam past the canoe. The snakes' wave-like movement propelled them swiftly, rippling the stagnant water as they passed. Sulfurous stenches sometimes belched from mudflats, and an odorous wet dog smell constantly emanated from the peat bogs. Despite the repulsions of the swamps, Chioke remained upbeat and enjoyed Catori's company as they paddled and talked.

⧗   ⧗   ⧗

Four days and nights passed. The wetlands appeared never-ending. They would canoe all day; the landscape would change constantly and yet appear the same. Cypress forest, meandering streams, tiny patches of dry land, wetland prairies, followed by more cypress forest, and motionless water everywhere. They would find a dry scrap of land at night, build their camp, light a fire, eat, and try to keep the mosquitoes away. It was a laborious journey.

Suddenly, the landscape changed. The swampland gave way to open forests, and pine trees superseded the ever-present cypress trees. More obvious Yamasee trails could be seen throughout the pine forest, and the meandering streams ended. The malignant odors dissipated in favor of the lemony tang of pine needles. Squirrels, deer, and turkeys replaced the snakes and alligators.

After their trip around Okefenokee, they found a decent place to conceal the canoe. It might be needed again by a Yamasee band heading the other way. The spot they picked was well-marked by prior campsites and nearby tracks. It was doubtful that the subsequent users would have the same challenges they'd experienced. Though, who knew if it was left as long as it had been before they recovered it.

Catori identified the overland route from Okefenokee, heading toward St. Augustine. It was still four days of hard-going foot travel before they arrived. Knowing the way ahead would be much easier; they set about their travel with much enthusiasm. Walking briskly and occasionally running through the forests, they made progress quickly. With unerring perception, Catori led the way. She stopped sporadically to read the signs of the forest but soon continued knowing exactly where to head next. As the journey progressed, they happened upon well-used Yamasee campsites, which they used to camp each night. Often, Catori would inspect the campfire's charcoal to assess when the spot was last occupied. Gradually, timeframes narrowed from a few weeks to a few days, and they fully expected to meet another band of Yamasee soon. It was not a surprise when it happened.

As they exited a compact forest of pines into a meadow area, a group of warriors could be seen in the distance. Catori stopped briefly to inspect the party to ensure they were friends and not foes. The headdresses, hairstyles, and outfits confirmed they had reached another band of Yamasee. She signaled with a high-pitched hoot and received a reply. The two groups raced across the grasslands, hurdling mounds as they went. The welcome was warm. Traditional greetings were shared, and arms were grasped. Chioke knew that the days to follow would be hard on Catori. She would relive the bad moments crossing Creek enemy territory and fall back into a stupor, blaming herself for the loss of their comrades. He promised to stay by Catori's side while she reported back to the chiefs and to help her through the moments of self-examination and reflection. She had been a blameless and effective leader, leading a dangerous mission that had gone wrong unluckily. Chioke wanted to ensure she knew it and that he would protect her reputation amongst the tribe's warriors should questions arise.

Chapter 31: Futch-Kitt

The morning sun flashed through the lodge's open side. Its sudden warmth awakened Tom. The air smelled of an earthy, wooden smell, peaty like mushrooms. His head pounded as if he'd been hit over the head with a carpenter's hammer. Tom felt an odd tingling sensation across his temples like ants crawling around in his brain. Despite these undesirable effects, he had a strange sense of serenity. A perception of feeling outside himself, joyful, and positive for the day to come. He closed his eyes and tried to recall the disjointed memories that flitted within his mind. The ceremony was there, and there was alligator stew, singing, and dancing. The chief's transformation and the visions of alligator spirits swirling in the ether—dreams, strange and unreal. Tom sat and rubbed his temples intensely. He'd fallen asleep fully dressed near the fire, and the clan had left him to his hallucinations. The brew the chief prepared must have been a drug. Pungent and earthy, it was undoubtedly a strange taste and had done something to him.

As Tom rubbed stiff limbs, Hilli entered the lodge hurriedly, speaking his pidgin English, "Come, Tom, move, wake up.

It is time for trials; we only have a day. Oglethorpe leaves tomorrow!" Tom arose and followed Hilli. As they made their way to the tribe's sports field, Hilli shared the gist of what was happening. Unexpectedly, Oglethorpe, Mary Musgrove, and Toonahowi had completed their negotiations, and Georgia's delegation was due to leave. Pipes had been smoked, gifts promised, and the red sticks of war had been declared. The Lower Creeks had granted an alliance and would fight against the Spanish, Yamasee, and Seminoles once war was declared. For Tom, it meant he had to cram all his clan trials into one day to be initiated. It was going to be a taxing day indeed.

⧗ ⧗ ⧗

They quickly made their way to Coweta's *afvcketv* field. Pronounced Ah-futch-kitt-uh, Tom had never been able to say the Muskogean word and always called it Futch-kitt. All of Tom's trials would be undertaken in the sacred arena. It was an ample open space, warmed by the sun and compacted level over many generations of play. Mostly dusty, dry mud, it had infrequent patches of short grass and the odd hazardous divet. Pine trees surrounded the field on three sides. Well-worn paths traced directly from Coweta to the open side of the field. The pitch was surrounded by viewing areas, and from their size, Tom could tell games drew sizable crowds. Tom last watched the sport on a makeshift field outside Savannah. Consequently, he was surprised to see two ten-meter poles at each end of the field. Massive skulls with big, sharp canine teeth and numerous flat molars sat on each pole. Bear skulls, each painted vivid red, stood out from a distance. As they arrived, Tom spotted alligator clansmen gathered in the middle of the field, and a few children, primarily boys, were reaching one of the viewing areas. They hoped to catch Tom's performance in the tryouts.

Hilli led Tom to the center of the field, where he saw Sin, the alligator clan chief, and an assembled group of witnesses, maybe twenty warriors. Tom's prowess as a warrior was to be tested and his weapons sanctified. Sin welcomed his two friends, and the clansmen formally greeted him. Tom's head still ached, and his eyes gave off a weird, fuzzy feeling. The heightened sense of presence, though, caused by the hallucinogenic drug, might play to his advantage. As the warriors parted, Tom noticed his first test and was overjoyed. Two circular targets stood in the center of the field. Tomahawks were placed nearby. Soon, Tom was invited to throw his tomahawk at the smaller of the two targets. He played this game many times with Hilli, Sin, and Umphichi and had become reasonably accomplished. It was simple enough. You throw the tomahawk at the target and get points for hitting. The closer to the middle, the more points you receive. Tom threw his tomahawk three times; it hit the target dead center each time. Maximum points from his first test. His witnesses looked at each other, grinning, while some children jumped with glee and raced away toward town.

As the alligator clansmen set up Tom's next test, more children arrived, and a couple of warriors from another clan came with them. They all watched with anticipation. Tom was delighted to see what was next; it seemed almost unfair. He was to use his principal weapon to shoot the larger target from a distance. The test was usually done with a bow and arrow. Tom thought it wrong to use a rifle at such a distance; it couldn't have been more than thirty yards. After negotiation via Hilli, they lengthened the gap to one hundred yards and switched to the smaller target. Tom was allowed three shots to hit the target. He knew he'd only need one to hit the bullseye. He unslung his ornately decorated rifle and loaded it carefully. Ramming the shot down the grooved barrel took longer than he would have liked. Once it was primed, he lifted, aimed, and fired. The bullet struck perfectly. A flick of straw from the target provided all the evidence Tom needed that his shot was accurate. The target pitched over. As the warriors inspected his marksmanship, they were astonished. Hilli and Sin smiled and waved at him across the field. They knew how good Tom's shooting was and enjoyed seeing their comrades perplexed by the outcome.

More spectators arrived as news of Tom's successes drifted back to Coweta. The small viewing area occupied by the children was now packed with onlookers. He'd passed the first two tests exceptionally and had consecrated his weapons, but he wasn't sure what might follow. No training or preparation had been allowed, so he wasn't aware of everything that would be asked of him. The next one was entirely new. All the warriors were led to the field's far end, near the futch-kitt pole. It appeared that they were to race each other across the field. Tom knew how his Yamacraw friends could outpace any Englishman he knew and feared his performance might not stack up. The chief dropped a rag, and they all sprinted as speedily as they could across the field. It turned out Hilli and Sin were exceptional runners. They sped off ahead of everybody and arrived almost simultaneously. Tom had run with them often; having learned from them, he followed them closely. Several other warriors matched Tom's pace, but the remainder lagged, arriving several lengths behind him. Another trial passed. The crowd seemed converted to Tom's cause and cheered him on as he sped just behind his friends. More watchers arrived.

The tests followed in quick succession. Stick fighting, like the British single stick training for swordsmanship, but with a longer stick and using both ends. Another of Tom's strengths. Quick wins and embarrassment for Tom's competitors. Next wrestling. This was not something Tom had done before, but he was much taller than his competitors and had gained incredible strength from his carpentry work. Another series of wins and an additional initiation hurdle cleared.

Then, the inevitable happened—the final test and disaster. The game was called chunkey. It involved rolling a fist-sized stone across the field and immediately throwing a spear. The aim was to have one's spear land closest to where the stone stopped. Tom had never seen the game before; all the warriors were experts. He was embarrassingly bad at it. His first throw landed twenty feet away from the stone when everybody else's landed within a foot or two. Tom's second throw was better, but he rolled the stone poorly. He found it difficult to concentrate on the javelin and chunkey stone simultaneously. Everybody's spears were far from the stone, which settled barely twenty feet from Tom's toss. The alligator clansmen all moaned at him, and there was audible laughing from rival clansmen watching in the crowd. Tom had one more chance. Failure was a real prospect, and he wasn't sure what it could mean. With some trepidation, he ran forward, ready to roll the stone and launch the spear. Just as he reached the hurling position, disaster struck. Tom tripped over one of the field's many divots and fell. Desperately, as he tumbled, he rolled the stone and threw the javelin. Divine intervention must have occurred. As Tom scrambled back to his feet, wiping dust off his face, he was in time to see a pure fluke. The stone had rolled well, and the spear appeared connected, following its trajectory perfectly. As the stone came to a halt, the spear hit it. There was an audible thud. The crowd went silent and then shouted with delight. It was rare to score a hit, and Tom had somehow pulled off the impossible accidentally. Hilli and Sin hooted with delight; they'd always considered him a lucky warrior, and here was further proof.

The alligator clansmen congregated around Tom quickly, congratulating him. They were unusually affectionate, slapping him on the back, hugging him, ruffling his hair, and pinching his cheeks. Tom smiled broadly. It appeared they'd accepted him into the clan, and his trial was over. The clan's witnesses grabbed him and lifted him onto their shoulders. The group held him high and carried him over to the gathered spectators. While holding Tom up, the alligator clansmen chanted, sang, and hissed at the crowd. It was a challenge that all understood. A new alligator clansman had been initiated, which meant only one thing. The clan was defying their rivals to come and meet them on the futch-kitt field.

Runners were sent back to Coweta. Soon, all manner of folks were arriving. First to arrive, running in formation, were the remaining alligator clansmen; nearly forty warriors joined Tom's initiation witnesses. Dribs and drabs of townsfolk began to come, followed by small groups, and then huge crowds began to appear—all the field's viewing areas filled up with the hustle and bustle of thronged masses. Refreshment vendors turned up amongst the multitudes and started selling cornbread, turkey legs, and dried fruit snacks. A massive cheer occurred when the alligator's rivals arrived. Another clan of fifty-plus warriors jogged onto the field in battle dress. Tom could tell from their attire and the assorted pelts they wore that it was Coweta's beaver clan, and he was delighted to see Umphichi among them.

Tom was ecstatic. A game of futch-kitt was evidently about to happen and in his honor. He hoped he would be

314

allowed to play. It had been a dream since he'd first seen the game outside the gates of Savannah. Each clan began to prepare themselves for the contest. The warriors stretched and drilled all over the field, getting ready. The crowd whistled, hissed, and hooted, depending on which clan they supported. Clansmen across the field fetched sticks with nets attached and small deerskin leather balls the size of a fist. Preparing for the game, they began to throw the balls at each other, using the stick to launch the ball and the net to catch it. A few encircled the futch-kitt poles and practiced trying to hit the red bear skulls with the balls.

Sin told Tom, "You're a part of the clan now, so you'll be playing. Stay on the side and watch for a bit before you come on. It's simple, though. The clan gets points when it hits the other side's pole and more points if it hits the skull. You can run with the ball in your net or pass it by throwing it to somebody else. The clan must keep the ball and advance it up the field. The other team can stop a player from moving. When you're ready, join in. It's fun, you'll love it!"

Sin and Hilli raced off to begin practicing with the rest of the clan. Tom picked up a stick. About three feet long, it was made of hickory. It felt light in his hand and was flexible while also seeming durable. The net was small, just large enough for the ball, and circular. He couldn't tell what it was made of, and it looked like some wicker. Tom ran onto the field, selected a ball, and placed it in the net. He figured catching a ball moving at speed would be pretty hard. Tom called out to Hilli, got his attention, and threw the ball. Throwing the ball was easy, and Hilli expertly caught it. The moment of truth arrived when Hilli sent it back in Tom's direction. It went over some distance, relatively high into the air, arched, and then plummeted downward swiftly. Tom completely missed it, and the ball bounced towards one of the observation areas. He picked up another ball and tried again. On the second attempt, he clumsily caught it. Tom and Hilli continued to practice until the game started. After a few minutes of training, Tom felt he could throw the ball relatively well but knew he was a lousy catcher. Like most things, the game would require some time and experience.

Before long, the game started. Tom followed Sin's advice and crouched at the side of the pitch, watching and trying to learn what he could before entering the fray. The crowd was excited at the start of the game, and there was a lot of celebration. Tom had once seen a game of football between two villages in England. It was a brutal sport, with lots of physical contact, few apparent rules, and no referees. The ball had to get from one end of the field to another. Futch-kitt looked like the Creek version of English football but with much less contact. As Tom's sponsors, Sin and Hilli had the honor of starting the game. Sin fired the ball over to Hilli, who caught it seamlessly. He ran a few paces, jigged to one side, evading the stick of a competitor, and hurled it to another clansman.

As Tom watched, he got a sense of the game. The first noticeable difference was that there was no physical contact. English football could be brutal. Players got broken arms or legs as they fought each other to move the ball along. In Futch-kitt, the players moved, ran with the ball in the net, and passed it. The opposing team would try to stop them by knocking the ball out of the net with their stick. Occasionally, players would barge at each other or collide, but there was no deliberate aggression against another player. The other evident difference was that nobody touched the ball. In English football, players kicked, carried, and threw the ball and touched it constantly as they tried to move it or stop it from progressing. In Futch-kitt the participants only touched the ball with nets. They'd try to whack another player's stick to make the ball spill to the ground. They would sweep the ball off the surface with the net and use it to throw or catch it. No player touched the ball with a hand or other body part unless by accident. In English football, a team scored when they got the ball over the opposing team's goal line. Scoring in Futch-kitt required a lot more skill on the attacker's part. Tom saw several shots on goal that flew well wide of the pole and a couple of attempts at the bear skull that went too low. It took some skill to move the ball downfield with so many opposing competitors, and once it went downfield, it was tricky to score. Tom concluded that it was a much more civilized sport.

Tom had seen enough; he decided to join in. As he raced across the pitch to position himself near Hilli and Sin, the crowd roared their approval, and an entire field of competitors on both sides stopped and welcomed him. It was a special moment for everybody. He was a new member of the Lower Creek's alligator clan and the first Englishman to play Futch-kitt. As the game restarted, Tom settled in. There was much running and movement; the game required stamina and agility. It was fast-paced. The ball moved with speed. It whizzed through the air and bounced along the ground swiftly. It was technically challenging. Tom found throwing the ball much more difficult while being opposed. Angles changed, sticks collided, and the ball sometimes got swatted away by an opposing stick. Though little contact, odd bumps, nudges, and barges made keeping the ball tough. Catching the ball in a tiny net was already challenging, and it became much more so when those around tried to steal your catch.

Tom's first Futch-kitt game would not live in the annals of the Creek tribe other than the novelty of having an Englishman play. He dropped the ball several times. He missed it twice and only caught it once. He had one shot on goal that went embarrassingly wide to the left-hand side. Tom's only saving grace was his keen eye and athleticism. His ability to run endlessly at speed, scoop up the ball successfully, and throw it safely to a team member was noted by the tribe and his clan that day.

Chapter 32: A New Identity

Captain Lamine stood to attention as the sun dipped low over the parade ground. His eyes intelligently scrutinized the gathered ranks of the free black militia. Each man looked fatigued and yet steadfast. The militia bore the telltale signs of their latest hardships. Everybody's clothes were dusty. Faces were streaming with sweat, and the men's eyes held the tiredness that naturally accompanied countless training exercises. Lamine saw tenacity and determination in those eyes and something else, something new: a sense of togetherness. He felt a profound sense of pride as he admired the men. Since the beginning of training, many hardships had been overcome, and these had forged the militia into a unit, brothers-in-arms, tied together by a common purpose. It was clear what they aimed to do. Defend the liberty that Jemmy's rebels had shouted for during their long and unsuccessful march south to escape the clutches of slavery. They were free blacks, and they intended to stay that way. To do so, they would have to fight for the Spanish, protect St. Augustine, and ensure the British did not gain a foothold in Florida.

As Captain Lamine prepared to dismiss the gathered militiamen, he wondered about their success. Erstwhile enemies stood next to each other, ready to fight for each other. Mandingo, Fulani, Yoruba, Kongolese, and Igbo, among other tribesmen, endured together as one. Living together in Mose had already minimized old animosities, but the militia unit and their training had brought them a new sense of identity, simultaneously African and something else. Lamine wasn't sure what it was. They were not Spanish, but they would fight as if they were. He turned to Major Menéndez, who spoke to Lamine, "Captain, dismiss the men!". Once Lamine gave the command, the militia's fifty men relaxed their pose and departed the training ground.

Lamine had been impressed by Major Menéndez. The man would go far despite his Mandingo origins, the traditional enemy of Lamine's tribe. He'd spent considerable time with his commander, had shared stories about Jemmy's rebellion and the Edisto Battle, and was convinced that Major Menéndez hated the South Carolinians as much as Jemmy had. The man would fight with ferocity if the British did invade the south. He was intelligent, commanded loyalty and respect, and had a natural, uncanny strategic sense. They were fortunate to have such a competent commander, especially since none of them had been trained for this type of warfare.

Lamine reflected on the work they'd done. It had been several months since he was commissioned as a captain in the free black militia. Training had begun with many meetings. Major Menéndez and Captain Lamine had spent days and occasional evenings being briefed by Colonel Ramos. The colonel introduced them to Spanish military tactics. How to position musketeers in long thin lines to maximize the impact of musket volleys and in what way to reposition them into squares for defensive operations. He explained the purpose of the forts and castles dotted across the region: to protect trade routes and defend local territories. Colonel Ramos reviewed the tactics for withdrawing these forces to the Castillo de San Marcos if the British attacked in strength. He used drawings to explain how to protect and defend a fort and described Spanish artillery tactics. The colonel discussed the role of their Native American allies and how they were deployed as scouts, harrying in force and used for ambuscades. One evening, over a glass of wine, the colonel had advised them to buy heavy leather clothing "To protect yourselves from Creek arrows."

Once their tactical education as militia officers was completed, the Spanish called up the militia and began basic training. Major Menéndez's and Captain Lamine's first job was identifying and commissioning junior officers. They knew the men well and made decisions quickly and judiciously, handing commissions out across the tribes. A Yoruba lieutenant was to work with an Igbo sergeant and Fulani corporal, while a Kongolese lieutenant worked with a Mossi sergeant and a Mandingo corporal. They chose respectable, trustworthy, and intelligent men from the Mose community. Traders, storekeepers, medicine men, and bakers became officers. These new leaders were taught Spanish military tactics. After the officers were appointed, Major Menéndez formed the militia. All able-bodied men between sixteen and sixty were called to serve. The free black militia was composed of just over fifty men. Lamine noted that some had been warriors in their former tribes while others were weak and almost useless. He worked with the major to form some more formidable, elite units from these men. The other weaker detachments were allotted to be reserves or supply units.

Basic training began before the equipment was available. They fashioned fake guns from wooden branches and carved them into the same shape and weight as muskets. Drills started every day in the morning. The militia formed at daybreak and exercised for an hour by jogging and sprinting between Fort Mose and the Castillo. Their morning exercise included wrestling and spear fighting. The Spanish soldiers laughed at such antics, but the Africans knew the benefits of fitness. Speed, agility, and strength mattered when you fought in the bush. Despite the range of abilities in the militia, Major Menéndez didn't want to lose a single man because of his lack of fitness.

During the day, the militiamen returned to Fort Mose and fulfilled their civic duties, carrying out their regular day jobs. Late in the afternoon, they reformed on the parade ground and began to learn the Spanish infantry tactics. Without real weapons, these efforts started by simulated loading and firing of their wooden muskets and pretend bayonet stabbing practices. While the militiamen gained the basic principles of this form of fighting, it was alien to most of them, and the lack of real guns made these practices seem superficial.

At night, and away from the gaze of the Spanish, the militia shared and practiced traditional fighting methods from the various tribes. The Igbo taught traditional wrestling techniques, including unique tribal throws, holds, and trips. The Fulani introduced the militia to Sharo, stick whip matches designed to increase pain resilience, endurance, and courage. The Yoruba taught their martial arts with unique techniques for hand-to-hand combat. The Mandingo secretly introduced their approaches to fighting with blowguns and harpoons. Sharing tribal practices across the free black militia became a source of pride for many. Lamine observed that it served two purposes. It became a glue that held the men together while increasing the potency of the force they trained. No troop in history would have the variety of fighting techniques these men were learning. If only Jemmy's rebellion had been successful. They might have created a formidable free black army if they had more men.

As the days passed, the militia became much fitter and more proficient with the various tactics they were learning. Major Menéndez's and Captain Lamine's pride in the men grew as their competencies increased. Fashioning such a fighting force from everyday artisans, workers, and fieldhands was a profound accomplishment. Eventually, the Spanish supplied the militia with muskets, balls, and gunpowder, along with bayonets, long knives, machetes, and pikes. It was not enough to equip everybody, so Major Menéndez allocated them to the two units formed from former warriors. The powder was also at a premium in the colony, and they couldn't afford to waste it. So, drills progressed with loading and simulated firing exercises using the muskets they did have, along with using them for more realistic bayonet practices. Everybody had a turn, but the elite units became much more proficient and had the opportunity for a few practice firings.

At this point, Lamine's confidence in the militia took a significant hit. While they had learned how to load and fire quickly and were nearly as quick as the Spanish, their marksmanship was atrocious. Nobody hit the target in their first practice. Almost all the musket balls flew high or wide. They did not have enough shot or powder to practice enough to improve much. It was clear to Major Menéndez and Captain Lamine that the militia would be extremely dangerous at close quarters in hand-to-hand combat, but they might not be useful in a fixed engagement between infantries. They knew the British regulars had a prodigious reputation for firing speed and accuracy in such encounters. It didn't seem likely that the militia would be able to get to a point where it might serve well against such a foe. It was possible, though, that they might stand a chance against the Creeks or the British militia.

As the men worked on their duties and drills, the women of the community set about ensuring the resilience of the fortifications. They took pride in learning basic carpentry and fixed gaps, deterioration, and flaws in the fortifications and gantries surrounding the town. Other groups of women improved the town's wells and wooden aqueducts. They followed the lead of the Castillo and started to stock foodstuffs, dried fish, and smoked meat. Groups of children were sent out across the landscape to collect berries and nuts, which were stored in ceramic pots. Stews, soups, and broths were cooked to keep the militia fed while they trained. The women sourced new cloth, darned, weaved, and fixed old clothes so that the men were kitted out in rudimentary uniforms. Leather was tanned and fashioned into crude armor; leg, arm, and chest guards were demanded. The entire town entered a war footing, and the black community in Fort Mose was as active as the Castillo de San Marcos preparing for a possible British siege.

General Manuel de Montiano and Colonel Ramos had been so impressed with the progress of the black militia under the stewardship of Major Menéndez and Captain Lamine that they'd taken time out of their planning and preparations to address the men. It had been a day to remember. General Manuel de Montiano was an impressive figure; he bore all the characteristics of a veteran commander. A man of medium build, the general stood erect as he addressed the militia. His face was weathered by the Florida sun, and a neatly trimmed beard framed it. His eyes were sharp and watchful, conveying wisdom and awareness of everyone's qualities. Montiano wore the attire of a high-ranking officer: a richly ornamented uniform, complete with epaulets and a sash, symbolizing his rank. The fastidiously maintained uniform featured vibrant colors and intricate embroidery. A tricorne hat perched confidently atop his head added to his distinguished appearance, and he carried a finely crafted sword.

As Lamine watched the unit departing the parade ground, he remembered General Manuel de Montiano's recent and inspiring words, "I have come here today to look you all in the eyes and tell you, you have been noticed. We see you! We welcome you as freemen who have chosen to fight with us for a common cause. Your tireless drills, your tenacious training, and your daily efforts to prepare have been seen. You've built a resilient community here alongside us, and we value it. When the British come, and they will come, their lust for Florida will drive them here. We will be ready, you will be ready, and together we will repel them. We will send them back to South Carolina with their tails between their legs, and then we will reclaim the disputed lands; we will win back Gaule from the British! War is declared between Spain and Britain! The moment of our future has arisen. We will fight together against their yoke, against the oppression that follows them everywhere, and our freedom will prevail!"

Lamine knew they were well-chosen words. Despite the range of languages spoken, all understood the sentiment, and the free black militia celebrated as if freedom itself had been guaranteed. It was the first time Captain Lamine had met General Manuel de Montiano, and the impression would live with him forever. He was some leader, this general, and the colony of Florida was ready for the British invasion. They knew it would occur as soon as war was declared, and now it was only a matter of time.

Chapter 33: A Storm Approaches

Translucent shimmering depths surrounded them for as far as the eye could see. There was an ominous stillness that had alerted Captain Drayton. He marched up and down Freedom's deck, scanning the horizon with his looking glass. The captain's red hair and vibrant beard made the man stand out from a distance. O'Sullivan was perched in the crow's nest, watching the captain and scanning the skyline. As far as he could tell, there was no sign of a gale despite the odd stillness of the wind. The crew was visible across the ship's decks and rigging, preparing her in case the captain's fears of a hurricane were realized. Morning mist hovered across the waters to their stern. Freedom's oak hull, weathered by her many voyages, creaked as she slid through the seawater. The unrelenting corrosion of salt and brine had taken a toll, and the ship was overdue for a return to harbor. Three towering masts and sagging sails surrounded O'Sullivan as he continued to scrutinize the clouds and vista. He picked up the signal flag and once again waved it. Captain Drake acknowledged the negative observation but continued pacing the deck and preparing the crew. The captain's instinct and experience had heightened his anxiety, and the man was rarely wrong about dire weather.

Freedom was on her return journey, and O'Sullivan was grateful to be heading toward Florida. The crew had become suspicious of his French accent and backstory. Many sailors had histories, so they'd not snooped into his affairs too much, but it was enough for O'Sullivan to become cautious. At the end of the day, he was a Spanish spy trying to avoid capture by posing as a sailor on a British merchant ship. His ruse had risks, and O'Sullivan didn't fancy being hanged from the yardarm. He'd resolved to jump ship the moment the opportunity arose. Fate had, however, dealt him a terrible blow. They'd just heard from a passing fishing boat that war between Spain and Britain had been declared. It had been a sore blow to everybody. The Freedom's captain and crew profited from trade between the British North American colonies and the Spanish colonies in the Caribbean. War meant this trade had ended, so the ship was returning to South Carolina, the last place O'Sullivan wanted to go. War also meant the captain wouldn't go near Florida's waters and couldn't trade with the colony. There was no chance for O'Sullivan to flee back to his spymasters as he'd intended. He'd have to find a way to escape before the Freedom docked in Charles Town or he was likely a dead man.

O'Sullivan resumed his watch. As the morning mist cleared, the air became thick with an oppressive humidity. The distant sky, just moments earlier a tranquil blue, had begun to transform, and menacing, swirling grays could be spotted. O'Sullivan raised a new signal, confirming Captain Drake's nervousness. Orders were given, and the crew became a hub of activity as they began to furl and store the sails. O'Sullivan watched the brewing storm as the sails were gradually reduced across the ship. Sailors climbed the rigging and yanked ropes as they tied up the canvases to secure them from the coming tempest. With little to do but watch as the squall developed, O'Sullivan's mind wandered, reflecting on his recent experiences with the vessel.

He had been reassured when the Freedom had put out to sea from Charles Town's port. He had known that Governor Bull's net was likely closing around him and his spy network. Since then, he'd experienced moments of regret. O'Sullivan had left women he cared for and children behind. Perhaps the unintended casualties of his plotting. He didn't know and couldn't tell what had happened to them. The hope was there that they'd been spared or were thought to be non-essential aides in the conspiracy. His remorse sometimes went deeper, and he occasionally prayed for forgiveness for leading Jemmy and his followers to their deaths. The images of the rebellious slaves' skulls mounted on pikes often haunted his dreams. He was repentant but also aware of his aim to defend and elevate the true Catholic faith and fight Protestant heresy.

O'Sullivan's ruminations were interrupted as he noticed a gentle breeze buffeting the crow's nest. It was a light gust but carried foreboding of the coming hurricane. The ship began to rise and fall, evidence that the flat sea had turned and was becoming restless. O'Sullivan's perch began to move, undulating with the sea's movements. He held on more tightly. Being thrown overboard had as much attraction as dying on the gallows. Both were dreadful ways to die, which he intended to avoid. Returning to his thoughts, O'Sullivan reflected on Freedom's journey. They'd first headed up the coast and delivered their cargo of rice and tobacco from South Carolina to the port in New York, where it was picked up by another ship headed for Britain. It was a prosperous and vibrant city, full of merchants, sailors, and a hustle and bustle that O'Sullivan had seldom experienced elsewhere. The Freedom's crew spent many days visiting the pubs while loading the ship with illicit trade goods. It took much work to remove the ballast stones, open the inside of the ship's hull, and stash the highly prized cast iron products sought after by the Spanish. Eventually, the vessel was full of contraband, the hull was reinstalled, and the ballast returned. Freedom then left New York City.

As time ticked by, the wind began to pick up. O'Sullivan noticed a whistling as it blew through the ship's rigging. The waves grew more intense, and the little crow's nest bobbed back and forth more forcefully. O'Sullivan signaled to the captain again. It would soon be time to go. Descending would become increasingly precarious as the wind and waves pounded the ship. Carefully surveying the incoming flashes of lightning that illuminated the darkening sky, O'Sullivan felt he had a while longer. Captain Drake wanted to know when the storm would hit and wouldn't appreciate him abandoning his post precipitously. There was a distant, deep, resonant growl of thunder, giving more cause for concern. O'Sullivan didn't want to stay too long, but the storm was some distance away, and there was no rain yet. He noted that the crew had most of the sails wrapped up and were starting to tie everything on the deck down.

O'Sullivan momentarily returned to his thoughts. After New York, they'd headed to the Bahamas and begun the worst part of the voyage. Captain Drake went ashore with his first mate and a few of the crew. They'd purchased a batch of slaves to convey to Cuba and aimed to profitably trade under the Asiento de Negros, while using the slaves to further hide the smuggled goods. The irony hadn't escaped O'Sullivan. Despite the necessity of his subterfuge, Stono Rebellion conspirator turned slaver wasn't an epithet he'd welcome on his grave.

Fighting for others' freedom was far more attractive than transporting the enslaved in bondage to yet another unfamiliar place.

Suddenly, the storm was no longer a distant threat. The swells were becoming more severe; the motion would make return to the deck extremely risky. The mizzenmast almost seemed to sway like a twig in the strengthening wind and the mainmast felt like a giant was pushing it away from the incoming thunderstorm. O'Sullivan saw heavy rainfall sweep toward them like a wall. It was time to go. He raised the final signal and heard Captain Drake's distant commands. Sailors finished tying down the remaining ropes and sought cover below deck.

O'Sullivan took one last glance at his panoramic view of the inbound storm. It was going to be nasty. He gripped the hempen rope with his calloused hands, took a deep breath, and swung his legs over the edge of the nest. He found his first foothold on the ratlines. The ship reeled suddenly, and he was almost catapulted into oblivion. Though this was a practiced skill, it wouldn't be a typical descent. The rain was starting to whip across him. It made the ropes slick and slippery. The wind tore at his clothing, trying to drag his feet and hands away. Step by step, he climbed down. The wind continued tugging at his clothing, shrieking with increasing intensity through the rigging. Rainfall pummeled him like wet shrapnel. The ropes creaked and groaned in the chaotic confusion. The lurches and jerks became increasingly dangerous but less extreme as he went down. He'd timed it about right. If O'Sullivan had left it any longer, he surely would have been flung into the ether. Glancing down, he saw he was halfway there. He paused momentarily, took a deep breath, and then continued steadily. The gale hit the ship with full force as he reached the deck.

Rain swept the deck horizontally, and the wind smacked it with incredible force. Massive waves were thrown high across the starboard deck and crashed violently; seawater flooded everywhere. The vessel lurched, crested, and fell like a cork bobbing in colossal breakers. Captain Drake was the last man on deck, and he greeted O'Sullivan with an exhilarated smile. The captain was leaning into the gale, fighting to retain his footing, and his wild red hair and beard blew ferociously, but he was unconcerned. The captain grabbed O'Sullivan by the arm as he reached the hatch. No man could be left on deck alone in a storm, the captain's rule. They struggled with the hefty wooden trapdoor. Each time they raised it, the wind blew it shut. There was a chance they might get stuck on the quarterdeck just as the captain's grin began to fade. Sailors from below pushed hard on the hatch door and held the two men as they balanced perilously and navigated the steps down into the ship's hold.

Below deck, the crew began to wait out the storm and the tempestuous seas it had brewed. Freedom was flung around, dipping, dropping, and rising through the various swells. Adrift in the turbulence, the vessel creaked and moaned as if under immense pressure. The wooden hull was battered and beaten by the waves; sounds from the impacts were thunderous.

Inside the hull, the air was thick, dense, and hard to breathe. The stench of unwashed bodies, mixed with sweat and the fetid odor of human waste, persisted from the ship's last cargo. Left to fester in the heat, the aromas assaulted the senses with a nauseating relentlessness. The vile staleness and memories of captives shackled and confined led O'Sullivan to volunteer for the risky duties of the crow's nest. He'd suffered many things in his grim life, but he wished never to witness or smell a ship full of slaves again. It was only a short trip between the Bahamas and Cuba, nothing like the unforgiving Atlantic voyages, and the hold was only half full. Nevertheless, it had been a horrid business. Sickness had quickly penetrated the crowd of captives as they were cramped into the suffocating space. The ship had swiftly become a floating hell as illness descended, and it had been impossible to remove the pungent cocktail, which now lingered below deck. It was a cruel and inhuman trade, and O'Sullivan was thankful when he was permitted to climb up the mainmast and begin his work above the vessel. The light Caribbean winds drifting lazily through the sails had offered an olfactory escape from the nightmare below. It was a blessing none of the captives could hope for.

Despite the inhumanity of the tactic, the ruse worked. O'Sullivan reflected as he held forcefully to a bulkhead, trying hard not to be thrown around by the rollers. As they approached Cuba, the dreaded Spanish coastguard caught them. Three fast sloops suddenly appeared on the horizon. With incredible speed, they had chased Freedom and overtaken her rapidly. Their smuggler's timing had been fortuitous. War hadn't been declared, or the declaration hadn't yet reached the Governor of Cuba. The ship wasn't seized, nor was the crew arrested. The Guarda Costa boarded their vessel, though, looking for suspected contraband. O'Sullivan was astonished to see the fabled coast guard leader Fandiño commanding the three vessels and was tempted to desert Freedom immediately. His usual cautiousness and watchfulness made him pause. As the Guarda Costa crew boarded the vessel, it was apparent that this outfit was best avoided. It was a brutal-looking band of mulattos, mestizos, the formally enslaved, and natives. Hardened weather-beaten sailors who you might wish to avoid in a port's dark, narrow alleys. O'Sullivan regretted it now that they were headed toward Charles Town, but at the time, he'd chosen to take his chances with Captain Drake and the Freedom's crew.

A sudden lurch downward reminded O'Sullivan to hang on tightly as the storm buffeted the ship. He was almost thrown across the floor but quickly returned to his recollections of the Guarda Costa. They'd corralled Freedom's crew in the vessel's stern while they searched for the stashed trade goods. Even the indomitable spirit of Captain Drake was curtailed by the ominous presence of Fandiño. The man was fleshy but had a hardness underlying it that suggested immense power. He was dirty and unkempt, but the cutlass hanging by his side hinted at a brutal streak. Astute eyes, a disconcerting lack of blinking, and scars crisscrossing his face and hands told a story of a long, dangerous life at sea. The desiccated ear that hung around his neck, his long black hair, and his beard made him the picture of a pirate in O'Sullivan's mind.

Freedom's crew were surrounded by an evil-looking group of Fandiño's men while others searched the vessel. Despite ripping everything apart, the Guarda Costa failed to find anything. Captain Drake knew his business and was rich for a reason. The combination of efforts to hide their items worked. The disgust from the stench of the slaves and the inability to move them from the hold made the searchers work too quickly and overlook recent changes to the hull. The ballast, which was heavy and difficult to move, meant the stashed goods were hard to access. Finally, the replaced oak boards concealed all evidence of the smuggling. It was proven to be an effective technique. It confused Fandiño's men, and it worked once again. After a period of bluster and threats, Fandiño gave up and let Freedom go.

O'Sullivan noted that the pitches and swells of the storm were beginning to dissipate. It would be past them soon, and they could return to their duties above deck. Before long, he'd climb back into the crow's nest and could get away from the stale reek. It seemed the ship would never again be free of it. As he contemplated climbing the ropes, he recalled the final moments of their smuggling efforts. They'd got to Cuba, spent a few days working with their collaborators to remove the slaves and sell all the goods, both the slaves and booty, and then set out to sea again. Their timing had been providential; the notice of war must have arrived soon after. The hairs on O'Sullivan's neck rose to attention, just contemplating what might have happened if Fandiño's coastguard had caught up and boarded them again. It would have been a bloodbath, and O'Sullivan probably wouldn't have had enough time to switch sides and reveal himself as a Spanish spy.

Chapter 34: Guerra del Asiento

Hernando stared at the glistening creek. The skiff knifed through the spray, urgently seeking out its destination. His unit was on a critical mission, perhaps the first engagement in the War of the Agreement. Moments like these convinced him he was a coward. It wasn't the impending skirmish that worried him but the water. It was everywhere. They had paddled up the creeks, rivers, and inlets from St. Augustine and now were near Amelia Island. Hernando had been scared the whole time. The brackish, silt-filled swamp water was omnipresent. It seemed never-ending. His constant fear of water and drowning reminded him of his days standing outside the inquisitor's door. The awful sound of a victim dying from a wet rag being forced down the throat had never entirely left Hernando. He sometimes awoke from terrible nightmares brought on by those memories. Those nightmares continuously provoked fear of drowning. As they had rowed up the coastline, he'd constantly dreaded that their skiff might be overturned. Each little swell from the coastal waves brought on a debilitating inward panic.

Hernando had other fears now. War had been announced and it seemed unlikely that Juana, and his beautiful children Isbel and María, would get to settle in Florida. There had been occasional letters, but contact was trying. Now, the soldiers' families were destined to stay in Spain, at least until the end of the war. He missed his family terribly, and all of the soldiers were depressed by the news. General de Montiano had promised that loved ones would follow and be allowed to come to Florida. It was hard on everybody, but they all understood that trips across the Atlantic would be precarious amid a war between two major naval powers.

Hernando scanned the skiffs as they meandered through a creek. Sergeant Moreno-Rodriguez was in the front boat alongside Lieutenant Sánchez with the first unit of their squad. Hernando's unit occupied the second craft. Juan paddled at the front, constantly cracking jokes. Alongside Juan, Miguel and Rodrigo laughed, as inseparable as ever. The big butcher Antonio smoldered in the center, increasingly irritated by Juan's jests. The youngsters Alvaro and Benito sat on either side of the huge man. Since the fights in Cuba, they'd become increasingly attached to Antonio, as if his vast bulk could protect them in battle. The rest of the unit, Gonzalo, Francisco, and Hernán, joined Hernando at the back. These were his family now. They did almost everything together and he knew they would fight to protect each other. Alvaro's and Benito's trust in their giant protector wasn't misplaced. Antonio would put his life on the line to prevent any harm to the two rookies. Each man felt the same way. They were brothers in arms and had committed to a lifetime of dedication to each other.

The two skiffs sculled along the leeward side of the island. It was a verdant paradise of lush greenery. Magnolias sat alongside ancient oaks, which were clothed in Spanish moss. A few pines were dotted amongst the trees. Palmettos lined the embankments; their fan-shaped leaves rustled softly as the two craft passed. Salt marshes stretched along the island's edges, and tall grasses bent in the light breeze. Across the island's sky, egrets flew, sailing low over the marshes. As he pulled at the oar, Hernando spotted an osprey hovering over the open cove, scanning the water for fish. He'd heard that giant sea turtles and dolphins could be observed hereabouts, but they'd seen none yet. The sounds of nature were everywhere: crickets were chirping, frogs were croaking, and the calls of various birds added music to the land.

The squad's mission was simple. They'd been dispatched to reinforce the makeshift fort that occupied the island's northern tip. A small British observation post had been set up nearby. It was a small log cabin that had sat on the island for some time. Since war had been declared, they were also ordered to neutralize the surveillance post. It was early morning, and mist stretched across the marshes, so they hoped to creep up on the site and surprise the occupants. Sergeant Moreno-Rodriguez was convinced the plan would work. The cabin had been there long, and the lookouts would likely have become careless. Hernando took one last fearful gaze at the swamp water and focused on the task. They would arrive shortly, and a quick skirmish was likely. There were over twenty men in the attacking squad, and only two Darien highlanders were expected to defend the site. Hernando checked his gun; it was loaded and primed. Unconsciously, his hand reached for the bayonet strapped to his webbing and he patted his gunpowder horn. After months in Florida, their breastplates were discarded as impractical. Hernando was grateful for this blessing. They were too heavy and hot to negotiate the Florida wilderness, and he was often scared that the weight would drown him, should they ever capsize.

The modest log cabin could be observed in the distance. Smoke billowed from its chimney, and haze surrounded its vegetable gardens. Tall deer fences had been installed to stop the animals from stealing the highlander's produce. Lieutenant Sánchez made a signal to command silence. The relief on Antonio's face was a picture of satisfaction as Juan's joking abruptly halted. While their offensive force would be overwhelming, they didn't want to take any chances of casualties. General Montiano's directions were clear. Every man was needed to defend St. Augustine, and no lazy mistakes would be accepted. Sánchez couldn't afford to alert the defenders needlessly. So, Sergeant Moreno-Rodriguez stared threateningly back at the men behind, just in case anybody had forgotten their orders. The Spanish soldiers quietly propelled their craft towards the embankment south of the log cabin. It had been used regularly. Hernando assumed to resupply the outpost.

There was a sudden thud as the first skiff hit the verge. Moments later, Hernando braced himself as his unit's boat hit home. A moment of panic flooded over him as he feared being flung overboard. He had no time to worry about it. In an instant, both units disembarked and crouched low behind some underbrush. The sergeant sent Gonzalo, Francisco, and Hernán to scout around the hut to check for booby traps and other dangers. Moments passed as they waited. Hernando could hear some crickets chirping nearby; their sound was thunderous. His breathing seemed loud. The two noises together felt like they could awaken a giant. Hernán returned to report the way clear. The scouts had removed all the entrapments designed to alert the highlanders of an approaching attack. Sánchez ordered the squad to encircle the hut. No risks would be taken, and overwhelming force would be used.

The surprise was complete. Twenty soldiers surrounded the observation point, and the defenders had no chance. The Spanish readied to fire. Just as they prepared, one barely dressed highlander exited the hut, preparing to undertake his morning trip to the privy. The shock on the man's face as he gazed at the barrels of numerous escopetas was eerie. Perplexed perhaps, resigned maybe, but not fearful. There was a steeliness in the highlander's face and an air of disdain. He possibly knew his fate yet headed toward it with an unbridled sense of dignity. He called out to his fellow, "Aodh, thig agus faic" (Hugh, come and look).

Hernando detected a strange language, not English, maybe Gaelic. A second highlander, also wearing undergarments, came to the door. He laughed out loud when he saw the Spanish. It was a genuinely perplexing response to their presence. Hernando watched as the two youngsters, Alvaro and Benito, responded, aghast. He could understand why. These highlanders were giant men, almost the size of Antonio. Their chests were covered in dense hair, muscles bulged, and their faces were contoured, chiseled, and worn. Thick beards covered their chins, hanging down to the nape of their necks, and long, bushy hair was tied back, running down their backs. The Spanish were in for a tough war if these men were the archetypical defenders of Georgia's frontier. Despite their predicament, the highlander's eyes betrayed only contempt. Hernando had a new fear to add to his growing list. Facing Scottish highlanders in battle didn't seem like a great idea. Unarmed and outnumbered, the Scots had no option but to raise their arms and surrender.

The turn of events had added a new complexion to the mission. In the first act of the war, they had been ordered to obliterate this long-suffered infiltration of the Spanish island. They weren't expecting to take prisoners. They hoped to set fire to the place and kill the spies in their beds. The Scots were roughly taken and tied up. Meanwhile, Lieutenant Sánchez and Sergeant Moreno-Rodriguez discussed their options. Taking prisoners south had limitations. Their boats were overloaded, and St. Augustine's castle was packed as the colony was preparing for siege warfare. Taking the spies to the small Spanish fort was highly risky. The outpost was poorly fortified, and should one of the Scots escape; they would surely take information about its weakness back to General Oglethorpe. Eventually, a decision was made.

Sergeant Moreno-Rodriguez pulled Antonio aside and engaged in a short conversation with the squad's butcher. Hernando dreaded the worst. If Antonio was to be deployed, it could only mean one thing, and nothing good would come of it. Moments later, Antonio headed toward the skiff and returned with his massive battle axe. It had a long oak handle designed for two-handed combat, a brutal hammer edge on one side, and a wicked-looking axe head on the other. It had been in Antonio's family for decades, and belonged to the medieval era. The axe head was sharp and regularly attended to, though it had a few nicks from prolonged use. Antonio marched up toward the log cabin, featuring a stern expression that betrayed his orders to all.

Lieutenant Sánchez had concluded these men were spies and not combatants. They'd lived on Spanish lands and spied on Amelia Island's Spanish garrison. They would die accordingly. Francisco and Gonzalo found a large log, and a group of soldiers moved it to the center of the yard. The two Scots were violently dragged across the yard. Despite the indignity of their treatment, the men continued to act resiliently. As they were kicked and cruelly beaten, the highlanders barely made a sound. The men's eyes became vacant, as if they'd accepted their fate and decided to withdraw from the scene. The first man, Aodh, was tugged to the log and held. His neck was exposed. The man didn't struggle. Antonio stepped up, looked down, and then swung his axe. It happened quickly. Antonio's great strength and the sharpness of the axe ended the man's life in seconds. The head was severed from the body, his last expression etched across his face. A strange look of serenity that seemed misplaced in the circumstances. Blood gushed out of the gaping wound across the trampled grass.

Hernando looked away as the second Scot was manhandled to his execution. The slaying spot was already a gruesome sight, and he'd seen enough. The second highlander swore quietly in Gaelic. It felt like a witch's curse, poignant and vituperative. Hernando heard the axe swing again and the telltale thump as it split muscle, tendons, and vertebrae. The second head fell to the floor, and the deed was done. As Hernando turned, he saw the look on Antonio's face; whatever spell the highlander had made, it had hit home. Antonio, a man of little expression, looked forlorn. He'd been jinxed, and he knew it.

As if to confirm the witch's curse, Hernán shouted and pointed across the cove. Another boat was several hundred yards away in the expanse of water. Several green-clad men sat in the boat, and it appeared they had just seen the Spanish executions of the two Scotsmen. They were too far away for a musket, yet there was the sudden retort of two weapons. The shots were incredibly accurate. One hit Antonio in the head, bursting his skull into smithereens, while the second struck him in the heart. He was dead instantly. The Scotsman's curse instantaneously came to pass. Recognizing it was outnumbered, the British ranger's boat retreated. The Spanish loaded the two bodies and severed heads of the Scotsmen into the cabin and set the building on fire. Hernando's squad picked up Antonio's colossal body and carried it to Amelia Island's fort for immediate burial. Losing their best man in the first action of the war seemed like a dreadful start, and the entire unit mourned Antonio's loss.

Chapter 35: Highlander Fury

Events had progressed quickly. After Tom's clan initiation and Futch-kitt game, he joined Oglethorpe's delegation for a speedy return to Fort Frederica. The trip home had been long but uneventful. Oglethorpe had fully recovered from his malady and returned to his usual energetic self. War was afoot, so Oglethorpe's time was dedicated to preparation. The formal declaration had arrived via courier just as they returned to Frederica. It seemed Oglethorpe was planning to invade Florida and take St. Augustine as soon as possible. The Yamacraws were dispatched to return Mary Musgrove to her trading post in Savannah and bring the rest of the Yamacraw warriors south. Following Oglethorpe's negotiations, their small unit of rangers had been accompanied by a large force of Lower Creek warriors, perhaps as many as two hundred strong. These men escorted Oglethorpe's skiffs and scouted along the banks of the river home. Consequently, there were no more Yamasee attempts on General Oglethorpe's life. Small detachments of Creek warriors were also now continuously scouting south of Fort Frederica in case the Spanish tried to attack. Tom occasionally spotted groups of warriors associated with his new clan, but as Hilli, Sin, and Umphichi had gone north, his interactions with the clan had been minimal.

The news they received on their return to Fort Frederica had been personally exhilarating and professionally depressing. Tom received a letter from Noble Jones sharing Mary's pregnancy. Tom was ecstatic; a rush of emotions surged through him. He grasped hold of the letter tightly in astonishment—a wave of joy, disbelief, and love washed over him. Warm emotions were suddenly followed by trepidation and fear of the responsibility of becoming a father in the middle of a war. His joy was tempered by the fact that he could not return to Savannah to be with Mary, to hug her, and to show her how happy he was. Tom's duties would keep him on the border waiting as the invasion force gathered. The rangers stepped into the void and took him to one of the local pubs, getting him drunk to celebrate. Afterward, thick with a hangover, Tom scribbled a letter to Noble Jones to read to Mary. Tom professed his love for her and shared his delight regarding the addition to their growing family. He hoped Uga was behaving, reminded Duke that he was almost a full-grown man now, and that he should help Mary around the house and gardens.

The news for Georgia was far more disheartening. There was no sign of the South Carolinians, and General Oglethorpe was apoplectic. The South Carolinian militia and rangers hadn't assembled at Fort Frederica as expected and were being held back by the colony's politicians. The army couldn't advance quickly on Florida without those forces; time and initiative were being lost, and coupled with this bad news, the colony learned of Tomochichi's death. The Yamacraw leader had been a stalwart supporter. Though well into his nineties and declining, Tomochichi had always brokered the relationship between the

Yamacraw and Georgia's settlers, even becoming a Christian. It felt like an era had passed, and all took a moment to reflect on the importance of the wise old owl's contribution to the founding years.

Oglethorpe ordered a military funeral for his friend and quickly departed for Savannah to organize it. Tom heard from an aide-de-camp that the general intended to head from the funeral to Charles Town to coax the South Carolinians to send their troops south so the war against Florida could begin.

⌛ ⌛ ⌛

So, here they were, back to their duties supplying the small highlander outpost on Amelia Island. Tom's unit had taken the usual route through the creeks and inlets past Jekyll and Cumberland islands. War had been declared, and they were entering Spanish Florida, so they were more alert than usual. Tom and Hill had loaded their rifles while Coleman and Sanders rowed the boat. It was an unusually crisp morning. Mist was rising, wispy and translucent across the marshlands. A covert of magnolias lined the bank; moss hung verdantly from each tree's branches. Salt marshes were vaguely visible through the fog. It was unusually cold, and a gentle breeze blew across the water. Tom rubbed his left arm. It had begun to tighten from the long period of holding his rifle. Hill fidgeted; he'd also become slightly uncomfortable. Despite the cooler weather, Coleman and Sanders were sweating. It was still hard work rowing, and undoubtedly, it would become hot and humid as the day progressed. Even though it was autumn, it remained oppressively muggy. Tom had concluded an age ago that early morning jaunts down to Amelia were best. It was much cooler, and there was less chance of being discovered.

Hums of crickets and frogs croaking joined the din of many birds calling their greetings to the new day. As they approached the Scottish hut, the craft steadily sliced through the gently undulating currents. They were a few hundred feet away when Tom heard a strange thud. It was a distinct sound of a boat hitting an embankment, and Tom recognized it instantly. His reaction was instantaneous. He quickly commanded the squad to stop rowing, observing the highlander's cottage from across the water. They gently rolled up and down as the tides moved the boat aimlessly. Hill and Tom were vigilant, guns at the ready. Something was wrong, and they all sensed it. Tom's breathing slowed, and the vapor from his lungs curled lazily like a haze in the crisp morning. A distinct but faint rustle drifted across them from the hut's garden. It was too early in the morning for Angus and Hugh to be up and about. Though it was tough to hear and be sure, the noise sounded alien. It didn't come from a deer, squirrel, or other animal Tom stalked. Then, there was another sound. Similar, perhaps, possibly a scuffed boot on rocky ground. Tom's senses were alive; something was amiss, and the squad knew his awareness was elevated. They observed the hut and its environs.

Moments later, the cottage and gardens were a hive of sudden activity. Several Spanish scouts abruptly appeared from nowhere. Positioned adjacent to each corner of the hut, they crouched and aimed their long muskets at the building. Hill pulled his gun to his shoulder, readying to shoot. Tom immediately cautioned him; it was too soon to engage. It was the correct decision. Rapidly, the scouts were followed by an entire squad of Spanish soldiers, perhaps as many as twenty men. Angus and Hugh were in trouble, and Tom's squad was outnumbered; they could not save the highlanders. It looked as if the Scots would become the first prisoners in the war.

Just as the squad surrounded the building, Angus emerged, stretching, welcoming the new morning. Surprised by his Spanish visitors, Angus called Hugh, who soon appeared. Both men were in their bedclothes, having just awoken. Unarmed, they raised their hands and surrendered. The highlanders were bound and guarded by several soldiers. Tom considered whether his squad might sneak up on those men and save their friends. Others soon joined them, and he concluded it would be a forlorn task that would fail.

The Spanish officers seemed to be in a discussion. The awful reality of that conversation was soon realized as soldiers were dispatched, soon to return with a huge log. The highlanders were dragged across to the center of the cottage's garden while being kicked and punched. Tom and Hill raised their rifles. So many Spanish surrounded the captives the rangers couldn't identify a clear target. A huge man was sent off and returned with a wicked-looking axe. They hauled Hugh over to the log, and things started to look desperate. Tom feared that they were about to witness an atrocity.

The Spanish soldiers gathered around, faces visibly curious with morbid anticipation. The bulky figure of the executioner stepped forward; his axe gleamed ominously. Even from a distance, the axe appeared sharp and menacing. Hugh was forced to kneel, his head and neck exposed, ready for the chop. It was over quickly. The colossal soldier raised his weapon, and then the axe fell, fast and callously. The sound reverberated across the water to Tom's boat. It was a sickening thwack. Hugh's head rolled onto the floor, and his body became a limp corpse. There was nothing Tom could do. His men looked on in disgust and anger as they witnessed the first brutal act of the new war. They tried again to get a clear shot, but none was offered. The Spanish soldiers moved Hugh's decapitated body and then hauled Angus up to the killing ground. Angus muttered something, but it was inaudible from a distance. The axe fell again, and the second outrage of the day was concluded. Tom was bereft. The two highlanders had become friends over the many months his unit had run supplies to them, and Tom's men would feel the loss keenly.

At that moment, the opportunity they'd been waiting for arrived. The soldiers began to move the bodies of the two dead men and opened a clear shot. Now that the highlanders had been executed, Tom didn't need to worry about collateral damage. He preferred to assassinate the commanding officer, but the man who committed the act would do. As the Spanish soldiers moved, the huge axe man became visible across the water. It was well over a hundred yards, and a gentle swell rocked the boat—a challenging but not impossible shot. Tom commanded Hill angrily, "Now's our chance for justice! Take down that big oaf and let's get out of here!" Just as they prepared to shoot, there was a yell from onshore; the axe man turned and faced them. They fired simultaneously. The rifle kicked into Tom's shoulder as the flint struck the frizzen. Sparks showered around them as the powder ignited. There was a harsh crack, a haze of smoke, and an echo of two rifles' retorts. As Tom peered through the cloud from the two guns, it was evident that their shots were accurate. The big man was down, and the squad of Spanish soldiers sought cover. Tom's squad was too far away for the Spanish muskets, but they were outnumbered, and it was time to leave. A small token of retribution exacted for the deaths of Hugh and Angus. Tom's unit left the scene speedily. He didn't want to take the risk that the Spanish would follow and overwhelm them. As they left, the outpost was set on fire, and they saw flames licking the outside of the building and smoke billowing from the roof.

Tom's unit headed straight for Fort Frederica; the Spanish had attacked, and he must raise the alarm. It took a few hours of hard rowing. They were exhausted by the time they returned to the fort. Captain Mackay was hurriedly informed about the extrajudicial murders of Angus and Hugh. Tom had never seen the man so incensed. The captain assembled a combined force of the 42nd regiment and a substantial contingent of Darien Highlanders. He requisitioned craft to carry the sizable attacking force toward the Spanish fort on Amelia Island. It took hours to assemble. Tom's unit, shattered from their morning of rowing, wasn't expected to join the expedition. By the time the British attackers arrived, the Spanish fort had been set on fire, and the Spanish had retreated. The highlanders' revenge for the Spanish murders would have to wait until General Oglethorpe's return with the South Carolinian militia and rangers. The men from Darien were outraged by the atrocity. It was an insidious start to the confrontations that were to follow.

Chapter 36: Political Gridlock

Williams' visits to the old cemetery had become increasingly common. He often sat and talked to his friend, sharing the details of Acting Governor Bull's latest furies. Williams regularly tended the grave, which was becoming as pleasing as the graveyard itself. He'd planted some miniature roses; their white buds were starting to appear. Alongside them was a bed of azaleas and camellias. The slighter pink flowers of the azaleas lay alongside the profusion of white camellia blooms, with their grander and more complex petal structures. The abundance of floral scents from the garden was almost overpowering. It was not unusual for Williams to sit eating a poor lunch of oat cakes and jerky while talking to his long-dead friend. As he chomped on a chunk of overly salted beef jerky, he reflected on the latest political gridlock that was making Bull angry. Williams knew Colonel Bull was livid again by the number of items he'd thrown recently. The volume and velocity of objects propelled at him had gone up. Bull was a hard taskmaster, but Williams had finally gotten as accomplished as Evans, anticipating the man's fits. He was becoming adept at dodging the projectiles, too.

The Acting Governor was furious with South Carolina's Assembly. General Oglethorpe's request to raise the militia and send them south to Fort Frederica for an invasion of Florida had been met with unending debates in the assembly. Though no friend of Oglethorpe, Bull knew his duty to the crown. After all, first and foremost, he was a military man who understood the necessity of speed and the importance of initiative in war. Once war was declared, Bull had quickly complied with the request to send South Carolina's rangers and militia south. The Commons House of Assembly, though, had created an unending delay by debating but not approving his request to raise the militia. Weeks passed, and they continued their childish bickering.

The causes of the delay were well known. The recent rebellion and battle had depleted the militia and threatened the colony. Many feared sending South Carolina's forces to Georgia and worried that the invasion force would leave the colony exposed to another slave revolt. Though the rebellion had been put down in an extreme fashion, the slave population still outnumbered the colonists. Many important residents had been killed, and concern grew about the risks of losing more citizens in the upcoming war. Williams had much empathy with the argument; after all, his best friend Evans had been slain during the conflict. In contrast, Acting Governor Bull was furious. As far as he was concerned, there was no room for disobedience. For better or worse, the King had commissioned General Oglethorpe, and the man commanded the colonial troops in the south. Despite its debates, the assembly had no right to prevent or delay these forces from forming and joining Oglethorpe's invasion. Bull was so angry that he'd almost dissolved the assembly several times. He'd stopped short of the decision, knowing that dissolution would delay matters further. There was no time for the Commons to disband and be replaced; war had been declared. Instead, Bull just fumed and threw more things at Williams.

Matters would come to a head soon, though. News had reached Charles Town that General Oglethorpe was traveling north for a meeting with Colonel Bull and was aiming to address the assembly. Williams didn't think the assembly could hold out much longer, especially if there were a direct and in-person request from the general. He remained surprised the politicians had refused Bull's requests. The Acting Governor wasn't a man you turned down lightly. Williams waved a fly away from his lunch and took another bite of the jerky. He slowly chewed the tough, leathery, salty texture and continued to ponder. Bull and Oglethorpe had become concerned about the delay to the invasion of Florida. They knew General Montiano lacked sufficient forces to defend the colony, but the longer they delayed the attack, the greater the chance that troops would reinforce Florida from Cuba. The invasion was a calculated risk, and both men grew concerned that delay would make the endeavor harder. They needed the invasion to begin soon.

The church clock chimed. Williams noted the time, finished his lunch, and bid his friend's grave a fond farewell. Williams missed Evans. He didn't think he would have such a close friend again. The man's death was such a wasteful loss; crushed by your horse didn't seem a great way to go either. Williams left the cemetery and went through the streets of Charles Town to return to the Governor's mansion. It was midday, and the roads were packed with traffic. Gentlemen's steeds gracefully carried them, weaving past ponies and hauling carts full of produce. Store owners arranged their curbside displays while children ran in the streets. Servants loitered while running errands for their households. Womenfolk, dressed in lacey finery and long dresses, perused the stores for bargains. Williams traced his way through the cobbled streets.

Though it was autumn, the air was humid and oppressive, and a scent of saltwater could be detected. In amongst the crowd, Williams spotted the occasional weathered face of a sailor. Residents' homes followed the bustle of the stores; their facades were painted in lively colors. Many sported petite front gardens decked in autumnal blooms. The city was booming despite the impending war. The populace's prosperity was evident along every street and captured by the beauty of each house. Despite the wealth, Williams could sense concern etched in the faces of the citizens. Such an exuberant moment often preceded periods of austerity; all sensed the coming trials that war with the Spanish would cause.

⧖ ⧖ ⧖

The Acting Governor's reception for General Oglethorpe was cordial but tense. The mansion house had been a hub of activity for days before the general's arrival. Despite the rise of Georgia as a rival, South Carolina remained the most powerful colony in the South. Colonel Bull intended to remind his colleague about the importance of the colony. Oglethorpe may have sucked away large parts of the Indian trade and secured his generalship through Viscount Percival's parliamentary machinations. Still, South Carolina was more prosperous than Georgia and offered a more significant military contribution to the invasion of Florida.

Williams was delighted to see General Oglethorpe again. It had been many years since he'd last seen the man. Williams had joined Georgia's founders when they first navigated the

Savannah River and scouted Yamacraw Bluff, the site that was now the vibrant colonial city of Savannah. It was remarkable how much Savannah had developed in the few years that had passed. It seemed like a time long lost when Bull and Oglethorpe considered each other friends. As Oglethorpe entered the mansion with his aides, Williams observed the physical changes in the man. Oglethorpe had always been tall, elegant, and agile—his underlying dynamism disguised by a graceful deportment.

Much to Bull's irritation, Oglethorpe wore the full grandiose uniform of a British general—a magnificent red coat with gold finishes, bright buttons, and golden embroidery. The coat fitted snugly over white breeches, which were tucked into black knee-high boots. A blue and gold sash across the chest, a tricorn hat edged with gold trim, and a gold-encrusted sword completed the outfit. Despite the splendor of his wardrobe, Williams noticed a visible aging of the general. Dark bags surrounded the eyes, further accentuating the man's prominent nose. His face was drawn and thinner, and the eyes were missing some sharpness. Oglethorpe had noticeably lost weight, and he was already a slender man; he'd somehow become leaner. It wasn't tighter, more sculpted muscle; it was the wasting of an illness. He appeared tired, somewhat lacking his former vigorous energy.

The official reception was a typically splendid affair. All the great and good of the colony had been invited. A drinks reception preceded an opulent five-course dinner, which was followed by a dance. The best food, drink, and music had been supplied while the servants darted in and out of the event, ensuring all were kept merry.

After the official duties of the reception, Bull and Oglethorpe retired to the lounge. Sitting across from each other in two comfortable chairs, they started their conference. Williams and two of Oglethorpe's aides were invited to attend them. No longer restricted by the formalities of the governor's reception, both men relaxed and enjoyed a glass of sherry. Conversations soon turned to matters at hand, and both men were candid about their views. General Oglethorpe soon moved beyond the pleasantries and courtesies, "Thank you for receiving me, Acting Governor Bull. We have left it too long. Next time, let us meet on better terms and as friends instead of in our official capacities. Time is of the essence, so I will be frank with you. As you know, we are assembling the invasion force at Fort Frederica. We have Georgia's militia and Georgia's rangers. We have our allies, the Yamacraws, and the Creeks. I have received news that Commodore Pearce is on his way to Fort St. Simon with seven British warships. Supplies for the endeavor have been gathered. Yet, I have not seen a single South Carolinian. We cannot wait forever; if we leave it much longer, St. Augustine will receive reinforcements from Cuba. So, on behalf of the King and his Parliament, I am here to officially ask why your forces have not moved south to join us?"

At the mention of the King and Parliament, Bull noticeably winced. Williams knew the situation vexed the colonel; he was not in the habit of disobeying orders, and the Commons Assembly had placed him in an untenable situation. Bull leaned over, emptied his pipe, refilled it, and lit it again. A ruddiness had reached Bull's cheeks, and Williams knew he was angry, but the colonel controlled it well, which was a necessary civility in the circumstances. After the deliberate pause, Bull replied, "Sir, as you know from my letters, the recent rebellion and battle have affected us. I suspect Spanish influence, but I have not been able to prove it beyond doubt. My people have become cautious. They fear another revolt, they fear further losses, and they are blocking the militia from being raised."

Oglethorpe seemed perplexed: "You are the Governor, at least the Acting Governor. You have the King's commission here. How is it that you cannot raise the militia when you command it?"

Again, after a moment of silence, Bull composed himself, "Sir, as I have tried to explain to you previously. We are not a company with a Board of Trustees. I do not have the same power over the colony that you have over Georgia. South Carolina is a royal colony; it has an elected Commons Assembly. They have a say in our governance, and they've been dragging their feet, holding up the vote to raise the militia. If it were purely my decision, you'd have the rangers and the militia by now."

Oglethorpe digested this for a moment, "Your people must understand how essential this invasion is. It is not just for Georgia's protection. We seek to defeat Spain in Florida so it cannot be used as a base to invade Britain's North American colonies. If they defeat Georgia, then South Carolina will be next. We have a common cause, and the King has commissioned me to lead our forces against the Spanish. We are at war, sir, and we cannot afford to delay this further! I am expecting you to send your rangers south with my aides. Commodore Pearce will arrive soon, and we need the land forces ready to move with the fleet. I will speak to your Commons Assembly; they must be persuaded to raise your militia, or all might be lost!"

As the bright red hues expanded across Bull's cheeks, Williams could tell the colonel felt boxed in between General Oglethorpe and his invasion and the Commons Assembly and its obstructions. Maybe the man would welcome the arrival of the new Governor once Parliament had finally settled on its choice. Bull's eyes narrowed as he decided, "I agree with you. I have waited too long. Colonel Palmer will head south immediately with our rangers and your aides. I command those men; the assembly has no say regarding where they go and what they do. I waited for the militia agreement before dispatching them. Clearly, that was my mistake. The Commons has tied my hands about the militia. I recommend you address the body directly. Perhaps a direct appeal to their patriotism will unlock enough votes. Behind the scenes, I will threaten to dissolve the assembly and take executive action. It will cause a huge controversy, but if that is what I must do, then so be it!"

General Oglethorpe smiled and leaned across the gap between them. He grasped Bull's forearm, "Thank you, sir. I know this is a trying state of affairs. You have always been a friend of Georgia; I'll not forget it. I will put the case in front of your Commons Assembly on the morrow. I have dreadful news to share with them. Hopefully, it will sufficiently convince the stalwarts to change their opinion against raising the militia." Williams listened as Oglethorpe shared with Bull the recent atrocity on Amelia Island. He was aghast. The first actions of the war broke all the protocols. It did not bode well, and the assembly was sure to be incensed.

⌛ ⌛ ⌛

The following day, Oglethorpe addressed South Carolina's Common Assembly. Williams watched on as the eyes and ears of the Acting Governor. Oglethorpe's oratory was a new side of the man, a skill perhaps honed as a parliamentarian. His speech simultaneously lifted the crowd to a higher purpose, threatened disaster in war, and provoked the citizens' loyalty to the crown. It was a masterful performance, culminating with a story of Spanish brutality on Amelia Island. As Williams had predicted, the assembly was enraged and immediately passed the ordinance to raise the militia and send them south under General Oglethorpe's command. Colonel Vanderdussen accepted the signed order from Acting Governor Bull in person, and the South Carolinian forces were finally free to join the invasion of Florida. Lieutenant Williams was sent with them as Colonel Vanderdussen's aide and Bull's correspondent.

Chapter 37: Reinforcements

A light breeze wafted gently across Lamine's face. Granules of beach sand were captured in the current, and they scoured his cheek coarsely. Lamine rubbed his eyes. The salt from the mild gust brought on momentary tears. Even with the cool draft from the ocean, it was a magnificent day. The sweltering, hot, and humid summer days, with their regular storms, had given way to a milder, more temperate climate. The weather chilled in the mornings and evenings but remained sultry during the day. The sun shone brightly and warmed Lamine's face. It wasn't an oppressive heat, but it was hot, and Lamine sweated as he walked. The climate reminded him of winters in Futa, his long-lost African homeland. Intensely hot periods had often been followed by lesser extremes. Florida had a similar pattern but benefitted from its location next to the ocean, so he welcomed the breeze, even when it was sandy and salty.

Lamine took a circuitous route from his hometown, Fort Mose, to the Castillo. He was due at the castle parade ground in the afternoon to lead more militia exercises. The Free Black Militia were now thoroughly drilled, so their mornings had been redirected to masonry, carpentry, and other work designed to prepare the community for siege warfare. Though weather-beaten and accessible, the path was rarely used. He preferred it to the more direct road, with its carts and passersby. Lamine valued the time to think undisturbed. As the route skirted the river, he could observe the new forces from Cuba. General Montiano and the senior officers had been ecstatic when these reinforcements arrived. The general knew the Spanish position in Florida was precarious, hence the efforts to recruit the populace of Mose into the militia and the blockade mentality that had driven the colony's preparations. Though the reinforcements only provided another two hundred soldiers, these were seasoned veterans from the regular army. Far more important, though, were the six half galleys that had arrived from Cuba with the regulars. These vessels patrolled the three rivers and guarded the St. Augustine inlet. They provided valuable defensive benefits should the British Navy attempt a seaborne attack.

Lamine had never seen Spanish half-galleys, but he was impressed and knew why General Montiano was pleased by their arrival. One of the half-galleys was patrolling the Tolomato River, sitting in the quiet waters across from Lamine's trail. He stopped and observed it intently. It was a slender, sleek vessel, much lower in the water than a Spanish Galleon. The hull was long, narrow, and built from solid-looking oak. Flying Spanish colors and painted red and black, the craft was perfect for navigating the tight confines of the St. Augustine estuary. Though smaller than many ships, the half galley had three tall masts. The mainsail was trussed, while the jib sail remained visible. Below the main deck, a row of oars poked out of the galley, smoothly propelling the craft downstream. The deck bristled with cannons, twelve iron beasts on the starboard side, their muzzles jutting out threateningly. Two smaller swivel guns were also noticeable, each on the bow and the stern. A few seasoned sailors seemed busy maintaining a cannon while others secured the mainsheet.

The vessel gradually drifts further away, moving faster than Lamine can walk, and back toward St. Augustine. The strategic significance of the half-galleys is immediately apparent. Though much smaller than British frigates, their river navigability gave them an advantage that open seas wouldn't usually afford. Lamine imagined the six ships blocking the entrance to the St. Augustine inlet or fighting the British in the tight confines of the rivers. He didn't think a British ship would enjoy trying to break such a barrier; running past those smaller vessels with their arsenal of guns was sure to inflict mortal damage on a taller ship's hull and could sink her. There was no question. The reinforcements had strengthened Montiano's chances of defending Florida.

As the vessel gradually disappeared down the river, Lamine continued his trek. Clumps of pickerelweed dotted the edges; at points, they had begun to grow across the pathway. Sawgrasses and spikerushes laced the river's embankment, while thick bulrushes grew abundantly around the shallow waterways. The path meandered, following the course of the Tolomato River. Lamine enjoyed the peacefulness of the walk and its rambling route. However, it was time for him to pick up the pace; he'd be overdue if he dawdled much longer.

⧗　⧗　⧗

Lamine approached the Castillo de San Marcos from the northeast. The castle always dominated the inlet, and the ancient fortifications looked renewed. General Montiano's energy and enthusiasm had driven the community into a frenzy of revitalization unheard of in other Spanish colonies. The massive coquina walls had been patched up and repaired by the stone masons. Lighter crushed seashell cement lay within the darker, older coquina of prior eras. The fort appeared impregnable, and Lamine couldn't imagine the British capturing it. Four diamond-shaped towering bastions topped the symmetrical star-shaped fort. Each bastion held multiple cannons; their black barrels watched over Matanzas Bay and guarded against a land attack. Assaulting such a fortress would take ingenuity. A forty-foot-wide moat surrounded the southern, western, and northern sides, while a steep slope protected the lower walls from cannon fire. As Lamine hiked along the river toward the castle, he could see the improved water battery. Montiano had insisted on its redevelopment. On the eastern side of the fort, it had been recently reconstructed, and it bristled with new cannons that had arrived from Cuba with Florida's reinforcements. Despite months of prior effort, the masons and carpenters continued busily fixing the remaining weaknesses in the ramparts and gantries.

Lamine skirted the moat's edge and took the path underneath the expansive walls of the castle. At least thirty feet high, there would be no way to scale them. Only a concerted effort with cannon batteries and consistent fire from ships could conceivably breach those walls. Even then, it would take weeks of controlled fire to create an opening that could be stormed by infantry. The Castillo de San Marcos was surely invulnerable. Based on the siege measures, Lamine assumed the general intended to retreat into the castle and hope to survive a blockade. It would be a risky tactic. The British Navy had a reputation for breaking such maneuvers by simply lingering, starving the defenders by stopping supplies entering.

There weren't any better options; though the reinforcements had strengthened the colony, they expected to be considerably outnumbered by the British invasion force.

Lamine continued along the path, passing underneath the northern wall of the castle. Knowing that the Spanish would be fighting from within the fortress filled him with immense confidence. As he contemplated the ramparts, a note of empathy washed over him. The poor souls who'd have to assail the fortress were in for a nasty surprise. After the Stono Rebellion and Edisto Battle, Lamine had no love for the British. Yet, as he gazed up at the massive fortifications, he was filled with awe, trepidation, and compassion. Hate and pity were simultaneously felt, and they were mixed emotions indeed. Lamine would always loathe the British for what they'd done to the African people, but he remembered individuals and friends who'd shown him mercy and companionship. He couldn't imagine those people having to fight their way into this castle. It would be a bloody mess, and surely many would die.

The northern end of the moat began to turn at an acute angle as Lamine passed the diamond tip of the castle. He now followed the roadway to the makeshift parade ground the troops had used for drills and exercises. The street became much busier with the comings and goings to and from the castle. Many carts full of produce were steadily heading through the gate to stockpile the castle's storerooms. Despite his meandering route, Lamine arrived early. A few of his militiamen loitered nearby, waiting for their appointed drills, and he bid them a good afternoon. Major Menéndez had also reached the grounds promptly, and Lamine joined his commanding officer. The major concentrated on the training ground and the newly arrived soldiers who'd occupied it all morning. Lamine nodded a silent greeting and cast his eye over the scene.

One company of Spanish soldiers, numbering just over two hundred men, were finishing their training for the day. Row upon row of men stood to attention, waiting for a dismissal. Each soldier's uniform was well used and maintained, exposing these men as the veteran reinforcements recently arrived from Cuba. The blue, white, and crimson uniforms were festooned with brass buttons. White leather cross belts, glinting swords, and tricorn hats completed a stunning appearance. Muskets, looking clean and ready to use, rested upon the men's shoulders while bayonets hung from their waists. As Lamine examined the company's equipment, he wished his troops could receive such a quality kit. The militia used assorted older gear, and consequently, they looked mismatched and unorganized.

Despite the professional look of the Spanish regulars, the men's faces stood out. Not a single fresh recruit amongst them. The soldiers' faces betrayed stern determination, eyes forward until the dismissal command was given, tanned, battle-hardened, grisly, fierce faces throughout. Many sported beards that were slightly flecked with grey. It appeared Cuba had sent their best company to defend Florida from the British. These were the elite, all veterans with significant service under their belts. The officers were magnificent in their uniforms, gold epaulets and cobalt blue sashes marking their rank. As they strode amongst the company, their competence and influence were evident from the keen way they surveyed the soldiers, offering occasional compliments and admonishments. Quick flashes of acknowledgment on the men's faces were proof of their esteem for their officers. As the final row was inspected, a bugle call signaled the end of their morning's drill, and the soldiers departed the field in an orderly fashion.

There was no other word for it; Lamine was impressed. After many months of training, the militia didn't come close to the discipline and precision of the Spanish regulars. These reinforcements were welcome. He turned to Major Menéndez, asking, "Are these veterans as good with their muskets as they are on the parade field? We have a lot of work to do with our men if they are to get anywhere close to this!"

Major Menéndez frowned and answered, "It's good to set ambitious goals, but let's be honest with ourselves. The regulars have almost grown up, loading and firing muskets. I don't think our men have a hope of matching the speed and accuracy I just witnessed. The militia are still firing high after months of training, and I'd say those regulars loaded their weapons ten seconds quicker! Mind you, I'd wager my mother on our men if it comes to hand-to-hand combat."

Lamine agreed, "Yes, sir, they've learned much from sharing and working together. Hopefully, the Spanish officers recognize our strengths. It would be a shame to waste the militia trying to match the British gun for gun. I hear they're even faster than the Spanish on the battlefield. What do you think about these reinforcements?"

Menéndez smiled, happiness showing in the creases of his face. His response confirmed Lamine's observations, "Very timely, very timely indeed! Those six half-galleys and the improved water battery will make life challenging for a waterborne attack through the bay. I don't think the British Navy will be too keen to run any of their ships past a floating barricade combining those two. If the half-galleys don't sink the frigates, the battery will surely get them. And these veterans look fantastic, but I fear we don't have enough infantry or artillery for a real standing battle. We'll likely hunker down in the Castillo. No question, though, our chances of surviving a British attack improved immeasurably when this lot arrived from Cuba!"

Chapter 38: Forces Assemble

The smaller of the two forts had been Tom's home for several months. He'd occasionally gotten to check his property north of Fort Frederica, but work on his house and grounds had been slow and laborious. With war looming, his time was occupied with preparations for the invasion. General Oglethorpe had been concentrating his forces on St. Simons Island, and he'd cast a wide net to amass provisions for the invasion. Tom's marksmanship and hunting skills had been fully deployed, accumulating a horde of dried meat for the army. The time spent pursuing prey had benefits, as Tom's friends Hilli and Sin renewed their scouting efforts, working with him almost daily. Their presence helped as Tom and his squad continued to mourn the extrajudicial deaths of the two highlanders. They'd quietly sworn an oath to exact revenge against the Spanish soldiers. Captain Mackay remained livid about the murders of Hugh and Angus. It was a bad start to the war, and Tom feared that further atrocities on both sides would follow the awful precedent he'd witnessed on Amelia Island. At least they'd taken down the executioner; that was one less Spanish combatant to worry about.

Fort St. Simon was the smaller twin of Fort Frederica. It guarded the entrance to Jekyll Sound and was designed to be the first line of defense against a Spanish attack. General Oglethorpe and Captain Mackay had situated the fort on the island's southern tip. It looked out from Georgia's coastline, bristling with cannons aiming out to sea. The fort was surrounded by thick wooden palisades cut from the local pine forests. These were formidable battlements offering satisfactory protection against an infantry assault. Tom didn't fancy they'd stand long if faced with a severe bombardment from Spanish Galleons, so the protection was likely illusionary. Inside the fort, a small barracks housed Tom and his men and a detachment of Oglethorpe's regiment. A series of storage buildings and a command post clustered together in the center of the fort, adjacent to the barracks. Cannon platforms lined the interior of the wooden barricade, and the iron barrels were maintained constantly, ready for action in the case of a naval threat. A small moat surrounded the fort, and the heavy marsh air was thick with the rich mixture of decaying vegetation and the salty odor of brackish water. Though the lesser of the two forts, Fort St. Simons was well-constructed and defensible.

They'd been moved to Fort St. Simons when more forces arrived. Oglethorpe's regiment of British regulars had been stationed at Fort Frederica, dominating the barracks and outbuildings. Meanwhile, Colonel Palmer had arrived with a contingent of South Carolina's rangers and had been accommodated nearby. It was rumored that the colonel had fallen out with Captain Mackay, apparently over who held the higher rank. The captain's commission had been in the British army, while the colonel's was in a colonial regiment. A heated argument ensued, and the two men were now scarcely talking. Tom considered it a trivial distraction; both men were excellent officers and would be needed when they headed south. Tom had also heard from some rangers that General Oglethorpe had resolved the dispute with South Carolina's Commons, and a large body of the colony's militia was now heading south. It wouldn't be long before the entire invasion force was assembled, and they could begin the attack on the Spanish and exact some revenge for Hugh and Angus. It had been too long, though, with many months of agonized waiting. Tom suspected the lengthy delay would come back to haunt them.

Tom turned the letter over in his hand and inspected it. The crisp envelope was slightly mottled, and the bright red wax seal held Noble Jones' insignia. He was grateful for Noble's constant correspondence. Mary's pregnancy had progressed in his absence, and it seemed likely he'd be away fighting when she gave birth. Tom broke the seal, unfolded the paper, and read the letter slowly. Reading and writing were rare skills for former servants, but that had been one of the few benefits of his terrible life as a carpenter's apprentice. He'd been instructed so he could keep a tally of the customers' bills and correspondence.

As Tom digested the elegant cursive, he promised to practice writing; sometimes, Tom's was barely legible. He also vowed to teach Mary to read and write. Their communications were stilted and bland, as they could not impart true feelings, while Noble facilitated the letters. Tom wanted to profess his true love and hopefulness for the birth of their first child, even though he would struggle to find the right words. However, he knew that Noble would read aloud to Mary, so he was much more formal than desired. Likewise, Mary's letters were somewhat functional and leaned heavily on Noble's medical knowledge. The new letter was no exception. Mary was in the third trimester; she was finding it more challenging to move around, constantly got heartburn, regularly had deadened legs, and, at times, breathing was proving difficult. Despite these symptoms, she was doing well, and Noble assured him that everything was progressing normally. Mary light-heartedly moaned about Uga. Apparently, the dog was chewing everything in the house. Duke was growing quickly, practicing his militia drills with the older boys, and doing his chores. Mary feared the boy might have to fight if the war lasted long. Tom felt sad that he'd miss the birth of his first child; likely, he'd be laying siege to St. Augustine when the baby arrived. Tom wished he could hold Mary in his arms and witness the birth.

Tom perused the rest of the letter as Noble moved on to other news. Commodore Pearce had arrived in Savannah with his fleet of seven warships. The flagship, a magnificent ship of the line, had been escorted by two frigates and several smaller vessels. By Noble's accounting, it was a formidable armada. The decks of each vessel bristled with cannons, and the sailors and marines became a hub of activity as the ships arrived. The masts of the flagship dominated the skyline, and its sails billowed as the fleet maneuvered. According to Noble, after a short stay resupplying the ship, Commodore Pearce had set off again, heading toward Charles Town to rendezvous with General Oglethorpe. The end of Noble's letter reported the gradual arrival of the South Carolinian militia. It appeared they were steadily arriving across the river, stopping in Savannah for a few days, and then setting off again south. Though he could only speculate, Noble assumed that the commodore would pick up General Oglethorpe, Colonel Vanderdussen, and a significant militia contingent before returning to reunite the fleet and heading toward Fort Frederica.

Though Tom hated to destroy the letter, with its updates from Mary, he recognized the sensitivity of the content. Picking up a candle, he lit the paper. It caught suddenly, and for a moment, flames licked his fingers. He dropped it onto the stone floor and stamped out the blazing correspondence. Clearly, the invasion was now imminent. Tom left his quarters to find the rest of the squad and share the important news. Of Mary's condition and the impending arrival of General Oglethorpe, the armada, and the remainder of the troops.

⧗ ⧗ ⧗

The anticipation in Frederica and its two forts had hit an all-time high. The army's renewed action was palpable after the dull months of waiting, preparing, and provisioning. The air was filled with excitement and chatter. A bustle and urgency had entered everyday activities. Just walking through the streets of Frederica, one could sense it. Tom had seen many new faces over recent days as the South Carolinian militiamen arrived. He was relieved that his men had quarters in Fort St. Simons; finding accommodation was becoming increasingly challenging. The land had been cleared, and many new arrivals camped outside the town. Strange accents started filtering through the noise of the town's thoroughfares, and Darien highlanders visited more regularly, their harsh Gaelic sometimes evident among the crowd. The uniforms were likewise varied. The 42nd Regiment of Foot, Oglethorpe's regiment, as they were often described, were ever-present. The soldiers' iconic red coats, brass buttons, white linen facings, crossbelts, and breeches were ubiquitous. Groups of regulars patrolled the streets and overwhelmed Frederica's few pubs and eateries. It was almost impossible for Tom's squad to get an ale now. These regulars were now overwhelmed by the arriving South Carolinian militiamen in their assorted clothing. The militia dressed in their own clothes, but noticeable due to their muskets, bayonets, webbing, and long knives. Dotted in amongst the swarm, one occasionally spotted the green coats of the rangers and the tartans of the highlanders. Tom was glad to see more rangers. He valued these men's sniping and scouting capacity and was happy to see more sharpshooters and their rifles. The highlanders, though few, were also a welcome addition. These men had grown up fighting and could easily form an elite troop, even more formidable than the British regulars.

As Tom, Hilli, and Sin hunted on Tom's lands, seeking out the increasingly shy prey, they happened across a large party of Lower Creeks, almost fifty warriors. It was exhilarating for Tom to greet some of his fellow alligator clansmen. They celebrated with a small feast of venison, and caught up with each other. The Creeks had been broken into smaller units that had patrolled south, harrying their Yamasee enemies and snooping on the Spanish forts. Their arrival and concentration near Frederica further spoke to the nearness of the invasion. The Creeks reported that the Yamasee had retreated south of St. Augustine and had completely removed themselves from the region. It was somewhat perplexing and disappointing that their foes had fled the fight.

The Spanish had similarly abandoned their small settlement on Amelia Island after the Darien highlanders' beheadings. They had holed up in two forts down the St. Johns River. Tom wondered at the news; he'd never heard of the forts. Sin translated for him, "They say the forts guard the trail between Pensacola and St. Augustine. There's one fort on each bank; it's a key supply route. The Creeks are sending word to General Oglethorpe that the forts need to be destroyed before an attack on St. Augustine can be attempted. Otherwise, there will be enemies behind the British forces, who might counterattack north and capture our forts."

Tom digested this information. He'd assumed that General Oglethorpe planned to pack most of the force onto Commodore Pearce's ships and take them straight down the coast. These forts must be neutralized first, which would likely mean an overland assault.

⧗ ⧗ ⧗

A few days later, Tom was patrolling the ramparts of Fort St. Simons when a massive cheer rippled through the fortress. Defenders quickly gathered along the ocean-facing bulwarks. Tom peered across the Jekyll Sound and glimpsed the unmistakable sight of an approaching British fleet. The flagship's giant masts appear over the horizon first, their imposing, towering poles bedecked with windblown sails. The Union Jack was flying at the masthead, announcing the Navy's arrival. The colossal oak hull, majestically demonstrating British martial dominance over the seas. The exterior is painted black and ochre, and it easily cuts through the waves toward the coast. Three rows of gunports line the flanks. The flagship was guided by a pilot, helping the flotilla enter the port. Alongside the flagship, no less impressive, are two British frigates. Their decks are a hive of activity as the sailors begin to furl the sheets so that the vessels can navigate into the Jekyll Sound's harbor. The sailors, dressed in blue and white uniforms, act with disciplined precision as they prepare the ships for their landings. Behind the warships, two smaller supply vessels escort the fleet. The soldiers in Fort St. Simons cheer again and wave at the sailors. The atmosphere is festive as General Oglethorpe's remaining forces arrive with the commodore's fleet.

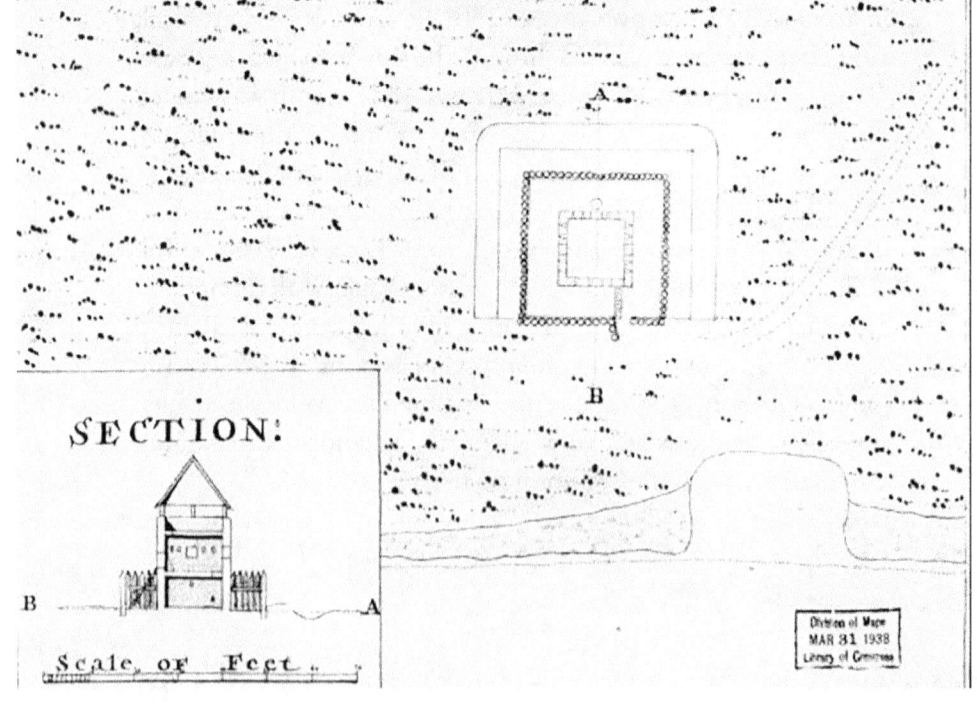

Chapter 39: Fort Picolata

The stronghold on Amelia Island was a misnomer, a poorly constructed blockhouse that had been left to deteriorate badly. When they reached the site, it was immediately apparent to Hernando that the place would be vulnerable. It was only a little more substantial than the highlander's outpost that they'd just attacked and set fire to. The few defenders present were the type of men you sent to the wilderness. Poorly disciplined, shoddily armed, and likely to run as soon as a fight started. The new arrivals set about digging a grave for Antonio and fortifying the location as best as possible. Hours passed, but it was not enough to address years of neglect. Even with the sizable force accompanying Lieutenant Sánchez, it was clear to all that they'd have to abandon the site and retreat south.

They had barely finished burying Antonio when the Darien Highlanders arrived. Fortunately, Gonzalo and Francisco, the unit's scouts, were as alert as ever and raised the alarm before the attackers could surprise them. Driving fiercely down the tepid waters of the St. Mary's River, the enemy combatants suddenly turned the bend and rowed rapidly toward their location. The highlanders must have recruited every man in Darien and requisitioned all the boats available. It was a significant corps of battle-hardened men, and it was instantaneously apparent that the Spanish troops were out-manned and out-gunned. With no real alternative and mindful of the general's orders to avoid losing men unnecessarily, Lieutenant Sánchez ordered a retreat. They scrapped their hastily constructed defenses and set fire to Amelia Island's blockhouse. The question then became whether they could outrun their pursuers.

Hernando didn't have time to be scared. The Spanish had to withdraw on foot across the island. There was a chance that they would be caught before they could get back to the boats. Lieutenant Sánchez began the retreat with a salvo of musket fire. Though unlikely to do any damage, as the distance was too far, it was intended to keep some space between them and slow the Scots down. As soon as the barrage was discharged, Hernando's unit ran along the island's trails joining the entire squad in its flight. The terrain was challenging, and he'd never run so fast, but their lives depended upon it. Given the decision to behead the two highlanders, they expected no quarter and were likely to be given none. Consequently, their progress to the boats was rapid.

Initially, there was some confusion when they arrived. The additional men from the Amelia blockhouse made it a tight fit. Following a sharp rebuke from Sergeant Moreno-Rodriguez, the disorder was overcome, and they knuckled down, rowing furiously. Now, it was a question of speed and endurance. The skiffs laced through the water rapidly. It appeared Lieutenant Sánchez's plans for the retreat might work. The highlanders had been delayed and were cautious after the musket fire and tracked the Spanish at some distance. As they progressed further down the Amelia River and deeper into Spanish Florida, their pursuers gave up, recognizing they'd lost the race. As the immediate danger dissipated, Hernando became conscious again of the water and his fears of drowning. It would be a long journey back down the inland waterways to the St. Johns River.

⏳ ⏳ ⏳

Hernando was in the third boat, bracing himself against the occasional swell as the men rowed into the mouth of St. Johns River. They were paddling hard and covering the distance from Amelia Island quickly, motivated by the reminder of the highlanders' pursuit. The river's gentle undulations remind him of his fears. He peers over the boat's edge into the silty river, praying to return to dry land. The mouth of the river is a broad expanse of water, the currents gentle as the freshwater mixes with the salty water. The riverbanks are indistinct as the marshes spread widely across the edges. Cordgrasses waft gently, blowing in the wind that drifts inland off the sea. Coppices of mangroves pepper the landscape, their root systems looking like old, haggled whiskers. Gulls, herons, and pelicans dash and glide in and out of the marshes. Despite the winter, the sun shines brightly, and the sky is clear. It was a beautiful scene if only Hernando's squad had time to dally.

They kept rowing furiously toward Fort Picolata. The word fort also seemed a contradiction. Like the blockhouse on Amelia Island, its upkeep had been neglected. The two forts, Picolata on the east bank, and San Francisco de Pupo on the west bank, defended the supply route from Pensacola to St. Augustine. They had been constructed to protect the river crossing and prevent ships from going upstream. The dilapidated state of the defenses appeared to undermine their purpose. Picolata, especially, was falling apart. As they swiftly covered the remaining distance to the fort, the actual state of its repairs became unmistakable. It must have been constructed eons ago. Individual stockade timbers were visibly rotten. Occasional gaps in the ramparts were noticeable where the hewn tree trunks had completely weakened and collapsed out of the structure. The remaining parts looked damp and were covered in olive and jade-colored mosses as evidence of the structure's weakness. Assorted wild mushrooms grew around the wooden foundations. Various mushrooms grew higher out of crevasses created by the constant river breezes. As a further indication of mismanagement, holes dotted the structures where woodpeckers had pecked incessantly, searching for grubs.

Lieutenant Sánchez's forces grounded the skiffs on the verges below the fort's battlements. There appeared to be two rusted cannons pointing out across the mouth of the river, but they didn't look functional. Finally, free of his qualms, Hernando was thankful to jump out of the boat and onto solid ground. He helped his unit pull the boats ashore and retrieved his possessions. The soldiers gradually trekked up to the fort, grateful for a rest from sculling.

The lieutenant scowled and swore as he inspected Fort Picolata. They'd expected to use the fort as a northern outpost against a British invasion, but it was a lost cause. There was one old rusty mortar to defend the fort's landward approaches and two rusty cannons to guard the river. None of the guns were operational; all had been left to corrode badly. The wooden structures inside the fort were as poorly maintained as the external walls; the storage house had collapsed completely. The small skeleton crew left to man the fort received a seemingly unending reprimand from Lieutenant Sánchez and were put under house arrest.

The fort's defenders looked as pitiful as the fort itself. Poorly uniformed, unclean, and unkempt, they were undoubtedly the dregs of the Spanish army. Hernando felt sorry for them, though they'd been negligent in their duties, they were underqualified, and there were too few to maintain the defenses properly. Lacking proper leaders, the defenders had declined into an unorganized mess. Sergeant Moreno-Rodriguez marched the men away. Hernando later saw them that day scrubbing the cannons and mortar with wire brushes, the Sergeant trying to recover the guns. The soldiers from Amelia Island's blockhouse soon joined the recovery efforts. Evidently, they were also getting disciplinary duties. Preserving defensive fortifications appeared to be the Achilles' heel of the Spanish forces in Florida.

Hernando's unit had some time to recuperate from Amelia Island's assault and retreat. Lieutenant Sánchez kept the men busy cleaning and tidying the fort for their occupation, but he made no attempt to repair the battlements. Sergeant Moreno-Rodriguez admitted openly that the fort would be abandoned and burnt to the ground. They didn't want the British to capture it intact, though, in truth, it would have little use to their enemies.

Hernando and the unit finally had time to mourn Antonio's loss. One night, they sat around a campfire and told stories about the big man. He would be missed, and they all shared fond memories. Antonio's penchant for fights emerged as a theme. Stories revolved around him cracking opponents' skulls, dragging foes across floors, and saving other unit members from nasty situations. The time to talk and grieve made everybody feel better. Though Antonio couldn't be described as respectable, to be honest, he had been a malicious and cruel man, but everyone valued his fighting prowess. He was worth two of any of them in a battle, and everyone knew they'd miss him once hostilities truly began.

⧗ ⧗ ⧗

The searing of the nostrils was the biggest surprise as Hernando breathed in the acrid, sharp scent of the fort being consumed by flames. The burning timbers gave off a pungent odor of resinous sweetness as the earthy woodsmoke billowed from the internal structures. The smoke was dense as it rose, alternating black and grey spirals circulated in strange vortexes. The rotten logs precipitously collapsed as the fire grew, validating the decision to abandon the fort. Hernando felt an intense heat searing his exposed skin; his face felt the full blast of the hotness as the flames grew, and clumsily, he stepped backward. All their possessions had been loaded onboard the boats, and they had already shipped the cleaned, repaired cannons and mortar to Fort San Francisco de Pupo.

The destruction of Fort Picolata had taken longer than expected. Lieutenant Sánchez was a diligent officer, and he'd recovered everything of value before setting fire to the outpost. They'd salvaged guns, provisions, lumber, wrought iron tacks, and anything that could be used to strengthen the defenses of the other fort. After weeks of stripping Picolata, only decayed and useless items were left. Crews had been constantly loading the boats with weighty and bulky articles, sometimes strapping them across several boats and propelling them to the west bank. Hernando was thankful he hadn't been assigned to those duties. The contraptions capsized several times, and the crews were thrown overboard. One man had drowned, as a heavy piece of lumber had slammed against his skull and sent him to the depths permanently. Once everything of value had been retrieved, they built large pyres around the inside of the fort, using the rotted boards from the crumpled storage house. The few items their enemies might conceivably use were flung onto the bonfires, and finally, they were lit. Though it took a while for the flames to take off, the soldiers watched as the fire danced towards the heavens. The smoke was thick, and the fire unrelenting as it ferociously consumed the remnants of Fort Picolata.

After some time viewing the fires, mesmerized by the pirouetting flames, they turned and boarded the skiffs. They didn't take long to paddle across to the west bank and Fort San Francisco de Pupo. The second fort was a little better than the first. It was undoubtedly better suited for defense. The battlements were perhaps less worn, the guns were reliably placed and maintained, and the soldiers were dependable. Sergeant Moreno-Rodriguez had been working this side of the river, and the men were keenly drilled and well-managed. Every item shipped over from Fort Picolata had been put to worthy use. Small holes from nesting insects and pecking woodpeckers had been filled. Work parties had been relentlessly treating the fortifications with creosote and varnish to reinforce the ramparts. Guns had been conscientiously cleaned and pointed out of bulwarks toward the burning fort across the river. Salvaged wrought iron was melted down and reformed into cannon balls now stockpiled near the guns. Gunpowder and other provisions had been shipped up the river. Gantries had been built from the spare lumber to aid defensive musket fire, and internal structures were repaired for the defenders' quarters. Sergeant Moreno-Rodriguez was a hard taskmaster, and Fort San Francisco de Pupo had patently been under his stewardship for a while. The fort was a hive of activity when the men abandoning Fort Picolata arrived. Everything that could be done had been done to prepare the remaining fort for the appearance of the British.

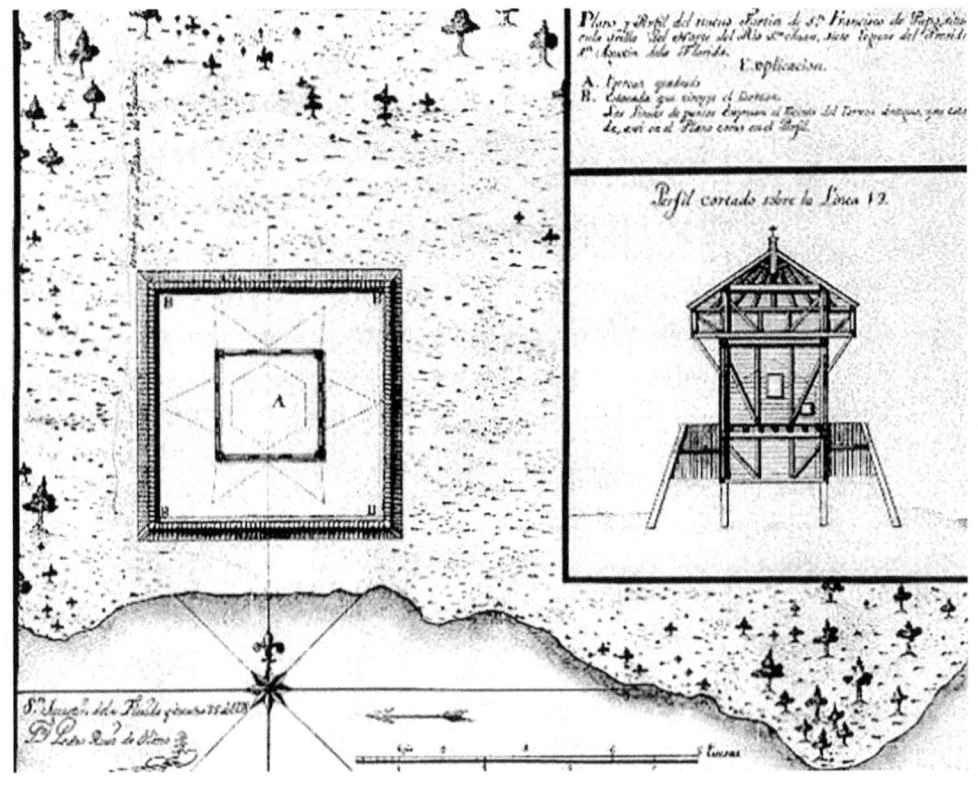

Plano y Perfil del nuevo Fuerte de S.n Francisco de Papa, sito
en la orilla del Norte del Rio S.n Juan, seis leguas del Presidi.
S.n Agustin de la Florida.

Explicacion.

A. Terrear quadrada
B. Estacada que ciñe, y el Fortin.
    Los lineas de puntos expresan el Recinto del Terreo Antiguo, que está
    de, asi en el Plano como en el Perfil.

Perfil cortado sobre la Linea 1.2.

S.n Agustin de la Florida, q Enero 28 de 1737
D.n Pedro Ruiz de Olano

Chapter 40: San Francisco de Pupo

Frederica and the two forts guarding St. Simon's Island were already a hive of activity before General Oglethorpe's arrival. With the entire invasion force assembled, the scene was frenetic. No soul relaxed; nobody slept well; the work was demanding. No idle hands, even women and children, are actively involved in the preparations. No men are spared from the martial planning. Every gun, axe, sword, and knife are requisitioned, cleaned, and sharpened. Soldiers are drilled relentlessly. Citizens collect, dry, and store foodstuff for the army; little is left behind for the populace. Nothing is left to chance. The army is fit, well-provisioned, prepared, and ready to begin its endeavors.

Tom learned his unit's arrangements from Colonel Palmer's orders. Georgia's rangers are to join forces with South Carolina's rangers under the command of the colonel. They will head south overland with General Oglethorpe, the 42nd Regiment of Foot, and the Creeks, engaging in a commando raid of the forts along the St. Johns River. Meanwhile, Colonel Vanderdussen with South Carolina's militia and Captain Mackay with the Darien Highlanders will go with the British Navy. Tom considers it a wise decision. The general had simultaneously split the quarreling commanders and curbed future atrocities by keeping the highlanders away from the Spanish regiment who'd beheaded their compatriots. He'd also picked the Creeks and rangers for the task, the best men to use for an overland assault through Georgia's and Florida's forests and marshes. Tom's only reservation was Oglethorpe's decision to haul three 42-pounder cannons through the forest to lay siege to the forts. It would be a two-to-three-day march along the Indian trails without them, but with the guns, it could take far longer. The paths must be cleared for the cannons to pass, and the marshes must be crossed. It wouldn't be simple. Though there were plenty of men for the job, the going could be challenging, and the speed of their assault would be slowed. For no apparent reason, there was hesitancy in taking the British Navy up the river to blow up the forts. Tom was no tactician, but that seemed the best and easiest course of action. At least the Creeks had cleared the region of the Yamasee, which will undoubtedly limit the defender's capacity to harry the attackers as they haul the cannons south.

General Oglethorpe wasn't known for dilly-dallying, and the ground assault began days after his arrival. The squad left the horses in Frederica. They'd be useless along the narrow tracks or within the forests. The rangers were deployed on foot along the army's flanks while the Creek Indians scouted ahead. At least they'd avoid the duties of hauling the great guns. That would be a burden left to the regulars, the artillery captains, and the engineers. First, they maneuvered around Turtle River along well-worn tracks used previously by the garrison. Occasionally, Tom glimpsed Oglethorpe at the head of the procession, his general's ornate red coat obvious. Tom judges that the man has learned nothing from his near-death experience. The column stops twice so the engineers can assess a stream or gully and determine how best to move the cannons over the obstacle. Later, as they hit the dense forest, crews of the 42nd are organized into several working groups operating in shifts to clear debris and widen the path for the army. As Tom predicted, it was slow going. His squad had little to do but watch for the enemy and witness the toil of the soldiers as they hacked into the forest.

During the first day, they skirt Turtle River, cross the Bluff streams, and arrive on the banks of the Satilla River. It was evident that moving the cannons overland was a mistake. There was a short delay while the engineers discussed the problem with the officers. After a brief hiatus, they decide to move the cannons via the inland waterways. It took two days to construct three large rafts to take the weight of the guns. Units of the British army are assigned to guard particular rafts, and the army set off again. The rafts head down the Cumberland Sound, the East River, and into the Amelia River, past the burnt-out Spanish blockhouse and the highlander's charred outpost. Eventually, the guns enter the St. Johns River and head south toward the forts. There were a few hiccups along the way, and one of the guns almost pitched into the St. Johns River as a raft became unstable. However, the cannons, their crews, and defending soldiers arrive at their planned destination without significant incident.

Meanwhile, the remainder of the army heads along the Indian trails, widening them as needed and constructing bridges when necessary. It takes them six days to arrive, longer than expected. As Tom arrives, he understands the necessity of the overland expedition. The forts are far deeper into Spanish Florida than they'd expected and some distance from the mouth of the river. No British ships could make it this far inland, into enemy territory, while exposed to attack. It would've been suicide for them to try. As he gazes at the site, Tom realizes the two forts were constructed to defend the trade route between Pensacola and St. Augustine rather than to protect the river itself. However, one of the forts has been burnt to the ground.

The officers survey the Spanish positions as the army unravels its long snake-like column, and the engineers maneuver the rafts, leveraging the cannons onto the riverbank. The Spanish defensive arrangements left the British leadership puzzled. The Spanish had abandoned and razed the southern fort on the east bank of the river. Instead, they'd opted to defend the more northern fort on the river's west bank. It was an oddity that was debated in General Oglethorpe's headquarters, and it raised many questions. Why would the Spanish choose the fort across the river from St. Augustine rather than the one closer to the fortress, cutting themselves off, with the river impeding their retreat? Indeed, that choice would also make reinforcement more challenging; reinforcements must cross the river, while defenders must retreat across it if defeated. They soon learned that the remaining fort was San Francisco de Pupo, while the charred husk was the remains of Fort Picolata. It didn't matter much; the remaining fort wouldn't stand long against a combined artillery and infantry assault. There couldn't be more than forty Spanish defenders. The attackers were much more powerful and had three forty-pounders. To Tom, despite the efforts expended, the wisdom of bringing the guns now appeared justified.

However, the mysterious decision to abandon one of the forts led to cautious decision-making. Perhaps reinforcements were on their way from Pensacola, or maybe there was a reason for the destruction of Fort Picolata. While the situation was assessed, the arriving British forces stayed concealed within the forest. The guns are positioned on an outcrop and fortified behind breastworks. The artillery officers' position and sight them, preparing them to fire on Fort San Francisco de Pupo.

Tom's squad and a body of Creeks under the leadership of Toonhowi are sent across the river to investigate. The Creeks scout the burnt-out fort's woodland while Tom and his men inspect the scorched remains of the fort. There are times when Tom's training as a carpenter is valuable, and this was one of those times. A quick inspection of the fort's remnants showed no sign of iron tacks, spikes, or braces. All the cast iron had been removed. An accidental inferno hadn't consumed the fort. It had been methodically dismantled. Coleman first noticed the telltale signs of recent felling and the hewing of nearby trees. The defenders had been trying to carry out repairs. Finally, Sanders found an old piece of lumber that seals their deliberations. The timber is rotted, dotted with holes from woodpeckers' jabbing, and infested with fungi. They all agreed. The fort had been forsaken, given up because it was decaying and vulnerable. With this intelligence, they returned to the army to impart the vital news. It was unlikely that Fort San Francisco de Pupo was expecting reinforcements from Pensacola. The Spanish are exposed because they'd had to accept the loss of the better-positioned fort due to its disrepair.

☒   ☒   ☒

Tom wishes there were bagpipes. Along with their fighting prowess, Tom misses the highlanders' bagpipes and the warbling timbres escorting the Tartans into battle. The scene is impressive as Oglethorpe's regiment steps out of the forest's cover and faces the fort, standing shoulder to shoulder. It is a warm, intensely humid Florida morning, and mist spills across the ground. The silence is omnipresent; the birds seem to pause their morning goings-on. The red coats stand motionless and ready. Formed line upon line in the haze. Discipline and determination are etched across the soldiers' faces. Their coats are bright scarlet, and their buttons and white cross-belts are immaculate. It is hard to imagine they'd spent days crossing forests and negotiating marshes, streams, and rivers. Tricorn hats, white cockades, muskets, and bayonets are all positioned precisely. Black boots are polished. It is an extraordinary display, further enhanced when the regimental colors and Union Jack unfurl. Young drummers and seasoned officers stand poised to command the advance.

Many of the soldiers are familiar with Tom; consequently, the display of military exactitude is even more stirring. He'd never seen a regiment of British regulars take to the field like this, and the moment would be immortalized in his memory, forever. It hadn't been long since the 42nd Regiment of Foot had arrived from Gibraltar in an undisciplined mess. They'd rebelled over pay, been disgruntled about their dispatch to Georgia, and had almost assassinated Oglethorpe. Half the regiment could have been hung for mutiny. Yet, here they were, perfectly disciplined and ready to march toward a Spanish fort in Florida. It was a true testament to General Oglethorpe's leadership that he'd turned the regiment around, even covering their pay himself. The 42nd Regiment of Foot was unrecognizable, no longer an unwanted rabble but now a military machine about to embark on its first major combat.

Tom's reflections are disturbed by Colonel Palmer deploying the rangers into skirmish formation in front of the regiment's front rank. In green uniforms, the rangers carrying longer-barreled rifles dart swiftly and silently to their forward positions. Coleman is to Tom's left and Hill to his right, some twenty paces away. Tom feels nervous. It is his first real battle, and he is unsure what to expect. He touches his tomahawk. A slight edgy twitch betrays his unease. Randomly, sweat begins to form across his forehead. He wipes it quickly and crouches, rifle loaded, awaiting orders.

They face Fort San Francisco de Pupo in battle formation along its northern barricade. The land in front undulates slightly. Various grasses and bushes provide limited cover but are open, flat, and arid. At least there are no marshes to break the attack's formations. The fort looks impenetrable. Its palisades had been recently repaired. Without ladders, scaling the ramparts could be impossible. The Spanish occupants are just waking up to the danger. Sudden voices shout in a strange language. Tom assumes they are raising the alarm. A bell within the fort begins to peal unremittingly.

General Oglethorpe was fond of the theatrical, and Tom saw his old friend march along the regiment's front rank. He speaks a few words to the occasional officer. A couple of muskets fire precipitously from the fort. A British officer, aiming to avoid an unnecessary response, shouts, "Hold your fire!"

As the general reaches the end of the rank, he waves his sword melodramatically at the artillery, and a bugler picks up his command. A deafening roar breaks the field's silence as the three forty-pounders fire. Tom detects the distinct stench of sulfur and saltpeter from the gunpowder as the guns discharge cannon balls. The battle scene slows as the cannon balls arch their way across to the fort and smash into the timbers. Dense smoke drifts across their positions, momentarily masking the fort's location. As the view clears, it is evident that the three cannons cause total annihilation to one section of the fort, which immediately ruptures. Tom notices a few defenders are blown apart as the section is blasted into smithereens. The artillerymen have sighted their weapons expertly, and two more shots from each cannon destroys an entire segment of the ramparts. Big enough for the infantry to breach.

The surprise for the Spanish defenders is total. Anticipating an attack from the river, their cannons point in the wrong direction. There is no time to bring them to the northern side of the fort—the mortar fires once, blowing up an unfortunate drummer boy and taking a leg from an infantryman. The blast is across the field from Tom, but ghastly, nevertheless. Some small arms fire flicks shot across the field toward the regiment, but it was inconsequential. Colonel Palmer commands the riflemen to fire. One expertly aimed riposte silences several defending soldiers, and the shooting from the fort ends. That's the battle for Tom. One shot, and he has no idea if has hit anybody. Sanders brags later that he'd shot a Spaniard, but as the rest of the squad knew, the man's claims were unreliable.

Oglethorpe commands the general advance, sending the infantry toward the breach in the fortifications. Moments later, a white flag emerges, flying from the ramparts. As the attackers pause, boats launch from behind the fort. They are heading across the river. Tom grasps that some of the Spanish soldiers are desperately attempting to escape. The brief battle of Fort San Francisco de Pupo is over.

Chapter 41: Escape

A dense mist drifts across the landscape. The Florida mornings are starting to lose the crispness of winter; the early morning felt clammy. Hernando could tell it would be another hot and sticky day. He'd been patrolling the northern ramparts of the fort all night and was tired. It was another uneventful, boring, and mundane night, and he was keen to roll into bed and get some kip; the sunrise is commencing, its glow obscured by the fog. Beams of sunlight shine through, fleetingly lighting up the fields between the garrison and the forest. Hernando yawns and rubs his eyes. The quiet of dawn is gradually interrupted by the twittering of morning birdsongs. Suddenly, the tweeting stops, and quietness descends once again. It is a strange occurrence; Hernando is immediately alert. He peers across the open land. Some noises catch his attention, a cough perhaps, and maybe a metallic clank. Then, the impenetrable mist lifts for a moment, and Hernando is horrified. Stood across the field is an entire regiment of British soldiers. The rangers are running into their skirmishing positions. There are drummers, officers, and flags. Worse still, there are guns. It's a shock, and Hernando cries loudly, "Sound the alarm! Sound the alarm! The British are here!"

Other guards along the northern ramparts almost simultaneously take up the call to warn the sleeping defenders. Sergeant Moreno-Rodriguez runs to the fort's bell and begins to ring it, constantly pulling on the cord to ensure no confusion. An attack is imminent, and there is little time to react. The fort, asleep moments before, is now a hive of abrupt activity. Soldiers run out of the barracks, half-dressing, while grabbing their weapons. Alert guards patrolling the eastern and western fortifications shift positions, running to face their British foes. His squad's brothers, Miguel and Rodrigo, race to join Hernando, raising their weapons at the British. A few useless and precipitous shots are fired. The distance is too far for their muskets. Lieutenant Sánchez appears in the fort's enclosure, bringing order to a hasty mobilization. The Spanish guns are pointing out to the river. It's too late to move them, so the lieutenant requisitions the fort's mortar and begins to sight it. The mortar is unlikely to stop the attack, but it's the only gun available.

Then, the British guns fire. Hernando hears the retort and soon sees the smoke. The conspicuous whizz and bang of the shot are dreadful. Unexpectedly, a vast section of the wall explodes into splinters. Bits of wood fragments are flung everywhere, and flames appear out of nowhere. The initial blast is near Hernando; smoke obscures his view, and the sound of the explosion causes his ears to ring. The fires are close; he feels the heat. Hernando loses sight of the British regiment but sees parts of Miguel and Rodrigo all over the place. The two brothers have been eviscerated. A big chunk of the fort is missing where they'd stood. Expecting another round of fire, Sergeant Moreno-Rodriguez shouts for the remaining defenders to move. There is a delay while the British reload. The Spanish mortar fires from the fort's courtyard, adding to the noise, smoke, and smells of fire and gunpowder.

Hernando jumps off the fort's ramparts onto the roof of a nearby warehouse. His timing is opportune. A second burst of cannon fire hits the fort in the exact same location as the first. More of the timbers are obliterated. Forewarned, the defenders avoid casualties, but a massive hole in the battlements opens— another short delay and a third detonation. The artillery are experts. Hitting the same spot, they've opened an indefensible breach. The defenders rush to the opening but hold back, concerned that another blast from the guns will blow them up. While the Spanish mortar reloads, Lieutenant Sánchez reviews the scene. Hernando sees him staring at the attacking forces, trying to assess the danger. He calls for the defenders to fire. Their efforts with the first musket discharge are inconsequential. No damage is inflicted. The enemy's rangers shoot and injure several more of the Spanish soldiers. Lieutenant Sánchez recognizes the impossibility of defending the fort. It's ruptured beyond defense. They're facing overwhelming British infantry forces, men who will soon surge through the gap created by the cannons. The lieutenant makes the only sensible decision. Retreat for two-thirds of his men, while those who remain buy time for their compatriot's escape by surrendering. He hopes that this ruse will enable some of his command to make it back to St. Augustine and thus strengthen the defenses of the Castillo. Evidently, the British invasion has begun.

Hernando's luck continues. He's chosen to join the retreat and will escape capture. A white flag of surrender is being rushed to the ramparts; its contours curl as a soldier climbs up the gangway and hoists it up the fort's flagpole. Hernando joins a thirty-strong body of Spanish soldiers as they exit the fort and board the boats. Many soldiers are not fully dressed, leaving with what they can grab quickly. There is a sense of panic. A small group pushes past Hernando. Sergeant Moreno-Rodriguez issues stern commands, which bring back order. It appears that the sergeant will command the retreat. Lieutenant Sánchez, meanwhile, is staying with the injured and some volunteers to surrender the fort to the British. The youngest in their squad, Alvaro, is among those staying with the lieutenant. Hopefully, the captives will be treated well by the British, and no retribution will be sought for the highlanders' executions.

As Hernando climbs into a boat, he recalls the brutal deaths of Miguel and Rodrigo. The shock had led him to forget. It was a devastatingly sudden way to die. Their small squad has now lost three men, and Alvaro will become a British prisoner. This expedition is taking quite a toll on their group. At least they're returning to St. Augustine and the Castillo. A sense of relief washes over Hernando, even though he's aware that getting across the river and marching along the trading road might have risks.

Hernando turns around and takes one last look at the brave defenders, giving themselves up so the rest of the Spanish can flee. The white flag is flying from the fort, and the sounds of battle dissipate. He turns and, along with his crew, thrusts the boat off the riverbank. They quickly paddle across the river. The St. Johns River is easygoing at this spot, and they get across it easily. Somewhat perplexingly, the British don't try to prevent their departure; perhaps the deception has been entirely successful. It felt too easy, though. Hernando looks back across the river at the fort. The British infantry is taking possession of the fortifications, and he can see redcoats in the parapets and along the walls. No musket or rifle fire comes their way, which once again seems odd. The Union Jack is raised above the fort, and the white flag is lowered. As the boats hit the river's opposite bank, the Spanish soldiers disembark and are formed up into marching order. They aim to march briskly along the trade route between the forts and St. Augustine. Thankful for the escape, a positive urgency permeates Sergeant Moreno-Rodriguez's force. They move quickly, at double pace, realizing that it wouldn't take long for the British to mount a pursuit.

The way ahead offers a well-used track. It's almost a road, arrow straight, crossing the Florida forest. As the main trading route between Pensacola and St. Augustine, it is well-used, footbridges have been constructed, and the path is compacted from years of traffic. They move hurriedly. After a mile, they realize why the British let them go. The Florida jungle surrounds them. Oaks, maples, and cypress grow along the edges of the trail. At points, redbuds, myrtle, and holly are dotted in the marshland. They are surrounded by densely packed trees with undergrowth that could camouflage many threats, so they run straight into the trap. It is a well-positioned and concealed ambush.

The British allies, the Creeks, had been waiting for precisely this eventuality. Hernando is in the middle of the column. A sudden whoop and scream is the first he knows about the attack. Sudden and horrifying. Creek Indians rush into the column from the forest. A few arrows arch into them. A couple of men close to Hernando fall. One has a white-plumed arrow stuck out of his chest. Then, warriors race through the column, hatchets swinging. Another defender falls nearby, his face vacant and his head bloodied. Hernando hears his sergeant's commands, raises his musket, and fires aimlessly into the forest. Who knew if they'd hit anything? Desperately, he pulls out his long knife; he has no time to reload the musket; the melee is sudden and ferocious. Men are fighting hand-to-hand combat across the column.

The Creek Indian who faces him holds a tomahawk in one hand and a machete in the other. Fully decked in red warpaint, headdress, and tattoos, the man is terrifying. Hernando would have run if there was anywhere to go. The warrior swings the tomahawk. Hernando ducks just in time as the axe slices his left earlobe. He parries the sudden thrust of the warrior's machete with his long knife and stabs hard at his assailant's chest. The man pivots at speed. Hernando misses. The warrior's speed of movement far surpasses Hernando's capability, and he knows he's doomed.

Then, there are more distinct war cries, and a second group of Indians smashes into the column and joins the fray. They are dressed differently from the first group; hairstyles, clothing, and tattoos mark them out as a new tribe. Hernando understands they are Spanish allies, maybe the Yamasee. Their allies have timed the counteroffensive perfectly, and the Creeks' surprise is complete. A tall, ebony black Yamasee combatant jumps between Hernando and his Creek opponent. The man wields an oaken staff, spinning it with both hands at incredible speed. The Creek Indian attacks. It is an ambitious and ambidextrous move, cutting the tomahawk down with the right hand while thrusting the machete with the left. The Yamasee's whirling shaft strikes both attacker's hands almost simultaneously, disarming him. As the Yamasee aims a killing blow at the Creek, the man is joined by two companions. Each wielding a tomahawk. In the blink of an eye, the Yamasee also disarms these men.

Then, an odd thing happens. The Yamasee warrior seems to recognize the other two and speaks faltering English to them. Surprise crosses the faces of the two new Creeks, and suddenly, they grin. It is a wholly unexpected event. They swiftly gather their weapons and haul their compatriot away, leaving the killing ground for the victorious Yamasee. The small battle is over. Only minutes have passed since the beginning of the ambush and subsequent counteroffensive. The Spanish column is largely intact, saved from inevitable defeat by their native allies. Four men are dead, and there are several injured, but they've avoided total annihilation. The Yamasee have protected critical troops that will soon be needed to defend St. Augustine.

Chapter 42: Flamborough

Lieutenant Williams was surrounded by opulence. In truth, he was getting used to it. His lodgings, on the British flagship, the Flamborough, were even more luxurious than the Governor's mansion. He was surrounded by red velvet drapes, exquisite oak floors, oak panels, and silk cushions. The room boasted flawless carvings of mythical beasts and expensive pictures, figurines, and other accouterments of the aristocracy. Williams' accommodation was in the ship's stern, adjacent to the captain's quarters. Usually reserved for titled passengers, it was used by Colonel Vanderdussen, South Carolina's military leader. Williams had been appointed to become the colonel's aide and the chief correspondent with the Acting Governor Bull. It was hardly the riskiest job going. His work was observing the action, sending personal observations to Bull, supporting Vanderdussen, and writing letters. Frankly, Williams was expecting it to be boring, but he craved something more dangerous.

The vessel was undulating gently. It was an annoying pitch and roll that took some getting used to. The British flagship was an enormous frigate; gigantic masts were masked by full sails that billowed in the placid tropical wind. The Flamborough was cutting through the moderate swells caused by the leading frigates. Hence, the slight undulations. Williams preferred something more severe. Bracing oneself against vast storms at least tells you you're at sea. The ship was part of Commodore Pearce's squadron. Three of the British Navy's finest frigates and four support craft. It was a formidable fleet heading toward the St. Johns River. Having loitered in the Jekyll Sound, it was rendezvousing with General Oglethorpe's army. South Carolina's militia and the Darien highlanders were aboard the fleet. The Navy's marines and sizable artillery of thirty or more guns completed the forces sailing for Florida. All were sent to assist in the invasion.

Williams had just digested the latest news. Several letters are lying across his desk. The first was a letter from General Oglethorpe to Colonel Vanderdussen, Commodore Pearce, and Captain Mackay. Oglethorpe's commando raid along the St. Johns River has succeeded. A contingent of his 42nd Regiment of Foot have occupied Fort San Francisco De Pupo and intend to hold it, cutting off the trade route between Pensacola and St. Augustine. The Creeks and Colonel Palmer's rangers are heading inland, chasing some retreating Spanish and clearing the forests of Yamasee patrols. Meanwhile, General Oglethorpe, his regiment, and their cannons are moving up the river to meet the fleet at its mouth. It appears the first phase of the invasion is complete, and Oglethorpe's tone in the letter was celebratory.

The second letter was from Acting Governor Bull and was only for Colonel Vanderdussen's eyes. It had led Williams to gasp in astonishment and lean back in his chair in contemplation. The letter laid out the conditions set by the legislature for South Carolina's engagement in the upcoming involvement in the conflict. Bull's tone was formal, but Williams could sense anger and sarcasm in the colonel's tone. He wondered who was scribing the letters now that he was absent. Despite the danger from flying objects, that was a cushy chore, and he hoped to get it back on his return.

The letter's contents were fascinating. They laid out South Carolina's reluctance to be involved in the attack. It appeared that Oglethorpe had been badgering them for months before Chief Tomochichi's death. The general had estimated that he did not have enough men and materials to conduct the invasion with Georgia's resources alone. He'd exhausted his personal funds but offered to loan money to the cause if South Carolina joined it. The legislature had refused him many times. Only after the atrocity on Amelia Island and eight months of debate had the legislature agreed to South Carolina's involvement. Oglethorpe had agreed to loan four thousand pounds secured against Georgia's future tax income, while South Carolina finally committed significant funds and the South Carolina militia under Colonel Vanderdussen's leadership.

The cause of the delay, though it had endangered the endeavor, was well known. Oglethorpe's personal commitment was a surprise, but it was not the reason for Williams to sit back in a chair aghast. The conditions the South Carolina Common Assembly had extracted from Oglethorpe were hefty. He wondered how they might impact the mission's success. Oglethorpe had received only half the troops he'd asked for. South Carolina's militia had been committed to serve for only four months and not six, as usual. This meant the operation would have to be undertaken more quickly. However, the last condition seemed the worst. General Oglethorpe wouldn't be granted complete military control over these troops. He would have to share command with Colonel Vanderdussen. Lieutenant Williams was new to the officer class, but splitting authority was a known elementary mistake. He worried about Vanderdussen's fastidiousness and penchant for administrative detail. Would the colonel have the flexibility to cede to Oglethorpe when needed? He doubted it.

Williams reflected that South Carolina's delay and the requirements outlined in the letter weren't ideal. Oglethorpe had already lost some of his Creek allies after the death of Tomochichi, and now he'd received a much smaller part of South Carolina's militia. Williams surmised that the Stono Rebellion was likely the cause. Residents of the colony were still fearful about another rebellion, especially if the absence of the militia would further weaken the community.

It was Bull's unveiled comments to Vanderdussen, though that were the most startling, "I am convinced that the Common Assembly is angry with our friend Oglethorpe. Georgia's longstanding prohibitions against slavery and rum have created much controversy in political circles here. They think he is becoming a progressive autocrat who doesn't understand our ways of doing things. It's conceivable they've dragged their feet and given him a poisoned chalice as a deliberate snub. Be careful, my friend; you must understand some key political nuances here. Don't give control of South Carolina's militia to Oglethorpe unless you wish to acquire some powerful political enemies. Only agree to military actions you deem wise yourself."

Williams leaned forward and picked up the letter. He reread these words. They didn't make sense. Why the delay? Why the conditions? The King and the British Parliament had given Oglethorpe the generalship. It didn't seem right for the South Carolina legislature to circumvent these powers. Yes, the man was decisive, and everybody looked to his leadership in Georgia, but describing him as dictatorial seemed to stretch reality somewhat. Yet here it was. Williams also knew

Oglethorpe's edicts over rum and slavery in Georgia had been highly unpopular in its sister colony. So, this underlying root cause for the delay did make sense. Neither item bothered him much, but he'd sat through enough debates in alehouses to know that citizens across the colony resented Oglethorpe for these regulations. However, Williams learned from talking to Acting Governor Bull that these bans mattered much less to South Carolina than Georgia's efforts to monopolize the Indian trade. Though he saw it daily, stuff like this made him want to avoid politics. Based on these machinations, South Carolina could hardly be described as rooting for Oglethorpe's success. Yet, South Carolina was equally exposed to Spanish retribution if the invasion failed. None of it made sense to Williams. It was time for a break. He locked the letters in a desk drawer and left his chambers.

⧗ ⧗ ⧗

The climb up the gangway was brief. After a few moments, he emerged onto Flamborough's poop deck. The fresh air was exhilarating. There was a light breeze off the sea. It was a hot, sunny day. Though it would be muggy inland, the air wafting across the ship was salty and pleasant. Gulls squawked as they followed the vessel; their presence seemed never-ending. Flamborough's giant masts and sails towered above him. They were in full sail. All the canvases were tight as they propelled the frigate through the open seas. Williams moved to the taffrail log at the end of the poop. It was wet, having been used recently.

There were four supporting vessels following the flagship. They were smaller but no less imposing, with significant gun decks and humming with activity. The other day, Williams saw the two escorting British frigates from the foredeck. Virtually the same size as the Flamborough, their three decks bristled with cannon, and their rigging, masts, and sails were as complex. Again, they were teeming with sailors, marines, and militia. Undoubtedly, they'd assembled a formidable armada, which was on the verge of entering Florida's waters.

Williams noticed that gentle, irritating, undulating motion again. At least on deck, the air was refreshing, unlike the stagnant fetid air in the cabins. He'd never suffered from seasickness, but he wondered about that. These gentle swells made him speculate that he might be susceptible to it. His stomach certainly churned at inopportune moments. As he breathed in deeply and enjoyed the fine air, he considered another of the operation's perplexing aspects. Colonel Vanderdussen had agreed with Commodore Pearce a slow sweep of the seas between St. Simon's Island and their liaison with Oglethorpe at the mouth of the St. Johns River. There was no urgency in their movement. Though no navigator, Williams realized that they were zig-zagging their way south. He couldn't fathom the reason. Were they deliberately moving slowly? Were they patrolling for Spanish shipping?

The only conclusion he could reach was that they were requisitioning supplies and men. They'd stopped several British merchant ships, taken supplies, and stripped them of men, many of whom had been forced to join South Carolina's militia. Williams thought that perhaps Colonel Vanderdussen was trying to add to his manpower before arriving at their rendezvous. Such sailors were tough and might add some backbone to the militia, which was still suffering from its prior losses.

The last ship they stopped was heading toward Charles Town. It was leaving Florida's waters, which raised suspicions.

The vessel was called the Freedom, and a heavy-set, red-headed, and bearded man, Captain Drayton, led her. The crew was a mixed bag. Some South Carolinians and some French from New Orleans. They were a typical British merchant craft but with an unusually far-ranging route. Vanderdussen had told him that they'd been as far north as New York and south as far as French New Orleans. Until recently, they'd traded in the Caribbean with the Spanish. It looked like they were smugglers and slavers, as well as traders.

Now that the war had arrived, they were fleeing Spanish waters, and their business dealings would be disrupted until the war ended. The captain had been a wily old soul who knew how to play the situation. He gave up half his crew to the militia and shared his ill-gotten goods with Commodore Pearce. It wasn't long before the Freedom sailed north with a skeleton crew and significantly less wealthy captain. The man's type was obvious, though. He'd continue to prosper, plying his trade around Britain's Northern American colonies. His losses would be a minor blip. However, future profits would be more challenging now that the war was progressing. The unfortunate sailors who'd made up the captain's crew might not be so fortunate. They'd been incorporated into South Carolina's militia units and were destined to join the fight.

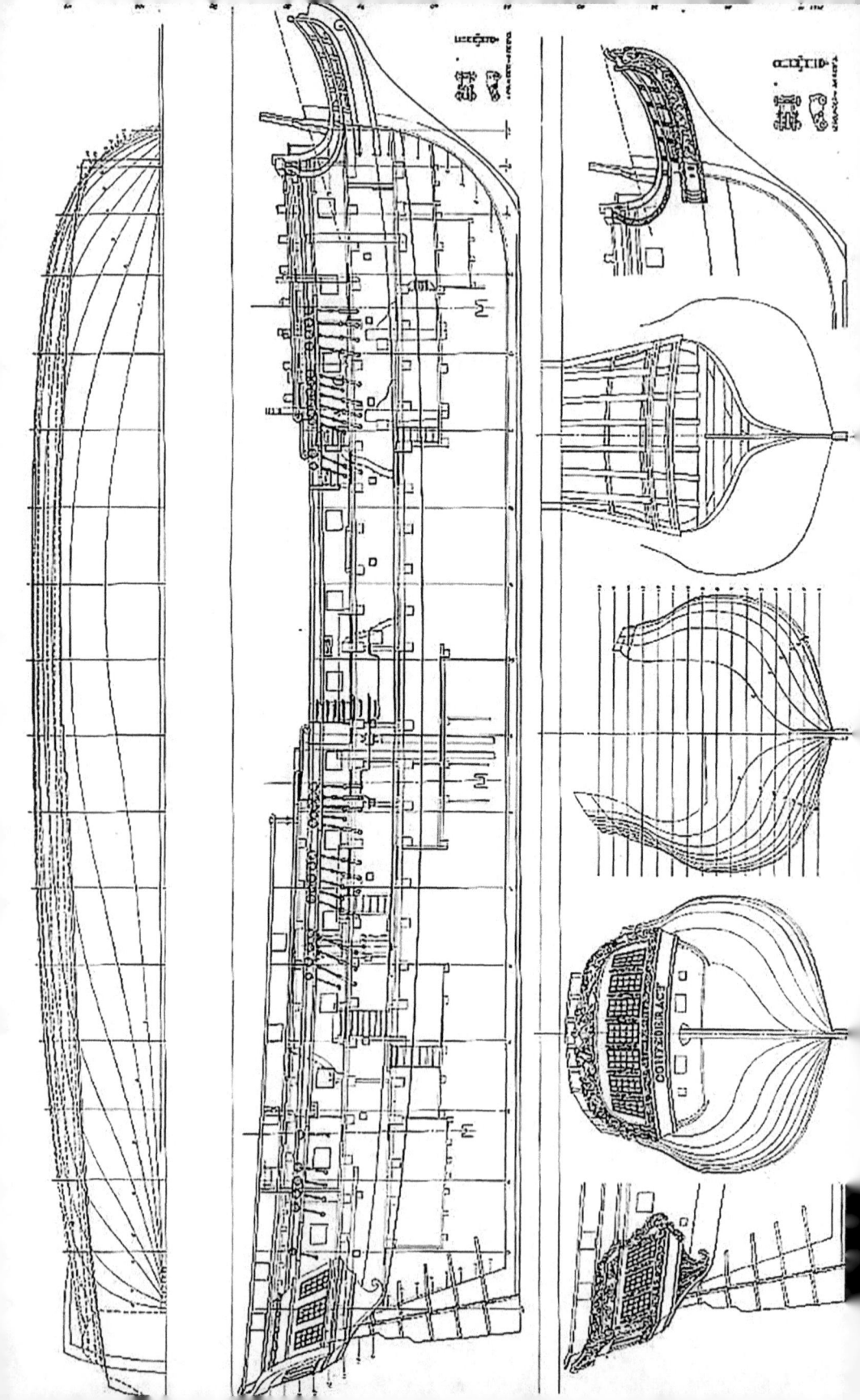

Chapter 43: Enlistment

The crow's nest job had become boring. O'Sullivan had initially relished it. Being away from Freedom's below-deck stench had been a compelling motivation to volunteer for the assignment. After the storm, the odors began dissipating, though, and now he was constantly swaying up above the vessel. He was alone, and his duties were tedious. O'Sullivan was constantly on the lookout for new storms or potential adversaries. His eyes were often strained, watery from the salty air and the continual staring at the cerulean sea and sky. On the plus side, at least he didn't have to endlessly strain his voice, putting on a fake Frenchman's accent. The isolation did have some merit alongside its increasing dullness.

Occasionally, the monotony was broken by seabirds. O'Sullivan was getting adept at identifying them. The gulls were common and followed the ship everywhere, waiting for waste to be thrown overboard. With their black heads and grey bodies, Terns often flew out from the coast, and he spotted them frequently. Less common were the cormorants, oystercatchers, and turnstones. It broke the tedium when he caught a glimpse of these. The ocean depths were translucent and smooth. There was no hint of bad weather. The sky was clear, and the sun was scorching. O'Sullivan could tell they were heading into the summer months, and his already baked skin would get further crispened. He certainly looked like the archetype. A weather-beaten sailor with a long, greasy mop of hair and a bristly, unkempt beard. His clothes were tatty, patched up, and dirty. At least he would pass for a mariner when they returned to Charles Town. Perhaps he would remain hidden, though the risks of detection were still high. If he got lucky, they would stop in Savannah, and he could jump ship there. There was a much lower chance of being recognized in Georgia.

The day was humdrum. O'Sullivan had only seen gulls and had nodded off somewhat. It was a precarious thing to do, harnessed up in the crow's nest a hundred feet above the deck. As his eyes flickered open, he saw several dots on the horizon. It awakened O'Sullivan from his dozing, and he stared at the specks with sudden intensity. As he watched, they grew. It was definitely ships, but who's? He signaled to Captain Drake that vessels were approaching. First, he could see three, then five, and soon there were seven. There were three immense ships in front, possibly British frigates, hopefully not Spanish galleons. The other vessels were smaller, perhaps supply ships. Captain Drake was on the Freedom's foredeck, craning across the gunwale with his looking glass, trying to discern the nationality of the approaching fleet. O'Sullivan spotted it first. The Red Ensign flew from the leading ships. The red of the flag became visible. As the British Navy's fleet came closer, O'Sullivan could see the hated Union Jack in the left corner of the flags. It appeared to be a British invasion taskforce heading into Florida's waters. He indicated to Captain Drake that the incoming vessels were friendly. Friendly for the captain, perhaps, but not for O'Sullivan.

As the British frigates closed in on the merchantman, they began to tower over the Freedom. Captain Drake's vessel wasn't a small ship, but it appeared tiny in comparison. The frigates had three rows of guns and could have easily blown the merchantman up. The lead frigate signaled their intention to board the Freedom. Captain Drake cut the sails and slowed the ship. One of the British frigates tacked alongside and then dispatched a boarding party. Several small boats were launched and were rowed expertly toward them. O'Sullivan observed the British vessel closely; its name was the Flamborough. With little need for him to be in the crow's nest, the captain called him down. O'Sullivan skillfully descended the mainmast's rigging to the deck. A large party of British marines had boarded, and a British naval officer was in a heated conversation with Captain Drake.

The crew tried to appear busy. They sensed that all was not well. The captain was a jovial, pleasant man; being so animated was unusual. He grew increasingly sweaty and lively as he debated with the officer. It soon became clear why the captain's exchange elicited such concern. As they often did, the British Navy planned to requisition items from the Freedom. More marines boarded and began to strip the vessel of needed items such as rope, rigging, and spare canvas. Captain Drake pulled an ornate chest from his captain's quarters, and it was spirited across to the Flamborough. Then, the true dreadfulness of the commandeering became apparent. Over half the sailors were to join the navy's fleet, and Captain Drake was to be left with a minimal crew. They drew straws, and O'Sullivan learned he'd be one of the men who would leave imminently. He glanced at the crow's nest at the very tip of Freedom's mainmast. Perhaps boring wasn't so bad after all. After the British Navy had taken everything they wanted, Captain Drake and the Freedom were released. O'Sullivan meanwhile joined the vast majority of Freedom's crew who were taken across to the Flamborough.

☒　☒　☒

The trickiness of O'Sullivan's situation did not emerge straight away. It was common practice for the British Navy to impress men into their ranks. O'Sullivan had assumed that would be their fate. A much more ruinous state unfolded, at least for O'Sullivan. The crew was to join and reinforce South Carolina's militia. Many of the commandeered men were overjoyed by this outcome. It meant they would serve for four months and then earn freedom, returning to South Carolina. Impressment would have been a much harsher and indefinite fate. However, for O'Sullivan, this development was unwelcome and presented many challenges. First and foremost, there was a real chance he'd be identified. Most of the militia were from Charles Town, and he'd operated his spy network in the city for years. He looked altered, but the chance of being found out remained. If somebody did recognize him, they'd know his old persona, not his new one, and the difference would likely raise immediate alarm. Meanwhile, Freedom's crew had already begun questioning his story about being from Louisiana and his bogus accent. The odds of being caught had grown with his secondment to the South Carolina militia. If feasible, he resolved to start a new guise, something simple, but the decision depended upon his enlistment. Which unit of the militia he was allotted to and whether other crew members joined him would influence his decision. Keeping multiple personas going could be draining, and there was always the chance of getting caught up in the complexity of maintaining them.

O'Sullivan's luck held. The crew of the Freedom was dispersed across multiple units of South Carolina's militia, many of which were accommodated on other ships. He was alone in joining his new unit and stayed aboard the Flamborough, allowing him to cast off his prior façade to adopt a new one. Along with this good fortune he was drafted into a unit from Port Royal. Though he'd maintained a spy network in the city, he'd rarely visited it and was unlikely to be known by anyone. It was a risk; he might still meet sailors from the Freedom, but he decided to switch to a well-practiced dialect. His Irish heritage made its adoption easier. O'Sullivan became a former fisherman who'd once lived by the shores of Tintagel, Cornwall. His accent became rich and melodic, flowing with a gentle lilt. The musical quality of the intonation was comfortable, and it came to O'Sullivan easily. He was relieved to forego his prior, more challenging accent with its French undertones. Being Cornish was almost natural, and it would put less stress on his vocal cords.

Port Royal's militia were accommodated below Flamborough's orlop deck, and O'Sullivan joined them there. They were cramped quarters. Four bunks were strung up over each other. Men had little space for their possessions and even less room to roam. The air wasn't as bad as it had been after the Freedom had transported slaves, but that wasn't saying much. It was stagnant and stultifying. The sweaty stench of too many men confined together overwhelmed his senses. He closed his eyes and imagined being ensconced in his crow's nest while the breeze blew gently in his face. O'Sullivan knew it was an image that he'd have to return to if he was to maintain his sanity in these conditions. At least the seas were calm, and nobody was adding seasickness to the olfactory disaster in the cabin.

Captain Lewis was his new commander, and Lieutenant Robinson was his unit leader. The squad had slightly over twenty men. O'Sullivan was supplied with a musket and bayonet but little else. The unit had some meager supplies, and they shared food with him. O'Sullivan kept himself busy cleaning the gun and sharpening his knife and bayonet. He barely spoke to anyone. Better to let others do the talking. It was a tactic he'd learned years ago when trying to escape British atrocities in Ireland. They had little to do but talk, play dice, and gamble. Occasionally, they were allowed on deck, strictly following a predetermined schedule. O'Sullivan learned a lot. His bunk companions, Harrison and Walker, were particularly talkative. Truth be told, they didn't seem to know much of any consequence. The militia had been called up for the invasion of Florida, they'd joined the fleet and were headed south to meet the rest of the army at the mouth of the St. Johns River. That's all they knew. The moment O'Sullivan had seen the armada from the crow's nest, he'd figured that much out by himself. At least he'd be back in Florida, but how he was to escape and return to his Spanish spymaster continued to be elusive.

Fortunately, there were only a few days of suffering in the overcrowded, foul, stinking quarters before they arrived. The vessel noticeably slowed its speed. It proceeded at a snail's pace. O'Sullivan knew from his years as a mariner that the Flamborough was being piloted into its mooring. Four guns fired. This meant they'd arrived at their destination and would soon disembark. The captain's orders to pack haversacks and gather weapons confirmed the news. There was excitement among the militia. The first phase of their mission was complete, and now they could begin the next. Harrison and

Walker chattered incessantly. O'Sullivan was sure they'd be a liability in a battle and thought he might have to silence them. He'd then have two fewer Brits to worry about. His value as an implanted spy was much more significant than two trivial deaths, so he restrained his urge.

Their disembarkation seemed to take an age. Hours passed, and the excitement descended into quiet boredom. Even Harrison and Walker managed to descend into a sullen silence. Eventually, they were allowed to go ashore. They made their way up from the orlop deck via the gangways, ladders, and stairways. Navigating through the maze and warrens of a sizable British frigate took time, but at least they were moving and would soon hit the fresh air. They were stunned by the scene when they finally made it onto the upper side of the orlop deck.

The three frigates were moored in May Port's harbor; the supply ships waited patiently in the mouth of the St. Johns River. South Carolina's entire militia was landing. There were hundreds of troops as far as the eye could see, columns of men filed across gangplanks and onto the shore. Each ship had upwards of twenty gangways. Men waited while others crossed. On the landward side, lines of militia streamed away from the harbor. Some of the guns had been unloaded and guarded in an artillery reserve. An officer walked his grey horse over a widened bridge, carefully hiding the horse's eyes so it didn't panic. The man whispered into its ear to calm it.

In the distance, along an invulnerable plateau, there was an encampment of British regulars. Regimental colors and the Union Jack flew provocatively over the site. Two hundred or more tents were spread across the hill. Redcoats could be seen milling about. Cooking fires were alight, and smoke billowed into the air. Some of South Carolina's militia began to sing a Welsh ballad about adventure and adversity. Ar Lan y Mor resonated, their mood captured the moment, and others took up the song. The singing spread across the landscape. An omen of the devastation that Florida would soon face.

O'Sullivan's sentiment differed. Inwardly, he seethed with hatred. Here they were, his loathsome enemies, the redcoats. The men who'd raped, stolen, and broken his beloved Ireland. The protestant riffraff who'd given up the true faith. These vagabonds now sat on the edge of his adopted homeland, Florida. Ready to invade it. Ready to bring their unique taste of devastation to it, just like they'd done to Ireland; yet here he stood on the wrong side of the dividing line. How can he get back? How can he help defend Spanish Florida? These questions consumed him as he crossed the gangplank onto dry land.

Chapter 44: Anastasia Island

Catori's embarrassment was short-lived. The Yamasee knew her qualities and quickly forgave her mission's losses. It had been a forlorn hope that they could assassinate the British general before he sealed an alliance with the Lower Creeks. Chioke appreciated how close it must have been. His arrow had grazed the man's arm, and surely its poison had done some damage. Not enough, it appeared. The British were invading Florida, and General Oglethorpe was commanding them.

Chioke had stayed close to Catori. As well as her lover, he had become her protector and righthand man. His power and physical prowess were an ever-present shadow, following her everywhere, demanding respect from her tribe's warriors. The Yamasee were no fools, though; they recognized superior leadership, and thus Catori gained followers despite the failure of her previous assignment. She led a band of some twenty Yamasee fighters. It had been a challenging time for the Yamasee and their Seminole brothers. The success of Oglethorpe's negotiations had led to wave upon wave of Creek attacks across Northern Florida. The Lower Creeks and their Yamacraw allies were winning, pushing the Spanish-allied tribes backward across the region. The assaults followed the native way, deep forest warfare of the most brutal kind.

Repeatedly, Catori had proven herself over the months following their return. Feint, followed by ruthless onslaught. Cunning traps were set in advantageous gorges. Fake retreats drew enemies into terrifying counterattacks. Pincer moves clamped foes into the jaws of overwhelming raids. Chioke had witnessed all of Catori's tactics, and though he was an experienced warrior, he was duly impressed. Though the Yamasee and Seminoles had gradually lost the overall battle in the face of overwhelming numbers, Catori had demonstrated her leadership.

One recent success had further enhanced Catori's reputation. Another equal number of Seminoles had joined her Yamasee troop, and they had designed another trick for their Creek opponents. It was simple enough. Yamasee scouts had observed the British landing north of the Spanish forts, but their surveillance was too late to be helpful to the Spanish defenders. The British were also too powerful to attack, having at least a regiment of British regulars. As the Yamasee advanced up the trade road, their scouts discovered a smaller band of Creeks who had crossed the St. Johns River. The Creeks evidently hoped to cut off any retreat from the Spanish forts and had quietly set up an ambush along the road. Catori, as tactically astute as ever, set up a counter-ambush. Though her Spanish allies may not have appreciated being used as bait, this was Catori's intent. Allow the Spanish to be drawn into the trap and hit their Creek enemies when least expected, when they thought they were attacking and winning an important victory.

Chioke was astounded that Catori's plan once again unfolded precisely as intended. The Spanish retreated across the river and moved at pace up the trade road toward St. Augustine. They were disciplined and organized yet still rushed straight into the Creek ambush. As the Creeks attacked, Catori released the counter move, and the results were devastating. Overwhelming numbers of Yamasee and Seminole warriors counterattacked, almost obliterating the Creeks. The maneuver saved the Spanish from certain annihilation and secured a few days of extra control over the forests between the river and St. Augustine. Catori's successful feat had even reached the grateful ears of General Montiano himself, as the general knew he needed every available man to defend St. Augustine.

The elation didn't last long, as the British sent a more significant force across the river, effectively cutting off the supply route between St. Augustine and Pensacola. The combination of colonial rangers and Creeks proved too much to hold back. The Yamasee and Seminoles themselves retreated. Ultimately, the British won. They'd captured the forts and the western approaches to the Castillo.

As Chioke mused about these battles, he fondly remembered his surprise. It had been unexpected and happened as he'd launched himself into the fray trying to rescue a Spanish soldier from certain death. He was about to dispatch the man's assailant when, to his utter surprise, two familiar faces popped out of the forest. Chioke saw Hilli's grinning expression first and then Sin's frowning visage. Though both had aged, Chioke knew them instantly; they were his Yamacraw friends. The realization stopped his killing blows immediately. Though now mortal enemies, Chioke owed the two warriors his life. They had escorted him away from his slavery and incarceration in Savannah and had become companions on the journey to the borderlands. He was indebted to them and so shouted at them to leave before other Yamasee warriors joined the fracas. They grasped their predicament, grabbed their friend, and retreated into the forest.

Only a few moments had passed, and they were gone. Safe to fight another day. Chioke considered the episode a debt paid but hoped none of his Yamasee brethren had observed his mercy. Such clemency was not permitted in the tribe's warrior culture. It was now weeks ago, and he could breathe more easily. Other than the Spanish soldier, nobody had witnessed his act of grace—at least nobody who was courageous enough to challenge him for it. Next time, though, he wouldn't take such risks; the debt had been fully repaid.

After the battle, they escorted the Spanish retreat. The damage to the withdrawing column had been minimal, with a few dead soldiers and several injured. In contrast, the cost for the Creeks was significant. They'd counted ten dead and several others mortally wounded. The Creeks had retreated and taken their deceased and injured with them. Despite the perils, Catori's gambit paid off. They'd taken a chance using their allies as a lure. It might have endangered the alliance if it had failed but it succeeded spectacularly. The Spanish regulars had reinforced the Castillo, and the general was content with the outcome. The Yamasee had consequently lost Northern Florida and the lands west of St. Augustine. Knowing they needed to be on hand, Catori's force thus joined the Seminole encampment on Anastasia Island.

⌛ ⌛ ⌛

Anastasia Island was stunning. Chioke rarely preferred Florida to his home, Igboland, but the island rivaled any he'd visited. The ocean breezes that drifted across the terrain provided happy relief from the intense heat of Florida's jungles.

The wind rustled through the leaves of the ancient oaks. The forest was dense and full of life. Sandy dunes and iridescent seashores amplified its beauty. Spanish moss hung from the oak branches, gently swaying. The air was thick with salty brine.

Chioke was residing in the Seminoles' camp and had taken time to explore the island. It served as a strategic point for the Spanish and guarded the Matanzas River from marauding ships. A battery had been constructed at the island's tip to defend the river's entrance. It had been recently improved as part of the general's efforts to strengthen St. Augustine's fortifications. The legendary coast guard commanded by Fandiño had assembled a fleet of half-galleys. These small shallow drafted vessels fitted out with nine-pound cannons patrolled the bay, shoals, and inlets approaching the city. They were constantly busy maneuvering around the waterways leading to the Castillo. The bay's shallow waters were intended to provide further protection against invasion. It was said that British warships could only attack with difficulty, with the chance they would be holed if they ran Fandiño's barricade. Chioke had heard rumors about this Fandiño. He was apparently notorious for cutting off Jenkins' ear and still wore the ear around his neck.

Chioke was hiking around the island with Catori when they discovered the coquina quarry. The mine had been used in the construction of the Castillo. Chioke marveled at the landscape. There were open pits surrounded by crags where segments of coquina had been detached and removed. The walls of the quarry displayed the stratified layers of shells. Its composition was strange—soft, porous limestone of compressed shells and fragments bound together by a rough textured material. There were distinctive hacks in the faces of the cliffs, where miners had cut stone blocks away. Telltale signs of removal were etched into the ground where ponies had dragged slabs. The quarry was overgrown in parts, but mining was ongoing in other sections. Presumably, rocks were being taken to repair the Castillo.

Chioke and Catori finished exploring the quarry and were returning to the Seminole encampment via one of Anastasia's pristine beaches. Suddenly, three British frigates appeared on the horizon almost out of nowhere. Soon afterward, the entire British fleet materialized, heading straight towards the island and the entrance to the Matanzas River. Where there was a fleet, there were cannons, sailors, and marines, and who knew where the army might be? They raced along the beach back to their Yamasee squad. Anastasia Island was about to be the focus of the British Navy's attention. As the armada closed, the two native tribes broke up camp. They knew that a retreat from the island was likely. Anastasia's battery prepared for the assault. Artillery officers sprinted from their quarters to their stations, preparing to fire on the approaching ships. Fandiño's half-galleys blockaded the river's mouth. They were a hive of activity as they prepared for the British to arrive.

Events unfolded swiftly. It looked as if the British Navy would slam straight into Fandiño's barrier, overwhelm it, and head upriver to lay siege to St. Augustine. A few well-timed cannonades from Fandiño's crews dissuaded them from this direct course of action. The British ships replied with a couple of return salvos, but these made little impact on Fandiño's smaller vessels. Most shots went high, there was only one direct hit, which caused minor damage. Then the Spanish battery open-fired and scored several hits on the British flagship. Recognizing the risks, the three British frigates veered away from the island's tip and maneuvered away, out of distance from the cannon fire. It was Chioke's first experience of large numbers of cannon firing swiftly in quick succession. The roar was thunderous and deafening as each cannon exploded and propelled its projectile. The air across the island was thick, and the acrid smell of gunpowder and the fog of war billowed across the bay. The ground seemed to shudder under the might of the discharges. It was a stupendous sensory overload that started and finished rapidly. The result was a stalemate. Fandiño's crew and the battery had deterred the British Navy from heading straight into the Matanzas River, but they had inflicted little loss. The entire fleet was intact and ready for its next attack.

Through the white smoke that drifted across the bay, Chioke could see that the British had dropped anchor off Anastasia Island. They were deciding what to do next. It didn't take long for them to engage in their next stratagem. Considerable numbers of small boats were launched from the British frigates and their supply ships. There were too many boats for Chioke to count. Each was jam-packed with marines. It was plain they planned an amphibious assault. It was a simple gambit, but the defenders didn't have an answer for it. The boats would land on Anastasia's long beaches, and the marines would fight their way inland, aiming to capture the battery. It was immediately apparent to the Spanish defenders that they'd been outmaneuvered. Fandiño's vessels couldn't afford to engage the British Navy in open waters as that would lead to inevitable defeat. The British ships were out of the cannons' range, so the marines were safe from bombardment. The incoming attackers far outnumbered the defenders despite the presence of the allied tribes. As they were under strict orders to preserve their forces, the Spanish commander made the only decision available. The order to retreat was made. The battery was abandoned, the guns spiked, and Fandiño's half-galleys transported the defenders across the river to strengthen St. Augustine's defense.

As Chioke and Catori joined the withdrawal, he considered the snare that was tightening around them. The British had closed off the west and removed the tribes from the North. They had captured the forts and blocked the supply route between Pensacola and St. Augustine. Now, they had captured the East. The British would likely strangle supplies or reinforcements reaching St. Augustine via the Atlantic coast. The British Navy clearly intended to stay and lay siege to the city, but where was the British army? And what was their intent?

Chapter 45: Fort Diego

Seeing an entire army uncoil, ready to march, and prepared to fight was a splendid sight. From Tom's vantage point on a nearby hill, he could see the whole scene. Oglethorpe's regiment had been camped on a plateau near the river, and they were breaking camp. Individual companies descended the plateau as units; their red uniforms marked them as the army's regulars. The day before, South Carolina's militia had disembarked from the British Navy's fleet. Many men in diverse civilian outfits had made camp in the valley. They were now forming into militia companies to the rear of the 42nd Regiment of Foot. An artillery unit of at least twenty guns was situated between the regulars and the militia. The artillery's ponies were being hitched to the guns, getting ready to haul the guns along as part of the column. Several artillery officers were gesticulating at their men animatedly, clearly concerned to protect their guns from harm. A pony was whipped harshly as it refused its bridle. Other artillery units were dotted throughout the army's unwinding spiral.

The supply train could be spotted at the far rear of the army; quartermasters were urging the suttlers to load up the wagons more hurriedly. Meanwhile, the Darien highlanders were forming the vanguard of the army. The burly highlanders, their tartans, drummers, and pipers comprised the ostentatious and colorful front ranks. A couple of Darien bagpipers began to play a stirring verse, adding further drama. The 42nd's buglers enhanced the musical mix, along with a few of the regiment's drummers and some militia fifers. The army was awakening, and it would be an eventful day. Tom was excited to see the entire military might of Georgia and South Carolina unfurl into a great beast, ready to devour Florida.

Colonel Palmer's rangers packed up their camp and headed toward their positions. Along with their Creek allies, the rangers would scout ahead of the army and protect its flanks. Tom led his unit to the front of the column beside the highlanders. The pipers' warbling tones could be heard above the din, and Tom was grateful. He loved bagpipes and hoped they would play all day. They inspired him, drawing a fighting spirit into his soul. As Tom examined his men, he saw contrasts. Like him, Coleman looked dangerous, enthused, and ready to engage in battle. Hill appeared reflective, withdrawn, and contemplative. Sanders was white, skittish, and perhaps scared; he looked like he might even throw up. It was strange how one's personality came to the fore during times of stress. He could see each man's quirks chiseled into their faces. Coleman's fighting disposition. Hill's creative, thoughtful side. Sanders, as they knew him to be, superficial and cowardly.

Tom and his unit sat on the grass verge as they waited for the army to finish forming. The army was due to march down a roughhewn road that led from May-Port directly to St. Augustine. It was another of the Spanish trade routes connecting the mouth of the river to the Spanish city. Marching the British army down this road made sense. It was wide, well-used, and compacted. They'd have little trouble moving down it, even with the volume of troops, ponies, horses, and cannons that would need to pass along it.

The route was a well-chosen attack, though perhaps lacking guile. It didn't take a genius to understand the general's strategy. The commando raid attacking the two forts had cut off St. Augustine on the westward side. Oglethorpe had left a garrison in Fort San Francisco de Pupo, ensuring the Spanish couldn't recapture it without significant cost. The Creeks and Palmer's rangers had cleared the west and north of Spain's native allies, the Yamasee and Seminoles. So, there was no chance for guerilla attacks on the army as it progressed toward St. Augustine. The British Navy, some artillery, and a component of South Carolina's militia had been sent to lay siege to St. Augustine via the Atlantic coastline. Meanwhile, the British army would advance on the city from the north. It was a claw designed to grasp the Spanish neck from three sides. Tom expected the city and Florida to be British within a few days. How could they possibly defend themselves against such overwhelming force?

The preparations took an age, which was to be expected; it was a vast army. As time progressed, Tom could tell that the officers were becoming impatient because of their increasing hollering and badgering of the men. Eventually, the vanguard moved forward down the St. Augustine Road. Tom directed his men to spread out, and they took their positions along the Darien highlanders' right flank. Tom was alone as he scouted the bushes alongside the road and listened to the bagpipes and drums. It was a noisy but rousing way to make war. After twenty minutes of marching, they paused again for the 42nd Regiment of Foot to follow and close the distance. Progress and pauses continued as units formed along the road behind the vanguard. Officers began to gallop along the flanks, encouraging more urgent action. Eventually, the entire army moved as one down the road, beginning to make quicker progress.

After an hour or so of marching, the army reached its first impediment. Fort Diego lay in the army's path. It was a small fort, not much more than a farmhouse surrounded by a wooden enclosure. An insignificant garrison of Spanish defenders protected the fort. As Palmer's advanced scouts came across the fort, Tom heard the retort of small arms fire. The defenders and the rangers were trying to pick each other off. Though the constant pop of guns continued for some time, and the stench of cordite wafted across the vanguard, it was an inconsequential skirmish. Palmer's scouts returned and reported to the commanding officer, Captain Mackay. The captain ordered the highlanders into an attacking line and then went to observe the fort from a nearby hillock. Tom noted that the highlanders appeared keen for their first action and some revenge for lost comrades.

The Darien Scots would miss out on their vengeance. Captain Mackay had no intention of losing good men to an unnecessary attack. It was barely more than a ranch, with just a few defenders. He would drag some guns up the hill and bombard them until the Spanish surrendered. Tom saw movement from a small squad of artillery to the left of his position. Four immaculate twelve-pounders, their wagons, horses, and crews raced to the captain's chosen site. It was a modest mound, and the guns were hauled up swiftly. Colonel Palmer and a unit of the rangers went to guard the artillery. Several other officers joined them, seemingly keen to watch their first engagement of the war.

Before long, the cannons were firing; their constant booms echoed across the valley, and smoke drifted over the waiting highlanders. Though much smaller than the massive guns

Oglethorpe had used to assault Fort San Francisco de Pupo, they rapidly began to destroy the Spanish farmhouse. Firing in succession, the cannons blew up a dairy barn, then a sheep pen. The bombardment tore an enormous hole in the stockade. As the barrage continued, a fire flared in one of the haybarns. Another explosion took out one of the farmhouse walls. The Spanish could do nothing in response. Aimless shooting flecked across the base of the artillery's mound, but the distance was too far for the Spanish muskets to be practical. An oak door burst into smithereens as a cannonball hit it directly. A couple of blue and white uniformed soldiers lay still in the open doorway and were likely dead. Unable to do much, the Spanish capitulated and raised the flag of surrender. They'd done enough to avoid being accused of cowardice, but not much more. Though faced with the entire invading British army, Tom didn't think one could expect much. However, if the war continued like this, they'd be home in a month.

As the artillery hitched their cannons back to the gun carriages, the Spanish vacated the farmhouse. There couldn't have been more than twenty men who'd successfully blocked the British army's progression for several hours. Orders were dispatched, the highlanders reformed into a column, and the military weaved past the ruined farmhouse. Hay continued to burn out of control in one of the outbuildings, and rubble from the farmhouse's collapsed wall suddenly gave way noisily. Scouts were sent in to look for supplies. As Tom's unit passed, he noticed that there appeared to be little evidence of food. The animals had been removed ages ago, and despite the flames, the burning haybarn didn't look as if it had been particularly full.

The army marched along the road for several hours before reaching its next impediment. It was much more substantial than the farm. A town sat on the road to St. Augustine. It had been fortified and was heavily garrisoned. As the British army's vanguard arrived, they encircled the town. Tom's unit joined the division of highlanders as they went northeast toward the Tolomato's riverbank. Once again, they flawlessly maneuvered from a marching column into a battle line, three rows deep. Captain Mackay's supporting artillery found another more sizable knoll and unhitched their guns. General Oglethorpe ordered his regiment to face the barricaded town from the north, and he sent Colonel Palmer and the contingent of South Carolina's militia to surround the town to the northwest. Upon a sizable rise, Oglethorpe positioned his headquarters just behind his regiment's front lines, slightly to the northeast. The bulk of the artillery and the officers joined him there. Two artillery units, each hauling four twelve-pounders, were sent northwest to strengthen the militia's position. These cannons guarded the plains between the town and the militia's lines and they were supplied with plenty of canister shot. Oglethorpe had ensured that an early evening Spanish attack on his weakest position would end in utter disaster for his enemy, should they try it. Any attackers would be flayed by the enfilading fire of guns loaded with anti-personnel ammunition.

The sultry Florida evening was drawing in. The heat had that intense breath-sucking quality, and Tom knew the summer season would soon arrive. Mosquitos were a constant headache on their march, and they descended on the men in swarms as the army halted and assessed its next steps. Camps were being set up across the lines, and fires were set. The soldiers hoped the billowing smoke would keep the bugs away. Clearly, there was no intent to attack the town this evening. Tom's unit assembled within a grove of palmettoes close to the highlanders' billets.

Tom ordered them to make camp while he crept through the reeds to get a closer look at the town. He'd not seen anything like it. The town was composed of perhaps fifty or sixty houses. A recently constructed palisade surrounded it. The barrier included towers and gantries, which appeared to be well-built. The houses were laid out like some of the older towns in Yorkshire. They were all higgledy-piggledy as if they'd been thrown there randomly. To an untrained eye, the town looked like a slum. Buildings were built using cheap, readily available materials, and there was no rhyme or reason to the positioning of houses, and the streets meandered accordingly. Each home seemed to have its own style. Tom's training as a carpenter led him to an entirely different conclusion. He saw a town full of unique buildings applying varying construction methods, many of which he'd never seen before. There was a freedom and inventiveness about the place. It seemed like some outlandish African tribes had come together in a great fusion of creativity. Yet, Spanish overtones in the newer buildings and barricades offered a European flavor to the settlement. Somewhat perplexed, Tom carefully crawled backward out of the reeds and headed for his unit's encampment.

Hill had put together a makeshift bivouac while Sanders had lit a fire. It was gradually catching. A waft of smoke spiraled upward from some twigs and leaves while tiny flames licked the edges of the pile. Coleman arrived from collecting wood for the fire, his arms full of brushwood. Tom remained puzzled: "What's this town? It's very odd-looking, and they've only just built fences around it."

While the others frowned, Coleman answered, "According to the Scots, it's called Mose. They say it's been here for decades. Apparently, the South Carolinian militia are itching to attack. The place is full of their escaped slaves. They're desperate to burn it to the ground and kill everybody, bloodthirsty lot!"

Tom realized Coleman's gossip made sense. He recalled Lamine's and Chioke's flight from Georgia. They'd intended to head south to a free black township called Mose. This must be it. The Spanish had lured escapees to freedom in Florida, and this must be their home. As night was drawing in, Tom assumed the British attack would start the following morning. Surely the militia would get their way, and Mose would be demolished at daybreak.

Chapter 46: An Irish Marine

The twists and turns of fate hadn't spared O'Sullivan. They'd spent the night camping in May Port with the British army, only to reboard the ships the following day. It seemed he would be heading back to St. Augustine after all. Lieutenant Robinson briefed them as they filed into their cramped quarters, "That's it, lads, back onboard, take your old bunks. We're joining Colonel Vanderdussen's militia division while Colonel Palmer takes the others with the army. Promoted to marines, lads, bloody marines. I hope you lot can swim!"

O'Sullivan appreciated their night on land. It had been a long time since he'd been off the ship, and the fresh air, though stifling, had been welcome. During the night, he'd been tempted to sneak away. Though fantasizing about murdering a few redcoats in their sleep before departing had been an equally compelling urge. Returning to the overcrowded quarters with its distinct aromas hadn't been high on his list. However, O'Sullivan knew his duty. The Spanish couldn't have many embedded spies in the British force, so he needed to stay concealed until he could be useful. Perhaps he'd have a chance to assassinate General Oglethorpe or pass along critical invasion secrets. Though his anti-redcoat yearnings wouldn't abate, it remained essential that he didn't betray himself by acting on them too soon.

O'Sullivan continued to play the quiet, shy, impressed sailor originally from Cornwall while he listened and learned more. It didn't take long; Harrison's and Walker's senseless nattering soon revealed their mission. They'd learned it from the sailors, and it was an open secret onboard the Flamborough. The British Navy was heading straight for St. Augustine and was due to start the castle's bombardment. Colonel Vanderdussen, with half the South Carolina militia and a contingent of artillery, was commanded to capture Anastasia Island's battery and turn the guns upon the citadel. So, the lieutenant's gibe made more sense; his squad was to become marines. They would make a waterborne assault, land on the beaches, and take the island. The assault would probably be carried out in the face of cannon fire, and the fighting after they landed would be intense. O'Sullivan didn't fear the attack; he would do what he had to and take the required risks. Others in the squad were afraid. Several couldn't swim, and as a civilian militia, their training for such adventures was limited. Their instruction was simple marching, land-based maneuvers, and practicing firing muskets and stabbing bayonets. Landing a small boat on a beach to storm and capture an island, while faced by a battery, had many rightly scared. Consequently, the scent of fear was added to the atrocious odors in their tight cabin. O'Sullivan knew it would only take a day for the armada to reach St. Augustine. So, no training would be offered, and the squad had little time for their fears to take hold.

⧗ ⧗ ⧗

The whistles demanding their immediate attention started early the following day. Few had slept well as they worried about the assault expected to unfold at daybreak. O'Sullivan wasn't one of them. He'd had a cozy night and dreamt about his old house in the city. Refreshed, he jumped out of his bunk bed, dressed quickly, and gathered his few possessions. The preparations onboard were chaotic. Men rushed everywhere in the cramped quarters, preparing for the militia's muster. Several tripped and fell. Others shouted urgent questions about lost equipment. Officers barked orders, and slowly, a semblance of calm descended over the disorder.

Soon, the Port Royal militia ascended Flamborough's stairways and emerged onto its decks. Other units of South Carolina's militia likewise appeared across the entire vessel. O'Sullivan could see similar events occurring onboard the other British frigates. The entire militia was being readied for the attack on Anastasia Island. The three frigates were a hive of activity. O'Sullivan associated the marshaling of forces with legions of rats suddenly scurrying around the ships. It was the brown civilian garb of the South Carolinians that had sparked the image. He unintentionally grinned at the thought; it seemed like an appropriate analogy. Hopefully, many of them would die like rats today.

The sailors were equally as busy, scurrying about preparing the vessel for battle. Meanwhile, the navy's gunners were called to the cannons, and some began to load and prime the guns. The militia was formed into units of twenty men. Each unit was adjacent to one of the skiffs dotted along the deck. A pulley system fastened them to the side of the frigate. A sailor was stationed alongside, ready to manipulate the mechanism so the boats could descend into the sea. The militia were commanded to stand to attention and wait. O'Sullivan groaned when he saw that Harrison and Walker had been allotted to his boat. Just his luck!

Like all the prospective marines, O'Sullivan had little to do but observe proceedings. They stayed at their stations while the entire fleet readied its attack. The British frigates were sleek, magnificent ships that glided through the ocean. Each posed a commanding presence. They were immense vessels bestowed with towering masts, stunning sails, and a spiderweb of ropes. Three rows of guns poked out of their gunports along each frigate, ready to fire. The sailors were veterans; all looked prepared and on top of their tasks.

One ship alone would intimidate a foe, but three, with their escorts, was an armada. The three vessels maneuvered into an attacking line as O'Sullivan waited and watched. The flagship led the way. O'Sullivan could see the coast approaching. To maximize the surprise, it seemed the British Navy had gone out to sea and then darted back in toward Anastasia rather than following along the coastline. The familiar islets, inlets, and beaches of St. Augustine's environs were materializing into view. It was O'Sullivan's home, and he was glad to see it despite the circumstances. The intent of the raid was as clear as day. The British Navy aimed to head straight into the Matanzas Bay and lay siege to St. Augustine's castle. Meanwhile, the South Carolinian militia would capture Anastasia's battery and neutralize the danger it posed. It would be a brutal fight. O'Sullivan expected many would die, even before they launched their boats and stormed the battery.

The commodore's plan unraveled before everybody's eyes. As the fleet approached the bay in attack formation, they saw six Spanish half-galleys blocking the entrance to the Matanzas River. They were relatively small vessels with one row of six-pound cannons. In open seas, they wouldn't pose much danger.

The British ships would have simply obliterated them. However, the shallow waters of the Matanzas Bay were another matter. Adding the half-galleys' guns to St. Augustine castle's and the battery's changed the offensive calculations. The odds of British success had just decreased significantly. Inwardly, O'Sullivan celebrated. Seeing that these were Fandiño's coastguard gave him even greater joy. The rough, burly, and frightening crews who had boarded the Freedom outside of Cuba. These men were a tough bunch. There was no chance they would flee in the face of a British onslaught.

As the vessels tore toward the six half-galleys, the British commander made last-minute adjustments to the tactics. Instead of breaking the barrier and heading into the Matanzas River, he adjusted course. The other frigates followed the flagship's lead. The Flamborough skirted past Fandiño's coastguard and fired a broadside salvo. It was deafening, and the vessel felt as if it moved as the ship's cannon fired as one. A strong smell of cordite and the fog of war momentarily obscured O'Sullivan's view. When it cleared, the problem facing the British Navy became obvious. Most of the volley went high. The rigging and masts of two of the coastguard half-galleys were hit, but not much else. Fandiño's vessels returned fire. Again, a thunderous discharge echoed across the bay. Smoke drifted towards Anastasia Island, and the whizz-bang of cannon balls surrounded them. Several exploded on the deck, and two hit the ship's hull. Sailors raced to put out fires and secure damaged rigging. A unit of militia was hit, and several men were blown over the gunwale. As they passed out of range, the danger facing the British fleet became palpable. Fandiño's vessels lay much lower in the water. The frigates risked being holed if they got too close, while the British guns would find it challenging to sink the smaller Spanish ships. As if to prove the point, the two following frigates discharged volleys and barely damaged the Spanish ships.

Improvising the fleet shot past the battery and the tip of the island. The battery fired a couple of shots, but none hit. The entire fleet came to anchor off the island's eastern shore. A long, inviting beach immediately attracted the commodore's attention. Soon after, anchors were dropped, and the marines were dispatched. They would still launch their amphibious assault and capture the battery and the island. As O'Sullivan's unit climbed into their skiff, he considered their good fortune. Instead of landing on the island's western side, rowing into the face of the battery's guns, they landed away from its defenses. It would be simple to land their boats on Anastasia's beaches and fight their way toward the rear of the battery. The cannons faced out to sea and the British would quickly overwhelm the defenders. O'Sullivan knew this part of the island well. It was near the mine, and plenty of well-worn tracks went from the mine to the battery. Anastasia would fall without a major fight. It appeared he'd live to be helpful to the Spanish another day. The idea of being blown up by his own side while pretending to be his enemy hadn't been particularly attractive.

The sailors gradually lowered the militia's boats. It ended up being the riskiest part. Loaded with men, the small boats were precariously balanced. One tipped and dropped a few unlucky fellows into the sea. O'Sullivan saw one man flailing around in the water, drowning. Consequently, those in O'Sullivan's who couldn't swim held their breaths and prayed. They hit the water with a thud. The boat's boards creaked and moaned with the impact. Each crew started rowing fiercely toward the shore. For most, the night's fears were replaced with adrenaline, and they used the burst to propel themselves swiftly. The militia's skiffs spread across the sea, racing each other to the beach. O'Sullivan heard an occasional pop, whiz, and splash as musket balls were propelled in their direction. Nobody was hit, and the small arms fire soon ceased.

O'Sullivan's crew navigated the tricky swell as they crashed through the waves and skidded through the surf onto the sand. It was a sudden stop, and Harrison was jettisoned overboard face-first into the wet silt. Many of the men laughed despite their potential exposure to musket fire. It was funny, but O'Sullivan also noted Harrison's lack of popularity. So, it wasn't just him who found the man's constant chatter irritating. The front group of men jumped out and pulled the boat ashore. Before long, hundreds of South Carolina's militia landed, armed and ready to assault Anastasia's battery. It turned out to be a pointless exercise. The mere threat of attack had led the defenders to retreat. Not a soul was left; the island was deserted. The battery's guns had been spiked, and the battery had been set ablaze. They found evidence of a sizeable Seminole camp, but it, too, was abandoned.

Colonel Vanderdussen ordered the militia to occupy the island. They doused the battery's flames and recovered what ordnance they could. Artillery was shipped across from the fleet to reinforce the position. Instead of facing seaward, the cannons faced inland, aiming at St. Augustine's castle. Militia squads began to work the mine, fetching stones to build breastworks. Then O'Sullivan heard the cannons fire at the Castillo for the first time. Before long, the explosions became repetitive, incessant, an ever-present background noise. The siege had begun. His home city was under attack, and all O'Sullivan could do was fume inwardly, forever concealing his true feelings and hoping that his time for revenge would come.

Chapter 47: Mose Ablaze

Utter despair sucked the joy from Lamine's heart. He knew he should aim to appear more resilient in front of his men. However, there was no escaping the sorrow he felt. Tears cascaded down his cheeks as they trudged toward St. Augustine's Castillo. His heart was sick with loss. Lamine needn't have been embarrassed. As he cast his eye across the Free Black Militia, he noticed similar dejection casting its pall over everybody. Shoulders were slumped. Nobody moved with ease. Despondency clouded every move. Others were crying too, unashamed grief acceptable in the circumstances.

The cause of the misery was easy to find, though not easily viewed. Behind the retreating militia, their hometown, Mose, was burning. Flames spread across the horizon, consuming every ounce of the town. Smoke drifted, rose, and curled into billows, creating a haze that transformed the panorama into a hellscape. The grey fumes of the blazing palisade danced devilishly with the dark black fumes of the militia's houses as the firestorms ate them. Thick, acrid smoke stung Lamine's nostrils. A distinctive charred wood aroma was mixed with the choking caustic odors of burning furniture, fabrics, and clothing. As the town was razed, the militia were losing their homes. The houses devoured by the fires contained all their personal belongings, memories, and treasures. Everything was lost as they retreated and were ordered to withdraw without a shot fired. It was depressing to see the unique town of Mose being destroyed in one act of wanton aggression. The mosaic of houses and streets was disappearing in the flames.

The officers of the Free Black Militia knew this would be Mose's fate. It was still a bitter pill to swallow. Lamine's tears dripped onto his collar as he led the men along the principal road to the castle. They knew they must leave when the British army appeared and surrounded the town. General Montiano's orders were clear. The Spanish defense of Florida depended upon the concentration of forces in the Castillo. They would have lost too many valuable men if they'd fought for Mose. So, they withdrew and now watched as the British army invaded their town and burnt it to the ground. Lamine could see the redcoats on the hill while the South Carolina militia rampaged around their community, setting fire to everything. Every movement seemed filled with the pleasure of evil men engaged in evil deeds. Undoubtedly, the South Carolinians had dreamt about this opportunity to destroy the free black town. It was a beacon of light for many of Lamine's brethren, and now it was going up in smoke. Lamine couldn't help but think about Jemmy's failed rebellion. If those escapees had made it south, would they have changed the outcome? It was hard to say. Maybe the South Carolinians would have been too weakened to have joined the foray into Florida. It was an irksome question with no answer.

Suddenly, it occurred to Lamine that, in their grief, they were acting stupidly. The long, slow-moving line of disheartened

456

militia was a prime target for British cavalry. He imagined the horses hitting them at speed while they were strung out along the road. The swish of the rapiers, as they swung, was a sound he was unlikely to forget. Just a few mounted men had destroyed Jemmy's defense. Imagine what an entire unit of cavalry would do. Recognizing the danger, Lamine wiped his tears away and shouted, "Form-up! Into tighter columns, men! Move at double-pace! Stop lingering back there! Do you want a cavalry sword in your back?" The militia began to move more hurriedly, casting off their despondent state as the danger dawned on the rest of the men. Fortunately, it appeared the British didn't have cavalry, and the Free Black Militia made swift progress along the road to St. Augustine. Behind them, Mose continued to burn. It wouldn't be long before the British army followed them.

As they approached the castle, they heard the boom of cannon fire. Its constant retort was ever-present. Lamine tried to count the number of guns. There were at least twenty firing in a continuous series of explosions. Somehow, the British had maneuvered along the coast and captured Anastasia Island. The island's battery had been defeated, and the guns turned on St. Augustine. It appeared that the general's careful preparations were warranted; the siege had begun. The fog of war drifted across the landscape in odd tufts of smoke. Incessant detonations became louder as they approached. New orders were given. The perils of artillery fire had displaced the danger of cavalry. The militia spread out again, aiming to minimize the carnage should they get hit by cannon balls. Moving at double speed had tired the men, so they slowed to a walk.

The Castillo's coquina walls were a welcome sight. They approached along the northern road heading towards the northeastern sallyport. It was their first mistake of the day. One of the British battery's mortars had spotted them. It hurled ordinance in a high arc across the Matanzas River. The first explosion fell short, well to the left of their column. The second detonated in the middle of their long line and killed two men instantly. One moment, they were marching as part of the militia; an instant later, there was little evidence that they'd existed at all. The mortar had sighted them, and they were now in mortal danger. Lamine made his decision automatically, "Off the road! Move! Take cover! Head to the northwestern gate!" The militia were well-trained and acted immediately, saving many lives. Their tribal instincts also helped, as they used the available cover to hide in the bushes, trees, and gullies alongside the road. Carefully, they crawled and shimmied in the marsh, slowly sneaking away from the artillery fire.

Lamine hid in a deep ditch while corralling his men and ensuring they escaped. As he waited and counted, he watched the artillery bombarding the castle. It was one of the strangest experiences of his lifetime. Something peculiar was happening to the British cannonballs. As they whizzed over from Anatasia Island, they barraged the castle. Lamine heard the retort of the cannon, saw the smoke drift across the river, and listened to the eerie whistling, high-pitched whoosh as the ball sheared through the air at velocity. Nothing amiss there. It was the impact that was unexpected. If the cannonballs came in at an angle, they seemed to bounce off the coquina walls and then ricocheted across the moat and into the open farmland. It reminded Lamine of stones skimmed over the water. The balls were taking out trees and hedges and making a mess of the fields but doing little damage to the castle.

Even more perplexing were the direct hits. About one in ten shots hit the castle perpendicularly. These direct shots were literally embedding themselves into the coquina walls.

Instead of blasting the stone away, the castle walls absorbed the impacts like sponges. As more direct hits were taken, the fortress began to be pitted with cannonballs. Each stuck where it had impacted. Lamine realized that the coquina stone was exhibiting unexpected qualities. Maybe there was a chance; perhaps the Spanish could survive the siege.

Lamine's last soldier edged past him in the ditch. It was time for him to leave and make his way to the gate, away from the artillery fire. The mortar attacking them was still sending random shells in their direction. It was aimless and did no damage. However, Lamine was careful not to betray his location and become an obvious target. He continued to crawl along the ditch, covering his withdrawal. It was a route most of his men had taken. The dyke snaked along the edge of the fields and eventually joined up with the castle's moat. Lamine was exposed for a moment while he climbed the side of the channel and rolled unceremoniously into the moat. He heard a whizz and bang to his rear as the mortar continued blasting their position. Lamine was dripping wet from the boggy mud. The moat added to his discomfort. It stank of stale urine and feces. No doubt dumped into it from the castle's parapets. The western wall now towered above him and protected him from further fire. He stood and jogged steadily along the wall's edge to the castle's entrance.

Lamine encountered chaos as he reached the gate. A heaving mass of Mose's militia were trying to enter the castle. They pushed at each other, their entry to the castle blocked. This gate was the only one protected from the British cannon fire, and it thronged with civilians seeking safety. Aware that the long-expected British invasion had arrived, the entire populace of St. Augustine had fled to the castle. Lamine saw an older man sitting in a ditch, nursing an injured leg. Mothers cried loudly for help and held their youngsters away from the fray, afraid the little ones could get trampled. Men jostled, trying to get ahead of the crowd, all sense of decorum lost. Two were in a full-blown fight, raining down blows on each other. Handcarts were being pushed along amongst the bedlam. Citizens were trying to save their possessions, but the presence of the carts blocked the road. One cart was overturned, and its contents spilled, further inhibiting the panicked citizens. Castle guards prodded people with their muskets and shouted. Lamine couldn't hear what was being said; the confusion at the gate was all-embracing. Meanwhile, the disorder was continually punctuated by the earsplitting burst of cannon fire.

Captain Lamine appeared to be the first officer at the scene, and it fell to him to bring some order to the chaos. His entire squad had been sucked into the mayhem, their training entirely forgotten. Clearly, it was one thing to practice on the parade ground and another to experience actual combat. Lamine grabbed three of his men from the back of the logjam. He pulled them away from the scene and yelled, "Soldiers, load and fire in the air! After three. One, two, three, fire!"

The sudden retort of several muskets blasting together and echoing off the gate's ramparts was sufficient to reduce the commotion. Mose's militia regained their orderliness. Lamine commanded, "Stop those men from fighting! Pull the men out of the crowd and have them move those carts! Women and children to the front, get them into the castle!"

Once Lamine had control of his men, it didn't take long for a semblance of order to descend over the pandemonium and panic. The carts were moved off the roadway. Their contents would only clutter up the castle. With the entire community sheltered within its confines, there wouldn't be enough room for the castle to safeguard people's possessions; it would be packed with citizens, soldiers, and provisions required for a lengthy siege. Such belongings had to be abandoned. With the militia and the city's menfolk standing to one side, the women and children filed into the castle safely. As calm was established, fears about the cannonade were replaced with the realization that the western side of the castle was shielded from the blasts. They could go about their duties without getting blown up. Soon, most of the backlog of fleeing citizens was cleared, and Lamine and his men entered St. Augustine's castle.

A new challenge was evident as they filed through the castle's coquina walls. The Castillo was packed with people. The citizens of St. Augustine were milling about the interior bailey, trying to get themselves situated. Camps were gradually being built, but the populace had little room. Mose's militia were given quarters within the battlements, but space was tight. General Montiano's tactics required the Spanish troops, St. Augustine's populace, and Mose's militia to shelter within the castle's confines for an extended period. Who knew how long that could be and whether the strategy would work? The British had arrived, and the siege had begun.

Chapter 48: Reunion

Boredom aboard had set in for Williams. Though surrounded by the plush trappings of power ornamenting Colonel Vanderdussen's quarters, he had almost nothing to do. There was an occasional letter to write to Acting Governor Bull, but few communications arrived. Williams had no military job beyond observing and listening to the officers in charge of Florida's invasion. He longed to be off the ship, leading a unit of South Carolina's marines as they captured Anastasia Island and fought the Spanish. Williams' new commission as lieutenant seemed like an illusion. Everyone knew he was a political appointment and wouldn't go anywhere or command anybody. He made use of his tedium by overperforming at Bull's assigned task. In some respects, he was a spy. Sent by Bull to gather intelligence about the fate of South Carolina's troops and to assess General Oglethorpe's leadership. Some more astute officers had realized this and were unusually careful what they said. After a time, though, they'd been no match for his Welsh charm. Perhaps this was why Bull had chosen Williams; he was a remarkably likable chap. They all share key information eventually after a few beers, a couple of card games, or rounds of dice.

Williams was putting the pieces together for another dispatch. He stared at the beautiful, ornate mahogany desk as he considered framing what he'd learned. Things were decidedly not going to plan, and Oglethorpe increasingly looked lost. Worse, Williams was convinced the general was severely ill. The man's orderly described the symptoms over a game of dice. Oglethorpe had regular chills and fevers. He'd fainted twice. Other times, he had relentless headaches that throbbed for hours and pounded his skull. Sometimes, Oglethorpe was incapacitated, unable to move; his limbs ached as if crushed by an invisible force. Blurred vision and disjointed thoughts seemed to follow these symptoms. It appeared that the mysterious illness was impeding his judgment. Several officers who worked with him closely reported his spirit of urgency and decisiveness had diminished. Oglethorpe was curiously indecisive, repeating his commands unnecessarily and getting confused during key moments.

Who knew whether this illness was impacting the campaign or not? Williams felt it probably was, and he said so in his letter to Bull. Williams continued considering the implications as he scratched these comments with ink and quill. The operation had undoubtedly stalled. The broad pincer that Oglethorpe had planned had failed. The British Navy was supposed to enter the Matanzas River and lay siege to St. Augustine's castle using the full force of their guns. Instead, they sat in the bay, bobbing around uselessly, afraid of a few Spanish half-galleons. The British army had been largely successful, destroying several forts, but now it faced the full might of the Spanish with one arm tied behind its back. It couldn't possibly be expected to capture the castle alone without the Navy's help. Consequently,

Oglethorpe was dithering and unable to develop a new plan. Some of the blame sat with Commodore Pearce. He was risk averse. If he'd been more audacious, he unquestionably would've devised a tactic to break the Spanish barricade and get at the castle with his ships.

Instead, all was delayed while South Carolina's militia contracts ticked on. Acting Governor Bull would be fully aware of the implications. Williams noted the lull's import. If Oglethorpe and the commodore hesitated much longer, the South Carolinians would demand to return home. The army sat outside the castle, the navy drifted in the bay, and the artillery bombarded the fortifications from too far away with little to no effect. Time was ticking, and a new plan was needed. That was Williams' honest assessment, and he finished writing it. He tried to close his letter positively, "A leading officers' conference has been called to address the issue, and a new strategy will likely be agreed upon soon."

The letter's close was more optimistic than he genuinely felt; perhaps the conference would solve the dilemma the British faced, but he doubted it. There were too many disagreements between the officers and no clarity regarding overall leadership. While General Oglethorpe was nominally in charge, Colonel Vanderdussen had been given a separate commission reporting to Bull, and surprisingly, Admiral Vernon had not signed over the commodore's command to Oglethorpe; the man was acting under an independent command. It was a recipe for indecision and disaster. Williams hoped his optimistic tone was justified as he waxed and sealed the letter, ready for the courier.

Moments later, there was a knock at Vanderdussen's cabin door. Williams had been sitting at the desk too long scribbling his letter to Bull. Consequently, it took him an instant to rise and cross the compartment. He swore all this desk work was terrible for him, causing weight gain. Unintentionally eyeing his gut as it protruded over his girdle, he was clearly suffering the consequences of a sedentary life. Williams dragged the oak-paneled door open to face his antithesis. The aging, grisly Colonel Palmer stood outside. The man's eyes were sharp with intelligence, and his face was sunburnt like leather. His bushy beard and hair were bristled and curled from the humidity. Clothed in the green and tans of South Carolina's rangers, Palmer appeared trim and rugged, all hard muscle, quite unlike Williams' increasingly portly build. His rifle was slung over his shoulder, and a long knife and tomahawk were hung at his waist. Sweat beaded down his brow. A vaguely familiar ranger stood behind him.

"Lieutenant Williams! Good to see you, man. I trust you're keeping the Acting Governor current with affairs?" Not waiting for a response, Palmer and his colleague strode into the cabin and continued, "Well, you can tell him this! The army has just taken Fort Mose. Burnt the bloody town to the ground, and good riddance! Our escapees have nowhere to aspire to go now; it's ashes. The entire population has decamped to St. Augustine's castle, though. It'll take months to extricate them now. We'd have them all if that damnable commodore would do his job! Stuck, that's my report! We don't seem to be gaining anything or going anywhere! The army is camping, the navy is sailing around in circles, and the artillery has no effect whatsoever! I'm already hearing complaints from the enlisted men. It doesn't feel good, a total debacle, and nobody seems to know what to do about it!"

As Colonel Palmer unloaded his frustrations, Williams watched the young man who'd escorted him. Palmer's report didn't add anything new; Williams had already included it all in the letter he'd just written. Now, he was sure he knew this young ranger. The lad was in his early twenties, strapping, tall, and solid-looking, like he'd seen much physical work. The man's long dark hair was tied in a ponytail. He was outfitted with the green and tan of a ranger's uniform. A wicked-looking cleaver of a tomahawk hung at his belt. Then Williams saw it and put two and two together. The rifle was a distinct weapon; this one was legendary, with its ornate gilded stock. South Carolina's Assembly had gifted it to Oglethorpe on the founding of Savannah, and it was donated to the first of Georgia's rangers. Williams suddenly realized this was his old friend Tom Ellis, and he undiplomatically cut the colonel off, "Colonel Palmer, thank you for your report. I will pass it along to Acting Governor Bull. Now, please allow me the opportunity to welcome an old friend! Tom, what are you doing here?"

The colonel recognized immediately that he was in the way of an old acquaintanceship, "I'll make my apologies and leave you two to catch up. I assume the meeting is in the commodore's quarters?" Not waiting for an answer, the colonel left, inadvertently leaving the door ajar.

Tom stuck out a hand of welcome, Williams didn't accept it. He brushed the hand aside and gave the lad a huge bear hug. Pulling back Williams inspected his old friend, "Well now boyo, you've certainly matured! The last time I saw you, must've been four, maybe five years ago! If I recall correctly, you were a gangly whippersnapper, with a keen eye for shooting that rifle! I can remember the first day you were practicing. You took down two ducks without even thinking about it. I'd never seen such accurate shooting! And you picked it up so quickly! Look at you now, a fine young man, and a corporal. Well, I never. I didn't expect to see you here!"

Williams ushered Tom further into the cabin, pulled out a chair, and beckoned him to sit at the mahogany desk. He poured a generous measure of rum from Vanderdussen's personal supply, "A cause for celebration, don't you think? I'm sure the colonel wouldn't mind sharing. He'll be too busy to appreciate it anyway. Now tell me what you've been up to?"

Williams and his old friend Tom Ellis caught up on the news while they waited for the senior officers to finish their meeting. Both knew it was an essential strategic gathering of the top brass, that it would likely get heated, and could last for hours. Tom carefully swilled his glass of rum. He was careful not to drink too much. For all he knew, they could be hours away from an all-out assault on St. Augustine's castle. A little courage wouldn't damage his fighting capacity, but he dared not get drunk. Williams began to tell the story of their mutual friend's demise. Poor Evans, he'd been a kind fellow. Getting crushed by your horse seemed a particularly awful way to die. It sent shivers down Tom's spine. He was only just becoming a competent rider and remained quite fearful of the whole thing. Slain by a horse falling on top of you added another dimension to his concerns. Tom could tell that Williams truly missed his dear friend Evans. He talked for an age about the loss, about the small churchyard where the body had been laid and his frequent visits to the grave. Though talkative, Williams knew his place, and didn't share much about his job, or discuss the politics that were bubbling up underneath the British campaign. The talk was incessant, like long lost brothers meeting after a lengthy time.

Williams soon goaded Tom into sharing his news. Tom shared his betrothal and the news of their imminent arrival. His excitement at the prospect of becoming a father was palpable. Williams teased him, "Well sonny-boy, I guess my invitation to the wedding got lost then, did it? I will be waiting for the Christening invite. Godfather Williams, has an agreeable ring about it, don't you think?"

Tom, familiar with the man's Welsh wit, smiled and chuckled generously. Their storytelling continued. Tom updated Williams on his experiences in Savannah. The founding of the city, the battle for Fort Argyle, his fight on Trustee's Island, and his run in with the exiled Christie. Williams was surprised to hear that Cameron and Horn had returned to Georgia after disappearing from the settlers' ship. Hours seemed to pass, while Tom tentatively sipped his rum. In contrast, Williams enjoyed demolishing Vanderdussen's supply of rum and was beginning to get quite tipsy.

⧗ ⧗ ⧗

After several hours, the cabin door suddenly and violently swung open. The door crashed into the oak paneled wall, making a terrible racket. Colonel Palmer barged back into the compartment, red-faced and angry. Having drunk a little too much, Williams was perhaps braver in the circumstances than he should have been, "My dear Colonel Palmer, whatever's the matter?"

The colonel seemed close to boiling over and there was a tense moment, when Williams wondered if he'd overstepped the mark. A pause and a deep breath followed, as Colonel Palmer contained his rage. Slowly the man gained control, but his response was almost shouted, "You can tell Governor Bull that these men are idiots! Complete fools! I have lost all respect for General Oglethorpe; the man is a waverer. I have never seen him act so indecisively. As for Commodore Pearce, we might as well send the British Navy home, he has no intention of doing anything with those ships. He's the most risk-adverse man I've ever come across!"

Williams paused, grabbed another glass, and poured a generous helping of rum. Handing it to Colonel Palmer he replied, "Drink! It'll help. Now what exactly is wrong? I will need to correspond with Bull, so don't leave anything out."

The colonel reached out, took the glass, and almost downed the rum in one swift swig. He turned the glass around, scrutinizing the remaining liquor's viscosity. Noticeably calmed down, he answered, "This isn't bad. Vanderdussen has a first-class taste in rum. That man has gone up in my esteem. Always thought he was a parade ground colonel, with his obsessive cleanliness and drilling of the men. He was the only man in the room who offered anything sensible. Apparently, Pearce must take his ships and leave before we have finished the blockade. He's scared of storms now! He won't do anything to attack those half-galleys. Vanderdussen came up with a great idea, to attack the half-galleys using long-boats, and about a hundred sailors and troops. The commodore refused! Worried it will leave his ships shorthanded and open to a sneak assault. Then Vanderdussen suggested setting up a battery to command the entrance to the St. Sebastian River, to stop supplies reaching the castle. The man refused that too! General Oglethorpe seemed to be at a loss and didn't seem to be able to sway the commodore! The situation is useless, without those ships."

As Palmer took another quick mouthful of rum and swallowed the remainder, Williams asked, "So what's the decision then?"

Palmer's face reddened again, "Well, that's the rub of it! General Oglethorpe, in his infinite wisdom, has ordered me to march the men around north of the castle. Somehow, it's supposed to lure the enemy out into the open so that we can have a pitched battle! Total idiocy, it'll never work. And, to top it all, I'm to have a joint command with that damn highlander Captain Mackay! That shitbag thinks a captain in the regulars is higher ranked than a colonel in a colonial regiment!" The colonel's anger had returned, he slammed the glass down on the mahogany desk, and stalked out of the cabin, forgetting Tom. Tom and Williams bid each other a hasty and fond farewell, before Tom rushed off to catch up with the colonel and return to the troops.

Chapter 49: The Duke of York

Around and around in his head went the rhyme. It was an incessant and irritating ditty that was stuck on repeat. Tom recalled fond moments before his apprenticeship with his family, reciting it. They'd often sit before a warm fire and recall many poems from the War of the Roses. While it had unearthed some pleasant memories, it was now becoming annoying. So, off in his mind, the poem played again, "Oh, the grand old Duke of York, he had ten thousand men. He marched them up to the top of the hill, and he marched them down again. When they were up, they were up, and when they were down, they were down. And, when they were only halfway up, they were neither up nor down."

It was hardly surprising that this specific rhyme was disturbing him. Tom felt like one of the Duke of York's ten thousand men. General Oglethorpe had commanded Colonel Palmer and Captain Mackay to march a significant contingent of his army across the northern approaches to St. Augustine's castle. At the same time, the artillery continued to bombard it. The mission was a makeshift mixture of Palmer's rangers, the Darien Highlanders, a company of Oglethorpe's 42nd Foot, and the Creeks. It was led by two feuding officers, with no clarity over the outright command. Not ten thousand, though; there were about one hundred and fifty men. They'd been marching across the fields, swamps, and woods, making as much noise as possible.

For the first few days, it had been fun. Tom loved his bagpipes, drums, and fifes, and they played constantly. The force waved flags, fired occasional volleys, and engaged in mock bayonet charges. After three days, everything and everyone was caked in mud. The gnats and mosquitoes grew into a nuisance, and they started to get tired. Any amusement gained began to dissipate. After six days, the drums became ear-splitting, and the intense Florida humidity made them sweat copiously. Some of the less resolute soldiers began grumbling. After eight days, even the bagpipes that Tom loved became irksome, and many quietly groaned about the effort. By the tenth day, they were covered in bites, reeking of stale perspiration, and had aching muscles that felt like they'd been stretched on the rack. Nobody was happy, and the pipes fell quiet. The landscape was all torn up by their constant passage, and every path they took was heavy underfoot. Their boots, moccasins, and leggings felt as if they were cast in stone. Every step inflicted an additional toll on their throbbing physiques.

Somehow, they'd expected to lure the Spanish out for a pitched battle. General Montiano wasn't falling for the ploy. He'd withdrawn all his forces into the castle for a reason, and their antics weren't changing his mind. The Spanish general had decided to hunker down behind his battlements and see out the siege. No amount of marching up and down, to and fro, would break his resolve, and so all knew their efforts were fruitless. Hence, Tom's ceaseless mind replayed the Duke of York's rhyme inside his head again. There was nothing else to do. March, be bored, think, reflect, rerun the poem, and repeat. Done to utter pointlessness.

Even the officers were beginning to get dejected and sluggish. On the tenth night, Colonel Palmer returned to the remnants of Fort Mose to set up camp. In the following nights, they began to establish a more permanent base. The soldiers recovered burnt timber, dragged the useful debris out of destroyed dwellings, and built crude shelters. Tom considered it risky and kept his small squad of Georgia's rangers out of the ruins. Oglethorpe had been explicit that they shouldn't stop twice in the same place. Doing so was also against Palmer's usual policies. Clearly, the colonel had given up their mission as a lost cause. They were all tired of the useless marching and needed a comfortable sleep. After five nights of denying the urge to build a more permanent camp in Fort Mose and after much moaning from his men, Tom capitulated. He allowed them to enter the scorched town to secure more comfortable quarters.

When they entered, Tom saw that the town's fortifications hadn't been destroyed entirely, but it wasn't defensible. There were many gaps where the fires had consumed the entire timber wall. The earth near these holes was charred extensively. Some of the openings were huge, wide enough to walk a company of soldiers through. Much of the remaining woodwork was singed, fragmented and split, pointy and misaligned, like shattered teeth. The reek of burnt wood permeated the site. An unpleasant, distinct, earthy smokiness, acrid with a subtle bitterness, devoured any residual freshness from the already dense air. The soot and carbon created a haunting aroma that gave Tom a horrible sense of foreboding.

Ashes from the conflagration lay everywhere. They dusted the remnants of the outer wall, covered the few dilapidated structures left, and encrusted the site. It was a mystery why the others wanted to set up their encampments within the scorched town. Tom didn't understand it; a covert would have been preferable. Though only a few combatants had died defending the town, it felt haunted, as if those spirits craved to see their enemies gone. The hair stood up on the back of Tom's neck. It didn't feel right, and he noted the Creeks were avoiding the location altogether, preferring a nearby meadow.

As Tom's unit entered the remains of Fort Mose, Coleman went ahead to look for a suitable spot for their encampment. The interior vestiges of the town were no more attractive than the ramparts. The same stench of the recent fires overwhelmed his senses, and the layer of the inferno's residue coated everything. Many of the homes had been destroyed. Occasionally, some more robust structures still had upright staves, boards, planks, and beams that had somehow escaped the blaze. These had already been ransacked for valuable lumber that the British soldiers had used to build crude shelters. Some leftover lumber had been hacked and collected for the soldiers' campfires. It was plain that the occupants had already gathered most of the valuable materials over the previous nights. As they searched for a campsite, they saw small groups of men all over the town. They were assembled in groups. Evidence of defensive fortification and pickets was negligible. Each squad had amassed what materials they could and built camps, including some more robust shelters that appeared semi-permanent. One unit of British regulars laughed and joked as they sat around a bonfire. Their swearing and teasing were overly loud, and Tom wondered if they were drunk. Other groups of Oglethorpe's 42nd were camped nearby but kept their distance from the disturbance. Most soldiers were preparing dinner, cleaning their gear, or talking quietly with friends as they prepared to relax for the evening. The British regulars were often arrogant and held significant contempt for the colonial soldiers, so Tom's squad looked for another location to rest for the night.

Bypassing the British regulars, they entered the center of Mose. It was evident that the flames had been most intense in the middle of town. None of the original structures stood. Shelters erected there had been constructed from lumber dragged from other parts of the site. Colonel Palmer's command tent had been erected within a large clearing in the heart of the center. It had been thoroughly cleaned. Crews must have worked hours to remove the ash deposits, and no sign remained of burnt-out buildings. Tom spotted several of Palmer's officers and wished them a good evening. There was no sign of the colonel; the man had probably retired to his tent.

Coleman reported back, "Corporal Ellis, I don't think there is room for us to join South Carolina's rangers. This space is occupied. I have found a spot nearer to the highlanders." He pointed to the north of the center. Tom wasn't surprised by Coleman's assessment. Even though Georgia's rangers had been attached to Palmer's command, none of Tom's squad had much affinity for the South Carolinians. They all preferred the company of other Georgians. Despite the communication problems and their inability to speak Scottish Gaelic, they'd all favor being near the Darien highlanders. The squad trudged on. It was getting late, and the day's marching began to exact a price on their exhausted bodies. At least the constant Florida humidity was starting to dissipate as the night closed in. A cooler night would be welcomed.

As they moved north within the town's blackened remains, the evening light started to lessen. Tom looked across the horizon. It was beginning to offer an incredible sunset. The sun was dipping low, casting an eerie glow across the sky. Hues of orange and crimson softened into tints of pink and lavender. The clouds lingered in ghostly formations athwart the heavens, catching the sun's rays and blazing golden light upon their silver edges. The cloud configurations looked like a pack of wolves chasing a herd of deer. Though beautiful, it was also portentous, and Tom could only wonder what his Creek friends made of it. There was an ill-omen about everything this evening, and it worried him. Turning to the squad, he requested, "Coleman, where's this site? We don't have much time before we lose the light. Sanders and Hill, can you pick up some of this discarded wood? We'll need it for a fire. Let's move!"

With a little more urgency, despite their tiredness, Tom's men set about building a camp. It was situated just south of the highlanders, between them and Palmer's rangers. In the distance, they could hear the melodic and rugged accents of the Scottish. Occasionally, they would burst out into a Scottish folk song accompanied by bagpipes, and these moments were often punctuated by laughter. They didn't appear to be too affected by the many days of marching.

As Coleman and Tom cleared the site, Sanders and Hill collected what firewood they could. The ominous sunset and its peculiar cloud patterns offered some light as they worked. Now, the clouds appeared blood-red, pushing Tom into an intuitive and more profound sense of foreboding. The sun descended further, and the horizon was painted with the cooler tones of indigo and twilight blue. Shadows were growing longer, and silhouettes fleetingly danced across the landscape. His men soon returned with enough firewood, and they quickly lit it before the night settled in.

More fires were being ignited across Fort Mose, and the woody smoke and acrid aroma of campfires began to mix with the crispness of the night air. They didn't have enough time to build a shelter before nightfall, so they stretched out their sleeping mats beside the fire. Florida had temperate nights. So, smooth ground and a snug campfire would be sufficient until the following evening. As it took hold, Hill began to cook a mixture of beans and bacon fat for their evening dinner. For a few moments, Tom daydreamed about his many hunting outings with Hilli and Sin and wished he had some turkey or venison to eat. He recalled eating alligator with his Creek friends. Even that would be preferable to more beans. Though, Hilli would surely have rolled out his relentless jokes about beans and unexpected odors. Tom wished he had more time to visit. They were just across the meadow with the other Creek Indians, no doubt enjoying considerably better fare than his squad was consuming.

Hypnotically, Tom was drawn to the fire's flames. They danced, flickered, and moved unpredictably. The movement was graceful, chaotic, and mesmerizing. Orange and yellow coalesce as hearts of blue leapt within. Irregular bursts of red glow white-hot. Curling tongues of flame retreat and reform, while the crackle and pop of wood charring adds to the allurement. As Tom stared, he could not ignore further harbingers. Unusual green hues cast an eerie spell. Unusually erratic movements and flames jumping wildly presage a predictive sense of chaos ahead. For luck, Tom feels compelled to touch the cleft of his tomahawk to check its sharpness. He picks up his rifle and begins cleaning it religiously. Coleman and Hill both note his unusual concern, scrutinizing him quizzically. Coleman is the first to break the silence, "What bothers thee?"

Unable to hide from his intuitive gut feeling, Tom confessed to his men, "I can't place my finger on it, but something isn't right here. Do you think it's haunted?" They all smiled at him, relieved it wasn't more serious.

Coleman saw the etched creases across Tom's forehead and his genuine expression of concern. He knew not to ignore the telltale signs of his corporal's instinct, "So if it's ghosts, why are you cleaning your rifle and checking the sharpness of your tomahawk?"

Tom had no answer: "I don't know; it just felt right." The men eyed each other, picked up their weapons, and started to check and clean them. Tom's fight at Fort Argyle was known, and they'd learned never to ignore the man's sixth sense.

Hill was first to offer, "I'll take the first guard duty." They fell quiet, ate dinner, and settled down to a disturbed night of watchfulness.

Chapter 50: Sallyport

Hernando murmured in his sleep. The cold sweats of fear consumed him once again as he saw the blade sweeping past his head and taking away a chunk of his ear. Sometimes, in the dream, the Yamasee warrior doesn't appear. He wakes up suddenly as the Creek's machete is thrust into his chest. Other times, his savior kills the other with a whirling staff and fades into a peculiar otherworldly mist.

Hernando woke up suddenly, covered in perspiration. Sitting upright, he rubbed his eyes and tried to dab sweat away from his forehead. It's always the same when Hernando wakes up. He is running out of vocabulary to describe the racket. Crash, wallop, boom, bang, crack, thump, and thud are all options. Though interchangeable, they all describe slight variations of the same phenomenon that has been ever-present since the siege began. So much so that it has almost drifted into his background consciousness. The crashes and wallops were cannonballs embedding themselves in the castle's walls. The booms and bangs are mortar shells dropping on the battlements from a vast height. Cracks, thumps, and thuds are balls ricocheting off the walls and into the nearby fields. Hernando listened carefully; another crash reverberated around the castle's interior. The British artillery was getting more skillful and better at identifying the more vulnerable targets. Of late, they'd aimed at the towers and were slowly grinding them down. The castle was largely untouched despite the damage, and no viable breaches had been cleaved into the structure. The walls, battlements, and sallyports were intact, and few occupants had been killed.

As Hernando arose, the constant barrage of noise drifted away, back into the background where it had been for many weeks. There was insufficient room in his cramped quarters. It almost felt as if they were sleeping on top of each other. The whole castle was the same. The entire garrison, the withdrawn soldiers, the free black militia, and the entire populace of St. Augustine were packed within its thick walls. Moving from one part to another was sometimes impossible without stumbling across a sleeping body. People were tired and increasingly hungry; despite the general's diligent planning, food was getting scarcer and was carefully rationed.

The noxiousness was something else entirely. All those bodies pressed together created a dense cocktail of stale perspiration, musk, and salty stagnant air. To make matters worse, many of the deaths had occurred near the tower latrines, some of which had been blasted into oblivion by the bombardment. Consequently, the castle's occupants were using what they could for privies and not discarding waste over the walls as often as they should, fearful they might get killed by the continuous shelling. The resulting stenches were atrocious. A pungent mix of ammonia, decaying organic matter, and sour, acrid air permeated the castle, causing significant olfactory discomfort. At least the castle's thick walls kept them all cooler during the humid Florida days.

Hernando dressed and gathered his equipment. They'd been commanded to muster at the northwestern sallyport. Something had changed. Instead of guarding the battlements, policing the occupants, or clearing the debris from the siege, they'd received this unexpected order. Over many weeks, little changed in their duties. They'd spent hours undertaking the risky assignments of clearing the battlements of wreckage or repairing damage to ramparts. A few men had been lost during these efforts, as the British gunners were happy to have moving targets, something more interesting to focus on. These tasks were carried out mainly at night to limit their losses. The Spanish soldiers had been instructed to keep the populace busy. So, they led older men and boys during these undertakings. Seeing the free blacks committed to the more dangerous work was also not unusual. Sometimes, the labor was more mundane. Clearing the castle of human waste. Distributing rations with careful measurement and observation. Making sure defensive gantries and corridors were safe and clear in case an outright assault began. They continued to undertake guard duties and spot the enemy's offensive maneuvers.

On one occasion, Hernando had been spying on the British arrangements from a loophole when something notable happened. A significant contingent of the British army began to march around the fields north of the castle. They made a great show, banging drums and waving flags. Scottish bagpipes even accompanied the force. Hernando noted the mix of men in the force as the senior officers were alerted. Rangers, Scots, and a group of Indian allies joined British regulars. Hernando couldn't make sense of it, in any case. It wasn't the entire British army or even a force the size of the one that assaulted Fort San Francisco de Pupo. It didn't make sense; surely, they didn't intend to assault the castle. As he'd observed the marching around, Sergeant Moreno-Rodriguez joined him. The sergeant observed wryly, "Fools! They think marching around making a fuss is going to draw us out for a fight. Thank God our general isn't an idiot. He will let them enjoy the Florida heat and sit tight in the Castillo!"

Sergeant Moreno-Rodriguez's observation proved correct. The British continued their show while the Spanish observed. They marched and countermarched. Occasionally, a sudden retort of muskets surprised the defenders, but no offensives followed. The British even tried to look like they would charge the castle with bayonets drawn, only to veer off when they got within range of the castle's guns. It was a ridiculous exercise in futility. The days passed, and the intense Florida mugginess sapped the enemy's energy. The Spanish sat and watched, increasingly perplexed. As time passed, it was evident that the British knew their tactics were ineffectual. The noise became less enthusiastic; the music slowly died off. The men's marching became more labored. Then they made an error. Every night, the British troops returned to the burnt-out carcass of Fort Mose to sleep. Their tiredness had sucked out their wits. It was a tactical blunder of epic proportions. Even Hernando could see it. Sergeant Moreno-Rodriguez captured it perfectly, "Well, that's the dumbest thing I've seen them do! I thought we would lose this siege, but now I am not so sure. Our provisions are getting low, and they've just given General Montiano the opportunity he needs to get stuff into the castle. Mark my words; we'll see action in the next few days!"

As Hernando hurried to the sallyport, barging past people in the castle's gloomy corridors, he supposed this might be the action the sergeant assumed was coming. They'd all been ordered to assemble there, in full dress uniform and with weapons. Every able-bodied regular in the garrison was involved in this morning's gathering. He'd heard that the Free Black Militia were likewise rendezvousing at the northeastern sallyport. Evidently, something momentous was happening. Hernando's adrenaline pumped as he rushed down several of the castle's stairwells. It could only mean one thing: the Spanish were finally preparing to attack. No more retreating, no more hiding in the castle, and no more timidity. They would venture out and exact some revenge for lost comrades. The arrogant British had finally made a misstep. As he jumped down several steps simultaneously, Hernando voiced a silent prayer for God to protect him so that he could see his family again, while giving vengeance to his enemies—an eye for an eye. Let them suffer for taking the lives of Antonio, Miguel, and Rodrigo.

The preparations went on all day. Nearly three hundred Spanish soldiers assembled near the sallyport. The castle's courtyard had been cleared of St. Augustine's citizens to accommodate the overflow. They broke into companies and began to assemble gunpowder and provisions for their commando raid. Sergeant Moreno-Rodriguez would lead Hernando's company, while Captain Antonio Salgado took overall command of the raid. Many grinding wheels were set up so the men could sharpen their blades. The constant grating and scraping noises of knives, swords, and bayonets being honed were ever-present. The soldiers diligently cleaned their escopetas and muskets. They were meticulous. First, they disassembled the weapons, separating the barrel, lock, and stock. The barrels were scrubbed using ramrods and cloth. The lock mechanisms were wiped clean with soft brushes, and the guns were reassembled. The sergeants thoroughly inspected everybody's weapons. Boots were polished, uniforms were cleaned and adjusted, and tears were fixed. There was no time to look slovenly during a Royal Spanish offensive. Kitchens were set up in the courtyard. Copious portions of bread, broth, and meat were provided from the stores. An attack was no time to hold back the rations, and the commandos wouldn't be allowed to go into the field hungry. It was early evening before everything was ready.

The leaders and non-commissioned officers were summoned to a conference with the general to review the tactical plan. Hernando lined up for dinner with the remainder of his squad. Juan was his usual jovial self, keeping them amused, while Gonzalo, Francisco, and Hernán quietly waited for their chow. It was their last meal, and they enjoyed the canteen's beef stew—a luxury indeed, given the declining state of the castle's provisions. Sergeant Moreno-Rodriguez returned from the officer's meeting as they sat down to eat. He quickly jumped to the head of the row and returned swiftly with a generous portion of the evening's grub. They regarded him quizzically as he stuffed chunks of meat into his mouth, desperate to learn their orders but unwilling to interrupt the sergeant's meal. Eventually, he put down his bowl and wiped his mouth clean. The squad waited in anticipation while Moreno-Rodriguez drew out the moment. Juan couldn't contain himself any longer and broke protocol, "Well, sergeant, are you going to tell us or not?"

Fortunately, the sergeant was in a positive mood and didn't take offense at Juan's lack of decorum. He examined them intently and then spilled the beans, "It's a simple strategy. The British keep staying the night within the remains of Fort Mose; tonight, they're using the same place. We get a good night's sleep and then attack them at dawn, aiming to maximize surprise. The Spanish force will engage in a commando raid straight up the main road and into Mose. The black militia is taking the river route and striking north of the town. With luck, we will defeat them before they wake up, and the militia will cut off their retreat. It's time for revenge." The sergeant pulled out a flask full of rum and passed it around. Each man took a draft and spoke earnestly, one after the other, "Venganza! For Antonio, Miguel, and Rodrigo!"

⧗   ⧗   ⧗

Hernando's sleep is intermittent. A mixture of excitement, nervousness, and trepidation keeps him awake. The night is simultaneously long and suddenly over. Juan sleeps soundly, but the others are uneasy. The officers rouse the troops long before dawn. The sallyport is open, and they file out of the castle for the first time in months. Hernando's company is the second to exit. Captain Salgado leads the way. Sergeant Moreno-Rodriguez pats Hernando on the back as they reach the sallyport's gate. Despite the cooler temperatures, he's tense, and sweat drips from his brow. The noise of the departing combatants is excessive; might they be heard? Their boots hit the hard pavement of the road, causing a scuffing sound of leather against gravel. Those in front pat the wall of the sallyport for luck as they pass, hoping it will help them survive the mission. Hernando follows their example; the coquina wall is cold.

They follow the Fort Mose Road; the raid is gaining momentum. The pace picks up. They march at double-time, planning to hit Mose before sunrise. Shadows from the night linger, casting a stillness; there is an uneasy motionlessness. Hernando wonders if the tranquility is prophesying death, hopefully not his own. He prays to survive. A soft light is coming up on the horizon; they'd better move quickly. The officers whisper commands, and their tempo picks up. Boots again sound loud. The air is calm and quiet, and there are a few tentative chirps from morning birds. They can see Mose now; there are no pickets! What were the British thinking!

They rush forward. Officers are waving them into the breach, encouraging them to strike their enemy hard. There are big gaps in Mose's fortifications that were destroyed by the fire. Hernando's company passed through one of these openings. Discipline is lost. Now past the outer wall, men fan out of the column and run headlong into Mose. Hernando is running with them. They encounter the first tents, and there's screaming. It's our men; their rage and tenseness spill suddenly from their mouths into violent yells. Hernando cries out with them, his odd howl echoes in the still night. The sudden uproar breaks the quietness; all about them is clamor, tumult, and action.

The British are sleeping; their tents are under attack. A head pops up out of one nearby camp, a hint of a red-coated chest. The man's head suddenly disintegrates into a bloody pulp. The splatter whips across the tent's fabric. Chunks of gore everywhere. Shot from close range, the musket ball destroys the man's head and tears a hole through the tent. The body collapses to the floor with its skull demolished. Another redcoat tries to fight, three Spanish soldiers bayonet him, and he dies quietly. Blood spurts from each wound and spills onto the floor. The leading company of Spanish soldiers surrounds the other shelters. British redcoats try to fight, but have no time to fetch their weapons. They're butchered swiftly in their beds. Some manage to leave their camps holding knives. Immediately, they are overcome and surrounded, bayonets stab viciously, and the defenders fall to the ground. Two redcoats get off shots. One lucky bullet blasts a Spanish leg, and the man goes down shrieking in agony. First blood of the morning flows into Mose's ashes, and the Spanish add to the town's ghosts—retribution for the deceased.

Hernando's company isn't required to subdue the redcoats; the leading company took the honor. His squad passes the initial fighting and advances into town. They are running and yelling, seeking somebody to fight. Sergeant Moreno-Rodriguez is leading them. Juan is in front; Gonzalo is beside him. He can hear Francisco and Hernán behind. They stay close, brothers in arms, who are ready to protect each other. Hernando is perspiring profusely and breathing heavily. Running makes his heart race. Then, out of the misty morning, green-clad warriors appear. The element of surprise is gone. They are fully armed and menacing, rushing into the fray unafraid. It's the British rangers. One swings his rifle up to his waist and fires at point-blank range. The bullet swooshes past Hernando's company. A Spanish soldier falls behind them. As they race into the pack, another ranger throws his tomahawk. It flies, embedding itself into Juan's right shoulder. He cries in pain. Blood from the wound flecks Hernando's face. Juan goes down.

They have no time to react. Hernando's entire company is thrust into battle with the British rangers. His squad is in the middle of it. Bayonets are used as the two sides clash. Green uniforms are everywhere, fighting face to face with the blue and whites of the Spanish regulars. A couple of muskets shoot sudden retorts. Guns are useless, though; men are using them as clubs, battering each other. Long knives, machetes, swords, and tomahawks are drawn. It's close-quarters fighting, hand-to-hand. The swirl of blades and the clangs and clatter of knife edges clashing surround them.

Hernando has no time to process the scene. As the two sides collide, a grisly old officer and two compatriots race from a large tent and come straight at Hernando's squad. The officer has a sword in his right hand and a tomahawk in his left. Ambidextrously, both hands appear to move simultaneously. Sergeant Moreno-Rodriguez parries the sword once, twice, thrice. Gonzalo steps into Juan's place beside the sergeant and stops the lefthanded sweep of the tomahawk from gutting the sergeant. One of the officer's men flies at Francisco, while the other attacks Hernán. Miraculously, Hernando is free to act. He stabs his bayonet straight into the chest of the British officer. Hernando's training comes into play; he jabs, twists, and withdraws the bayonet. An intense sucking sensation momentarily grasps the blade, he pulls harder and manages to pull the bayonet out. It's a mortal wound, hitting the man in the heart. As the officer falls, blood pumps out onto his green uniform. His eyes glaze over, and a milkiness descends across his eyeballs. The body slumps to the floor. Hernando stares down at his victim, shocked at how quickly death can come.

Sergeant Moreno-Rodriguez immediately turns on Francisco's attacker and runs his short sword through the ranger's midriff. Meanwhile, Gonzalo smashes the second ranger over the head with the butt of his musket. The fight is intense but swiftly over. Hernando's squad pauses for a few moments as the intense commotion around them dissipates, and then they turn to look for Juan.

Chapter 51: The Battle for Mose

The order to assemble the men came late in the afternoon. Lamine was commanding a unit of the black militia as they moved the castle's ruins from its accumulated piles following the shelling. He'd been included in the officers' meetings, along with Commander Francisco Menéndez, and knew the assault on Mose was likely looming. A sense of eagerness surged through him. His adrenaline-stimulated muscles renewed his energy, as they heaved the remaining debris away from the sallyport. The castle's northeastern tower was closest to the British battery and had taken a beating. The constant retort of cannon fire and the whiz bang of mortars was ever-present. Cannonballs were endlessly smashing into the walls along the upper ramparts of the gate. There were occasional shouts of alarm as another cannonball hit and disturbed additional chunks of the coquina wall. As they fell, the men desperately sought cover, seeking safety from the falling lumps as they smashed into the ground, only to generate more rubble for them to move.

Captain Lamine's squad had the unenviable task of keeping the gateway unobstructed until the morning's attack. The Free

Black Militia was scheduled to strike out of the northeastern sallyport, so it needed to remain free of impediments. As he often did, Lamine worked with his men, not standing idly by directing the effort, as some officers tended to do. It was sweaty, hard work in the Florida humidity, but they knew how important the task was and labored vigorously. The dust from the destruction caused problems. Men were coughing it up and getting sick. Most were wearing bandanas to protect their faces. Occasionally, the squad burst out into song, singing the tunes of the assorted African tribes. For Lamine, it was another sign of the tribal fusion among the free blacks. The music helped them keep up the relentless donkeywork. Each time they successfully unblocked the gate, another British barrage would add more for them to remove. It was dangerous work. Several men were crushed by falling masonry, their limp bodies swiftly removed to the infirmary, more casualties of the war.

His knowledge bolstered Lamine's efforts. They would attack the British in the morning, and revenge was near. Lamine was a peaceful man at heart, but he couldn't forgive the South Carolinians for their treatment of Jemmy and his rebels. Neither could he excuse them for burning his town to the ground. Mose had been a unique place, and now it was gone. He hoped they'd face the South Carolinian militia when they ventured out. Vengeance was in his heart, and it wouldn't be quenched until blood was spilled. The town's militia was itching to fight. Siege warfare was tedious, and the monotony and unsatisfying labor had lasted too long. They craved action, and they wanted retribution. They were ready to bring hellfire down on their enemies. Prepared to cast their lives into the sea of uncertainty, to risk everything, and take action to avenge the past.

Lamine considered the men as they toiled. Mandingo, Igbo, Fulani worked side by side. Many tribes had melded into one. Brothers who would defend each other and fight for a common cause. It was a revelation of uncommon clarity. They had become something new. A tribe of free Africans, perhaps. Mose's destruction and their shared militia training undoubtedly influenced this new identity, but there was something more. Lamine wondered if it might be slavery. These men were all hardened by it. They were the survivors. The ones who'd lived to see others die and be cast overboard. Most had labored under the yoke of violent and oppressive slaveholders. Yet, all had somehow lived. Moreover, these were the few who had escaped slavery and who'd travelled many leagues to start a new life as freemen. The hardened discards of a wicked institution. Pride washed over Lamine as he reflected. He was lucky to lead these survivors and live while this new identity formed. These men would fight like fiends. They would take everything into this battle and expend every ounce of their lives to gain victory against their former oppressors. Tomorrow would be a splendid day. It was their fight for liberty that Jemmy and his rebels yelled for when they'd marched south toward Mose.

Lamine's thoughts and his squad's labor were interrupted by the arrival of the relief crew. It was Francisco Menéndez with the other half of the militia. They greeted each other briefly. Menéndez held Lamine's arm as he spoke, "It's confirmed, we'll attack them in the morning. The fools are still camping in the remains of the town. The general's adamant, it's time to strike them while we've an opportunity to do so. Take your men, get food, and as much sleep as you can. Everybody needs to be ready before dawn. It will be a bloody day tomorrow, and we must make the most of it."

Lamine dreamt of Jemmy. The hordes following the rebel leader were shouting "liberty" repeatedly, as they marched into battle. They attacked like demons, washing over the British position like an army of ghosts. A translucent mist disguises the apparitions from the defenders, who fall to mystical, deathly sickles wielded by the ghostly forms. Each swish decapitates the head of a British foe.

The dream dissipates as Lamine's sleeve is tugged. As it recedes, he wonders if it was a vision of what might have been or a prophecy for the morning's offensive. Perhaps the phantoms of his lost friends would stand alongside them today, as ghouls seeking retribution. The tough, sunbeaten face of Menéndez suddenly appears over him, "It's time. Wake your men and form up at the sallyport." As Lamine rises, the irritating buzz of flies surrounds him, and he shoos them away from his face. Near the busted northeastern sallyport's latrines, their beds are constantly infested with insects. As usual, the stench is rancid. They'd tried to fix the problem, but the cannon fire had totally imploded the walls of the privies. So, nothing could be done but tolerate the flies swarming around their chamber and ignore the ever-present reek.

Lamine rose, rubbed his eyes, dressed quickly, and grabbed his weapons. Unlike the Spanish regulars, his musket was old and barely functional. His bayonet had been bent and took some effort to straighten. Like the rest of his men, he'd worked hard to get the weapon working adequately. Likewise, his blade was ancient, and over many weeks, he'd spent hours cleaning off the rust and fashioning a sharp edge. After considerable sweat and exertion, both weapons were ready to be taken into battle. No plush officer's uniform for Lamine either, the free black militia owned only the clothes they'd been wearing when they retreated from Mose. The British had burned everything else. They didn't look like much, a poorly fitted troop of former slaves. However, Lamine knew better. After months of training, they'd been honed into an effective force and were ready for action.

Lamine roused his men. Many were already awake, unable to sleep, knowing what lay ahead. Others stirred quickly and moved with determination. Nobody dawdled; all understood the urgency of the moment. As they gathered their equipment, they filed down the stairwell into the inner confines of the sallyport. Lamine fondly slapped the last man on the back as he left their sleeping quarters, following as the man descended into the sallyport's interior. The free black militia gathered there, readying to sally out and join the Spanish raid. Over forty men were gradually shifting into ordered formations for their venture. Lamine picked out many familiar faces. Men he'd known as neighbors, shopkeepers, and craftsmen. Others were newer colleagues, thrust together into the militia's squads. Many emotions were visible. Determination, anger, doggedness, anxiety, and even joy were painted across those faces. The anticipation of the attack was palpable. The men had been training for this opportunity for many months, and an expectant sense of vengeance percolated among them.

Lamine knew the tactics; they were straightforward. Before daybreak, the militia was to depart from the northeastern sallyport. It would be a coordinated offensive. The Spanish regulars were to exit the northwestern sallyport and thrust up the main road, hitting the British encampment while they slept. Meanwhile, the militia and a large body of Seminoles were to take the river route and hook into the northern approaches to Mose, to cut off the British retreat and force a complete defeat or capitulation. It was an elegant plan, and Lamine expected it to work. They'd completely surprise and would attack the British with overwhelming force. They outnumbered the defenders three to one. It was going to be a bloodbath, and the militia were keen to begin the onslaught.

⌛ ⌛ ⌛

When the order arrives, everybody is ready. A few men are nervously playing with their weapons, checking triggers and firing mechanisms, or running their fingers along the sharp edges of their blades. There is a hush of silence as the courier delivers the letter. Commander Menéndez inspects the wax seal and approves; it's the general's insignia. He breaks the seal, opens the letter, and reads it briefly, handing it back to the courier. There is no conversation, no grand speeches. The commander points at the sallyport's door. It swings open. Menéndez's squad files out of the sallyport's archway. Men are moving quietly now. Steely determination crosses everyone's faces—no more hesitation, anxiety, or joy; just an unwavering focus on the present. As the last of Menéndez's men depart the castle, Lamine steps forward. It's his squad's turn to head up the river path towards Mose. They follow the vanguard in columns, two men abreast.

As Lamine marches, he sees their Seminole allies. It's still dark and gloomy, with the long night drifting shadows across the landscape, but there is unmistakable movement. At first, it's just the odd movement in the ditches or through bushes. Lamine's eyes are getting more accustomed to the predawn light. A cloud covering the moon moves on, and a new glow bathes the fields in softer hues. The countryside is suddenly filled with movement. Hundreds of stealthy shifting bodies cast shadows everywhere. The Seminoles are advancing alongside them. There are hundreds of them, too many to count. They pass through the terrain like the ghosts in Lamine's dream. Mist from the river drifts across the scene, and the image disappears. Did he imagine it? How did they sneak past the British artillery?

They pass several of Fandiño's half-galleys as they progress up the path. The vessels sit sleepily in the foggy river. Not a soul is seen. Evidently, they aren't employed during this morning's actions. One of Lamine's men sneezes, and it sounds thunderous. Lamine stares back, can't the fool do that quietly? It is too late, and his punishment must wait; more pressing issues are ahead. The culprit might not even survive the day's combat. Fandiño's ships are disappearing into the haze. Lamine recognizes the path; he's traveled along it many times and sees the bends, contours, and shrubs along the route. They're approaching Fort Mose and must soon hook westwards. As if Lamine was predicting it, Commander Menéndez suddenly takes his troop off the path and into the fields heading toward Mose. Lamine follows with his men and brings them alongside Menéndez's squad. Gradually, as they'd been trained to do, both units shift from columns into lines. Forty free blacks ready to smash into the British, seeking revenge for the destruction of their home. Out of nowhere, hundreds of Seminole warriors join them. The ghostly figures were real after all. Armed with wicked-looking tomahawks, bows, short knives, and old muskets, the warriors are ready for war. Faces are painted with war paint, and headdresses displaying adornments to celebrate former conquests are worn by the leaders. The Seminoles form a cocoon of strength around the militia, reinforcing the flanks and rear of the attack. Scouts run to the front, feeling their way forward, as the small army advances purposefully on Mose's northern front.

The battle descends into chaos swiftly. The Seminole scouts run straight into the Creek encampment and are immediately butchered. A few victorious cries are evidence of their sudden demise. The Creeks immediately recognize their predicament, see the more significant force approaching them, and instantly withdraw. A few shots are fired, with little effect. The small party of Creeks escape, racing to the northwest. A bigger detachment of Seminoles splinters away from the right flank and pursues their quarry. Lamine sees the first hints of sunrise. Dawn's shadows may not hide them much longer, and the sunlight may soon betray their surprise offensive. The militia continues to tramp onwards in a measured and disciplined way. Their sizable, allied escort matches them step by step.

As they close in on Mose, Captain Lamine realizes that they will have the fight of their lives ahead. The first indication of a problem is the bagpipes. The warbling melodies drift across the battlefield towards them. It's an eerie, otherworldly noise that echoes oddly. As they continue to approach the burnt-out ramparts of the town, they see their foe, and it's an unpleasant revelation. Ready to fight, and fully prepared, are the Darien Highlanders. The Scotsmen's tartans dot along Mose's dilapidated walls, and are arranged in battle formation. An officer in the middle of the line holds a giant Claymore ready to command the Scots to fire a volley. In the final moments, Lamine sees that there will be no chance for revenge against South Carolina's militia. The distinctive clashes, pops of musket fire, and high-pitched rings of weapons meeting suddenly flare up in the distance. The Spanish regulars have begun to attack.

Commander Menéndez takes five more steps and commands the men to halt. The order to present weapons is given, and then to fire. Lamine fires his ancient musket. The gun's retort is loud, and the butt digs brutally into his shoulder. A fog of war momentarily hides the town from view. The Scots wait. They've taken a few hits but not many. Menéndez gives the command to fix bayonets and charge. Within moments, Lamine and his men race across the field toward Mose, all order gone. He feels his heart racing; everything begins to slow down. The Seminoles charge, their yelps and hollas add to the cacophony. Lamine still hears the faint tones of the bagpipes. Then all sounds are subsumed by the Scots firing their own volley. It's brutally close. Though they have fewer men, the highlanders inflict considerable damage. Many of Mose's militia die or are injured in the musket fire. Lamine hears a couple of balls whizz past him. He sees two of his men go down mortally hurt. Several others lose limbs, instantly blown into smithereens. Blood and mud fly everywhere.

There is no time to think. The remainder of the attacking force is vying to make its way into Mose through the outer perimeter. The Scots wield deadly Claymores and fiendishly defend any openings. The blades whirl with stunning speed. A sturdy-looking highlander with blazing red hair comes for Lamine. His tartans swirl as his sword falls. Lamine parries the first thrust with his bayonet. Drawing his short sword, Lamine fortuitously defends himself against a stunning set of aggressive strikes—his blade withers under duress as the Claymore smashes into it. Two of Lamine's men come to his rescue, plunging their bayonets into the big man's chest. The Scot goes down, blood spurts everywhere, and he drops away from sight. Intense hand-to-hand combat takes hold inside Mose. They trained for this, and they go toe to toe against the British army's elite soldiers. The Seminoles are everywhere, hacking the Scots to pieces with their tomahawks. The militia is in the mix, and small, intense fights are breaking out all over Mose's ruins. They've surrounded the Scots, but the fools are still fighting, not giving up an inch.

Then out of nowhere, Lamine feels a shooting, excruciating pain pulse up his spine. The intensity of the agony is nauseating. Acidic bile forces itself up to his larynx, but he doesn't throw up. A lightness transcends his body, a faint delirium makes him want to rest and fall to his knees. He tries to bend, but a strange entity pins him, holding him upright. Lamine looks down, and reality dawns. A Claymore sword pokes out of his abdomen. Two feet of a broad blade visibly jut out from his body. Blood oozes from the wound and slowly seeps down his legs. Another violent discomfort occurs as the blade is wrenched backwards. He gags again as an audible sucking noise accompanies the blade's withdrawal. Suddenly, blood gushes from the wound, and he collapses to the ground, no longer able to support his weight. As he stares at the sunrise sky, he perplexedly notes the slowly fading melody of the bagpipes.

Chapter 52: Bloody Fort Mose

Tom's unit is having a long and watchful night. Coleman takes the first guard duty, after which they take turns. The night stretches over an eternity, and none of them sleep. Tom's sixth sense and agitation made them all vigilant. Tom is taking a turn as sentry when they all hear the telltale signs of a large body of men moving in the middle of the night. Initially, they aren't sure. They pick up a distant soft clink, metal tapping against metal, and then another. It's too faint to be certain, and they listen more intently. Hill stands and walks a few paces towards Palmer's encampment. Coleman cranes his head sideways, seeking further sounds keenly. Sanders picks up his musket. Then they hear a distinctive sneeze, off in the distance. It could've been anybody, and if they'd been half asleep, they might have discounted it as if coming from one of the highlanders. Alert, they immediately understand that it came from outside Mose's perimeter. They hear more revealing noises, a grunt, a heavy gasp, and more clanking of weapons clashing. There's an army approaching, and they instinctively know it.

Tom acts immediately, unflinchingly, not worried about raising the alarm unnecessarily: "Sanders, go! Get to Colonel Palmer's tent, tell him we're under attack! Hill, Coleman, you're with me. We must find Captain Mackay."

Tom's unit reacts with the urgency the revelation demands. Sanders sprints towards the colonel's position and disappears swiftly, running with his gun in one hand. Meanwhile, Tom and the others promptly gather their weapons and run north towards the highlanders. They leave behind a smoldering fire and their camp equipment; unnecessary encumberments should battle ensue. In seconds, Tom realizes that they are sitting ducks. Staying in the same place night after night, fires ablaze, showing their attackers where they are, and no pickets. He understands they'll be lucky to get out of this alive.

They dash past two small groups of highlanders, startling them. Tom shouts, "Get up, we're under attack!" The Scots are highly trained; they react immediately and begin to raise the alarm across the encampment. Tom's unit passes another group. Tom asks, "Where is Captain Mackay?" The Scots point to the commander's whereabouts, pick up their muskets and dangerous-looking Claymores, and head directly towards Mose's barricades. A general hubbub descends across the position. Men run back and forth, they wake up comrades, collect their weapons, and shout commands at each other. Tom's intervention might give them enough time to prepare for an assault. They find Captain Mackay. The Scottish commander, reacting to the general commotion, is already in full battle dress, waving his Claymore as he directs the Scots. Tom greets the captain, "Sir, we heard a large force moving along the river. I think they plan to hit our flank, along the northeast side."

The captain reacts straightaway and bellows, "Flag sergeant, to me! Officers, take your units to the northeastern wall. Bagpiper, play the Campbells are coming! Our enemy approaches!" A sudden orderliness descends on the chaotic scenes, as the Scots understand the nature and location of the threat. While officers lead their men to the ramparts, Darien's flag is unfurled, and the bagpiper squeezes his instrument. The tune begins as a low, droning hum, steady and unwavering, and then the first note breaks free, filling the air with a bold and piercing resonance. The lively and spirited melody boldly builds rhythm as the song progresses. Captain Mackay turns back to Tom, "Corporal Ellis, I believe. I'll need your rifles here. Prepare for battle!"

"Yes, sir!" Tom replies. He sees Hill and Coleman already busy loading their rifles, ramming bullets down grooved barrels. Tom starts to load his precious rifle. It's a laborious process, and he hopes they have time. He unconsciously touches his tomahawk for luck before loading the gun. Mackay's command post is on a slight incline within Mose's perimeter. As Tom loads, he sees the developing battlefield. The Scots had enough time to react and now line the outer boundary of the town— their enemy approaches in battle lines, less than forty feet from the Scots' defensive array. The advancing adversary is an odd concoction. A black militia, likely Mose's townsfolk, and a large contingent of Seminoles. Unusually for a militia, they appear disciplined, approaching in tight combat lines arranged in two rows. Perhaps forty or fifty militia and several hundred native warriors, hopelessly outnumbering the Scots. Tom gauges that the attackers have at least a three-to-one advantage over the defenders. Tom knows the Scots will be terrible opponents, battling harshly, but the odds for victory look poor. Finally, he finishes loading his rifle and waits.

Suddenly, the sounds of conflict are all around them. From the south, there is an unexpected cry of hundreds of voices charging into the fray. The distinctive pop, pop, and pop of musket fire reverberates across the town. Shrieks, yelps, and screams of men dying in their beds swiftly follow the initial shouts of the assault. Momentarily, Tom is concerned about Sanders; he's in the southern part of the town, warning Colonel Palmer. Further cries of anguish come from the east as the Seminole scouts run into the Creek encampment and are slain. Tom watches the Creeks hastily leave the meadow, a more significant Seminole force in pursuit. Tom's worries shift to his Creek friends; he could lose people dear to him today.

The militia halt and lift their weapons. Captain Mackay raises his Claymore, signaling the Scots to hold their fire. Flames dart out of the attackers' guns; a simultaneous deafening retort reverberates as the muskets fire. Musket balls fleck the defenders, and some of the Scots go down. Tom watches horrified as a nearby highlander takes a hit, his guts bursting out of his back. The enemy fix bayonets and charge. It's their only error. As they rush to within ten yards of the barricade, Captain Mackay swishes his sword, and in unison, the Scots fire. It's a devastating volley at close quarters and takes a severe toll. Tom, Coleman, and Hill join the slaughter using their more accurate rifles, trying to pick off officers. The lack of obvious insignia of rank makes it difficult to pick their targets. Many go down, dead or injured. However, it is not enough. The defenders are outnumbered, and the aggressors swiftly punch holes through the defenses, breaking the Scottish lines. Realizing their desperation, Captain Mackay turns to Tom, "Corporal, take your men north immediately. The rest of General Oglethorpe's regiment is encamped north of our position. Bring them here as quickly as you can!"

Tom knows it is too late for Oglethorpe's regiment to save the Darien Highlanders. He wants to stay and fight, but is bright enough to recognize a direct command and its intent. Captain Mackay aims to contest the battle to the end, hoping to delay the Spanish retreat and hold them long enough for the British regulars to stage a counteroffensive. It's a bold stratagem, sacrificing himself and his men to turn defeat into victory, and it might work. Understanding the risks the tactic implies, Tom answers, "Yes, Sir! It would be an honor."

As the hand-to-hand combat intensifies, Tom turns away from the confrontation and leads his men northeast. He prays quietly that they don't happen upon the splinter group of Seminole warriors chasing the Creeks. Undoubtedly, death will occur swiftly if they do. They tear away, and the battle clashes recede into the distance. He still hears the bagpipes calling the Scots to arms, and deep in Tom's soul, he wishes he could stay and fight. Then he remembers Mary and their unborn child and is grateful for the commander's order to send him away.

⏳ ⏳ ⏳

Tom led Coleman and Hill carefully. They ran speedily, but cautiously. Too slow, and the battle will be over before Oglethorpe's regiment arrives. If they are too hasty, they risk running into the Seminole warriors, thus failing altogether. It wasn't an easy task. Clearing the remains of Fort Mose was the simple part. Tom was sure the Creeks would have headed away from Mose, so it was unlikely that the Seminoles would have entered the town's remnants. Consequently, they sprint, weave past the burnt-out structures dotted in their way. His squad is fit, while sweat drips and they breathe heavily, their progress is rapid. Once past the town's ramparts, the trek gets trickier. Seminole scouts and raiding parties are everywhere, and Tom becomes cautious. The northern road would've been preferable, but it's too dangerous. They take a narrow culvert surrounded by forest, and splash along a gentle sloping stream, getting wet as they hop from one stone to another. As the culvert narrows to a point, they climb out of a steep gorge. Fingers are ripped apart as they clamber up the rock face. At the top, they run along a small hillock running parallel to the northern roadway. Tom notices that their Creek allies are down on the road, and in the distance, he sees Oglethorpe's regiment marching in columns south towards the battle. Maybe hope remains.

Tom's unit joins the reinforcements. He's happy to see that Hilli and Sin are safe. The Creeks had outpaced their Seminole chasers, and Toonhowi had briefed Oglethorpe. The 42nd Regiment was mustered and is heading directly into the fray. Though short of one company, the regiment ought to be enough to turn the battle's tide in the British favor. Tom, Coleman, and Hill take their customary positions, scouting alongside the column's flanks.

⏳   ⏳   ⏳

All hope vanishes when they arrive. They are too late, and the battle of Fort Mose is lost. The Spanish commando raid had succeeded, and the Spanish had returned to St. Augustine's castle. The battlefield is silent, except for a mournful wind and the caws of carrion crows. The morning mist hangs over the town, and the moist Florida air is heavy with the telltale odor of saltpeter. As they reenter Mose, Tom braces himself for what they may find. The mist shrouds the broken bodies of the fallen. The Scots are decimated. Tartan-clad bodies are spread everywhere, sprawled in unnatural poses, lying on the ground, and leaning against the few remaining structures. Men's faces are frozen in expressions of agony and defiance. Crimson blood cakes the ground and is spilled everywhere. Coleman mutters, "Bloody Fort Mose!" and Tom can't disagree with his sentiment. Scottish Claymores and British muskets lay abandoned, their owners dead. There are moans and grunts, and some of the bodies move. A battered Scot stands and staggers toward them, a bloody mess but living. There are no dead or injured attackers; they have been removed. They've arrived too late. Too late!

Oglethorpe's regiment scours the site and begins to collect the bodies and tend to the injured. Meanwhile, Tom and his men look for Captain Mackay. It was an honorable last stand and a shame it had come to nought. They found the little knoll the captain had commanded. The flag sergeant lay dead there, his eyes wide, staring. He'd visibly fought hard to defend Darien's flag, but the flag was gone, and the sergeant had died a vicious death. Multiple stab wounds punctuated his body; several assailants had taken him down. The bagpipes lay nearby, busted and discarded, with no sign of a bagpiper. They searched for the captain's body but couldn't find it and had to conclude that maybe he'd been captured. Their eyes became dry in the hot Florida sun as Mose's ashes dusted their uniforms and covered their faces. Hill eventually interrupted the search, "Corporal, we should go look for Sanders. He may not have made it."

Tom understood that in his shock and grief he'd forgotten his duties, "Yes, of course. Maybe Captain Mackay has been captured. I sent Sanders to Colonel Palmer. Let's check near Palmer's tent, perhaps some of the rangers survived." It was a forlorn hope. The battlefield was covered in British bodies, densely packed, lying one upon another in the center of the town. Crews were starting to untangle the stiff limbs and lay out the dead for burial. It was a brutal sight. They found a section of green-clad soldiers; all of South Carolina's rangers had been killed. Colonel Palmer lay there, accompanying his men, his eyes blank, and his form soulless. Next to the colonel rested Sanders. His green uniform was covered in blood. A chest wound from a bayonet was the cause of his demise. The man probably experienced a sudden death, as the bayonet's steel had ripped his heart into pieces. Though Sanders was unpopular, they each paid their respects to their former colleague.

As Tom surveyed the aftermath of the battle and reviewed the deaths of the redcoats, especially the ones still in their beds, he couldn't help but reflect on life and death. The captain's order to fetch the regiment had saved his life and the lives of his men. Had they stayed and fought, they would have been dead along with the others. Their bodies would be lying here with all the rest. Cast across Mose like the detritus of Fall, dead leaves piled one upon another, just another season of withered vibrancy, dying, decaying, and returning to the earth. The town's ghosts had stolen a cruel vengeance, and new British phantoms would join them to celebrate the carnival of war. Coleman had been right, bloody Fort Mose! And all for a man's ear, damn Jenkins' ear!

Epilogue

O'Sullivan watched the Spanish march back to St. Augustine victorious. They'd destroyed General Oglethorpe's troops at Fort Mose and were returning with captives. It was a total triumph for the Catholic cause. He was overcome with joy and almost gave himself away, until he forced himself to internalize his satisfaction and celebrated inwardly. He thanked God for the Spanish success.

As O'Sullivan gazed out across the bay, he saw the Spanish returning with their injured and dead. They'd lost many men, but nowhere near the death toll they must have inflicted. The returning raiders had preoccupied the entire South Carolina militia, who were watching from the island, unable to intervene. The artillery fired a few cannons at the returning Spanish troops, but to little effect. The retort of the guns was once again deafening.

O'Sullivan quickly spotted the opportunity the distraction afforded. Everybody was focused on the disaster that had just unfolded for the British army. This might be his only opportunity to escape, and he decided to take it. Quickly, he disappeared into some nearby bushes. He worked his way along the island's coastline to the north. Once adjacent to one of Fandiño's half-galleys, he discarded his weapons and other accoutrements, stripped, and launched himself into the river. He wasn't a great swimmer, but it was a short distance, and he was hauled onboard moments later. Perhaps he would join Fandiño's crew or return to his spymaster. This battle was likely over, and he didn't want to risk having to return to Charles Town.

⧖ ⧖ ⧖

Chioke and Catori were seated next to the great fire at the center of the Seminole camp, the evening following the Spanish victory. It's blazing hot, burning their cheeks, and blinding their eyes. Chioke was trying to celebrate while chewing deer jerky, but he couldn't hide his disappointment. The Seminoles had ventured out that morning and secured a remarkable win against the hated British. They'd returned with their war trophies, singing and dancing around the fire. Their epic stories would last for generations.

The Yamasee had been left behind, a spent force. They'd lost too many warriors from the many tribal battles with the Creeks, trying to defend St. Augustine's northern and western approaches. What warriors they had left were exhausted. It maddened Chioke. The Seminoles had done little for months, allowing the Yamasees to lead Spain's Indian warfare, and when the moment arrived for a major battle, they'd been deployed fresh, had won, and would take the honors. He tried to be pleased for them, but he was simply disgruntled and had to accept his feelings. Chioke hated the British with a passion. They'd enslaved him and treated him without honor. To miss an opportunity to take a few of his enemies' lives truly rankled. Catori sensed his anger and touched his hand to calm him down. This was neither the time nor the place for senselessness. The British had lost, and her Yamasee warriors remained guests among the victors. As it often did, her touch calmed his temper.

⧗ ⧗ ⧗

Francisco Menéndez knew his militia had been lucky. Nobody expected the Scots to be guarding the northern side of Fort Mose, ready for battle. The militia and Seminoles were just supposed to cut off the British retreat, capturing and killing the fleeing survivors of the Spanish assault. The Scots' positioning and readiness had exacted a terrible price on his militia. They only succeeded because of the overwhelming numbers of Seminoles and due to some of the Spanish companies driving their attack north into the Scots' rear. The arrival of the Spanish regulars had saved the militia from annihilation. The Scots had fought for their flag, inspired by their bagpipes, to the last man and with honor. Because of this character, once they were surrounded, the Spanish spared the leader, his bagpiper, and a few of his highlanders. They were now locked in the castle's dungeons and likely to be traded for Spanish prisoners. The Scots had been obliterated, though; hardly any had survived.

As he surveyed the bodies of his men, Francisco Menéndez accepted the reality that the eradication of the Free Black Militia was also a fact. Pitifully few of his men had survived the conflict. The bodies of over thirty men lay side by side inside the northeastern sallyport. As Menéndez inspected the dead, he noticed his second-in-command, Captain Lamine, lying lifeless with his eyes blank and his body contorted. The man had died of a stomach wound from a Claymore, not a pleasant death; his agony would have been prolonged before he passed. The man's loss was a symbol of the demise of Fort Mose itself. Lamine had been full of inspiring ideas, yet he was lying prostrate in the dirt. Mose was now like that. The town had been destroyed, burnt to the ground; it was lying in ashes. Meanwhile, most of its male populace were gone, taken away by the fighting. Menéndez realized that Mose and the ideals Mose stood for were likely dead too.

⏳ ⏳ ⏳

Weeks had passed since the battle of Fort Mose, and the siege had continued. Hernando and the Spanish regulars had been allowed to celebrate but soon returned to their regular duties. Juan was alive but still recovering from his wound. The British defeat wasn't conclusive. While the British were licking their wounds, supplies had gotten into the castle. However, the Spanish were precariously close to running out of food. All knew that surrender might soon occur, and there was a general sense of despondency. It was a shame to win such a famous battle, yet ultimately lose the castle and the whole of Florida with it. It now appeared inevitable that the colony would soon collapse into the arms of the British.

Then something miraculous happened. The British Navy sailed away and lifted the siege. It was a stunning development. The castle was on its knees, ready to give up the fight, and the general was close to announcing the Spanish capitulation. Immediately, Fandiño used the opportunity to resupply the castle, and everyone celebrated. Hernando would never forget how the bells sang. It was their liberation day. Spanish Florida would survive the British invasion after all.

Williams was poised with his parchment, ink, and quill. He was due to write a letter to Acting Governor Bull explaining the debacle, but he wasn't sure how to start it. Moreover, how should he finish it? In fact, he wasn't sure what to put in the middle either. Williams knew Colonel Bull would be apoplectic when he read the letter, and Williams was glad he'd be hundreds of miles away when the man opened it. He didn't have long either, as Commodore Pearce was kicking him and all of South Carolina's men off the ship. A simple, short explanation was likely best in the circumstances.

Williams began to scratch quickly with his pen, while occasionally dipping it in the inkwell.

The battle of Fort Mose was a disaster; all were lost. Colonel Palmer and his men are dead. The entire South Carolina Rangers' company was destroyed. General Oglethorpe unadvisedly split his forces and spent the entire time suffering with a mysterious illness. The Spanish raided the position and surprised Colonel Palmer. More bad decisions. They camped at the same site for many nights in a row, and no pickets were posted. Colonel Palmer and Captain Mackay agreed on almost nothing. Most were killed in their beds. Colonel Palmer is dead, Captain Mackay is missing, presumed captured.

General Oglethorpe continued the siege after the defeat. There was no need for the British Navy. Commodore Pearce has barely used them and just announced his departure and the fleet's return to Admiral Vernon. The commodore is worried about the hurricane season and will depart today. General Oglethorpe nearly hit the commodore. He felt we were close to success. The siege is over, and we return across land on the morrow. Florida remains Spanish.

Williams sat back and thought, well, that pretty much captured it. After a few years in the governor's employment, he knew enough about politics to understand that this fiasco was just the beginning. Colonel Palmer couldn't be blamed; he was dead. South Carolina was sure to blame Georgia, which meant General Oglethorpe was in for a rough time. Oglethorpe was certain to accuse Commodore Pearce of timidity, and perhaps there was fairness in the accusation. The general would probably fault South Carolina's legislature for dragging its feet and unnecessarily delaying the invasion. Commodore Pearce would make excuses. It was because of Fandiño's half-galleys or General Oglethorpe's unwillingness to assault the castle with the army alone, or because of the dangerous hurricane season, or the need to ensure his ships could return to Admiral Vernon's fleet for the Caribbean invasion. The blame game would soon commence, and it would surely be full of fireworks. Williams could already see the letters flying back and forth, along with the odd shoe thrown at him by Bull. What a shame. They were close to capturing Florida, and now they must wait to see what the Spanish would do.

Historical Note

The War of Jenkins' Ear (1739-1748) has largely disappeared in time because it ended in a stalemate. It was fought between the British and the Spanish across multiple localities, including New Granada, the Caribbean Sea, and the two empires' North American colonies. The name comes from Robert Jenkins, a British sea captain whose ear was severed by the Spanish coastguard leader Fandiño a few years before the conflict. In 1738, politicians in Britain used the incident to incite hostilities, and Jenkins' ear and his story was paraded in Parliament. However, the actual reasons for the war were more complicated. For the most part, Spain was upset with the British because they were using the slave trade to smuggle illicit goods into the Spanish colonies. Often hidden in ships used to conduct trade under the Asiento de Negros contract. The British, for their part, were offended by how the Spanish coastguard conducted searches of ships and mistreated their sailors while they rooted out smuggling. Under the surface, though, it was a lucrative trade; the Spanish sought to limit its flow, while the British sought to enhance it.

As often happens in war, Jenkins' Ear was used as a pretext and trigger. Wider pressures had built up between the two due to the constant competition between the empires. The British used the war as a naked attempt to capture Spain's Caribbean and South American colonies, aiming to destroy Spanish power in the region. If the war had been successful, the history of the Caribbean and South America would have changed, and the British would have dominated the entire region.

In the North American theater, the war took on a vital shape. Oglethorpe's success in persuading the British to start a colony in Georgia was hotly disputed by the Spanish. They saw the settled territories as Spanish and called them Guale. The British were concerned about the invasion of their North American colonies from Spanish Florida and had founded Georgia as a buffer colony, aiming to strengthen their southern territories. So, inevitably, as war began, conflict was expected between the American British colonies and Spanish Florida.

This book is focused on one part of the war, the British invasion of Florida. One of the major departures I have made from most historical accounts is to include the Stono Rebellion. As far as I can tell, historians don't connect the rebellion to the war or the invasion of Florida. The uprising occurred in September 1739, just a few months before the war started and destabilized South Carolina, and it was too much of a coincidence to ignore. Additionally, the rebellion was led by Catholic Africans from the Congo, who were inspired to seek freedom in Spanish Florida and hoped to settle in the free black town of Mose (called Forte Negro, indicated by a white circle in the map below), north of St. Augustine. When digging into some of the older historical accounts and letters, there is fleeting evidence that the South Carolinians suspected foul play and that Spanish spies may have actively encouraged the rebellion.

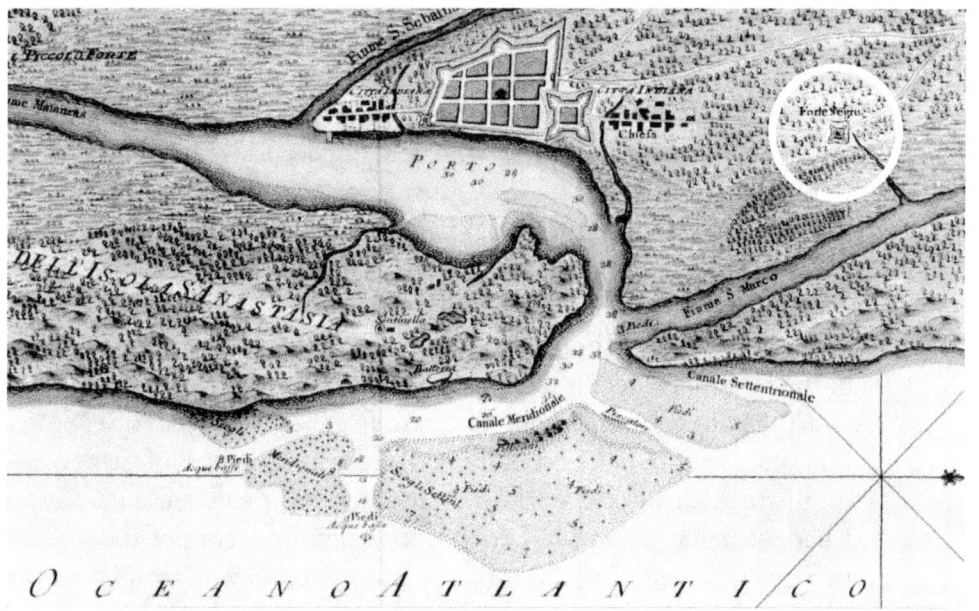

The Spanish keenly encouraged enslaved peoples to seek their freedom in Florida, while employing slavery in other colonies. Consequently, it seemed reasonable to connect the events. It is also clear that the rebellion led to some hesitancy for South Carolina to send men to support General Oglethorpe's Florida invasion, ultimately delaying the war effort and assisting the Spanish defense.

⧗ ⧗ ⧗

The Stono Rebellion and Edisto Battle were horrible episodes, and views on them can be controversial even today. This is one reason I chose to write this book from multiple points of view (POVs). Atrocities happened on both sides. The rebels, seeking their freedom, killed innocents and engaged in a scorched-earth approach as they progressed south. The South

Carolinian militia treated the captured rebels atrociously, cutting off their heads and mounting them on spikes along the roads to Charles Town, modern Charleston, to make a point and intimidate others who remained enslaved. Some were sold to other places, but most were brutally executed. The actions described are as close to the historical accounts as I could make them.

The invasion of Florida has many aspects that are almost lost in history, and I hoped to resurface some of the intricacies of the offensive. Details like the beheading of two highlanders and the capturing of minor forts are more or less accurate. Likewise, the destruction of Fort Mose and the siege of St. Augustine's castle are as close to the historical information I had available. Likewise, I tried to portray the tactics of the two generals genuinely. The British aimed for a swift assault and a comprehensive siege, while the Spanish intended to concentrate their forces in the castle and wait out the siege. In this case, the British tactics unraveled for all the reasons presented in the story.

Using different characters and POVs allowed me to introduce a range of events, some of which coincided. It also allowed me to present a variety of relevant perspectives and alliances. At this point in history, the major combatants (Britain and Spain) and the many native allies are taking varied and shifting positions regarding their relationships. Georgia has recently become a British colony, and tensions exist between it and its older sister, South Carolina. The native American tribes have many older grievances and traditional foes that play a role in the conflict. The British Navy was apathetic at best, seemingly more focused on protecting their ships for the invasion of the Caribbean. Consequently, I wanted to present the story through the eyes of varied protagonists to give more insight into the complexity and dynamics of the relationships between the actors.

As presented in my story, the invasion of Florida was essentially a disaster for the British. Due to South Carolina's concerns, it started late, allowing the Spanish to prepare, reinforcements to arrive, and Fandiño's half-galleys to join the castle's defense. The mission's leadership was never settled. General Oglethorpe didn't directly command South Carolina's militia or the British Navy's contingent. There was an order for Commodore Pearce to report to Oglethorpe, but it never arrived. Lack of clarity regarding the overall leadership of the mission probably contributed to its failure. Likewise, the book's reporting of disagreements between Colonel Palmer and Captain Mackay likely contributed to their failure in the Battle of Fort Mose. Such disputes were common between colonial officers and men commissioned by the British regulars.

It is also known that General Oglethorpe contracted malaria on his trip to Coweta, and this may have contributed to his uncharacteristic indecisiveness; he spent much of the campaign incapacitated. It is also fair to speculate that the strange qualities of coquina stone contributed to the siege's disappointment. As in a prior campaign, the artillery barrage was ineffective against the castle. The stone has concrete-like qualities but is also slightly malleable, hence the odd effects experienced by the cannonballs described in the story.

Oglethorpe and all the major officers described in the book are real characters of the period. I've tried to build them on available information. Tom Ellis features in my first book, *Yamacraw Bluff*. He is an indentured servant who came to Georgia with the original settlers. However, beyond that, he is purely fictional. My first book also briefly features Lamine, Chioke, Evans, and Williams. Lamine is the enslaved translator of Ayuba Suleiman Diallo (Job Jalla) and was a real person. The character's details and experiences in the book are figments of my imagination. Chioke, Evans, and Williams are all fictional characters featured in my first work, while *Jenkins' Ear* introduces the fictitious characters Hernando and O'Sullivan.

This story includes two unique cultures and towns that remain fascinating today. Mose, the first free black town in North America, was north of St. Augustine, and the Scottish settlement of Darien, with its Scottish Gaelic-speaking highlanders, was a unique frontier town in Georgia. Both communities were distinctive and largely destroyed because of the Battle for Fort Mose. Mose was burned to the ground, and both groups suffered significant losses of their male settlers, which may have undermined the long-term viability of the two communities. It's interesting to speculate what might have been. Mose was destroyed, while Darien still exists, though I don't know how much of its Scottish heritage remains.

I used many different sources for this book. My first go-to for this work and *Yamacraw Bluff* was *James Edward Oglethorpe: Imperial Idealist* by Ettinger (1936). Other valuable books have included *Oglethorpe in America (Spalding, 1977)*, *James Edward Oglethorpe (Blackburn, 2004)*, and *Creeks and Seminoles (Wright, 1986)*. As I finished my first book in the series, Robert Gaudi's (2021) book *The War of Jenkins' Ear* came out. It is a valuable contribution to this history, and I used it to help construct my story. If you want to learn more about the War of Jenkins' Ear, I highly recommend it. The book is a well-researched and well-written account of the entire war.

www.ingramcontent.com/pod-product-compliance
Lightning Source LLC
Chambersburg PA
CBHW071729110726
47908CB00006B/1541

* 9 7 8 1 6 8 3 1 5 1 8 0 7 *